R J PARKER

REQUIEM,
CHANGING TIMES

WHERE FANTASY MEETS REALITY

20 Twenty
Literary Group

ISBN
978-1-962868-52-5 (Paperback)
978-1-962868-53-2 (eBook)
978-1-962868-49-5 (Hardcover)

To my wife and children, who were always there.

Table of Contents

In the Not-Too-Distant Future

"Good evening. This is Nicole Wilsonland for your Channel Ten News. Our first and only story, of course, is about the virus's massive effect, causing economic turmoil that has now caused Andorra's government to declare bankruptcy along with Malta and Liechtenstein this week. The global crisis encompasses all nations scrambling to prepare for war with each other over human existence's political, environmental, and economic elements. The psychological diminishment and worldwide sustainability in question have kept Congress on its knees night and day.

With millions homeless, organized crime widespread, and thousands starving, many find themselves turning to faith for support and perhaps answers.

As world leaders become overwhelmed with countless people needing medical attention, marshal law has been declared in Asia, Africa, and, today, India.

Many religious leaders are accused of fueling the economic downturn and preaching hostile motivations against the governments and UN leaders. The heads of these different faiths have denied any such acts. Oddly, though, they repeatedly state that the hand of God may be looming over the world.

Armed civilians have assaulted embassies, and with people of every nation suffering, it seems to have started hitting us in our backyards. Masses of immigrants have started their long journey here to California. More are coming over our borders daily, hoping for a new life, some selling all they have for this chance and traveling by whatever means possible. Some are being met with hostility. Earlier today at a press conference, the President had this to say, 'To all those Americans living today within the reach of my voice, I call upon you to remember what is written on our

Statue of Liberty, "Give me your tired, your poor, your huddled masses yearning to breathe free, the wretched refuse of your teeming shore. Send these, the homeless, tempest-tossed to me, and I lift my lamp beside the golden door!'"

Although many people have opened their homes and arms to these new arrivals, with the number of homeless and vagrants on the rise, our law enforcement agencies have been pushed to the breaking point. We will have more on that later this hour. Now for sports with Dennis Bindley."

One

SPLIT PERSONALITIES

Sackson turned his television off now that the attractive news reporter had finished. His eyes lingered out of the hotel window at the palm trees swaying in the wind before returning to straightening his fake mustache and beard. Seeing himself in the mirror with a different-looking man in the reflection was nothing new. Still readying himself for the day, he allowed himself a quick scratch under his hairpiece while he pushed his false mustache to his face to ensure the adhesive would stick. Rounding his shoulders, he shifted his bodyweight suit that enlarged his waist and backside, cursing the new girth around him. In this climate, it always made him sweat more. He had to use the more expensive adhesive for his mustache and wig to stay in place. Leaning in closer, he examined every feature, pulling and pushing out his lips, straining every facial muscle from his forehead to his neck so nothing would be left to chance.

Satisfied with the altered image staring back at him, he moved quickly to bed. Pulling the comforter off revealed dozens of small weapons and dismantled guns. Circling, he carefully selected each weapon, trying to ignore the annoying swishing his suit pants made with each stride. Each weapon he chose was discretely secured on his person in perfect concealment.

Every act that morning was made with distinction and purpose until he retrieved a large briefcase by the hotel door. He paused with his hand resting on the doorknob.

"Car, 5 minutes and 58 seconds. Guards, one minute, two seconds. Door, 11 minutes, 34 seconds, mark, 4 minutes 3 seconds, mark, 9 minutes' decontamination, and change, 14 minutes 1 second, mark, 17 minutes until acquisition. No worries, an she'll be right with its ten million in me bum bag and all the esky from the bottle-o."

His eyes turned from the door to his rather large and unusual watch. Behind its hands was a digital picture of six Australian Special Ground Force Service Regiment combatants in military attire. All of them were holding each other arm in arm, smiling, drinks in each hand.

"Good on ya, mates. Ta for all," Sackson whispered. Feeling the buttons of his shirt stretch with a deep breath, his watch gave him two small electric taps that only he could feel. At that moment, his persona changed as he opened the door with an amused, goofy smile now showing on his face and the picture on his watch vanishing.

Swaggering, he entered the hallway, securing the do not disturb sign on the hotel doorknob behind him. Following the sound of the door shutting was the soft 'pop' of a metal can next to the bed, which spread an aerosol that would eliminate all evidence of his fingerprints and DNA. Once down the hallway, he raised his hand to ring for the elevator; he flicked his wrist sharply, triggering the electrical pulse to blind the camera above him. The elevator was coming down just as it always did, thanks to Miss Ford, who rode it every morning like clockwork to dine in the hotel's restaurant.

"Good day, Mr. Morgan. What floor, please?" The elevator attendant asked brightly. Sackson smiled, baring his fake teeth first to the short man and turning toward Miss Ford sitting on one of the two fine brown leather chairs.

"Take the lift to the lobby, if ya please," Mr. Sackson said smartly, tapping his right knuckle to his forehead in respect to Miss Ford as he positioned himself in the center of the elevator.

"What a salivating accent, Mr. Morgan," Miss Ford said airily as she resituated her thin frame on her seat. "Whereabouts in England are you from?"

"Manchester," Sackson said briskly. "But across the pond, we don't have any quite as lovely as you." Miss Ford giggled, running her hands down her skirt, smoothing it. She readjusted in her seat again, giving Sackson a flirty smile, and raised one of her overly plucked eyebrows.

"I guess I let out a little secret there, didn't I?" Sackson exclaimed, slapping the elevator worker on the back with his free hand. Under the itch of his hairpiece, he recalled that Miss Ford was recovering from plastic surgery in this hotel. She was from New York but told her husband she was on a cruise because she didn't want him to know about all the work she'd done to her figure. Tightening his grip on his briefcase, he prided himself on the background checks he'd performed on everyone in the building.

"The devil is in the details," he thought as his mind raced over all his preparation for this job.

"How are you doing today, Mr. Morgan?" The attendant asked keenly and added. "It is a little warmer than yesterday, and a slight breeze is coming in from the ocean."

"Same pleasure as always," Sackson said smartly.

"Have a good day, Mr. Morgan," the attendant said excitedly as the elevator doors opened, turned, and waved an arm out of the doors.

Sackson turned his back, hiding his face from the first camera in the lobby, blocking the door as he reached into his pocket.

"Excuse me one moment as I get a biscuit from the tin," Sackson said, turning to allow Miss Ford out of the elevator and showing his back now to camera number two. He leaned just right to block her way again as he handed the elevator attendant a hundred-dollar bill. He knew that if anyone was going to inquire about him, being a heavy tipper would make it challenging to be informed, and it also gave testimony that he didn't know American money.

"Thank you, sir, thank you," the attendant said happily. Sackson didn't wait for praise. He was already walking next to Miss Ford, using her as a human shield from the other cameras across the room.

Miss Ford was saying something he paid no attention to as he marked all the people in the lobby. Waving to no one in particular to block the third security camera, he slowed his steps, as he was five seconds ahead of schedule on reaching the carpet adorning the center of the lobby.

Through all the chatter, he gave Miss Ford another salute, not caring that she was still talking, and made his way to the front doors.

"Mr. Morgan, oh Mr. Morgan!" came a horrible woman's voice from behind him. He knew instantly who it was. Mrs. Goodwin was in the apartment across from his. She had let herself into his room when room service was being delivered and spoke to him at length about her money, her horrible driver who always made unwanted passes toward her, and the lack of restaurants left in the world that could make a decent foie gras. Miss Ford instantly disappeared at the sight of Mrs. Goodwin.

"Mr. Morgan!" She called again as she bustled toward him, pushing people out of her way. Every eye was on her, from her perfect overly tight shoes. She could barely walk in her fabulous three sizes too small dress.

For a moment, he considered walking on, but with every eye on her, his leaving would bring more unwanted attention. Not turning, he raised a hand in acknowledgment and waited for her to ensure he didn't show his face.

"Cheerio, Mrs. Goodwin," he called back. She didn't see that he was tapping his foot to keep track of each second he was behind schedule waiting for her.

"Oh dear," Mrs. Goodwin said almost mournfully as she grabbed Sackson's arm and wrapped it around her shoulder.

"I have forgotten all my manners, Mr. Morgan." She said, readjusting her handbag with difficulty under the strain of her dress, which appeared to be on the verge of exploding. "I wanted to talk to you about the abysmal cuisine they inflict on people here and to ask if you were available to share dinner with me," she added a long drooling laugh that made Sackson wish he could just move his arm back a quarter of an inch and break her neck.

Helplessly, Sackson tried to move her to the door, but she only grabbed his waist to hold him back. "Oh, but you are stronger than you look," she said, sounding like a cat meowing as she felt Sackson pulling her.

"Not at all, Mrs. Goodwin," Sackson said, loud enough for others to hear as he counted 45, 46, 47 seconds behind schedule. "It has been such a long time since such a fine-looking lady has accompanied me. But I must say, I am on my way out and…"

"Oh, ho, but you are a sweet one with such a nice accent. You must tell me which part of England you are from, Morgan."

"All in good time," Sackson said as he finally managed to get her out of the hotel. He tried vainly to free himself from her grip, but he couldn't without causing an unwanted scene.

"Car, sir?" Another hotel employee was asking guests who were coming out of the hotel. His eyes found Sackson, and his face broke into a full smile. He instantly stopped helping other guests and made his way toward Sackson.

"Ah, Mr. Laszio, how are you, sir? Your usual driver again, sir? He just pulled up a moment ago and is just around the corner. He is not in your usual car, sir, but in a Humvee; congratulations, sir, on a fine purchase." The doorman pointed a white-gloved hand a few feet up the sidewalk and indicated a left around the corner.

"Who is Mr. Lase-zio?" Mrs. Goodwin asked, looking and sounding like someone just told her they didn't carry a dress for her size.

Sackson smiled, clicking his shoe heels together. He jerked his arm away from Mrs. Goodwin and pulled out another hundred-dollar bill as a tip to the doorman.

"Merci, au revoir," Sackson said calmly as if nothing was amiss to the doorman.

Sackson's rueful smile grew as he saw the confused look on Mrs. Goodwin's face as he waved and said, "Bonjour Monsieur, and how is your family?"

"Well, sir, my family is well. Thank you for asking," the attendant said proudly, spacing his words as if he were talking to someone who couldn't understand English.

"I didn't know you spoke French." Mrs. Goodwin said excitedly, evaluating Sackson from top to bottom when the doorman took his tip.

"This is Mrs. Goodwin; she and I will take some time to see the city," Sackson said, still sounding French, winking at the attendant. The attendant winked back as their ride was pulling up. Sackson gently motioned Mrs. Goodwin down the sidewalk. She moved excitedly now despite her wardrobe restrictions until Sackson opened the door of the Humvee for her.

"I am quivering to ask," Mrs. Goodwin said as she made her third attempt to get into the vehicle. "How do you say, 'take this meal back and tell the chef to bring me something decent to eat' in French?"

Sackson's smile left his face as he lowered his shoulder and shoved her into the Humvee. She made a sound like someone had driven over a chicken and hadn't stopped until he got into the Humvee and shut the door. "Put a sock in it!" Sackson yelled, dropping all charm and not sounding like he was from France or England. Mrs. Goodwin's face pruned as she had just sucked on a sour lemon.

"How... how dare you!" she bellowed in disgust.

"Oy, mate," the driver called back as they slowly merged into traffic. "What did ya bring the old heifer for, mate?"

"HEIFER?!" Mrs. Goodwin shouted. Lunging forward, she started to slap the back of the driver's head clumsily, whimpering, "You stop this car, stop it at once. Do you hear? I will have your license revoked." She was hitting him with each word.

"Leave it, love, if ya don' cut that out, we'll be drivin' unda a buildin'. Oy, mate, strap the heifer down, will ya?"

Sackson grabbed her, pulling her back in her seat. "Let go of me, you multi-lingual pervert, lustful sinner!" she cried, reaching over his lap, desperately pulling on the door handle, whimpering.

"I think she likes you," Sackson said, laughing.

"Aint the first time you had a Sheila in the back seat who wanted me instead of ya."

"Let me out! You let me ou…"

Before she could finish what she was saying, Sackson struck her hard in the throat, crushing her windpipe. He was still looking at the driver, not even giving a glance to see her clutching at her neck, struggling to let air into her lungs. Blood began to bead on her lower lip as her eyes rolled up in her head. Sackson rested the suitcase on the floor and pulled a plastic bag from under his seat, showing no sign that he had just murdered a woman next to him.

"Ya never told me about her coming," the driver called back as he turned left at a busy traffic light.

"She was the banana kick in the game plan," Sackson said, smirking. He had taken off his suit coat and shirt and now was removing his bodysuit, asking, "How are we on time?"

"It's this San Francisco yank traffic. They drive on the wrong side, with steering wheels on the wrong side and a large Sheila off the line on the wrong side. So we are going ta be late ta the game, mate."

Sackson said nothing as he finished changing his clothes. He took special care that all his weapons stayed in place about him as he adorned himself in his American officer's uniform. Sackson finished changing and removed the last object from the plastic bag, pinning his fake military identification to his jacket.

"Why are we pulling over 'ere?" Sackson asked, looking around. "There's nothing around 'ere."

"Exactly," the driver said. "Push the Heffer off on the next block. Then I will get back on the highway."

"Hey, wait," the driver called out in protest as Sackson didn't wait for the next block but opened his door and pushed her body out then and there.

"I was going to slow a bit," the driver said, checking to see if anyone had seen them.

"Her perfume bothered me," Sackson said, with the air of someone who just took the garbage out to the street.

The driver changed his pants and donned a military hat and shirt showing the rank of sergeant while he waited for the traffic lights to change. Sackson's mood did not change until his driver called back, "Arrival in two minutes," as he turned by a sign that said, 'Alameda Naval Base.'

"Car, 5 minutes and 58 seconds. Guards, one minute, two seconds. Door, 11 minutes, 34 seconds, mark, 4 minutes, 3 seconds, mark, 9 minutes' decontamination, and change, 14 minutes one second, mark, 17 minutes until acquisitions," he thought.

They slowed to a stop in front of the first security checkpoint. Showing his identification, he was waved through after a moment. They approached their destination, following the path shown to them.

"Do you know why you're after this guy? I mean, this is risky since, in a few days, the president of the United States himself is supposed to come here. This much trouble to get to this guy; why not just wait and nick what we need at his home or something?" his driver asked, slowing down to ensure they arrived perfectly on time.

"You know what, the Americans watch all day with that guy who used to make you laugh enough ta make beer come out ya nose. If the price is right, mate. We do what they pay us for when and where they giv' the info about."

The late morning sun was climbing over the tops of the palm trees as they were coming to their second checkpoint. "Lieutenant Chisam," the driver roared, turning his identification tag that hung from his uniform so the guard could see it. "Driving Major General Whinzer for security check before the presidential arrival."

The guard eyed the driver's identity tag and then looked into the back seat, clearly impressed as he said, "Yes, sir. Sir, proud to have you, sir."

Once they passed the gate, the driver said, "Coming up on the first mark in 2 minutes and 50 seconds."

"Understood," Sackson said, taking the last explosive package that was on the floor and holding its timer button ready. He eyed his watch and waited till there was one minute to go before he pushed it and slid it under the driver's seat with his foot.

"See you at the rendezvous, Sergeant, as scheduled," Sackson said, now sounding as if he was from Texas.

"Sir, yes, sir, and good luck to you, sir." the driver replied, slowing the Humvee by a curb. "Time and location in… mark," the driver said as he stopped. Sackson pushed the button on his watch to start the timer.

Sackson opened his door and walked with his head high and shoulders back, saluting those he walked by with his suitcase-free hand. His driver drove away, parked the vehicle, and was gone.

Sackson approached the main entrance of the largest building on the base, the only one that bore no signs. Two sentries stood guard on either side of its only door.

Sackson was most concerned about this part of the plan as he was a high-ranking officer without an attending staff. His contact had only given him one set of false identification.

"Sir," the guard to Sackson's right said with a salute. Sackson returned the salute and held his identification out for inspection. When the guard looked down, Sackson checked around to ensure they were not being observed, when he felt two sharp taps from his watch. He had a ten-second window in security to act. The door lock clicked, and the security panel turned green. Both guards turned around in confusion. His programmed watch released a small needle from its base. Sackson struck out, quick and precise, injecting both guards in the neck. The effects were instant as both guards' bodies went rigid. With only five seconds to spare, Sackson moved the guards' arms, hands, and faces back to their sentry positions as they had stood before he arrived. He stepped through the door, and just before closing it, he reached back and forced the guard closest to him to show a smile. The door shut, leaving both guards as still and silent as statues as the security light next to the lock turned red again.

The door locked behind him, and the needle in his watch retracted. He walked on, giving no sign that anything was out of the ordinary. In this climate, the injection he gave the guards would only last two minutes. If someone approached them in their catatonic state before it wore off, he was dead. But if not, they would have no memory of him and be none the wiser for the rest of the day.

"11 minutes, 34 seconds," he whispered to himself, saluting a woman who sat behind a desk with thick security glass separating them.

"Sir, please place your hand on the panel and present your eye for a retinal scan," she said firmly, pointing her rifle at him. Sackson nodded and turned to his right, where there was a flat panel and station to set his face in the wall.

"Major General Calven R. Whinzer, security code Alpha 736-8987 Echo," Sackson said authoritatively into the screen as he placed his hand on the pad while a red light shone in his eyes. Once completed, a green light shone above him.

"Thank you, sir," the guard said, lowering her weapon and turning her attention to the security screens in front of her.

Everything went according to plan as he passed through the following two checkpoints, but he was behind schedule now. He quickened his pace until he came to the men's room and entered the end stall. Once alone, he opened his suitcase and set it on the toilet tank. He opened the briefcase's false panel and removed dark pants, a white shirt, and a tie with a lab coat. He began to change, listening intently as someone entered the bathroom. It sounded like whoever they were, they were washing their hands as Sackson finished dressing and placed his military uniform in the briefcase. He put on a pair of glasses from his lab coat and checked his new identification. Confident in his new appearance, he put his suitcase behind the toilet and pressed one of the number locks at its center. The leather case changed color from a dark brown to an eggshell white, blending and matching the paint color of the bathroom wall.

Opening the stall door, he proceeded to wash his hands. The other person who was now drying their hands was a guard with his back to Sackson.

"Warm today in't it," the guard said, disposing of his paper towel.

"Sure is," Sackson said nasally, using the soap. He was rinsing his hands when the guard turned toward him.

"Funny thing was I saw a guy with your build just come in here who went through all the checkpoints but the first. Our monitor went out at the time that you must have gained entry," the guard said, placing one hand on his weapon and the other on his radio receiver on his shoulder.

Sackson moved like lightning, throwing a handful of soapy water into the guard's face. Briefly stunned, the guard stepped back as Sackson struck, hitting the guard four times in the stomach and chest, forcing the air out of him, and following with a sharp uppercut. Sackson swiftly threw him a left hook, but it fell short when the guard had somehow taken out his legs on the slippery floor. Sackson would have hit the tile floor hard, but he caught the bathroom counter with his left hand. Unable to breathe, the guard fought to say anything into his radio and reached for his sidearm.

Sackson ripped off the sink faucet closest to him and threw it at the guard's face. Water sprung out from it like a geyser as Sackson lunged at the guard, planting his shoulder into the guard's gut. He lashed out, hitting him in the legs, aiming for the peroneal and femoral nerves. The guard slumped over Sackson now, hitting both sides of his ribs with his fists.

The guard's radio called out, "Come in, Yankee Seal 2159. Didn't read your last, over."

Sackson flipped his opponent over him, slamming him to the ground and turning sharply to kick him hard in the side. The guard caught his leg and twisted his foot, bringing him to his knees. Sackson hit the guard hard in the chest with his elbow and pulled the guard's gun from his holster. He pointed it in the guard's face as water pooled on the floor.

"I will pull the trigger if you don't stop now," Sackson said, cocking the gun.

"Come in again, Yankee Seal 2159. Do you copy over?" his radio called out again.

"Give the all-clear response, or your Big Mac-eating days are over, mate."

The guard slowly clicked the microphone 'on' switch and said roughly, "Yankee Seal 2159, all clear, just need a moment after bad shrimp, over."

"Roger that, Yankee Seal, good luck out there."

"Get up!" Sackson ordered, getting to his feet, still pointing the gun at him. "Sit down on the last loo and keep your hands where I can see them."

The guard moved gingerly, and as soon as he sat down, Sackson hit him hard over the head, knocking him out. His body went limp as Sackson emptied the bullets of the gun and clip in the toilet next to him. Flushing them, he shut the stall doors and tried to clean himself up as much as possible. His watch gave him two more taps, telling him he should be entering decontamination now.

"Bugger!" Sackson said, sliding on the wet floor in a hurry to get out of there.

He left the bathroom looking as orderly as possible. Nothing stopped him as he entered the last code he'd been given for the decontamination hall. As he walked out, he was thankful for the process, as his clothes were now dry and showed no sign of his fight in the bathroom.

"Sir," a lovely young lady wearing a lab coat said as the last decontamination door opened before him, "please take your name, leave your cellular phone, and join the others in the press room."

Sackson smiled, "Thank yuh, and where is that? It's my first time here."

"Yes, sir," she said, turning to her left. "If you would follow the yellow line on the floor to your right and pardon the noise, they are about to charge and fire the decelerator again."

Sackson took his false name badge to wear and, pinning it to his chest, said, "Hey, uh… when do yuh get off tonight? I just happen tuh have dis evenin' off and I know the best place tuh get lobstuh."

She glowered at Sackson and pointed at the floor to her left again. "Grill, girl," Sackson said, walking down the hall with eight different colored lines on the ground, all leading down the hall to a single door. When he came to the door and opened it, he was hit with a wave of bright light. Even though he had been training for this for months, nothing could prepare him for what he saw and heard.

He was standing on a metal walkway eight stories high in a room home to an entire underground city. There was a buzz of activity everywhere, with a maze of metal walkways over massive machines humming in use. Shaking away the awe-inspiring sight, Sackson followed the yellow line as it wound its way up, down, and around the amazing city. Even with his training, he started to lose track of all the turns he was making as other colored lines also appeared and disappeared until he came to a small, closed office-type room. It was also guarded in the same fashion as the ones he had passed, and there were about 20 people, all in lab coats, milling around the closed doors.

"Nathan Cassel," a rather pasty-looking man said, stepping toward Sackson with his hand outstretched, "from Ecole Nomale University?"

Sackson shook his hand vigorously, saying, "Oui, Monsieur, and 'ow are you today?"

"Glorious, just glorious!" the man said, shaking Sackson's hand. "You have a strong handshake there. They must be keeping you at the board too long on a triple vector, following the x and y components of the males and females in your halls," the man said and finally let go of Sackson's hand, smiling and laughing as if he'd just said the funniest thing in a pub.

"Mmmm, yes," Sackson said, not understanding what was wrong with this man. "How much longair?"

"Oh, any moment now," the man said, putting a hand on Sackson's shoulder and walking him into the crowd before them. Everyone waiting outside this office seemed to know one another, and not one of them wanted to be with the short, bald man with a huge mustache who had latched on to him.

With each word, Sackson was losing interest in the man and started picturing all the horrific ways he could silence him. From pushing him over the metal scaffolding handrails that separated them from an eight-story drop or waiting to see how long he could hold on if he just held him over the side.

Thankfully, the doors burst open, and he saw his target in the flesh for the first time. The room seemed packed beyond capacity as everyone spilled out, with those in the way parting before one strong man leading the pack.

"General Powell, you are being unreasonable," one woman said, trying to keep up next to him with two men hastening close behind her. "Just let our two team leaders, John Holden and Kevin Ferney, explain it, and I am sure…"

"Enough," the general ordered. His rugged military boots reverberated on the metal walkway as he pulled the crowd deeper into the facility.

"This just proves that some people can't explain how to put cereal in a bowl," the general said, taking a cigar from his vest.

Kevin Ferney caught the women's pleading glance and hastily spoke, "Si, sir, we jus just don't have the proo… proof that you, you want for the Presi—"

"I need someone who made it past a second-grade vocabulary," General Powell interrupted, keeping his head straight as he walked.

"Sir!" Mr. Holden shouted, lunging forward to grab the general's shoulder. The general stopped his march, causing everyone who followed to crash into each other. The general slowly turned to look him in the eye. Everyone else shrunk under his gaze except Mr. Holden. He was not a strong man, but he stood tall.

"You have my attention, and you need to tell me so I can tell the President and the American people what you are doing here. The order is myself, the President, the people, God, and if you touch me again, you will be seeing them in person in that order. Now speak up," the general finished by lighting his cigar. He looked like he was waiting for an answer to what was one plus one.

Mr. Ferney seemed to disappear when Holden squared his shoulders and raised his hands as he explained. "What we are doing is taking the possibility of the theory an antiproton and an anit-atom can be bound together with enough to compare the spectrum of light and emit it with regular hydrogen on a new level, with not just the elements of matter but changing it into doing it with DNA coding."

"Don't put a finger in my barrel," General Powell barked as he started to march away again. "I need to understand what you are saying and be able to pass it on to my superiors while they are playing golf, and what you are telling me will definitely change their handicap. So, if you can't tell me what is going on here in plain and simple terms, then find me someone who will."

"General, sir, you know what DNA is? What we have been doing is very complex. Deoxyribonucleic acid is the building block of everything, and it was discovered and scanned as early as the 1860s. But it never made a huge impact on science until the 1980s."

"That is more like it. Keep talking," the general called, as Sackson tripped up someone in front of him so he could get closer to hear and stay by his target.

"We can map something like you by your chromosomes, by dividing them into smaller fragments and then ordering them into different locations. Now, not only can we do that with you, but we can do that with anything by mapping it into codes like A, T, C, and G or numbers. Thymine, Cytosine, Guanine."

"You are starting to cost someone 20 yards on their drive swing, Holden…"

"All right, stop!" John shouted, coming to a halt and causing everyone and Sackson to bump into one another again. After taking three more steps, General Powell stopped and turned slowly around. He fixed John with penetrating eyes, making everyone's blood run cold. No one moved or made a sound until Mr. Powell took his cigar out of his mouth. He smiled, dropped his cigar on the metal walkway, and put it out with his foot.

"All right, Mr. Holden, I'm listening," the general said, folding his arms.

John was breathing heavily as Sackson noticed that he looked pale, almost sick, and had lost some weight compared to the pictures his client had given him.

"We know what makes us up, and now we find differences. We have one of the oldest human fossils discovered in Ethiopia, over 160,000 years old, found under two layers of volcanic ash. We have been mapping out dinosaur DNA, some 243 million years old. We have been studying and making a timeline from then until now, and we are seeing differences not only in evolution but also in finding the way they have been changed."

"Jurassic Park?" the general asked, standing motionless.

"Uh, kind of," John said as he walked forward. "For things like that, you need living bone composed of mineral components like calcium hydroxyapatite and organic components such as collagen, blood cells, etc. Right now, that isn't what we want you to understand. We want you to know that we are learning the difference between everyone and everything's DNA, from a dinosaur to the man who pressed your uniform. More importantly, we are learning how they changed and how we could change them. That is what we are discovering."

"That's operation Red Thorn?" The general asked. "So, what is going on with Operation Black Thorn?"

"That is something else, with respect to temporal displacement fields, regarding displacing DNA out of its natural reality and part of the Arc Project. If you just listen and give us the time to show you, I think what we have here will change this nation and the world."

Sackson was impressed at someone who looked so feeble, speaking up to someone who looked like he had eaten the heads of nations for breakfast. Maybe he would let this man live after all this was over.

"Doctor John Holden, please return to your office for a phone call. Doctor John Holden, please return to your office for a phone call." The loudspeakers rang out through the entire facility.

"Tell me this," the general said, not blinking, "Will Project Red Thorn be the answer to our intel on the bioweapon we discovered a week ago?"

"Sir, if we are right, this will answer everything."

"All right, son, you got your funding," the general said, taking out another cigar.

"Thank you, sir," Holden said. "Please excuse me."

Before he even turned, the general finished, "You got your funding if you are the one giving me and the President weekly reports."

Holden didn't look back as he went to his office, not answering the general. He walked quickly down endless turns until he reached the ground level, which had trucks, forklifts, carts, walkways, offices, endless machines, and vats of every chemical mixing and turning, and all around them, large electrical cables, like the veins of a giant.

John Holden slowed his long walk in front of a lone office in the center of the complex. After entering his security code and opening the door, the light came on, illuminating an office with a solitary desk in the middle of the room. The walls were covered in hand-written equations and computer screens showing loading screens, power levels, and calculations, still searching for a solution.

"Computer, answer the call," John said weakly. He was thankful to be alone momentarily as he pushed the door shut. Before it closed, something stopped it.

"There is no call waiting for you, John," the computer's voice responded.

Just then, before the door could shut, something hit him hard in the head. Lights filled his closed eyes as he fell. Someone pushed him hard in the back and shut the door with a snap.

"Who are you? How did you get—" John started to say but was stopped when Sackson kicked him in the gut. John coughed as he held his stomach. Sackson grabbed him by the collar and pulled him to sit at the computer desk.

"You know, you are not as smart as I thought," Sackson said, pulling a knife from under his lab coat. "If you were smarter, you would have known that if someone wanted to get in touch with you, they would have called you on your mobile and not back to your office."

John started to laugh between his coughs as he struggled to breathe. "We are hundreds of feet below ground." John choked. "You couldn't get a call from anyone down here, not to mention all the interference from the equipment, so if knowing that makes me dumb, what does that make you?"

Slam! Sackson pushed John's face hard down on the desk, causing him to become silent once more.

Sackson grabbed John by the hair and moved over to stand behind him. He pressed the knife against the back of John's skull.

"Now, log on to your computer," he ordered, sounding frustrated. With one hand ready to kill John, he started to take out parts of a gun he had hidden on his person and assembled it on John's desk.

John did not move his hands. He only sat limp and dizzy. Sackson didn't hesitate for a minute as he hit John in the back of the head again with his elbow. John's face flew forward and slammed against the keyboard on his dark brown desk. He didn't lift his head as cold blood dripped down his chin. The back of his head throbbed with unbelievable pain. Sackson grabbed John's hair and lifted his head while leaning over to speak into his ear.

"Now login with your code, and that will be all, and I will let you live," Sackson ordered, pressing the barrel of the gun he'd just assembled into John's neck.

Weakly, John lifted his heavy hands above the desk and set them on the keyboard. Sackson let go of John's head and, with his free hand, turned on the computer monitors, still holding the gun steady with his finger on the trigger. The monitors flickered with each key. John entered his login and password.

John hesitated before hitting enter. "Do it!" Sackson shouted as he pushed John's chair forward, pinning his chest against the sharp corner of the desk. John squirmed in pain, and after a moment, he hit enter. The computer screen changed to a startup screen showing John's family in the background.

Sackson grabbed the back of John's chair and pulled it out of the way with John still in it, pushing it hard into the corner of the room. John fell, hitting the hard floor. He could hear nothing from outside the office except for a faint tapping noise.

Sackson removed his watch, turned it around, revealing a drive port, and plugged it into an output on the center monitor. John struggled to lift his head to see what was happening as Sackson repeatedly said, "Come on, come on," to the computer display.

"You will never remove any files from that computer without the access co… How did you?" John didn't finish what he was saying as his computer showed files being copied.

"Clean your face up!" Sackson bellowed. Sackson watched as John rubbed his face off with his sleeves. A ding from the computer told them the download was complete. Sackson removed his watch and put it back on his wrist. Still pointing a gun at John, he waved the barrel up.

"Get up!" Sackson said calmly. "You are my ticket out of here." John shakily stood. "Where are you from? Your inflection is off."

"Move," Sackson called, lifting an eyebrow.

"I cannot comprehend what you took or needed from my computer, but there are only maybe five people in the world who could even understand it. Where are you from?" John asked bravely as he walked across his office, reaching for the door handle.

"You won't ever know the weather outside unless you do as I say. I said move. And remember one false move and…" Sackson finished what he was saying by just waving his gun in John's eye.

"All right, all right," John said shakily.

Sackson checked his watch for the last time and clicked one more button on the side of it. This one would start burning the briefcase he had concealed on his way in. As it burned, it would release a nerve gas that would paralyze anyone within a city block for one hour. That was more than enough time for him to make it out of the building, detonate the Humvee as a distraction, and escape.

John opened the door slowly, not taking his eyes off his attacker. Sackson followed him closely behind and shut the door as soon as they were clear. Nothing appeared out of the ordinary from when he had come in. John was taking Sackson back the way they had come. He moved more slowly, his sore side giving him problems standing upright as they climbed the narrow stairs.

They had made it up to the top level when Sackson could see the office room he was first sent to when he came in. The nerve gas should have taken care of everyone in the hallways, and as soon as he got there, it should be clear and safe to breathe.

"You are doing a good job," Sackson said, sounding again like a lab nerd. "You might just live through this."

They had just passed the office room and turned the corner when John came to a stop. Sackson almost bumped into him.

"That's what you think," John said lightly. Then he fell to the metal grating walkway.

"*Bang!*" The office doors behind Sackson were thrown open, and military guards poured out, all with rifles pointed right at Sackson. All of them were yelling at him, "Drop the gun, put up your hands, and get on your knees!" The walkway shook as more guards blazed toward them. He was surrounded before he had a moment to think.

Sackson slowly raised his hands, dropping his gun. As his hands reached his face, he removed the fake mustache and smiled. When his hands were up, John got to his feet.

"See, if you were smarter, you would have known that it was Morse code being tapped in the hallway letting me know to bring you here, that they were ready for you, and that they found your briefcase before anything else happened. So the only way you will live is by cooperating with us," John smirked, breathing a sigh of relief.

Sackson dropped his head and cracked a smile. He took a single step back, which made every gun move and every trigger finger flinch.

"Who are you? Who sent you?" John asked, taking a step forward. "How did you get this far in here? Who sent you?"

Sackson's heart was pounding as he took another step back. He was now pushed up against the side handrail eight stories from a solid concrete floor.

"You know, mate," Sackson said in relief. "I need a rest, and this hairpiece really itches."

"Who are you?" John shouted louder, inching closer to Sackson as each gun still tentatively pointed at him.

Sackson snorted briskly and laughed, scratching his head. He seemed unconcerned with the fact that there was no way that he could escape alive.

"You don't want to know who I am. You don't want to know your enemy, mate." Sackson was blindly leaning on the handrail that was just above his waist. He clasped his hands behind his head. "You Yankees only like ta put a face to your enemy after you kill them."

"Get down on your knees," the closest security guard ordered, stepping forward.

Sackson shrugged his shoulders and clinched his hands tightly, "Trying ta lighten the mood, mate. You don't know who you can trust when the enemies are within your walls."

Before anyone could act, Sackson had dropped his watch over the side of the railing. Everyone was transfixed watching it fall, and it was lost. Sackson was put in restraints and taken away.

Two

WHEN YOU'RE POPULAR

IN ANOTHER TIME
AND ANOTHER
PLACE…

"How many do you figure?" Banks gasped.

O'Neil took the time to fill his lungs with as much cold mountain air as he could, inhaling some of his beard. He leaned his short frame on a tree and held up a hand, signaling five.

"Fifty," Banks groaned as he rolled his eyes. "How far are we away from the border?"

O'Neil, lifting his bushy eyebrows, waved again with his free hand, showing that he was still unable to speak for lack of air. Unknowingly, Banks' tired legs started to bend, and he sat on a fallen tree. Wiping the sweat from his bald head, Banks weakly nodded to O'Neil. O'Neil understood it was all right to rest. He immediately fell to the damp earth, letting his gear drop everywhere around him.

"We have a few until they discover we doubled back up this gully." Banks said, breathing a little easier. "How much time do you think we have until they figure they're on a false trail?"

O'Neil didn't answer him this time nor indicate that he heard him. He just lay motionless, flat on the ground, looking up at the murky clouds that were starting to gather over them.

"That much, huh?" Banks sighed, knowing that his new friend had given his answer by not replying.

"You keep up pretty good for a dwarf," Banks huffed.

"And yoo almost don't run like a sissy for someone who is so old an' being six-foot-two. Yoo have tae be getting close to mandatory retirement from the service. Yoo look like yoo are still wearing the same clothes given yoo when yoo were me height. Didn't they have needle an' thread in that unforgivin' land yoo broke out of?"

"That's OK," Banks gasped, "being short and covered in hair is not too bad. Hair is beautiful. Don't let anyone tell you differently because your shiny uniform does wonders to contain all that hair on your back."

"How mony people," O'Neil huffed between deep breaths, "have told yoo that they were sorry that yer father ever met yer mother and brought yoo into this world? I know that I am one of them. The other group who likes ya, yoo can count them on one hand with missing fingers. Because after making yer acquaintance, I could kill ya with the rest of 'em."

The smallest of smiles appeared on Banks' dirty face. "They are good," Banks coughed, "give them about ten to follow the trail and about five to figure we backtracked on them. We have about thirty until they are on us again."

"After what mist have been an 'orrible pregnancy and excruciating birth yoo popped intae unfortunate people's lives." O'Neil didn't seem to pay attention to Banks as he lay sprawled out on the ground. "No doubt yer good parents tried to raise yoo but no mortal could stand yoo too long, so they had ta gave yoo up to save themsel's. Which is what I should have done."

Banks also didn't give any sign that he was listening to O'Neil as he was looking at the limbs of the trees above them. "The wind is in our favor, so they can't sniff us out."

"I can see it was difficult bein' so young and no one could stand the sight of yoo Must 'ave raised yoorself in the wilderness. Och, and I think yoor ugly too by the way," O'Neil growled breathing easier now.

"Unless," Banks moaned, "they have something waiting up there for us."

"Bein' so unloved and causing destruction where ever yoo went. Yoo ran tae the only organization that yoo could, the Military. But not even our finest could stand yoor stench, so off yoo were sent to the defense forces.

Once yoo must uh destroyed everything there they sent yoo oot 'ere where I just happened to find yoo."

"Maybe we haven't been so lucky after all," Banks moaned while he stretched.

"Lucky?" O'Neil exclaimed with a laugh, indicating that he was listening for the first time.

"The only luck ah think anyone has had with yoo is when they said goodbye. Yoor aboot as sought after as soberness." O'Neil groaned as he arched his short frame off the ground, stretching his back.

"These hit and runs. Rise and hides have been working well, but not if they are driving us towards something." Banks wiped the sweat from his face again and reached for his water skin.

"Has anyone left yoo and not felt good aboot it, even if you had a reflection in a mirror? Which I doot you have."

Banks took a long drink from his water skin and secured it at his side. He patted around his body as if he were looking for something. He stopped when he felt one of the smallest traveling packs he was carrying over his tattered clothes.

"Can't relax, can yoo?" O'Neil said, not looking at him, when, oddly, what appeared to be the brownest part of O'Neil's long beard seemed to move on its own. It came off his face and hurried down to his side. The lively hair turned out to be a squirrel. O'Neil, either from fatigue or familiarity with having a squirrel on him, gave no notice to it. The squirrel wriggled into O'Neil's knapsack and retrieved two small portions of dry bread. It then hurried up, dropping one in O'Neil's mouth, and gave the other two Banks.

"Thanks, Nuts," Banks sighed. "How did he know I was hungry?"

"Yoo are always keen for something tae eat. An' besides, it looks like we are going tae get that cloud cover yoo wanted. Storm is movin' in fast."

After looking up for so long, Banks rubbed his neck as he watched Nuts dart back onto O'Neil's round frame. Banks smiled again, thinking how lucky it was that O'Neil came across him. His mind went back to where it always did these past few days.

"Yoor think'en about him again, arn't yoo?"

"You're very fast O'Neil."

"It worn't your fault."

"I wish I never volunteered for this mission."

"Yoo took the words right out of where I insert me ale and mead!"

The moments came and went, waiting for one to say what must be said. "It wasn't yer fault that yoo were the only one tae make it here with the package and Heavy and the others didn't."

Their conversation paused again. "At least yoo both made it tae the rendezvous point with the package, which would be one pretty hard diaper tae fill."

"Wait," Banks said, looking confused. "Is that a good thing?" His body was so exhausted that he didn't have the strength to hold those memories at bay. He tried to raise his hand to wipe the sweat from his face again but was too weak to. He could see Heavy telling him to leave him behind after he could go no further. Blinking hard, he tried again to block that image out as he didn't want to relive what kept appearing in his dreams every night since it happened. The image of Heavy's face as he held his wounded leg, yelling at Banks to go as he held off the hunting party.

Banks slowly lowered his head as he twisted his face in concentration. His eyes were tightly closed, but he saw and felt everything again as if he were doomed to repeat it. The feeling of Nut's tiny claws on his leg drove those images back, bringing the small open grove where he was back into focus. Banks, blinking hard, could barely see the image of Nuts sitting on his knee, now offering a piece of fruit. Banks' trembling hand took it from the squirrel with a nod of thanks. He watched as Nuts scurried back to O'Neil, and with a grateful sigh, Banks saw that O'Neil hadn't noticed what he'd just been through. A fresh breeze from the approaching storm told him he was covered in a new layer of sweat. His muscles ached as they released their grip over him. He didn't know that he had been shivering until his muscles stopped, and he was reminded with a breeze that he was wearing clothes to blend into the environment in that were tattered and torn, while O'Neil's uniform was only showing minor wear.

Banks twisted his body around to remove one of the travel packs on his belt he had patted earlier. In it were two sacks that he was informed not to open until he had reached Karmaridon. From the time when both bags were given to him, he wished to peer into their secrets. One pack was cold to the touch, heavy, and elongated. The other felt warm, smaller, and seemed to be filled with small stones. Banks' eyes reflected the oddest thing about both packages. Both bundles illuminated a brilliant light on their own. The heavy one gave the soft glow of a deep red, while the other seemed a dazzling white; both could be seen even through the cloth that held them.

"Checking them again, are we?" O'Neil coughed, almost breathing normally now. O'Neil knew what Banks was doing without even turning to look.

Banks glared at O'Neil momentarily and then returned both bundles to his pack. He was about to remark that O'Neil's beard looked like he just had very long nose hair. But when he inhaled to speak, something in the air alarmed him.

"O'Neil." He whispered with urgency.

"No! Whatever it is, no. Ever since I saw yoo running from this hunting party of ten and I thought I was doing the right thin' tae jump in and drive them back tae save your skinny butt. Then that ten became thirty, tae forty, tae fifty. Tae... how many are after us new?"

"O'Neil."

"About two hundred, I think noo."

"O'Neil."

"There was no bonding time between me and yoo. Och, not nearly enough bonding time for this kind of stuff tae happen between us."

"O'Neil!" Banks grunted pleadingly as he grabbed his Long Bow Caster and got behind the mossy fallen log on which he rested his head.

"I think tis time that we reestablish our relationship. Because from the first time I saw yoo, I was not looking forward tae the second time I would see yoo. Then there is the noise and odder problems of sharing a campsite with yoo. Yoo are best viewed from afar. We need tae start over. That's it! Just forget that time I first saw yoo and thought that I might lose me job if I didnae help yoo."

"O'Neil!" Banks pleaded in a hushed, urgent undertone. "Any other dwarf would listen, O'Neil!"

"Yoo know that's why I did it, didn't yoo?" He croaked. "So they would have caught yoo, beat yoo fur a wee amount of time. Knowing yoo now. That would have been good for yoo. Yoo need a good beatin'."

"If you want to tell someone else who would care about this, they will be here in a minute," Banks called, hunching down further behind the log, readying his strength through his weapon. O'Neil still lay just where he was, sprawled out, looking up at the sky.

"Yoor always full of the bad news. Why do yoo have tae always give bad news? How much time do yoo think we got now?" O'Neil asked, the playfulness gone from his voice.

Before Banks could respond, dozens of dark plasma bolts shot over O'Neil. Leaves, needles, and twigs fell in their wake before cutting a hole in the trees and soft earth. Sparks erupted when they struck, causing Banks to take cover as they showered about him. O'Neil lay motionless and sighed, "Och, that much time… Figures with yoo here."

With a howl of rage, two figures emerged from the thick underbrush into the clearing just below Banks and O'Neil. The first was a female Orc who charged uphill toward them, brandishing a long sword over her head. A lean troll dropped a short plasma crossbow, charged, and leaped into the air at O'Neil, drawing short swords.

Banks rose from his concealment, charging his bow caster with a shot. Light started in his right hand as he pulled back the nock and string to his other hand and grip, revealing an arrow made of light. The Orcs' face changed oddly from one of delight to terror at the sight of Bank's weapon. She spun wildly down for cover, dodging Banks' shot as the troll landed on O'Neil with two short swords in his gnarled hands bearing down on him.

O'Neil caught him with his short arms holding the troll's wrists, stopping the points of both swords from stabbing him. O'Neil kicked out at the skinny troll, causing him to volt over his head. Banks' eyes left the sights of his weapon to find his friend, and when they returned, the Orc was leaning from behind a tree, winding up her arm with two daggers to throw at him. Banks fired again and fell to his side, letting both daggers fly over him.

O'Neil rolled, causing some of his equipment and weapons to fall from his pack and travel pouches. He got to his knees before the troll was on him again. The troll slashed and swiped at him with both swords, but O'Neil fell back, and the blows missed. The troll leaped again, but O'Neil was ready this time to catch his arms. Both were locked as before, the slender troll desperate to drive his weapons into O'Neil's face. O'Neil's arms were locked, holding the trolls, and this time, the troll stood over O'Neil in a wide stance so he could not be kicked. Banks charged another bolt as the Orc bounded behind another tree for better cover towards him. Banks fired again and missed, as sparks sprinkled over the Orc.

O'Neil let go with one hand and twisted, causing the long dagger thrust to miss. He then struck the Troll hard across the face. The blow caused the Troll to release the dagger he was still trying to force into O'Neil. Howling in rage again, he grabbed O'Neil's throat with one hand and pulled the dagger out of the ground, trying to stab past O'Neil's defensive grip on his arm. O'Neil felt the ground around him with his free hand, trying to find his axe. The troll's face twisted in anger, fitting O'Neil for his tombstone behind his eyes. Drops or his drool fell from its long tusks onto O'Neil's hairy cheek.

"Nuts, get me axe," O'Neil choked.

The squirrel bounded out from somewhere under O'Neil's arm, but when it got to the axe rod a few feet away, it squeaked and chirped in protest, unable to lift it. Nuts stood on its hind legs with both hands on its hips, chirping its complaints at O'Neil.

"Noow? Yoo want to talk about this noow?" O'Neil grunted. "I'm a wee bit busy at the moment."

Nuts waved at the axe rod and then to his thin arms, still squeaking in anger at O'Neil. Banks fired two more shots at the Orc, who dove behind the last tree separating him and her.

"Listen, yoo miniature throw pillow, we will blather on about whatever yoo want after I tend tae me current pressing problem. But if it's nae too much trouble? I have me hands full right now. So kindly get me something tae knock this blighter off with, or yoo will be looking for someone else to sing ye tae sleep at night!"

Banks kept his cover fire going to keep the Orc from gaining any more ground while Nuts darted around, searching for something he could lift to use as a weapon for O'Neil. The troll reared back and lunged forward with his wiry frame, trying to use what little weight he had as an advantage. O'Neil could only deflect the blows, causing the blade tip to hit the ground on either side of his head with each thrust. O'Neil heard Nuts squeaking approval as he came closer to his head. Nuts had rolled an apple close that had fallen from O'Neil's haversack. Seeing it, O'Neil rolled his eyes in disbelief.

Every time the orc popped out from behind the tree, Banks would fire a shot at her. The orc howled in frustration and rammed her shoulder into the tree. She slammed into the tree repeatedly until, with a massive howl and terrible crack, it started to break right where Banks's shots had weakened it. Fearing that she would cause the tree to fall on him, Banks jumped back.

As soon as he was exposed, the orc peered around the weakened tree and fired back. She threw dagger after dagger that landed in the soft earth on Banks's heels. With each throw, she limped farther out from under the damaged tree she had taken refuge behind. One of Banks's shots must have grazed her thigh as she was limping. Miss after miss, her frustration rose until she threw a small ax. Banks was able to crawl over a dead tree, which was large enough to conceal him and block the axe. In his haste, he dropped his bow.

Oddly enough, the troll and O'Neil stopped fighting as both watched Banks narrowly dodge the axe with their arms still locked in combat. The troll's long face turned and smiled widely at O'Neil. O'Neil eyed him and matched his smile for a moment. Unexpectedly, O'Neil freed one hand, and with one quick hit to the troll's throat, the troll opened his mouth wide. O'Neil reached out, grabbed the apple, and thrust it in the open mouth of the troll, causing him to gag on it. The troll's eyes bulged as he made an odd squawking noise struggling to suck air past the apple now firmly lodged in his mouth. O'Neil hit him hard, causing the shocked, gasping troll to fall off him.

There was no sign of Banks as the orc started charging, throwing up handfuls of dirt as she clawed her way up toward her prey. O'Neil, free now, snatched up his axe rod and, summoning his strength, invoked the axe blades to spring to life as he stood in an attack stance. The gagging troll was on his knees, hitting his stomach, trying to dislodge the apple choking him. The orc stopped climbing and brought up her swords, ready to take on O'Neil. Her smile froze as she followed O'Neil's gaze, which didn't fall on her but on his friend. She turned to see Banks's body lying on the log he was just behind. He had pulled out the axe embedded in it, and it was just leaving his fingertips, slicing the air toward her.

She howled in anger as she spun around, dodging the axe. She readied herself again in a fighting stance but was stopped by the look of joy on Banks's face. She was about to charge when a loud crack caused her to turn around. She had just enough time to understand that the axe Bank threw had hit the large tree where it was weak, causing it to break and fall right on top of her. Banks rolled back behind the log as the top of the fallen tree came crashing down on him. O'Neil shielded himself from the dust and earth that was thrown up in the air with his arms. Once he waved the air clear so he could breathe, he looked in horror at where Banks had been crushed. Thankfully, a moment later, Banks emerged from underneath the collapsed tree.

"Anyone tell yoo where yoo belong? Becouse I would loove for yoo to return there." O'Neil garbled as he wiped the troll's drool off his beard.

Banks extricated himself from the fallen tree, looking past O'Neil down the mountainside. He felt behind his hip to ensure the prized cargo was safe.

"Yoo just checked those wee things." O'Neil barked as he slowly picked up his scattered belongings. He gave no aid to the troll desperately reaching for him for help, his green skin now turning a light pink.

"Tae, continue what I was saying before," O'Neil said as he purposefully stepped on the troll's hand. "I liked yoo better from a distance. Ah cannae believe a'body stayed around long enough that could be called yoor friend."

"Well, you're still alive," Banks smirked as he charged another bolt and got behind a tree.

"Aye, despite yoor best efforts. But before yoo dream up another way for the rest of yoor lonely friends down there, tae come up and visit. How come they only sent two?"

O'Neil started to look over the dead orc more closely while Banks covered him with his bow. Nuts scampered up and sat on O'Neil's shoulder, holding his nose and waving a paw in front of his mouth.

"I know if he waited a wee bit longer, the rain would have given him his bath this month," O'Neil remarked. "No running pack or long-term gear."

Banks charged down his bow. "I don't like it. Only two on a one-way mission. I don't get it."

The troll had finally dislodged the apple from his mouth by falling hard on his back. The apple popped out with a stomach-turning, moist, popping sound. Banks and O'Neil watched him silently as he turned over, filling his lungs like he had never breathed. The troll laughed oddly with each wheezing exhale. He barely had enough strength to stand as he felt around for his weapons. Banks and O'Neil looked on, amused.

"Do you want him? Or would you like him to drool on you some more?"

Before O'Neil could respond, there came a strange new sound. Through the wind and darkening sky, a whistling was getting louder. Banks froze as the whistling got louder from above until a long shaft hit the troll right in the middle and embedded itself in the ground. It was right between Banks and O'Neil as they heard the troll give off one last sick laugh.

"Now there's a sight that will turn your heart sideways in ya. It's amazing yoo made it past when yoo was weaned," O'Neil groaned.

"Shrikes!" Banks yelled as he started to run up the mountain.

WHEN IT RAINS, IT POURS

The shrike embedded itself into the ground and, after a moment, erupted into an aura of darkness. It looked as if the aura were composed of gloomy, murky flames around the shriek on the ground. Banks and O'Neil both ran up the mountain as quickly as they could. The dark energy of the shrike built up, and then, with the sound of a whip-crack, it erupted, sending a black wave that radiated from the shrike like ripples in a pond. What was living in that radius instantly died, turning dark, devoid of life.

Banks scrambled on all fours, reaching and grabbing at anything he could use to propel himself forward. O'Neil's short legs hampered his efforts to keep up in the underbrush, but he made up for it with his superior strength. He leaped and bounded whenever it was possible to gain ground.

The whistles and whines of more shrikes came from below them, driving them up the mountain. The sharp sounds they made flying and the cracks of their eruption caused Banks to glance over his shoulder to see the area behind him. The mountainside below them was once lush and green. Now, it appeared dead, as if a fire had torn through that area months before.

Banks climbed on, but the price he had to pay to live through this mission began to take its toll. His body ached, his fingers started to give way, his strength was leaving him, and the cold was seeping into his tattered clothing down to his bones.

Banks gave no notice to his breath that he could see now in the cold. The soft earth that he was climbing on started to feel more challenging. The trees were thinning out as

Banks and O'Neil had climbed up to a rock line in the mountainside. Both climbed up the mountain, aiding one another as death washed below them, driving them on.

"We would stand a chance if we go over that high cliff," Banks puffed.

"I think that's a good idea. Besides, from the sounds of the party do'n there are about three hundred and I do't feel that friendly at the mooment," O'Neil huffed.

Banks again looked down as the sun's light dipped behind the opposing mountains. Darkness crept over them as tiny raindrops fell from the sky above. Torchlights were lit below, showing a group of about fifty. Then it appeared to be a hundred, then two hundred. With the sounds of trumpets and horns, the flaming lights started up the mountain toward them. Two lines of torchlights formed, moving to their left and right sides to box them in.

"Well," Banks groaned, out of breath again.

"Yeah," O'Neil grumbled in response as they both started climbing again as best as they could. The slope of the rocks was not steep, but their ruggedness hampered their movement.

"Did yoo promise them free drinks at the pub and skip out on the bill, because they really want yoo?" O'Neil barked as he helped Banks up a challenging rock.

"Less talk, more climbing," Banks puffed.

"Yoo have a tongue like a young pixen," O'Neil spat. "If yoo want tae use your lips other than for climbing, which they are big enough tae by the way, then don't be putting on the hate for those whose lips were made for kissing and taken a wee goldie now and then." O'Neil huffed as he changed hand grips on a slippery rock. "Since the only people who care tae hear from yoo is me, who yoo should buy a drink fer, and those who are coming up, whose only drink that yoo would buy is from a puddal. Why dae yoo be thinkin' they would use torches and let us know they was coming? Most of 'em see better in the dark anyway."

The fatigue in Banks grew from his heart to his fingers and lips. He didn't answer for some time as he forced himself to climb on. "See that big bluff rock face above us?" Banks panted as he lifted his body on and on.

"Aye," O'Neil barked.

"Our friends below us must have some company waiting there," Banks wheezed as the wisps of the shrikes began again. "I think you will finally be rid of me when we get there."

"Aye," O'Neil groaned again, but this time there was no joy in his tone.

The rain grew heavier as they climbed with new waves of cold wind. Their wet clothes were now sticking to their bodies as they helped each other climb the rocks that were growing increasingly difficult to navigate. The lights had now reached the death line of the first shrikes. However, the shrikes kept coming, and a few found places in the rocks to score a hit to erupt. There was nowhere else to go but up to face whatever was waiting for them.

They approached just below the cliff edge and slowed their climb while Nuts shivered under O'Neil's beard. "We fight together, one with his back to the ledge, giving the other time to rest." Banks gasped, spitting out rain from his mouth. "If there are too many, you go first and take the leaders while I shoot range."

"Wait a tick, that's all bum and parsley," O'Neil said as he twisted the water out of his beard. "Yoo, go first? I doona think so."

"What did you say when I first saw you? You're a long time dead. Besides, I have the package," Banks said, indicating his back.

"Arn't yoo the egg with a double yolk? I have not had a drop of the creature for two weeks and I am not dying without it, so if yoo think that I am going to die today, so I will go and take care of…"

"We go together!" Banks interrupted.

"Noo, I can't let yoo just…" O'Neil barked.

"Fine. On three." Banks nodded.

"On three?" O'Neil said mockingly, sounding like Banks. "Why should we both goo? The one who goes up there and makes it would sure be a coin for half a loaf. So why don't yoo hide, and I get me chance at glory and give them all what's coming? While yoo try and skip oout on da tab?"

Banks didn't pay attention to what O'Neil was saying this time and started to count.

"One."

"Yoo, make a better door than a window. So, shut it."

"Two," Banks said soberly and readied his bow.

"Noo, yoo, stay here. I have to kill at least five o' the Fury to keep me head up. Don't leave me with only…"

"Three!" Banks shouted and started to rise.

Crash! Before Banks or O'Neil could lift themselves over the ledge, a body was thrown over their heads. It rolled down the mountain until it came to rest on a sharp rock. Banks and O'Neil looked at each other, then the body down the mountain, and then back to one another in confusion.

"Or we can both go noo. I'm good. Aye, good noo," O'Neil sniffed.

They both craned their heads to peer over what was above them on the rock face. The rain was falling hard now, whipping in the wind and with the air illuminated with lightning. They both could see at least forty orcs, trolls, and imps in Fury armor waiting for them. But as they lifted themselves over the ledge, Banks and O'Neil were amazed to find that all of them were dead. Some lay on the ground, horribly killed, while others were impaled on the sparse trees, giving the appearance that they were still alive before meeting their gruesome fate.

"What happened?" Banks moaned, unaware that he was the one who said it.

"Well, I am not one to not kiss the winning pony before the race. Let's be off while we can," O'Neil said happily, clasping his wet hands together, already starting to move on.

"Somethings not right," Banks said, stepping over a large corpse to grab O'Neil's shoulder.

"What killed them?" Banks asked.

"Yoo're a wee scunner about this!" O'Neil said almost lovingly. "So, I say we change yoor head because we have a clear path to the border and I am with yoo till the end. But let's not keep your head here. Let's keep it moving as we have all those bloodthirsty, homicidal, bedwetting, ruthless, nose-picking, barbaric, pimple-faced, non-toilet trained, bad-breath sorority group that are coming dis way. All right? Soo, noow, let's be off," O'Neil said as he almost danced off, being careful to step on those who were dead.

Banks didn't move as the rain fell about him. He only looked down at those who had fallen.

"I don't see any tracks of whatever did this." He looked around at the tree line in front of him that O'Neil went through.

Shouts and cries from below were getting closer. Banks started to move on, but his mind didn't leave that spot for some time as the rocks thinned out, and his way up the mountain was easier. Whatever had done this was powerful, and as O'Neil kept reminding him, the mission was what was important.

Now That Is Bad

Atop a dark balcony far from the border stood a lone, tall, hooded figure taking in the sight of the last rays of the sun. He shifted his stance as another night was being born. Its birth spawned activity in the evil city beyond. Most out there hated the sun and used his kind to do their dirty work in keeping the unbelievers out of their lands. Despite that knowledge, a tiny flame of pride from all the Fury's accomplishments grew in his chest.

That flame was quickly extinguished when he felt the parchment in his hand again. He gripped it harder out of frustration every time he thought of it. It was a wonder that the words were still visible after he had read them so often. They were ordered to come to Necrotie at once and to transfer command of his troops to his subordinate. There could be only one reason for this. It must be because he lost those prisoners who escaped across the border. His rage changed to caution when a hissing voice behind him called, "Voscasss."

Voscass turned to the giant lizard who had bid his audience. He walked across the large, barren room, lit only by blue crystal slime creatures that oozed their way across the ceiling. The light showed his worn Hunter Officer traveler's uniform, but he refused to give up his sailor's heavy traveling boots, which knocked loudly on the stone floor as the seven-foot-tall lizard held the large wooden door open for him.

Voscass said nothing when he stopped before the massive scaly guard and glared at him with his one eye.

"You have been sssummoned," it hissed as it turned out the door swinging a large pole with a heavy blade on end balanced on its left shoulder. The inner building was vast and treacherous before them. Their steps echoed around them while faint calls of creatures came from distant directions. The noises surrounded them while they continued down the dim paths, giving no indication of where they had started. Neither of them spoke as they marched. They passed trophies of heads, skeletons, and skulls of every kind adorning the walls until they turned to a doorway that was large enough for a giant to enter.

Standing on either side of the door were two more guards. One was another lizard taller than Voscass guide, while the other was a shorter, stouter fish-like humanoid. It made a horrible slurping sound with each deep breath. They both held long lances before them that matched their gray armor. When Voscass approached, each sentry stared at him guarding the large wooden door behind them. All three sentries each waited in silence with all eyes on Voscass. Voscass could only pace to ease his tension. He pounded his hands together in fists, smashing the written orders. Before any new thought could enter his mind, the sounds of approaching steps grew louder over the shrieks from afar.

Another guard came in the dim blue light with a muscular steel-clad ape dragging a long mace behind him. Their watches opened the large gate with some difficulty as they bid Voscass and the ape to enter. When the gates parted, they released a blast of cold air that pushed Voscass back while his guards stood steady, accustomed to the wind.

Voscass stepped forward, taking his place next to his attendant again, not noticing the invitation to enter the room. "You are to go in together while we sstay here," his guard said as he turned and shut the door.

Voscass was not one to fear, but as he stood at the entryway of a large, darkened hall, it took him a moment to go in. He took both his swords by the hilt in hand that hung in their sheaths at his side. He stepped into the room, not noticing that he had dropped the parchment he'd gripped so tightly for so long. The grand hall had no windows but was lit by the elements strangely oozing on the walls and ceiling. They only gave enough light to bathe the room in twilight. The cold room appeared to have been the battleground for some skirmish years ago. Broken weapons lay untouched in the bony hands that once held them. Fragmented fixtures of tables, chairs, and tapestries bore the signs of years of neglect over the bodies of corpses from long ago.

The door shut behind him, leaving Voscass two steps ahead of his hairy companion. Voscass sniffed the air and used all his senses to scan the room. He slowly moved forward to peer at an oversized stone chair that was raised at the top of steps on the far side of the hall. He moved cautiously, not giving in alarm, seeing that the throne had tattered rags covering it. Over the sound of boots crunching through eons of dust and decay, a soft laugh sounded in the hall. His companion moved slowly, hunched over on all fours, parallel with him, giving no word.

Voscass poised himself for an attack as the room became even colder. His cohort took a defensive stance abruptly when his dark eyes found something moving. What looked like darkness in a prominent lone stone chair across the hall slowly stood. Its emotionless laughter started low and continued while it sluggishly descended the stairs toward them. It was covered in dark rags, revealing nothing of itself while it dragged its right leg as it came towards them.

Voscass was much larger than the one approaching him, and the ape with him was even bigger than them. He shared a weary glance with his friend, telling him he was tempted to strike first. Their adversary was hunched over and close enough to see its left hand's sharp white fingertips and a grayish snowy chin protruding under the dark garb. The room oddly grew colder with its approach as it dragged its right leg and drew sharp, raspy breaths.

"You have spirit, don't you both?" The hooded figure asked. The sound of that voice knocked the air out of him.

The shock caused Voscass to act instinctively as he dropped his robe to free his weapons. He drew his swords, holding them before him at the ready. Next to him, the ape growled, pounding his chest armor and readying his mace. Their rival in rags slowed to a halt in front of them. Whatever was under those rags had difficulty standing straight as it maneuvered itself to lean on its bad side. They stood five feet away from each other as Voscass wondered if losing those two at the border was enough for him to be killed.

The Fury only had one punishment. Victory meant life, and failure was for the frail. Nothing seemed right in this situation, as with what happened to all those who tried to test him. All that was above him in rank who were weak were shown his strength. If he were to be tested, why would he be ordered here, and why would he be faced with something that appeared as feeble as this? Voscass took a deep breath and tightened his jaw, showing his broken tusk. He gripped his cutlasses, readying himself for what was coming.

"You would fight for what little is your life, would you?" it asked. "That is good, isn't it?" the icy voice said.

"This be not the time to question me till my blade point feels your innards. My life has been me own, and it is my fate to change unless ye feel ye can take it," Voscass barked back.

The ape swiftly charged to his right and leaped to attack the ragged figure. It happened so fast that Voscass could only watch. Five hundred pounds of muscle rose, and just before the ape came down to crush what was holding up those shredded rags, a single white hand swiped at the ape. It sounded like the snapping of fingers when the giant ape fell to the hard stone floor. Voscass took a step back in shock. His strong companion lay on the ground, a motionless, shriveled pile of fur. He was dead.

"You are the one who hunted a human and another north, aren't you?" it asked. Voscass didn't answer but stood still, staring at what was left of his cohort.

"You don't have to worry about anything here now, do you?" the cold figure asked, taking one uneasy step forward. "Overall, you did well, leaving nothing to chance, did you?" His voice was getting lower as his breath grew sharper and rapid with excitement.

"It be too late to change what was done so bring what you have brought me here for," Voscass snapped back. He stood resolute for what was coming, his weapons ready despite the pain he felt in his hands and long ears from the cold.

"You took no risks with killing those you were after, did you? Do you still have the scent of the ones you hunted?" the mysterious voice asked eagerly.

"I care not for those I was sent after and what I have seen here. Belay talk on that perspective and tell me what you be after?"

"The scent!" it called tersely. His voice was not loud, but it carried a power like a rush of cold wind through the room. It came with the force to blow dust and drove the light creatures to hasten their crawl to the other side of the room. "The scent of that which you went after up the mountain. Do you remember the scent to track them still?"

"What if I did? Push on and tell if it would stay your hand to preserve me life."

"Answer, troll! Do you still have the mind to track them?" The hooded figure shouted, causing even the breath from Voscass to become visible in the freezing air. Then it added, almost lovingly, "While you still live."

"One scent still be on me mind but there were a pair and the tuther I never came across," Voscass said, still holding his swords before him ready to defend himself.

"That will do for now, won't it?" The hunched figure growled, panting slightly, showing small vapers of cold above his chin concealed in rags.

"It is time then for you to understand, isn't it?" it said, standing taller, its grayish chin stretching tighter in what could have been a hidden smile. Its left arm moved up, showing a gray dead hand with skin that was so tightly stuck to it that all the bones were visible down to the joints.

"Now is the time for you to join us, isn't it?" he said, bringing a new chill to Voscass's left ear as they were only inches apart. "We are about to take back what is ours. We will invade those who stole from us, aren't we?"

"What scuttle be this?" Voscass asked. "Un where will we be a'goin'?"

"We are going to take back what was taken from us. We are going to kill all those who oppose us. You will come with us to retrieve that which will turn the tide in our favor, won't you? We will rule all and never see anything, not ours again."

"What part of this be mine as those whom I was after be only two and long gone be they?" Voscass asked with more confidence in his voice. Now that it felt like his insides had returned, he lowered his swords, thinking that this was not the moment to show physical strength.

"Before long, we will have it. We will have the Requiem."

Voscass could not hide his amazement as those words filled him. "With the Requiem, noth…nothing could stop us," he stuttered.

The cold companion shifted to look over at Voscass while it rebalanced its weight to rest a cold hand on his shoulder. The hooded figure shuffled toward the door, leading Voscass with him.

"We are among those who will go and claim the Requiem and bring those who are feeble to their knees. We will find the Requiem for the Fury and, at last, rule what was taken from us," he continued while shuffling as Voscass walked beside him.

Still dragging his right leg, the hooded man began to breathe more heavily. It looked like snowy wind came out of his mouth as he said, "There will be opposition, but we will have some of the Counted with us, won't we, and you will track the one for us?"

"Ye are an Elemental, to be sure?" Voscass stated, feeling stronger as he followed him but being careful not to do it too closely.

"I am Larange," the Elemental replied as the large doors parted. Voscass didn't know how cold it was until the heat from outside washed over him.

Larange chuckled again, sending the light creatures to the other end of the room, and Voscass took courage from the looks of fear that the two guards gave as the Elemental went by them, with Voscass walking next to him as an equal.

"We will not fail," Larange said strongly, and he stated before the doors were closed behind them.

"We will find Clint Holden."

GOOD THINGS DON'T ALWAYS COME TO THOSE WHO WAIT

O'Neil couldn't remember how often he went to the window only to see the same view repeatedly. He had been isolated so long that he was tired of listening to himself. The anxiety of the past few weeks kept reappearing in his mind. Being hunted all the way to the border, engage, retreat, engage the enemy, and retreat again, sleepless nights, making cold camp, and having to endure field rations and no spirits for days. He screwed up his face at that horrible memory. No spirits, not even a drop, for days. They made it back alive and leaned on Banks as they gave the proper countersign for the gate to open. They were safe at last. All their hopes that they would finally be able to rest were fleeting as they were ordered past every checkpoint with all possible speed and rushed every minute until they finally came to Karmaridon. O'Neil remembered how his jaw dropped when he saw the massive city for the first time, and Banks asked if his beard was too heavy for his mouth and in need of a trim.

O'Neil shook his head while he turned his gaze from the window over to the table of food. He had never been in Karmaridon before, nor ever this far north. When they were let into the city and led to the military district, Banks and O'Neil were separated. It had been seven days now, being locked in this room with guards looming outside.

O'Neil started pacing again from the window to the bed, the table, and back. Over and over, with the orders of being rushed and hurried, and only now to wait with no word or information on what was going on, not being allowed to leave this room, with diverse leaders questioning him over and over. They asked him about his orders, how he had met Banks, and how they escaped. First, a Chairman of the Council, Chief of the Ministers, First Executive, Prime Senator Chairmen representative, and Vice-admiral who brought her entire staff. Then came the ones who just asked questions while those they brought recorded every word he said: a Banking Circle Leader, a Trade Party member, a hairy Colonel, a Chapter cadet with a Group commodore, and even some who were historians. All of them came and only asked questions with no explanation.

"I can't take this anymore!" O'Neil bellowed as he looked around his small room again, desperate to find anything to relieve his pressure and apprehension. Not finding anything, he hopped onto the bed and started jumping up and down, howling in madness with each bound.

He was so loud that he didn't hear the knocking on the door, nor the sound of it opening. With the crack of the bed breaking, Banks asked, "Following orders, or are you just trying to see things a little higher than your normal perspective?"

"I'm just thankful that I was not born tae be a skinny-malinky long leg who looks like a barrel o' fruit trying tae shift aboot on a pair o' toothpicks," O'Neil said calmly as he glided effortlessly off the broken bed.

"And I am glad tae see that yoo got the promotion that yoo are so unqualified for. You went from being a homeless Jimmy running on the wrong side o' the border tae hotel maidservant. Soo yoo should no' the bed is too hard."

"We have work to do," Banks ordered with a wry smile.

"Oh, is the building out of linen cloths, is it?"

Banks turned to leave O'Neil standing with a peculiar look on his face. Four guards quickly entered the room when Banks was out of the doorway.

"Sir, would you please come with me, sir?" a rather large minotaur in Home Guard armor called.

"If this is about the bed, would yoo believe me if I told yoo a giant came in here through yonder windae tae hop on the bed?" O'Neil asked, looking sheepishly. The other three guards wasted no time as they escorted him out. They forced O'Neil on, at a fast pace, following Banks.

They moved with authority down the halls, through the lobby, and into the busy street. O'Neil breathed in the fresh air from the sea and busy city streets. He couldn't move his eyes fast enough to see what midday city life was like for those who lived in this district of Karmaridon. A group of elves was busy bartering over bread. Some hobbits and imps enjoyed tea together. He barely had time to move out of the way of a group of fairies, each holding fast to essential papers as they whizzed by him in the sea breeze.

His guard all too soon started marching him on, following Banks, who had been parting a wide berth in the crowded streets. O'Neil saw some pixies and sprites switch their flower shop sign to show they were back from lunch and now open. A Redcap legal aid office had a weary-looking sylph walk out, bumping into a large nix. A Bugbear beauty salon had the oddest-looking window of hairstyles. A huldra opened the door for those entering a restaurant with a sign that read, "Domovois Dwarf and Elf food restaurant, come every day and try something new."

O'Neil had never been in such a place before. Not only were there humanoids everywhere he looked, but animals of all varieties were busy busying themselves on errands for their masters. A beaver was carrying some wood into a furniture store. His guards almost fell over a turtle carrying groceries with a harassed-looking toad frantically striving to balance them on his shell. O'Neil laughed hardily when he saw a zebra posing for an artist asking for funds for the borderline orphans. His guards' hurried pace brought him up to Banks as both groups merged.

"I have never seen so many fowks at once. Looks lik' an ant hill that some poor lad spilled his sugar on. How long have yoo bin a honey bee in this here hive?" O'Neil asked.

"We don't have time for that," Banks said, sounding almost worried.

"We don no have time for that?" O'Neil groaned while leaning out of the way of a giraffe's legs as it worked hard to keep its head stable, a rabbit on it endeavoring not to look down as he nailed a signup. "I have had nothing but time without a drop of the nectar of the gods, with so many who wanted tae know what happened tae yoo and I tae drive me aff me heid. So what is going on?"

"These gentlemen," Banks said, indicating the guards, "are here to escort you and me for our next op."

"What?" O'Neil coughed. "Yer aff yer heid! We just got here, and I have me own company tae get back to."

"You have been transferred under my command," Banks said smartly as he gave way to a large group of young kids crossing the street.

"What?" O'Neil asked, coughing again. "Hold the grave taps. Yoo've been promoted and not just in the maid service. Who has done this horrible thing?"

The guard to O'Neil's right handed him his transfer papers. O'Neil took them and started reading as he walked. If it had not been for Nuts waking up from under O'Neil's beard and redirecting O'Neil, he might have walked into a cart shop. Sadly, Nuts led him into an assorted fruit shop, where he was spared too much embarrassment by his guards, who extricated him and put him back on track.

"This cannae no be," O'Neil said to Nuts.

"I'm no' a man to participate in groups," O'Neil called to Banks. "And what's this part where it says, 'dispatched to unknown. Time dispatched unknown. Area dispatched to…'" The guards around O'Neil closed in tightly together, ordering him to keep silent.

"Our chaperones are also here to see to it that we don't say anything about what is going on," Banks added, still walking fast.

"Oh," O'Neil moaned weakly, still pressed between an insectoid and a cyclops guard. "Me mind is minced since it's been that long from me stay at the pub," he said apologetically to them.

The guards allowed him to breathe again as Banks walked them deeper into the military district. They passed their defensive placements and checkpoints. Again, O'Neil was amazed at the ease with which they passed. They went by training areas for recruits, and he saw them undergoing physical exercises, weapons drills, and communications. After walking for an hour, they were loaded onto large horse-drawn military armored carriages and rushed onward. O'Neil didn't mind as he looked at officers trained to spot different enemy installments in the air, land, or sea. Weapon manufacturing of everything he had ever heard was taking place. He was reluctant to say anything after almost being crushed by his honor guard, but once they reached another checkpoint listed as "Armament

Analysis, research and development branch level seventeen." O'Neil leaned forward in his seat, calling to Banks, "How much further?"

"Don't know," Banks called back as he showed his identification papers again at another checkpoint. Before they moved on, the guard who checked their papers waved them to a group standing just out of view. They were provided with a carriage drawn by large horses. O'Neil grew even more uneasy as all the windows were covered and blocked with black cloths. He was about to ask what was happening when the cyclops beside him smiled. That was enough for him to swallow the rest of his words and Nuts to cower in his chest pocket. All the guards with them left and were replaced with new ones wearing heavy homeland defense armor. With the exchange, they were off again. O'Neil found his voice when their carriage came to a halt sometime later.

"Have we been in 'ere for one hour or two?" he asked but was given no reply from the guards. Thankfully, they stopped, and the door opened, letting in some much-needed fresh air. O'Neil squinted in the sunlight and saw several rocs, hippogriffs, and Pegasus riders patrolling the air above them.

"Why are we here? To watch sky gauntlet air races?" O'Neil asked wearily.

O'Neil saw two lines of guards standing parallel, leaving a single path before them. O'Neil walked, ducking and jumping to see the wonders past the guard's arms and legs, who stood as fence-like sentries. They both walked on toward a single massive building. It appeared to be a giant mess hall, O'Neil thought as he mused that this time, Banks was the one who slowed his pace to stay beside him. Noticing that O'Neil had stopped scrutinizing the area and was eyeing him carefully, Banks quickened his step.

"This lot make better walls than windaes," O'Neil said softly, pointing a thumb at the guards to his left and right. "But they don't block your thoughts, so what aren't yoo telling me?"

Banks only smiled until they reached the wooden doors of the building they were led to. On either side of the door were pens for masters to leave their animals before entering the building. Banks stepped forward, causing O'Neil to slow momentarily before they entered.

"Before we go in, I should tell you something," Banks said calmly. "This mission we are going on is not going to be like anything you've ever done, and before I open this door, I want you to know that I'm in command."

"Aye," O'Neil said seriously. He seemed to feel Banks was going to say something else.

"I want you to know that you have also been promoted."

"WHAT?" O'Neil asked incredulously.

"And you are second in command of our team in this hall that we are going to brief."

Banks pulled open the doors before O'Neil could indicate he opposed his new position. Banks entered the room with a fresh air of authority about him. At least five hundred soldiers were waiting for them. Benches lined along the walls while windows high above them cast light, revealing the elaborate wood lodge. Some soldiers didn't even look up as they lay on the floor using their gear bags as pillows, indicating they had been there for some time. Others were tending to their equipment as if they had only arrived that day.

"I am Colonel Banks," he called after assessing the situation.

Everyone in the hall jumped to attention at his words while Banks put his hands behind his back, taking in the moment. O'Neil was still standing in shock behind him in the doorway. For a moment, no one said anything while the heavy doors closed, leaving O'Neil outside with a foolish look of shock. Banks glanced over his shoulder.

Suddenly the doors flew open as O'Neil bellowed, "Ah, this be Banks, your new I.O., and I am O'Neil second I.O. to yoo lot. We have been through a lot together an yoo don't look like yoo all couldn't make it across the street without holding someone's hand or last a day without a shiny teaspoon. I take your lives in me hands from noo on and am proud to say I feel like jugglin'."

O'Neil stopped talking after he marched next to Banks and saw the look he gave him that no one else could see. O'Neil met his eyes for a moment, and then his confidence deflated. Looking down, he saw the two small critical sacks he'd had when he first met him hanging from Banks's belt.

"At ease," Banks called as the doors were shut behind him. The tension in the room seemed to diminish as all present relaxed. Banks walked to one of the long tables in the room, climbed it, and opened his mouth to address the room. O'Neil nosily interrupted him after he was unable to climb up to stand by Banks. After the look Banks gave him, O'Neil settled himself in a chair. Banks opened his mouth again to speak but couldn't because of the sound of O'Neil dragging his heavy chair across the floor to lean it against the wall. Banks watched him until he was settled.

O'Neil sat with his chin down in disgrace, causing Nuts to reposition himself in his beard. Banks looked at him for a moment longer than was necessary. Then he cleared his throat, calling attention to return to him.

"Everyone, this briefing on the operation is secret," Banks stated, loud enough for all to hear. "I repeat, secret. Your attention is on me, or you will be subject to immediate court-martial. Those who go will be chosen for this composite op by chance and will be the first in a mission bigger than you can understand. All those not chosen will stay here isolated for at least one week. Those going on this spec op task force will have to get to know each other once there and follow O'Neil and my lead. With that understood, if any wish to leave, speak up now because you won't have a chance in a moment. Understand this; if anyone who is left behind so much as thinks of opening their mouths, they will find themselves in more trouble than you could realize."

The atmosphere in the hall was charged with silent emotions. Some looked afraid, while others tried to hide a look of worry behind a confident expression.

Banks only let a moment slip by before he spoke again, but this time, he sounded calmer. "This building is surrounded by armed guards who are ordered to kill anyone attempting to leave. Until the operation is completed, you will not talk, whisper, write, or even think outside this hall. Now, the objective of this mission is to use the means given to us by a deep-cover operative in the Fury territory to locate and retrieve the means of finding the Requiem."

Everyone could feel the tension of the moment. It was enough that O'Neil was going to jump to his feet to call all to order, but he only managed to fall off his chair with a bang, causing Nuts to give off a loud squeak and pull O'Neil's beard hard, at which he grunted sharply in pain.

Clearing his throat and coughing, he sat in his seat again, chin down with worried eyes.

"This will be a blind op, meaning charts, maps, or intelligence on where we are going will not be provided. All we must do is go in, find what we are looking for, and come home before the Fury knows we are even there. If you might be wondering why you have been selected for this and not a previous superior force, I don't want you to worry about that; just concentrate on the fact that you are here and going. We need the Requiem before the Fury gets it; someone must go, and you are the chosen ones. This will be difficult, so pack anything needed on a one-week op."

Almost everyone glanced at each other uneasily. One tall elf raised his hand and took a step forward. Banks started to pace on the table again as he nodded his approval for him to speak.

"Sir," the elf said very properly, "we are going to an unknown location, but do we know the enemy's strength?"

"No, but we are clear to engage on my order and my order only," Banks said flatly, and before anyone else could inquire more about it, he said. "Any other questions?"

It was noticeable that many wished for a more straightforward answer than what was given. After a pregnant pause, the same elf raised his hand once more.

"Yes," Banks called.

"Since some are staying here, and we are not allowed to leave this building, how will insertion and extraction happen?" the elf asked again, sounding as if he had practiced that question in front of a mirror. Banks kept pacing but eyed him wearily. He was one of the tallest in the room, with thick purple hair on his head and a sharp nose.

"We will return the same way we left," Banks responded quickly. "That will be clear to you by midnight."

The strain on everyone in the hall was palpable due to the lack of information. Banks either expected it or didn't care as he paced back to where he originally stood.

"Nobody will take with them any personal item containing individual information. Each person will carry enough rations for a week, aid packs, special gear for their own expertise equipment, rolling gear, signal flags, food, and care parcels for their second. Each person will take six fire flasks where able. I want everyone to report to O'Neil and then get some rest. We don't know what kind of night you will have. The ministers of each faith will come in for service each half an hour in the northeast corner. Dismissed."

Most didn't move, resembling the motionless figures in one of the large portages hanging high on the walls. Banks paid them no attention as he jumped and leaned to whisper to O'Neil. "I will make certain that everything is in order in the back room. Tend to your duties here."

"Yoo mean the kitchen over hither?" O'Neil asked excitedly.

"Not now," Banks responded quietly.

"Once I am done, I want you to check them all and quietly evaluate them. We don't know which ones will be coming with us. I need to know what you think of each one of them."

"What doo I think of them? I don't lik' them, that's what I think of them. No facts of locality, enemy, colleagues, clear mission objectives, and extraction. Just that we are going somewhere, somehow. Now yoo are tellin' me to wait and not goo to the kitchen for a touch of the daily dew? I really wished I left yoo in the forest." The usual tone of joy in O'Neil's voice was diminishing.

Banks and O'Neil shared a deep stare into each other's eyes. Neither of them noticed that everyone else in the hall was still motionless. The looks of disapproval bearing down on them brought their focus from each other to the rest of the room.

"If yoo are going tae command them tae fight and die fer yoo, then yoo will have tae give them more."

Banks grabbed O'Neil's shoulder with care. "I just need them. They will get more than anyone could imagine before this night ends." After saying this, Banks jabbed O'Neil in the chest and said happily, "Just get them ready."

Banks started to walk briskly to the back of the hall while everyone gave him a wide berth, except for one.

"Sir, a word?" the same tall elf asked again.

"Not now," Banks commanded. "You have your orders; see to it, legionnaire."

The elf let him pass but not without a long sigh of frustration in protest and muttered, "Oh, nice that. Hoggy Poggy right in the offset without a word."

Everyone watched Banks march on until he passed through the backroom and out of sight. No one spoke as everyone stood looking at the door Banks closed behind him. Then, all present turned their heads slowly and simultaneously towards O'Neil as if in a trance. O'Neil stood still as if he were facing a firing squad. He shivered momentarily and then took on a dignified stance as if he were being presented before royalty. He stood up and brushed any nonexistent dust from himself. He nobly helped Nuts to his shoulder and marched, parade-like, to the hall's center.

"Now, all you lot!" He coughed, clearing his throat. "Keep your heids up and bottoms doon. I want all of yoo tae line up in groups according tae yoor specialty after yoo have gathered up yoor belongings, and see me in the back. Just as soon as I inspect the spirits." he said, adding a wink.

I Just Feel Silly Using A Travel Agent

The irritable mood of every soldier filled the hall as O'Neil checked every type of combatant he had ever seen, heard of, or met. Some had enlisted when they came of age, while others had almost reached the age of dismissal. O'Neil wished Banks had not left and locked himself in one of the unused kitchens. It was difficult enough working with such a variety of personnel but having no further information was unfathomable. Some packed too many weapons, food, and rations, while others had no idea what they were doing. One of the last eager young soldiers next in line had about as much muscle on him as a walking broom. O'Neil shook his head as he approached with so many weapons and armor on him that he could barely stand under their combined weight. He stood quivering before O'Neil and gave him a shaky salute when it was his turn for inspection.

"Son, if you fall doon, just stay doon, all right?" O'Neil groaned and dropped his head into his hands. He saw the last person in line behind the shaking pile of armor and gear as he did. He perked up instantly when he noticed it was a very well-put-together young lady in majestic red garb armor. He did not recognize her insignia, which told what part of the military she was from, nor any sign of rank. But he could not wait to talk to her.

"Siiir,?" The soldier in front of him said, quivering.

"Aye?" O'Neil asked, not looking at him but transfixed on the woman behind him. She had her arms folded and paid no attention to anyone.

"Am… am… I… fit… fit and ge… ge… up… up… for… fo… Am I ready?" The young man stuttered.

"What? Oh, Aye, Aye, son, yoo will do grand, just grand." O'Neil moaned as he drew out a hip flask, his eyes still fixed on anything but who was talking with him. After he took a long gulp from its contents, he unknowingly waved the shaky soldier on.

O'Neil smiled and straightened himself as the soldier took four weak steps and collapsed noisily to the floor. O'Neil didn't care. He got up and passed everyone, going down the line. As he was about to open his mouth to talk to the young woman, the hall's main door opened, and superior guards entered on either side of the doors. When the doors opened, a single figure stood for a moment at the threshold.

"Premier Laygrim." Someone gasped from behind O'Neil. Everyone stood to attention as briskly as possible, except for a pile of armor on the floor. Just a weak, shaky hand lifted, giving a salute.

"I wish to address Commander Banks," Laygrim called. He had power in his speech, befitting one of his position. Nothing in his stature was weak, from his black hair down to his dark leather shoes and cap. He held his muscular arms behind his back, but his eyes seemed warm to all who met them. He was the most unusual-looking orc O'Neil had ever come across. It was so unusual that O'Neil hadn't noticed Banks was walking past him and had stepped over the armor on the floor, still stuck in a flat saluting position.

Banks walked up to the Premier as if he knew him and talked with him for a moment. The words they shared were so low that no one heard them until Laygrim called out, "What you are called to do tonight is uncommon, but I know that I can count on every one of you to do what is needed. For us all!" he ended with a roar. All those in the hall boisterously boomed back, "For us all!"

Premier Laygrim nodded, spoke with Banks for a few more moments, and left, his two honor guards closing the doors behind him. With them closed, it shut out the sun's last light setting beyond the high mountains.

Banks stood saying nothing as everyone in the hall waited in awe. A large timepiece hung above the main door, letting those present know they had three hours until midnight. He composed himself before calling, "Three hours until it's time to turn in your snack trays. Now that you've all held your hands, tend to your seconds if you believe they can go with us and service in any environment. If they can't, leave them here and let the guards know, and they will be attended to. You have two and a half hours to make peace with the voices in your head. After that, I will be the only thing you will hear."

Banks didn't look as he marched past them to a janitor's closet. Once he was in and locked the door, his robust and proud frame slowly hunched over. He clasped to his knees and washed his hands with his tears. All his training and experience were gone when he reached into his pocket. He pulled out the strangest piece of parchment he had ever seen. It was rough on the back and oddly smooth on the front, like glass that could bend. On the flat side, there was the most amazing thing he had ever seen. It was a picture of a family so accurate they could leap out of his hands to life.

"Sir?" came the soft call from behind the door.

Banks rubbed the back of his neck, returning the portrait to his pocket. It sounded like that same elf with all the questions, Banks thought as he answered, "Make it fast?"

"Sir, sorry to disturb you, sir. But this intel so far is a bit nitty," came the voice behind the door. "Everyone else out there has been picked by our leader, but I need to get to know you better before I follow you home."

Banks remembered being in front of the council when they gave him the picture as they explained every facet of his mission. How difficult it would be for him to keep the actual task from his men. He didn't notice his hands were trembling as he reached for the two leather sacks on his waist containing the objects he had almost died for.

"You will get all you need before midnight," Banks replied. "Dismissed."

Banks heard the tall elf respond, "Sir," and walked away. Banks watched the door as he listened to him go. Then, he examined what was in his hands again. He held them as every detail he was told about them filled him. He had learned more about history in the past three days than in his entire life. He saw the faces of his comrades, who gave their last light to retrieve them.

He stood up, returning the two leather sacks, and habitually checked his vital equipment. For the time being, he was glad that he was alone. Once he was ready, he cracked open the door to check the large timepiece in the hall. It was twenty minutes till midnight. He shook his head in disbelief at how much time had passed. Once he went through that door, there was no going back.

What made Banks different from most men was his lack of hesitation. He had his time, and now came the demand for it. His chin was out with authority when he went through the door to the main hall. His travel cloak flowed behind him as if carried by some invisible breeze. He rested his large hands on both his plasma long swords while he centered himself in the Hall. Around him was a beehive of activity in torchlight lining the walls and ceiling. The attitude had changed so tangibly that one would think it was a different hall.

"Line up the tables against the walls," he ordered. "And pass the word."

Everyone jumped to action as their animal seconds helped. A smile of admiration spread over Banks's face as he watched each one of them move with a purpose. He could see every face, every life, and hope that each one had. All of them now were his responsibility. He shook his head as a bitter memory threatened to creep in. The mission comes before the men, he recited, to keep it at bay. Why did this bother him now? He stepped out of the way of an elf and an avian with white feathers that looked so soft they could fill any pillow, moving a table next to where he was standing. Suddenly, passing several people, he saw Heavy. How could he be here? His hands started to shake as he saw Heavy's bloody hand reach out for him. Although Heavy was in the center of the room, no one else noticed him or acted differently.

"Yoo know, it's an avian you could kiss but it's the dwarf that yoo want tae take home with yoo," O'Neil said with a sigh.

Startled, Banks turned to look over his shoulder to see O'Neil. He quickly looked back and was amazed to see that Heavy was gone and was never there. Banks found strength and truth, knowing deep down that O'Neil was by him. Banks' thoughts shifted when he noticed that O'Neil had almost twice the number of haversacks he needed. O'Neil's attention followed where Banks was looking before he interrupted his thoughts.

"Steady noow. Are yoo seeing a mirage brought on by yoor terrible thirst?"

"Everything ready?" Banks asked, ignoring O'Neil's comment.

"Aye, but are yoo?"

"There is no ready for me. But you look more than ready. How much can you hold?"

"Yoo can talk about me drinking but yoo will never know how I'm plagued with the thirst in need for these fine bottles of medicine," O'Neil said shaking his head.

"Not all of us will make it out of this one. You need a clear head if I don't make it." Banks replied over the sounds of long seats and tables scratching the floor.

"Noow don't yoo be talking about yourself while yoo're here. We will surely be doing that after yoo leave and as long as I don't see the bottom of me bottle, I'll stand with yoo," O'Neil said.

"For us all," Banks said, almost sounding sad.

"Fer us all," O'Neil replied seriously.

Banks patted O'Neil on the back. O'Neil's strong frame didn't move. Banks rechecked the time before calling out, "Ten minutes to go. Line the walls, form a circle, and hold your seconds close." They did so remarkably quickly as Banks took both pouches from his side.

Banks did as instructed but was concerned that nothing would come of it. He knelt on one knee and slid the object out of its bag. He had never seen such an object as it was cumbersome for something that size. It was smooth on all sides but the one that was facing him. There were different colored switches on it with a hole at the top. What was most interesting was that the lower section had a panel with strange lettering glowed red. He read the name even though he was told what it was in his briefing, as he was amazed that such a wonderous object could exist.

Following the instructions given to him, he opened the other sack and removed one of its contents. They were small enough that he could do it with two fingers. It had the appearance of a large black pearl that glowed at its center. He set the larger object down and removed a short dagger from his calf. He cut his finger and held the radiant marble to the cut.

Doubt caused him to pause a moment. He had been told what would happen, but it didn't prepare him for what occurred. The small, smooth stone somehow absorbed his blood. After momentarily turning it in his hand, he inserted it into the other large device by the hole at its top. The readout panel changed momentarily and returned to displaying the original name it had shown before.

"O'Neil," Banks called as he waved for him to come over. He handed O'Neil one stone and instructed him to do the same. It had the same result.

"Everyone," Banks bellowed after exchanging a querying look with O'Neil. "We will pass these stones around you all. I want you to deposit some blood on the stone and pass it around, then back to me and O'Neil." Each one of them did so and passed them along. There were not enough for each one of them, so some had to share. As Banks collected them, he inserted them all into the rectangular object just as he had done before. He then set it at the center of the room and walked over to stand in the circle.

Checking the time, he had three minutes to go until midnight. "Whatever happens," Banks shouted, "those who go form a perimeter and await instructions. Sound off for equipment check." Everyone in the hall checked the person to their left and right and gave thumbs up before calling out their approval. All except for one who seemed to be asleep, covered in weapons and armor in a pile on the floor.

Time seemed to stop for everyone for the last few seconds before midnight. Once midnight struck, the object at the center of the hall radiated a wave that extinguished all light from the hall. The only light came from the object, showing the same name as before in red letters. The name it showed was "Clint Holden" before the readout panel started blinking the words "execute the initiative."

These words blinked three times and, after that, vanished, leaving complete darkness. Seconds of time seemed to become minutes when the device began rapidly ejecting stones. It was amazing how each stone gave off light for all to see and that the device could somehow hold them all when it did not seem big enough.

The stones rolled freely in all directions on the floor. Banks opened his mouth to order everyone to remain calm, but when he did, he couldn't hear his voice. He tried again, but nothing came out. He couldn't hear anything now as the stones rolled for a moment until they began to move oddly on their own. They seemed to jump left and right slightly as if they moved of their own free will. The light in them started to grow until they shined brilliantly as they were each also giving off smoke till everyone was enveloped in swirling fog.

Banks grabbed his throat in wonder until the mist grew so thick he couldn't see anyone in the hall. A small ball of light started to snake toward him until it struck as quickly as a viper at his heart. He let go of his neck and felt his chest, expecting to find a hole, but felt nothing out of the ordinary. Suddenly, he was struck with pressure on his ears, nose, and mouth. It felt like he was being sucked through the keyhole of a door until everything went dark. Then there was nothing.

HAZARD PAY

"**D**o you want another, Coop?" asked the bartender. Jason Cooper didn't say anything but raised his empty glass.

"That's your seventh, you know," the bartender said while he filled his glass for him.

"Are you on duty tonight?"

"What's the difference?" Cooper grunted with a heaving breath. "As far as dispatch is concerned, I'm never off duty these days." He nodded toward the television on the other side of the room behind the bar. The news was on with a pretty reporter recounting the day's events.

"Good evening. This is Nicole Wilsonland for your Channel Ten News. Our first and only story, of course, is about the virus's massive effect, causing economic turmoil that has now caused Andorra's government to declare bankruptcy along with Malta and Liechtenstein this week. The global crisis…"

"Do we have to watch this?" Cooper muttered.

Letting his mind wander, Cooper took a deep draw from his beer glass. Something of his thoughts must have shown on his face.

"All these newcomers givin' you problems?" The bartender asked while he was wiping a glass cleaner.

The radio at Cooper's hip interrupted him and attracted the attention of all those who had not passed out at their tables.

"Spare 1-6-5-4 come in," it squawked.

"Oh, for heaven's sake, no! Not again!" Cooper moaned, dropping his head to the bar with a thud.

"I take it you are spare 1-6-5-4?" the bartender asked, chuckling.

"Spare 1-6-5-4, come in," the dispatcher repeated.

Cooper didn't move, but he seemed to sag under the weight of his radio. A shiver ran up his back, causing his massive frame to jiggle while his forehead vibrated on the cold bar counter. The woman's voice came again, sounding more frustrated, "Spare 1-6-5-4. Do you read me?"

The bartender slowly leaned over so he was close to Cooper and said softly, "Would you like me to get that for you?"

"COOPER, you alcoholic toilet bug, RESPOND!"

"Why does your dispatcher sound like a Banshee over the radio?" the bartender whispered while Cooper rolled his head on the counter.

"Do you read me, Cooper, or are you four sheets to the wind?"

With an unmistakable look of disdain, Cooper reached for the handset attached to his left shoulder. He held down the button and shouted, "Yes! Yes, I can read you. Who can't hear your voice? Your shrill would even beat the worldwide emergency broadcast system! Now, what do you want? I was working on a nice healthy hangover before your vocal tune sounded like fingernails on a chalkboard," Cooper roared into his receiver.

The voice over the radio sounded calmer this time as she said, "Need you to check out the Bernard's farm again. Gladys has called in three times now about a disturbance out in their field, and Brian called us twice to come over to take Gladys away."

"Gladys?" the bartender asked, looking confused.

Cooper took his finger off the radio. "Walnut farmers with a few animals. The last time they dialed 911 was because she was screaming that someone was drowning in her tub. And it turned out to be one of her overweight cats who fell into a tub full of homemade moonshine. By the time I got there, she was out on her front porch trying to give her cat CPR. Either from her efforts, the poison it bathed in, or her breath, it still looked a little blue in the face. Mr. Bernard yelled at me, wanting to know where the ambulance was. She was lucky I didn't shoot the cat right there and put it out of its misery."

The bartender let out a laugh that sounded like a gunshot before the radio said again. "This is a confirmed report. We have three more like it in different locations and separate districts. Two just started in the woods off by a campground, and another in Mountain Brooks Golf Course."

"Why not just send over some fools from the fire department or the academy? It's probably just one of her cats trying to commit suicide. I mean, if I were one of her pets, I would do the same."

"This might be more than it seems," she told him. "Sarge on duty told me to give this one to you. Over and out."

"You going to make it?" the bartender asked. Cooper gave him a mocking sneer as the bartender looked worried and mildly amused at the same time.

Cooper got to his shaky feet while adjusting his belt over his expanding waist. He took out his wallet, flicked through its contents, took out some cash, and left it on the counter.

"Keep the tip to buy some soap for some of these people," he called, walking towards the exit.

Callaway took up the money and called back, "They're already lathered up pretty good." He put the money in the register with a chime and added to Officer Cooper before he left, "Give my love to the Bernards."

Opening the doors, Cooper realized how bad the bar smelled now that he had the cool night breeze in his face. Being an officer on the edge of one of the largest cities in the world had its perks. While helping others was what he had wanted to do ever since he was young, it meant that he also saw people at their nastiest and on their worst days.

Losing track of time in his thoughts, he was surprised that he got to the farm so quickly. It seemed he had just turned on the ignition when he pulled into the long dirt driveway to Bernard's old filthy farmhouse. It was never easy to pull up to this house without seeing the vast number of cats that roamed free around their farm, a loose pig or two, or the trash everywhere.

Eight

FUNNY THINGS HAPPEN ON THE FARM

The old wood steps of their front porch cracked and screeched under his weight. He rolled his eyes as the smell of the farm filled his nostrils. It was strong enough to peel paint, which accounted for all the peeling paint around the place. He was surprised not to see either of Bernard's outside. They usually were busy trying to explain the earth-shattering emergency of one of their cats having trouble with a particularly large hairball or that they were fighting over the television remote again.

Cooper straightened up as he opened the broken screen door before he knocked. He was expecting a yell from the back of the house for him to come in but none came. He knocked on the door again just as the porch light bulb fell out and shattered behind him.

Maybe the prayers of the entire precinct had been answered, and the Bernards had killed each other off. Knocking again, he turned around, trying to make anything out in the darkness. Still, there was nothing. He was about to return to his car when he thought better about it. His humor fading away, he decided to have a look around.

Cooper walked to the corner of the house, the wooden porch creaking with each step. He was worried that he would fall through any moment. Seeing nothing out of the ordinary for this place, he made his way back to look over the granary and milking shed.

Looking around in the dark, Cooper removed his flashlight and illuminated his surroundings. By the rickety old barn was the only usable car. An old Gremlin with wooden bumpers meant the Bernards must still be home.

Checking the other corner of the house, Cooper decided to give the door one more try before calling dispatch with an update. He walked back to their front door and opened the screen more quickly this time. He was about to knock again, but when he opened what remained of the screen door, it came off its hinges and fell with a thud.

"What next?" he said quietly, wondering if the entire building would collapse when he leaned the screen door on the side of the house. He had scarcely set the screen door aside when the blast of a shotgun from the inside blew a hole through the front door.

Cooper instinctively reached for his weapon, dropped to one knee, and turned to see Mrs. Bernard burst through the door, screaming. She was dressed in a red-spotted nightgown, her hair in curlers that had been there since time began. Huge galoshes three times too big for her covered her bony legs. Her awkward running carried her off the porch when out of the door followed her husband. Strangely, his screaming was even higher pitched than his wife's. Cooper had never seen such a large man move so fast before.

Mr. Bernard had one hand on his long shotgun, and the other held up his overalls, which was the only thing protecting Cooper from a horrible sight. Cooper couldn't help but watch them, open-mouthed, as both the Bernards dashed clumsily to his patrol car. When they reached it, both tried desperately to open the driver-side passenger door simultaneously.

One of them managed to open the door, and in amazement and amusement, Cooper saw both struggling wildly to jump in. First in went the skinny frame of Mrs. Bernard and then Mr. Bernard's larger form on top of her, causing her scream to elevate. Cooper came to and realized he had not moved as he saw one of Bernard's shaking arms come out from under the pile and shut the car door.

He got up and started walking toward the car with his weapon drawn, Mrs. Bernard's nest-like hair and Mr. Bernard's balding head creeping into view.

"Let me see your hands!" Cooper ordered the Bernards as he glanced over his shoulder to the house to ensure no one else was inside. In the car, he could only see both their faces from the nose up as four trembling hands came up. Seeing that it appeared safe, he lowered his gun as he approached the vehicle.

Cooper kept his distance and slid his gun back in its holster, trying to make out the frantic babble of shouts coming from them.

"Wait, wait, wait! What is going on? Who were you shooting at?" Cooper shouted.

"Where yo' been? Me and the Miss been unner attack!" Mr. Bernard bellowed enough that Cooper could finally understand.

"Keep your hands up while I open the door," Cooper yelled, again taking a step forward.

"No, no, no, no," called out both Mr. and Mrs. Bernard.

"You have just fired at an officer!" Cooper shouted.

In the same amount of time, it took for Cooper to reach for his weapon again. Mr. Bernard somehow lowered his arm, opened the door, dropped his short shotgun out of the car, closed the door again, locked it, and lifted his hand again into the air.

Cooper was amazed at his speed. He came closer and kicked the shotgun away, shouting, "Get out of the car."

"We ain't moving nothin' till yo' take care of them on the other side of our house!" Mrs. Bernard declared.

"What are you talking about?" Cooper said, staring at her tooth. She started to speak very fast, but either out of excitement or because Mr. Bernard's massive frame was forcing all the air out of her, Cooper couldn't understand her.

Irritated, Cooper ordered her to shut up. "Mr. Bernard, what is it this time?" he shouted authoritatively.

Mr. Bernard swallowed, apparently unaware his wife was deflating like a balloon under him. "I was gowin' about my nightly duties takin' care of Gluttonies. She hasn't been given a lot of milk lately, ya know. So I was out there given her a back rub when I heard this here noise like when

I start up our TV. Ya knows it takes a spell t'warm up. I looked outside of the barn when I saw those lights and I knows what it was right when I saw it. It was on that movie Close Encounters." He started nodding quickly, but not as fast as his wife.

"Them there aliens is har to probe us and Gluttonies for sur'." Mrs. Bernard told Cooper as she grew redder in the face, either from fright or lack of oxygen.

"Now, I grabbed my shotgun and ended Gluttonies so they wouldn't git her an' all our hens so theys couldn't implant their eggs into our minds. Then scooted to the house, firin' shots into my crop so they'd stay away. I keep shootin' and shoutin' at them aliens till we heard them around the house. So I barricaded us in, grabbed the TV, cats, house plants, an' TV guide an' took us to the basement ya know. Waiting there till we saw you a come up in the windah." Mr. Bernard finished, biting his lip with his green teeth.

"Right," Cooper said under his breath. Then, louder so the Bernards could hear him through the glass, "If I go check around the house, will you get out of the car?"

The Bernard's didn't say anything but glared at each other and then back to him. Cooper shook his head at both and started walking toward the house's side.

"He's a-gonna be probed for sure," Mrs. Bernard said breathlessly.

"Better'im than us. At least he will have a better chance than I did when Sasquatch came into mah tent reckoning I was his honeymooner, yo' know," Mr. Bernard replied so low that Cooper could not hear him.

Cooper turned his flashlight toward the tall weeds where the orchard of walnut trees began searching for anything out of the ordinary. He checked in front of him and every place his flashlight could reach. He took a deep breath and, given his past experiences with this home, was convinced that there was no threat. He held his radio up and was about to call and report to dispatch when his light fell on something odd-looking in the ground just at the edge of the beam.

Nine

OK, NOW YOU SEE, THAT'S WHY I AM NOT A CAT PERSON

It was toward the back of the house—a footprint set in soft earth between the sparse grass patches.

"I can't believe I have to keep coming out here in the middle of the night," Cooper said to himself as he walked around with his flashlight. "Why can't I get called to respond to the coast or something? Looking for concealed weapons on people in swimsuits."

He reached the back of the house, where nothing was waiting for him. No aliens were looming in the darkness. There were no death rays, no bright lights. There was nothing to indicate that anything was going to harm him. Shaking his head, he bent down to see the print, but if it looked odd, it was only because it was smaller than either of the Bernard's. He started to follow the path left when he stepped in something soft and smelly.

Cursing inwardly, he walked over in disgust to the dying lawn and scraped off the bottom of his shoe. "That's why I became a police officer. Not to protect the innocent but to be the hero to the only people who have animals that miss the outhouse! Why don't you keep these animals in their pens?" Cooper groaned.

As he scraped his foot in the grass, Cooper saw another footprint in the soft ground. He leaned down to get a closer look, turned off his flashlight, and took out a small camera to take a picture. After closer inspection, he noticed that it must have been from a small animal. He felt the footprint with his fingertips and realized it was more human-like. It was small, oddly childlike in shape. He peered at it, feeling that it must have been made with a bare foot. It was about four inches long, but the Bernards had no children, and no kid would come here unless they were playing some sort of prank.

Standing up, he looked around more seriously this time. The darkness was thick beyond the first row of short walnut trees in the field. There was a great deal of weeds and undergrowth, so it was difficult to make out what was tree and what was weed. The small footprints seemed to lead toward the horse coral parallel to the rows of walnut trees.

"Kids," grumbled Cooper. After cleaning his shoe, he started off away from the house, following the footprints. He kept tracking them but found it difficult due to the storms they had had over the past few days. The night was darker as he moved away from the house, which was the only other light source. The thought entered his mind that maybe he would scare the children as he tried to keep as silent as possible, his flashlight still picking up the small footprints here and there and where he pushed back the weeds as he moved his light from the field to the ground. He stopped as the path went deeper into the field, and his flashlight didn't illuminate more than thirty feet.

Cooper stopped and checked around behind him again. Once he was still, he noticed that something had changed in the air. The animals in their pens sounded nervous, anxious, and moved uneasily. Shining his light back into the path, he knelt to see if there were more tiny footprints.

"Must be more than one," Cooper said to himself.

Somewhere in the field came the sound of movement that made Cooper's training kick in again. He twisted around fast to shine the light on where the sound came from. The top of the weeds gave way to whatever was running. Cooper ran after it, taking his taser in one hand and his flashlight under it.

"Come out here," Cooper bellowed. "If you have a weapon, I will challenge you. So, throw it out now and come out with your hands up."

From the sound of it, the movement had slowed and then halted somewhere in the field up to his left. Cooper slowed to a walk, checking behind him again, hearing the farm animals still acting peculiarly. He was close to the next field's first line of trees. He stopped for a moment, shining his light down the tree rows. Feeling his heart pound, Cooper resumed his pursuit. The path the kid ran down was narrow and appeared to go right to the heart of the field. The noise of small insects died around him where he walked, but with every gentle breeze of the wind, a ripple in the leaves and weeds made his hair stand on end.

Step by step, he followed the way the trespasser went. In each row he passed, he shone his light down both ends, trying to make out where those kids were. He couldn't check the eerie feeling that he was being watched, and since he didn't hear anything running, that told him they must be hiding near him somewhere.

Suddenly, a rush of movement erupted right in front of him from behind a tree through a very high patch of weeds. "Halt!" Cooper yelled as he ran off after the suspect. The kid was agile as it darted around but it kept mostly on the path that it had left before. Cooper saw the child partly here and there when his light hit parts of it through the weed path openings as he pursued him.

"Get down on your knees! Stop!" Cooper bellowed between heaving breaths. "Stop with your hands up."

"Halt!" He coughed, feeling the beer in his stomach start to turn. His ribs and feet began to throb, but he ran as fast as he could.

"Halt means stop running, you little runt!"

Wham! Something hit Cooper hard in the back of the head. White light flashed before his eyes as he fell to his knees. Fog filled his mind, clouded with pain as he struggled to focus. He dropped the flashlight somewhere as he instinctively felt the back of his throbbing head. He felt the ground hit him as he fell hard, the weeds scratching his bare skin and the dead twigs and fallen branches digging into his back.

He rolled to his side, and for some reason, his vision was clearing up, but he could still see white lights. These were not right in front of his nose but far away. He looked around quickly to see who had hit him and saw his flashlight about two feet away, giving an eerie shine. It looked like a light fog around it, but shaking his head, Cooper was convinced that it was still just the effect of being hit in the head. He couldn't find the one who had hit him.

Instinctively, he reached for his radio. "Dispatch, this is spare 1-6-5-4, officer in…" He stopped when unexpectedly, a rope was thrown around his feet from nowhere, and before he knew what hit him, he was being dragged as if by a runaway horse. He screamed as loud as he could despite the plant seeds, dirt, and dust filling his lungs as he massed them down while being dragged. This was no longer an early Halloween prank. They had assaulted an officer, and he was not going to let them get away with it. Everything was a blur now that he could barely see or breathe until whatever was pulling him stopped.

The dirt and debris in his eyes forced him to keep them closed. Even through closed lids, he could make out a pulsing light that must have been floating about four feet above the ground. He spat out the dust and earth from his mouth, but before he could gather his senses, something struck him hard across the head again.

The pain washed over him so abruptly that it forced his eyes open. It was like looking through a dirty fishbowl as he watched three blurry figures fall on him. What little air he had in his lungs, Cooper lost as they bent and twisted him, causing him to cry out in greater pain. A sharp kick to his side caused him to instinctively roll over where they grabbed him, twisting him, and before he could even breathe right, his hands were being tied tightly behind his back to his feet.

Panicking, he found new strength, pulling hard to free himself. Wham! Pain coursed through his forehead, with more white lights erupting in his mind. Then there was darkness. He didn't know if he had blacked out or if it was pain combined with beer pushing his body to its limits, but suddenly, he vomited on the cold soil.

Spitting out what was left in his mouth, Cooper felt his chest burn up to his mouth. Coughing caused pain to explode all over him. The rope was cutting into his wrists and ankles. His back ached from being bent backward. His shirt had been pulled up, showing the scratches all over his skin where rocks, weeds, and branches had cut him from being dragged.

The light was still pulsating only a few feet away amid a swirl of smoke. He was in a clearing in what must have been the center of the orchard where the weeds and trees had mysteriously been flattened evenly. He was on the edge of the clear patch with the light at the center, and he wasn't alone.

It must be from the throbbing lump on his head, but what appeared to be next to him was a pig, three or four cats, and a cow. Blinking hard to make sure what he saw, they were all tied and gagged, squirming on the ground just as he was. Refusing to believe it as the brilliant light grew brighter, he swallowed hard, forcing his vocal cords to work despite the scorching of stomach acid and dust. When he tried, all that came out was a wheeze.

Somewhere deep down behind his stomach, anger began to grow. It grew until it consumed his pain, and all he felt was rage. "You little maggots," Cooper yelled as he thrashed against his restraints.

"Now listen to me, you little butt nuggets! You have assaulted a police officer, and you have vandalized, terrorized, and trespassed on private property, public property, and anything else I can think of. I might also make up some charges just for the fun of it! Now, you might think that you are having fun with a couple who you could probably knock on the door and ask for sugar in water and get away with blowing up their truck. But if you don't untie me right now, I am really going to get mad! Now let me go!"

Breathing hard, Cooper could hear someone talking behind him in a strange language. He twisted and squirmed to roll over but froze when he realized he had never heard anyone speak that way. What was even stranger was whoever was talking so oddly was being responded to by a cat and a pig. The three of them were having a conversation. Cooper suddenly started to laugh as the sound of pig grunts and cat meows conversing together was hilarious.

"What is going on here?" he called wearily as he chuckled. "Hey, Swahili-sounding happy meal, tell Piglet and Garfield to let me go!" Without warning, something rushed from behind him, grabbed and pulled him over on his back, crushing his arms and legs. He howled in pain, and when he opened his eyes again, he saw a creature with a small, skinny head, red skin, large eyes, and ears. The creature was staring at him hungrily. It had a small leather helmet perched between two horns that jutted out of the crown of his head. It grabbed Cooper by the throat with its long, slender fingers.

"What are you supposed to be dressed up as, a medieval Cabbage Patch Kid from the wrong side of the street?" Cooper choked.

The creature swung its large, sharp, carrot-like fingers right between Cooper's eyes. Then it spoke that strange language over to its right. Cooper looked over and saw two more things, like the one standing over him. They both had different colored skin from head to foot. One was blue, and the other was green. They all had the same nasty pair of short horns on each of their heads and as soon as he caught a glimpse of them, he knew that these were not kids. They both were conversing, one sounding like the pig he had heard and the other like the cat. Cooper strained to see them past the one holding him by the collar. They both had their backs to him and were doing something with their hands that he could not see.

"I don't know what happened to all three of you," Cooper choked, "but you're all products of what happens when you watch too much television and play video games all day. Is this your first time out of your parent's basements? Where are you guys from, Canada?"

Cooper stopped talking once the red-skinned one, still standing over him, grabbed his hair with its other wiry hand and pulled his head back. The red-skinned one's face smiled madly, with its large orb-like eyes glinting lustfully as it forced Cooper's mouth open. Cooper gagged as he saw the other two come closer. The green one appeared in his peripheral vision and knelt next to him. The other appeared to his right, and as it passed, he noticed the strange light hovering in the air growing brighter.

The blue one drew a short sword, and he held a peculiar, thick piece of string in his other hand. A horrible realization came to Cooper when the strings started to move on its own. It was alive.

Fear filled Cooper's mind as he started to thrash around again. The ropes were too tight and began to cut into his skin. Cooper tried to jerk his head left and right against the creature's grip but to no avail. Horror filled his mind as those horrible red hands held him tight as the blue and green ones brought that string-like worm toward his face. Cooper bellowed out like a wounded bulldog.

They held the four-foot-long worm in their fists and let their ends dangle low over his head. The green one moved his hand to Cooper's left ear while the blue one pointed the other end of the worm over Cooper's mouth. Cooper thrashed again when, with a small tingle, he felt the worm touch his ear and then his mouth. It was slimy and tingly, like a shot from the dentist. The side of his head went numb. The red creature gave the others a reassuring nod, turned its dirty face back to Cooper, and spoke.

"Imds, kipper," it said sharply, almost like he was giving commands to a dog.

Cooper tried to move his mouth, but his muscles were numb. The red creature released Cooper's head, and he held his hands out to the other two. Cooper saw that they put their heads together and held one of the worm's ends to their ears while the other was still touching his mouth or ear; he couldn't feel which.

The red one smiled, showing all his needle teeth, then put the end of the worm just like the other two did to his mouth and ear.

"Imds, kipper," it said again through the side of its red lips.

Gathering his will, Cooper said, "What are you?"

Nodding excitedly, the red creature said again, "Imds, kipper."

The red one glanced over to the other two and passed the end of the worm from his ear back to the other two. It moved its ugly face closer, almost nose to nose, then said once more. "Imds, human."

"What?" Cooper gasped, horrified.

The green creature seemed to be done with the worm and handed it to the blue one, who, like the other, put it to his ear. The blue creature started to talk fast in meows and hisses like an angry cat. The red creature slapped him hard, drawing his attention back to Cooper.

"Speak, human," it said clearly. "Speak more."

Cooper tried yelling but ended up sounding like he was some toddler speaking his first words.

All three of his captors nodded and gathered the worm back into their hands. In a jumble, they all stood up, holding the worm out so the red one could collect it. They each had an unmistakable look of pleasure on their faces.

"Good, we ready for him. It would be pain if we didn't," the red one said in a whimper.

The green one snorted pig-like in reply, but Cooper could understand this time. How could that be? Was it because his head was still numb? The Green one snorted, speaking again softly. "What we do with the natives? Should we start the fire? My insides ache with emptiness," it oinked, fingering a long knife and looking hungrily at Cooper and the other animals beside him.

"No, we wait for them that will be coming," the red one said, his face almost beaming, his ears slightly flapping.

"What coming?" The blue one meowed.

"Rare T's, little o's, big O's, a G, some special class and him," the red one responded.

Suddenly, the light started to gain strength, pulsating faster and faster. It was coming from the center of the clearing, brighter and brighter. Cooper squirmed his body over, taking his weight off his arms and legs to see better. The light was so brilliant now that it appeared almost noon, forcing the darkness to retreat.

IT WOULD HAVE BEEN BETTER TO HAVE BEEN PROBED

"Coming, they coming! Hurry!" the red one called as he ran back to Cooper. The others tripped over each other, following him. All three started fighting for the center position at the threshold of the light. They pushed, pulled, kicked, and bit one another to get the string-like worm all to themselves. The red creature won after a hit to the crotch of the green one and an excellent two-finger pull on the nostrils of the blue creature.

"Demonized three stooges," Cooper coughed.

The blue and green-skinned ones squealed and meowed loudly in protest, collapsing on the ground. Winning the battle, the red one held the worm close and knelt. In this terrifying event, Cooper couldn't help but laugh at the noises that sounded like a cat and pig in a death match.

The light was now almost blinding. Loud cracks of electricity erupted in the smoke. The smolder swirled around as the light grew ten feet, then fifteen, twenty. Cooper panicked as it was going to overtake him. Then, with a crack, something started to emerge out of the center of this disturbance. It was like watching a reflection in a foggy mirror coming closer and emerging through the glass.

What appeared first was a large, green leg. It was like nothing he had ever seen before. It was well-muscled with thin sandals wrapped around large feet and up its ankles. Its torso appeared adorned in animal skins. Cooper couldn't blink or even breathe as what he was looking at must have been ten feet tall, human-like, except for a sharp, upturned green nose and small ears with a tiny gold earring hanging from his right ear. It wore bone jewelry around its arms and neck. The monster was balancing a large club mace on its shoulder that was at least five feet long and must have weighed sixty pounds.

With a roar from its colossal mouth that could have broken glass. Cooper winced, quivering as he couldn't believe the two short tusks protruding from its bottom jaw. Opening one eye, he saw it roll its red eyes, penetrating everything around it. Those eyes dropped from Cooper to the three creatures that were his captors. The large green man-like animal moved its thick tree trunk legs and turned to face the light, kneeling on the right of the three trembling creatures.

Then, something else was coming out of the glass-like smoke. Another human-like creature appeared, but this one was shorter. Cooper squinted to make out its features with the light shimmering behind it. After it took a step forward, Cooper could see its skin was a lighter shade of green and skinnier than its predecessor. It walked forward holding a long bow with a nasty-looking glowing arrow ready in the taut string. Its face was oddly small with large ears and a nose that had many different-sized rings, a single patch over its left eye. As it moved to his left, Cooper saw that around its wrist, waist, and neck were strings that held what looked like horribly shrunken heads and tiny skulls.

Cooper's astonishment grew as another was coming out of the light. He noticed its emergence seemed easier than the others. It appeared to be an ordinary man except for the fact he was very well dressed, bearing no weapons, and had oddly pale skin. The man seemed to glide around rather than walk. He seemed to carry himself with excellent confidence.

The light gave birth to another similar to the second who had come, except it was a female with badly sagging skin. Next came a creature who looked like the first. This one also was just as large in stature but carried two great axes. After they had each come through, they took positions as if the animated light was an arena to which they knelt. More and more came, each one more threatening and menacing than its forerunner.

Two came out at the same time now. They were also humanoid but had dark green skin with upturned noses. They both brandished weapons as intimidating as their faces. They looked like something he'd seen in the movies: creatures called Orcs. One was male, while the other must have been female. They moved away quickly, taking different positions. They were both almost entirely naked save for the animal skins that covered them and held their weapons in place.

Once all of them knelt with heads down, Cooper tried to work one hand free, unable to watch what was unfolding before him. It felt like he was trying to rip his hand off as blood started to drip from the ropes, tearing into his wrists and ankles. The feeling in his face started to return, bringing with it the cold night air, making him shiver, not just from fear.

The light and smoke oddly froze briefly before it rolled back into itself. The very heart of it was growing darker, as if he were looking down a long dark tunnel. All at once, with a flash, it was gone. Cooper instinctively shut his eyes and turned his head away, expecting an explosion that never came. He kept his face down in the dirt, breathing deeply, and worked even harder to free his hands. Then, he heard something new. Something passed the wind in the trees, and his heart was pumping in his ears. It sounded like something was taking long, deep breaths. Blinking hard now that the light was gone, Cooper moved his head back out of the dirt to see what had happened. When he saw it, a feeling of fear filled his chest, enveloping him, making him forget everything as he felt that he was five years old and in the middle of a nightmare.

Cooper could see his panicked breath materialize before his eyes as, magically, the temperature of the night air must have dropped thirty degrees. Where the light had disappeared stood a large, black-cloaked figure that all those present knelt before. He felt the cold creep into his lungs, chilling his heart. The dark figure was heavily lopsided, leaning to its right. It walked slowly and stiffly as if its limbs were not made to move. It took a step, then dragged its right leg. It staggered toward the red creature holding the string worm as far above its quivering, bowed head as it could.

The cloaked figure reached out with its left arm, taking the worm. It lifted it under its hood as if observing it up close. It only moved its left side as its right side seemed to sink low as if heavy weights were attached to its shoulder.

After a moment, the hooded figure turned to the pig on the ground. The pig squealed madly until the figure turned to the cats, which also hissed and meowed in agony, as did the cow. Then, the figure turned toward him. Cooper's whole body went numb with fright as if seeing his worst fears come true. It was as if his eyes were locked onto whatever was under that hood.

Thankfully, the figure twisted away from him, and he sighed in relief as it turned to the three-horned creatures. The red one had removed his helmet, revealing bright, fine hair that seemed to erupt magically when freed. The black form limped its way right up to the red creature and tossed the worm to the large green man at its left. He caught it with his free hand while using his other to lean on his large mace.

He touched the worm's ends to his mouth and ear. After holding them firm for a moment, he passed them on until all his companions had done the same.

The hooded creature took a rough breath and looked up toward the stars. The hood dropped slowly and, without words, seemed to order the imp who trembled before him to speak.

The three imps looked up, and all started talking at once. It was in a ramble of words, cat calls, and pig grunts that no one could understand. All this passed over Cooper as his view remained fixed on the dark, cold figure.

All three imps went silent when the hooded being let out a long, clouded breath. It was remarkable how quickly their excited gestures and words left them with the merest glance.

The red imp was the one who attempted to respond. He raised his head and shook his short, red, untidy hair, and when he spoke, his eyes didn't leave the ground.

"All about secure, we see some humans," he pointed a red finger toward Cooper. "And some others lessers that we don't know. There is no site of the Alliance nor any other danger. We are with little detection, but…" the imp hesitated as his courage faltered. He looked around at his two buddies for some misplaced help.

"We don't know not where we be. Now, we did gather the ear and tongue of what they say here, but we don't know where here is."

Finishing, the imp fell flat on its face, and right after him, the other two followed suit. When the green one did, he sadly found that his forehead had hit a rock, almost knocking him out. Towering over the imps, the hooded figure looked again up into the night sky. As it did, Cooper could see a human chin as white as snow under that hood. It took a very long, uneven breath again that seemed to freeze the leaves and branches around it.

"What are all these things? What do they want? How can I understand them?" The questions raced through Cooper's mind with no answer. The hooded man spoke, making Cooper shift, still pulling and working hard against his restraints.

"We are where we are supposed to be to retrieve what was ours to begin. We will once more have the Requiem, and all will know it," it said between sharp intakes of excited breath. It shot a look over to the one in the circle with the large bow and a patch over its left eye.

"Voscass, go and find me the one we seek." It coughed and turned its attention to the nicely dressed human who had come with them.

"Reynard," he motioned with a wave of its long-cloaked arm for the man to come closer. Standing at once, the man strode toward the black mass of robes. Watching him walk in the twilight, Cooper could see his clothes were old, unkempt, with dark stains but of very high quality.

"Recruit, but stay close if needed. Stay hidden until we need the dead." The pale man bowed in response and walked a little way out of the clearing. Cooper followed the sounds of his footsteps in the field until suddenly, they were gone. Cooper didn't have time to think of this as he realized he couldn't trust his senses anymore.

"All others," the hooded figure ordered, "rise and make ready."

Cooper desperately struggled to free his hand until he felt something watching him. The imp turned its large, venomous gaze on him. Cooper instinctively played dead and closed his eyes, not daring to breathe. He waited for a moment as he listened to all the creatures rise to their feet and check their gear. Cooper couldn't help but peek through one eye as they each took up different positions in an odd line around the hooded figure. They knew where to go and stand without being told, except for the red imp.

The imp hurried to the hooded leader whose head was bent back, looking up again, examining the sky. It was preoccupied, muttering something under its breath that was still so cold Cooper could see it. The imp waited for its master to notice him before speaking. Something unsaid told the red imp that he had his master's attention because when his hood pointed down at him, the imp never looked up at him.

"Speak," ordered the cold voice.

Shaking, the imp replied, "Mas…master, what you want with the four kinds we got?"

What was under the hood directed its gaze back to Cooper. Cooper felt his skin crawl with a wave of goosebumps from head to foot. With relief, the hood turned back to the other tied animals. It was like a warm breeze on a winter's day for Cooper, but the pig, cow, and cats howled and shrieked once again. Without a backward glance at him, the hooded figure started to limp to the middle of the line, with two of the largest creatures flanking him.

"Take the two smaller ones, the human leave, with some…" it paused, taking a deep breath, "remembrance of what happened here. Kill the rest."

At once, the red and blue imps ran over to the animals. All Cooper could see were the pig's hooves struggling to free itself from its binds, its high-pitched squeals filling the air. Then suddenly, all he could hear were the imp's pig-like squeals as the earth around them grew darker with blood. With the shock, Cooper jerked hard and freed his hands. In his relief, he didn't notice the final imp coming toward him until it was right by his feet. His hands were free, but his feet were still bound together at the ankles. Cooper didn't move to keep the illusion that he was still bound. The imp hesitated for a moment, looking mad with anticipation. It took a small dagger in its thin, knobby hand, and with a cat-like hiss, it raised the knife high into the air over his head. Cooper was ready as he kicked out hard and stuck its midsection just as the imp brought the dagger down to strike. The imp hit the ground, and with a nauseating meow, he dropped the dagger.

As fast as Cooper could, he squirmed like a worm over to the dagger. The imp tried to get up, sounding like a drunken cat. Cooper raised his sore body as best he could but panicked when he noticed the other imps had been alerted. They dropped the dead pig they were carrying, and with a war cry, they rushed toward him. With seconds to react, Cooper took up the knife and struggled to cut the ropes holding his legs together.

One swift slice, and he was free. His whole body was stiff and stinging. He pushed himself into a crouching position despite feeling like his arms and legs were broken. The red and blue imps were almost on him, and their third companion was now getting to its feet.

Cooper automatically drew his gun and supported it with his other hand with the dagger in it. Its barrel lined up on the center target. As he controlled his breathing and felt the tension of the trigger, he heard a hearty laugh. The two charging imps skidded to a halt in the dirt and broken weeds. Then Cooper felt it. It was that same feeling, that same sickening, hollow, cold feeling. The three imps cowered away from him, giving off mournful meows, pig grunts, and whimpered groans. Cooper's instincts told his body to move, but nothing was working. In the shimmering starlight, the cold laugh was growing. Cooper's eyes were fixed past his sights now on the black hood.

For a few seconds, no one moved. Even the night seemed to have stopped. Slowly, a right arm started to rise under that black cloak. Its cold laugh was somehow more alive, sounding hungry now. All his subordinates bowed low, moving away, clearing a path between them.

"Stand down!" Cooper roared, seeing his breath in a frozen cloud come out of his mouth. A single finger came to rest, pointing at him from under those dark robes.

Cooper was shaking so hard from the cold he could hardly keep his kneeling stance. The cold was now almost unbearable, and he found it harder and harder to breathe.

Suddenly, ice erupted around his feet with the force of a small explosion. Cooper howled in pain as the ice block around his feet sent dozens of needles piercing deep into his skin. The pain was so sharp that he almost dropped his gun and knife.

Cooper struggled to keep his gun sight steady on his target, but his hand shook so severely that seconds seemed like minutes. Before his howl of pain ended, the ice burst around his hand, holding the knife. It was almost up to his elbow with the same razor needles clawing into him.

Cooper found himself screaming again. Miraculously, the pain caused Cooper to gain control of his senses as he pulled his trigger three times. He heard the bullets hit with an odd cracking sound, finally ending the laughter. The sound from his gun echoed in the trees, and when it had ended, there was only the sound of Cooper's whimpers of pain.

"The rest of you drop your weapons, get down on the ground with your hands…" Cooper was cut off as ice engulfed his gun hand. His hand fell helpless to the ground. His eyes bulged as he screamed in pain again, wondering what he had hit.

"This one has spirit!" he heard past his whimpers. All those around their leader looked on with bated breath, watching Cooper being frozen alive.

"Their weapons have no honor," their leader said. The air was uneasy as all watched as the night seemed to shuffle between hot and cold winds. In an aggravated yell, the leader called, "We will incapacitate him. He may serve us later. The Requiem will not wait. We will spare his life for now, won't we?"

Before Cooper could do anything except yell, the green imp came close again, overpowering his yell with its cat hiss and hit him sharply in the forehead with the butt of its dagger-like hammer. Blood started to drip down his face onto his lips. The floating, vague images of the monstrous band were moving off, vanishing from his dull sight. Blackness was creeping around everything he could see. Closing his eyes, Cooper could hear that frigid laugh grow fainter like someone was turning down the volume.

He couldn't move, not even his lips or fingers anymore, as everything turned black.

Eleven

Is This A Bad Time To Ask To Go To The School Counselor?

"Clint Holden!" the teacher's voice called out over the thunderstruck class. Her shout pulled everyone's eyes back to her and away from the clock perched above the only door in the room. "Will you stop laughing and pay attention!" bellowed Mrs. Christenson, sounding angrier with each word.

Trying to stifle a snicker, Clint replied, "Yes, Mrs. Christenson." It was probably the dull, drawling tone of his voice that made her stare him down.

Her eyes were full of a mad shine as her lips quivered. "Perhaps you can tell us all what is so funny about the question on the board?" she asked sternly.

Clint looked from her to the board, to his friend Corbin, who was sitting next to him at the front of the class, for any unspoken answer. Corbin was doing a much better job at not laughing. His friend's only betrayal was that his chest and stomach were still trembling in silent giggles.

"Well, uh, I was never really good at this kind of stuff, Mrs. Christenson," Clint replied bravely.

"This was your homework assignment from last night," Mrs. Christenson said as her glasses slid further down her sharp nose. "So, let's see what you make of it; please show us the answer on the board." At the end of those words, her expression changed as if the fat lady had sung.

Clint's smile left him as he felt she was two moves from checkmate. It was now Corbin who couldn't help but let out a laugh as Clint got to his feet. His hands and legs felt like someone had attached an additional twenty-pound weights to them. The whiteboard seemed to grow larger than he ever remembered. He had just taken three steps, and it was about the size of a billboard off the freeway. Slouching in defeat for not getting away with a little joke, he shuffled his death march until he was at the board.

As if this was not horrible enough, he could feel every eye in the class was on him, which meant that *she* was watching. Unable to control himself, he glanced at a young, very pretty blonde girl sitting at the side of the room nearest the door. Her dark eyes seemed to blaze in the same way that would typically make his stomach lurch. Looking back at the whiteboard as if it were his tombstone, he straightened up and puffed out his chest.

"You can't look too bad in front of her," he thought. Finding new strength, he had his signature George Clooney look of confidence on as he felt with his fingers to pick up a marker, uncapped it, and brought the tip to the board. His face plummeted when he remembered that his homework paper was still on his desk. Feeling stupid, he got the paper and went back to the board. He snuck another nervous look at the teacher, who watched venomously, her hair tied up in a bun that must have been a crank. It pulled her facial skin so tight.

Clint wrote the equation on the board with soft squeaks that made some of the class jitter in discomfort in their seats. The thought that he was never good at these types of questions kept barking in the back of his mind as he wrote. When he was done copying everything on the board, he wrote the answer below it. Knowing the worst was coming, he swung over to face the two-legged Hydra Teacher.

"So," she said in a sharp voice that sounded remarkably like the Sharpie did on the board. It had the same effect, making the students wince in pain.

"The question in our homework was if Johnny and Mary were both walking toward each other from a thousand paces and Johnny walked five paces every four seconds and Mary walked eight paces every six seconds, how long would it take for Johnny to meet Mary and how many paces should it take him?" She took a moment to observe Clint and then the class and then looked at Corbin, who was still failing to sit still, being overcome again by giggles.

"Your answer is correct," Mrs. Christenson said past trembling lips of defeat.

"Did all of you come to the same conclusion?" she inquired, turning on the rest of the class.

A fearful murmur of approval came from the class except for the ones in the back who were daydreaming and some who even looked to be falling asleep. Mrs. Christenson turned and walked behind Clint, squinting down on him past her needle-like nose, making his insides dissolve. The stare she gave him made him feel as if someone had just flipped open a door of panic behind his navel. She twisted around in her tight dress as if she were wrapped as an Egyptian mummy, with her overly large earrings like tiny wrecking balls as she examined each student.

"You all did your homework this way?" she barked again, through lips that looked like they were growing thinner and thinner as she retired behind her desk. The dread was building in Clint as her gleaming gaze bore a hole into the board where he had just written his answer. Out of all his teachers, she was the one he didn't want to get on the wrong side of. He felt in the place where his liver should have been that she was fattening them up for the kill.

Clint hesitated and then turned around to see her and face the class. He didn't like being this close to the creature teacher without even a desk to take cover behind. It was always best to keep her at arm's length, especially when you might be in trouble or when she could make up reasons for you to be in trouble. She was skinny, with skin that resembled the gray lunch trays in the cafeteria.

Finishing her examination of the class, she apparently seemed satisfied. The tension was building, and he felt the noose tighten around his neck; he had a hard time swallowing. His mouth was getting drier every second until she broke the silence so harshly that one of the two kids in the back, who was almost asleep, fell off their seat.

"If you all did it that way, why aren't you all laughing?" she snapped, shooting up from her chair.

No one spoke, as a fresh wave of anxiety washed over all of them as if someone had just told them they all would be force-fed the school's meatloaf. Corbin even stopped silent laughing and straightened up so fast that his desk chair jumped an inch into the air.

"You are the only two laughing, Mr. Holden and Mr. Jenkins."

Clint and Corbin exchanged curious looks with each other. Mrs. Christenson's lips twitched slightly, and Clint knew from sad experience that this was her way of smiling when she had a student right where she wanted them.

"So, what do you two find so funny?" she hollered, watching both with a steely glint in her eye. She first scanned Corbin like a hungry vulture waiting for what she was watching to die. Corbin tried to answer as the color in his face drained but only made faint gurgling noises. She seemed satisfied with this, and turned on her out-of-date high-heeled shoes toward Clint. She walked as if she was in the Miss America pageant, but her features resembled a drill sergeant.

"I am waiting," she said, sounding like her mouth was full of cottage cheese.

Rather than prolong this questioning, Clint knew that the teacher was at the peak of her anger. He decided to let the air out of the balloon and just tell her.

"Clint," Corbin whispered so only he could hear him. "When you show the wicked witch the ruby slippers, you don't yank them away from her before you start walking down the yellow brick road."

Clint shrugged before addressing the class and said, "Well when you were reviewing all our homework questions, you kind of slurred one word in there that made me question what it was about." He tried to sound brave, but in the back of his mind, he knew he would never see his parents again.

"And what word was it?" she hissed.

"Uh," his courage weakened under her bad breath. He couldn't say anything else but could only stare at Corbin for help.

She turned her look between them so quickly that it was amazing that the windows and door didn't snap closed.

"Well?" she asked expectantly.

Not daring to look her in the eye, Corbin's chubby face looked at his textbook as an escape tactic. His black, neatly cut hair started to shake. "I, I thought that, I thought that... that you... you..."

"Out with it, boy!"

"I thought that you didn't say paces," he said quickly.

Looking more like the Grim Reaper than a teacher, she waited as if his answer would determine his life span. Corbin finished knowing that he'd signed his own death warrant.

"I thought that you said something." He looked at Clint for help. All Clint could do was nod his approval to get it over with.

"She sucked the Ruby slippers off of ya," Clint whispered with a shrug.

Speaking very slowly and sliding as far back in his desk as his weight would allow him, Corbin said, "I thought you said something that, that, sounded like list, mist you know when someone takes, a, uh…"

Most of the class started to laugh, but they were cut short by that look that every child feared from a teacher. It was as if someone had just canceled Christmas.

"Thinking I must be wrong, I asked Clint if you said that… that word," Corbin said almost pleadingly.

"And what did Clint tell you I said?" she asked, turning to him.

Corbin's cheeks were quivering like a chipmunk. He looked like he didn't want to say it.

Clint looked at her and finished answering very quickly for him. Closing his eyes, he blurted it out.

"I told him that I couldn't take that many pisses if my life depended on it."

Then, opening his eyes, he hurriedly added, "Ma'am," in a shocked voice. The class started to laugh again but was cut short with just a turn of Mrs. Christenson's head. Clint kept his eyes down, but nothing he could do would stop the sound of her taking such a deep breath that it felt like airplanes overhead would have to lower their altitude because of the change in air pressure; at least that would explain why so many kids suddenly looked sick and fearful in the class now.

Not looking at them, Mrs. Christenson walked behind her desk and wrote on a piece of paper with almost incredible speed. A smile spread across her pasty face that didn't show any of her sharp flesh-eating teeth. She motioned for Clint and Corbin to come to her desk.

Clint straightened his back and held his head high as he walked over while Corbin squeezed his overweight frame out of the desk chair. He was about twice as heavy as Clint. It was always difficult for him to extricate himself, particularly when he was nervous. She finished writing as Corbin came to a halt next to Clint. He looked like he was going to the dentist to get his teeth pulled. The extraterrestrial teacher finished her writing with her hand moving so fast that her handwriting looked like something a three-year-old would scribble. Clint turned to see how his friend was holding up.

Corbin was his best friend in the world. They had been friends since kindergarten when their names were read out for roll call, and they had sat together ever since. This wasn't their first time in trouble, and it wouldn't be the last. Clint watched as Corbin was strangely bouncing and discovered that he was rubbing his knees together. Clint couldn't help but smile because he knew whatever happened to him didn't matter as long as Corbin was with him.

Clint looked on in appreciation until Corbin's poker face turned to shock. Clint saw Mrs. Christenson holding out a folded piece of paper for him to take. When he took it from her, he touched one of her bone-thin, cold fingers that had what looked like a four-inch-long fingernail at the end of it.

"Please take this to the principal's office," she said as if she were a loving parent asking them to go to the store to buy some cookies for themselves.

I Could get an Award in Visits to The Principal's Office

Taking the lead, Clint turned and started to the door. He did very well until he walked by Melanie's desk. Out of the corner of his eye, he could see just a little of her dark blonde hair, but in his mind, he could see all her face. That same face he tried to picture so clearly and failed but saw it everywhere else. He wanted to give her his quarter smile that he had been practicing for picture day, but all that happened was he almost walked into the door. Corbin grabbed him and directed him to safety at the last moment.

"Port sailor," Corbin groaned, rolling his eyes.

As soon as they were in the shelter of the hallway, Clint smacked himself in the face. "I looked so stupid in front of her."

Walking beside him now, Corbin smugly said, "Yeah, you did."

"Is that all you have to say?" Clint lowered his voice, trying to sound like Corbin, "'Yeah, you did.'"

"Well, you did look pretty dumb and don't give me that attitude. You are the one who made me laugh. You know you can't do that kind of stuff in her class. She would enjoy seeing two puppies like you and me drowned," Corbin replied.

Shaking his head, they strolled to the office. Everyone else was in their classes, the doors open with the hopes of letting the air circulate a little more to cool things off.

"I wouldn't have made you laugh if you didn't ask that stupid question," Clint said, his regret rising.

"There is no such thing as a stupid question," Corbin replied.

"No, just stupid people," Clint retorted.

"Would you rather I held up my hand and asked her directly? Besides, I do feel bad about that, and to make up for it, I saved you from walking into the door. I mean, you could have really hurt yourself with your eyes sticking out of your head like that at Melanie. You could have died. I just saved your life."

"Was it that bad?"

"Worse," Corbin said gravely.

They didn't say much for the rest of the way down the long halls lined with lockers by the gym and then the pool. It wasn't until they went down the stairs next to the lunchroom that Clint broke the silence.

"Do you think they'll have the Halloween dance this Friday?"

"How can you still be thinking about her at a time like this?" Corbin asked breathlessly.

"Time like what?" Clint asked.

"No way we're coming out of that office alive, you know that, right? Even if we do, our parents will chew us out until all that's left are our toes in our shoes because they smell."

They both slowed to a snail's pace, prolonging what remained of their freedom. The thought of Principal Miller's face made any child feel like they would need rash ointment. It was not the fact of the disciplinary action that was sure to come but the fact that they would have to be in the same room as the man. Principal Miller was tall with a slender frame except for a gut that showed his life from behind a desk. It was as if a signpost had swallowed a beach ball. The kids talked about him, saying he was born before people had full heads of hair. What was left of his dark red hair grew on one side that he combed over to make up for the round bald spot on his head. The only other hair he had was a bushy, full mustache that resembled an old wire brush. Any child who went into that office prayed that there was no food hanging off that mustache, which was known as an everyday event. His suits were the worst that had ever been made. He always looked like those hippy photos that Clint saw in the documentaries where people of that generation got married, surrounded by nothing but flowers and peace signs.

Coming to the door, Clint could see the tile was worn away by all the troubled students who had gone to their deaths before him. The thoughts of all the places that he wanted to see flashed in his mind. His parents would never let him live to see the light of day. Like all dungeon lairs, this one had its monster guarding the mouth of the cave. Daring to overcome his first obstacle, Clint mournfully walked past the archway to the office with Corbin close behind him. Behind the counter was a large head with enough untidy hair to hide hundreds of pencils and a bird or two. His large crown of hair left little room for a forehead but held enough space for two dark eyes magically magnified to the size of a pea by the inch-thick glasses that hung on a horrible nose that seemed to have grown around the curled frames.

"I'm going in," Clint said, low enough that only Corbin could hear him.

Standing bolt upright, the nightmare started. The hunched old secretary bent forward, leaning heavily on the desk before him and, hearing Clint clear his throat.

Coughing, Mr. Hogarth moved his beady, ugly pea-sized eyes over the two boys and, wheezing, said, "Ah, Mr. Holden, good, you have heard that… what is this you have?" Mr. Hogarth stopped and looked down at the letter that Corbin was holding out for him. Clint didn't know what was worse, the fact that his parents were going to kill him or watching those tiny eyes run over each word.

"Hey guyths!" came an over-enthusiastic voice from the other side of the room. Clint and Corbin knew that voice belonged to Zack. He was a tall kid at about five feet six and looked like he weighed about 20 pounds. He was sick all the time, but what energy he had was used to boost his brain power, so they made him a teacher's assistant. All the kids knew that it was the grownups' way to try and save him from being picked on so much.

"Oh, not the walking light bulb with zits," Corbin said quietly to Clint as both sat down on the worn plastic seats in the office. Then happily shouted, "Hey dude!" with an over-excited wave that anyone else would interpret as someone trying to flag down a plane for landing.

Zack could tell at first glance that something was wrong. He always had a nose for trouble, and his greatest wish was to tell someone in authority that a kid was misbehaving. Looking reasonably ashamed, both Clint and Corbin looked down at their feet. Zack didn't say anything but just looked at them and took a long snort of nasal spray. He took a breath as if to say something when the voice of the old secretary brought Clint's attention back in front of him. He was talking on the phone, apparently to the principal.

"Sir, we have two boys here that need to see you." He stopped talking with an arrested look under that mushroom-shaped hair of his. "Yes, sir. They are Clint Holden and Corbin Jenkins. All right, yes, sir, I will take care of it. Yes, sir. Goodbye, sir." Then, hanging up the phone, the secretary added in his slobbery old voice, "Old windbag." Getting off his stool with a grunt, the secretary went over to the file cabinets in the corner of the room. Pulling a cardigan that George Washington could have worn higher around his neck, the wizened old secretary retrieved two files and scuffled back to his desk. It took him six or seven tries to sit back on his stool comfortably. Clint became very interested in his shoes when the secretary, who looked particularly grim and tired, turned his attention to them.

Holding one of the files in a gruesome way, he pointed at Corbin. "You first," he said, wiggling the file in a threatening way toward them. Corbin got up and tugged the file out of the secretary's cold hand. Corbin's face started to grow redder and redder as he went to the door with the words written like a tombstone on the glass over the door stating, Principal Miller's Office.

Corbin took a moment and waved back at Clint. If this were in another time and place, Clint would have been overcome with mirth from Corbin's red face and sorrowful look. He gave his friend a reassuring smile as the call of "Come in" came from behind the door. Corbin went in and vanished from sight as the door snapped closed behind him.

Feeling some of his courage ebb away with his friend gone, Clint glanced at Zack, who was now coming over to take up Corbin's seat. With each step, his shoes squeaked horribly. Clint thought of standing up and walking around the office, but it was too late; Zack's skinny frame sat beside him.

"Isthn't it great to be in the seventh grade now?" Zack asked in a nasal voice.

"Yeah," Clint replied dully.

"Our junior high and highth school all in one and so far, the lessons are not all that difficult. This is the life for me and anyone else who valueth a good education, if you asthk me," Zack said rapidly. It was hard to make out some of what he was saying because of his retainer.

For the rest of his condemned time waiting in the office for his turn with the principal, Clint let Zack keep talking. It was nice to have something to distract him from what was waiting behind that door, and Zack was about as good a distraction as a walking headache. Clint sat there giving an occasional nod or responding to the gaps in what Zack was saying with a "Yeah" or "I know what you mean."

All too soon, the door to the principal's office opened, and a pitiful-looking Corbin came out of it. Jerking his head, he saw his best friend in a stupor. Corbin's mouth was open, his skin was pale, and his hands were shaking, holding a piece of paper. When he passed Clint, he didn't even look at him. He just went out into the hallway, muttering odd words to himself.

Through the open office door came the stale voice calling, "Mr. Holden." Collecting his thoughts, Clint remembered where he was and what was going on as he got to his feet again, but his heart felt like he left it on the seat behind him.

"Good luck," Zack called to him. Adding a soft laugh, he said, "Thereth going to be a thurprise coming that you won't believe. Saya!" He was still saying something in the wake of Clint leaving. Clint didn't hear him or give it a second thought as he dragged his feet toward the open office door. As soon as he passed the threshold, he felt a wave of heat and humidity hit him. It was like walking into a furnace that smelt like they had cremated children in here.

"Shut the door, please, Mr. Holden," came the principal's all-too-familiar voice that never wavered in pitch.

Not looking back, Clint shut the door, not noticing that Zack was still talking to him.

Thirteen

I Can Feel My IQ Getting Smaller

Closing the door behind him, Clint couldn't help but look around the gloomy office. There was only one place for students to sit, a single uncomfortable chair facing the front of an old oak desk. The office was the size of a regular classroom but only sparsely furnished. All the windows had their blinds drawn, not letting a fraction of happiness in from the sun. Various pictures hung around the old room, each dull and depicting remnants of all the previous principals standing in front of the school. More frames held a place of honor on the wall behind the desk, showing many different specimens of bugs with pins sticking out of each one. Clint's imagination was filled with the thought of him being hung on the wall like any other interesting pest, being put on display with pins holding his body in place, just like one of those bugs.

"Sit," the principal croaked from his squeaky chair behind the desk. Coming up to the chair he was supposed to sit in, Clint could see the desk was well organized, with a single sheet of paper right in front of the principal. It was the paper that his teacher had given them to show him. It must have been brought in while he was occupied with Zack. Sitting down, he found that his pants made an odd squeaking noise on the chair. Something like skidding a wet shoe on a tile floor. Suddenly, he found that all he could do was look at the bald patch on the principal's head, reflecting the dull lighting in the office. He was also starting to develop a headache from a light flickering in the left corner of the room.

Clint couldn't even look away when the principal held out a hand and asked, "File, please." Shaking his head quickly to clear it, Clint got up, handed it to him, and sat down again. To his shame and despite his best efforts, his seat made the same squealing sound as he got up and returned. Principal Miller got to his feet, making the old, worn-out chair squeal horribly as he stood and perused the file.

Clint wondered how in the world someone could survive in this heat, day in and day out. He squirmed in the uncomfortable chair as he watched Principal Miller thumb through his file.

Done, he shut the folder and didn't say anything but placed it in a perfect uniform position on his desk. He ambled to the window on the right side of the office. Parting the blinds, he said in that terrible monotone voice, "So we had quite the day today, didn't we, Mr. Holden?"

Looking subdued, Clint said, "Yes, sir."

Closing the blinds with a snap, Principal Miller started to walk around the office with his hands behind his back. It made his already oversized sphere of a stomach stick out even further. He walked around admiring the walls, not looking at Clint.

Clint looked up at the elegant but dull clock behind the desk and watched the hands as they refused to move. School was almost over, so all he had to do was last a little longer in this boiler room. He was lucky to be called to the office right before leaving school. He wouldn't have to suffer too long.

Principal Miller stopped pacing behind Clint and rested his hands on the back of the chair. In a surprisingly kind voice that caught Clint off guard, he said, "You have had a rough go of things, haven't you?"

This was not what Clint had expected from the chrome dome tyrant who had reprimanded him so many times before. Not knowing where Principal Miller was going with this, Clint asked, "Sir?"

"First your father dies in a car accident and then your mother recently remarries, bringing you to a new home," Principal Miller said taking his seat, leaning hard on his chair, making it fall back further giving off that sound like someone running over an elephant's trunk with a car.

"Uh, yeah," Clint said in rather a clipped tone, looking first at the principal's face, then the shine from between his combover.

Looking uncomfortable, Principal Miller started to pace around the room again. "I know your brother with his career on our football team. He is a fine youth. You have an older sister at college and one more biological sister, right?"

"Yes, sir." Now Principal Miller was coming to it, Clint thought.

"And your new father has two other children? Tamara, who is a year or so ahead of you, going to this school, and a younger brother who is behind you?"

"Yes, sir," Clint went on. It would have been easier to record 'Yes, sir' and have it keep playing on repeat than to keep saying it over and over again.

Principal Miller began tapping on Clint's folder with his fingers to a tone that seemed as dull as his tie. "You must understand that you cannot disrupt class, Mr. Holden. You may not want to learn for your own personal reasons, but if you inflict your bad attitude on others, you will have to accept the significance determined by this society."

Clint tuned the principal's voice out, rolling his eyes over to the clock. Only fifteen more minutes until school got out. He could last that long with a glazed look on his face. Principal Miller droned on for another five minutes until he leaned forward in his chair, causing a loud squawk that sliced through Clint's senses.

"Do you agree, Mr. Holden?" he asked.

"Oh, yes, sir, Clint agreed vigorously without the faintest idea what he was agreeing to.

"Mr. Holden, are you going to be proud of your family, proud of your community, proud of your country, or are you going to do bad?"

"Oh, I want to be good, sir," Clint said, trying to look as innocent as possible.

"Good. That is good, Mr. Holden. Now I will have to give you this note and have your parents sign it, and you bring it back to Mrs. Christenson tomorrow."

Looking up at the clock, he had about five minutes to go before the bell rang. It must be some sort of record to get out of the steam vault that quickly. His breathing was starting to return to normal. He stood up, taking the letter that Principal Miller had just finished writing. Principal Miller also stood up with another loud yell of complaint from his old seat.

"If you would be a gentleman and excuse me, I have an announcement to give to the school," he droned, indicating the door behind Clint.

Not waiting for another chance, Clint whipped around the lone seat in the middle of the room and headed for the door. When he opened it, a rush of cool air hit him like the sea waves on the shore. He wasn't aware that he had been sweating that much until the cool air confirmed it on his forehead and under his arms. Leaving the office and walking into the hallway, he saw Principal Miller return the files to the cabinets and head over to the intercom system.

Fourteen

WALKING THE MILE

Clint's attention was taken out of the office by an overweight body jumping on his back.

"We live to prank another day!" Corbin yelled, trying to look like he was riding a wild horse while on Clint's back. Half falling, half trying to look cool in this awkward moment, Corbin hit the ground on his butt and asked, "So did he hurt you, or did you put up a fight or just put the file between your legs and run around the room screaming?"

"If I had to stay in that office for another minute, I would have been a chicken nugget," Clint replied wearily. "I have a letter for my parents to sign. How did you make out?" Clint asked, extending a hand to help Corbin up.

Taking it, Corbin said as he heaved himself up, "Detention this Friday after school and a letter to my parents as well. You didn't get detention?"

"No."

"Must be your dad. I wish my father got the Nobel Prize. I know it's not because of your looks."

Clint started walking down the hall, "I will trade you any day; besides, he's not my dad. He's my stepdad, and I don't want him even that close to me. It's bad enough that I have to live with him."

"Well, at least you get to see him. My dad's only home once a month. All he does is scratch himself in places I didn't think he could reach, given his weight. I wish I had brothers and sisters." Corbin looked suddenly tired and worn.

"You have me," Clint said arrogantly and added, "so don't just stand there. You have exactly thirty seconds to change your expression to one of enormous gratitude for being in my presence."

"I must say you are a good…"

He was interrupted by the loud crackle of the intercom system throughout the school. Echoing down the hall and out of every room's speaker came the dull voice of Principal Miller. The sound failed and then came in clear as he started to speak.

"Attention, all students."

Corbin let out a long sigh, "He sounds worse over the intercom. Like Charlie Brown's teacher."

"I want to hear this, Corbin. He let me out of the office for this, so it has to be important. You know he likes nothing better than to overcook some kid in there," Clint said as he stopped walking. Corbin stopped next to him, suddenly looking like he had stayed up all night.

"Attention, all students." Principal Miller's voice came over the intercom again, "This Friday is Halloween. No costumes will be allowed during school hours on the school grounds. Students are all reminded that it is a school day and they should conduct themselves accordingly."

"He sounds like he is reading all of this," Clint snorted.

"He always sounds like he is reading something. He must have cue cards to read from when he orders drive-through. He's an idiot!" Corbin said, sitting on the floor with his back against the wall.

"With the subject of the Halloween dance," cracked the principal's voice, causing Clint and Corbin to look up expectantly.

"The dance will go on as we have in the past, but we will be adding new security, and Zackary Glass will inspect all costumes. So, dress accordingly. Also, it is a young ladies' evening. There will be no confusion; all young men will buy a ghost note inviting the young lady they wish to accompany to the dance. The ghost note invitations cost five dollars each, which will pay for the dance. This is a girl's choice dance, so when a young lady receives a ghost note, they can accept or refuse who they will go with. Ladies, please choose wisely, and young men may buy as many ghost notes as you wish."

There was an outbreak of applause and shouts of cheer from all over the school that poured in from the classrooms to the halls. It was quickly hushed by calls from the teachers.

"Friday?" Corbin called out, knocking his hand over his head as the intercom system shut off with another crack. "I have detention Friday. That's why Mr. Miller looked so excited when he told me about it. I won't be able to do anything before the dance."

"He looked excited? You mean his voice actually changed, and he cracked a smile?" Clint asked in disbelief as he started to walk down the hall again.

"No, he just walked a little faster around the room. For him, that's absolutely being ecstatic!" Corbin said with a wave of his hand.

The end-of-school bell rang, which was immediately followed by a cascade of students rushing out of the classrooms. Clint and Corbin retrieved what they needed from their lockers and started walking out of the school. Each one was waving their goodbyes when someone very noticeable caught Clint's eye, someone who made his heart skip.

It was Melanie. She was walking toward him and Corbin with a spring in her step, a smile on her face, and a crowd of friends following her. Even as his stomach felt like it was doing hula-hoops around his chest and the growing urge to run for it, Clint couldn't help but notice that she was beautiful, as if he had not seen her for months. Not like most girls around this school, she didn't need makeup. She didn't have to try to make her face look different. *She is perfect the way she is*, he thought as his mouth fell open. Her hair moved in the soft breeze coming out of a classroom door as other students walked by her.

Corbin took a step between her and Clint right before she got there and said, with a look like he was announcing that there was a snake at his feet, "Close your mouth or get a coaster for your lower lip!" Realizing how stupid he looked, Clint closed his mouth, trying not to look so desperate but cool and smooth.

"Hello, troublemakers," Melanie said cheerfully as she arrived.

"That's us. How are you, Melanie?" Corbin asked, smiling. Looking over his shoulder, he muttered low so only Clint could hear him, "You still look like you have a hook in your mouth."

"Fine. I hope that you didn't get in too much trouble. Mrs. Christenson has been waiting to make an example of someone so others will fall into line in her classes. What did she have you two do?"

She looked back and forth between Clint and Corbin, but Corbin was the only one who spoke. Although he was only a foot away, Clint heard every word but could only remember her tone. He just stood there in some strange, unblinking trance.

Corbin shook his head in despair and answered, "Clint had a hard time in the office, but we both got out all right. I got detention for Friday and a letter home."

"Did you get detention too, Clint?" she asked. Did she sound a little worried?

"Clint?" Corbin asked, trying to bring his friend back to life.

"Oh, uh," Clint grunted to Melanie and Corbin as if he had just woken up licking his lips, hoping to get rid of an unpleasant taste in his mouth.

"No, I didn't get detention, just a letter home, yeah, I didn't get one just, uh just, got one, he, him, uh, got one…" Clint was looking at Corbin, but his brain decided to run down to one of his shaking knees for some reason. He had utterly forgotten his best friend's name. They shared a moment where all three of them were as quiet as the grave, each wondering what was wrong with Clint. The only noise was that of students talking as they passed by and Melanie's group of friends, who started to whisper in hushed giggles at seeing Clint lose his mind. Corbin saved everyone by breaking the pause.

"Well, we better get home. If we're late, that will only make it worse. See you, Melanie." He started to walk off.

"Wait," she said. "Before you go, here are your books you left in class. I collected them for you."

"Thanks, Melanie," Corbin said, taking both books as Clint was still dumbstruck.

Clint didn't move. He was as still as a mannequin; every nerve in his body seemed to refuse to work. He wanted to say something very smooth and mature. But all that happened was to give off a slight smile. Melanie, who was already smiling, broadened it, showing her glinting teeth. Clint heard quick footsteps behind him, followed by a tight grip on his arm.

Corbin came back smiling and laughing over him to, Melanie. "He has to go home too, you know. He won't last long in his current condition." Corbin pulled Clint back to life. His jelly legs finally moved and held his weight. Then, to make it really bad, Corbin stopped, "Hey Melanie, remind me of your friend's name over there in the pink outfit?"

"Oh, that's Karin," she called back after looking over her shoulder.

"Think she would go to the dance with me?"

"You'll have to ask her and take your chance," Melanie said, smiling again. "It's not that hard to take a chance."

"Right!" Corbin said, waving goodbye with his free hand. He started to walk away again while keeping a firm grip on the quiet Clint. Was she just saying that to Corbin, or was she looking at Clint when she said it?

"Good to see you alive after the oven, Clint, bye." She turned and was gone into the sea of students. Something in the way she said his name made his spine tingle.

Feeling like he had hit a solid wall while running full out, Clint shook off Corbin's hand and straightened up fast, brushing his clothes off as if ants were all over him. "What did you do that for?" Clint asked sharply.

"You looked so dumb there with your mouth open. It was like you were Moana's chicken Heihei in the middle of the ocean, and besides, everyone was watching you. Even Amber stared at you like an escaped mental patient when she walked by," Corbin retorted.

"Amber? The cheerleader, Amber?"

"Is there another Amber worth mentioning around here? Yeah, that Amber. She was talking to a couple of guys from the basketball team doing that swish of the hair thing she does when she wants guys to pay attention to her and…" He stopped talking, and he even stopped walking. He stood still, tense, looking amused. "And, ohhhhh boy!"

"That's your Kool-Aid, man, not mine," Clint said as he stopped walking too.

"You have all kinds of things wrong with you on a number of levels. You don't like the best-looking girl in our school when you know she likes you, and you like some other girl. I swear you must wait for telemarketers to call you and ask them advice from them about the ladies," Corbin said jokingly.

Clint gave him an irritable glare.

"Not to say that she isn't good-looking or anything like that," Corbin exclaimed quickly. "You just have a problem with your hormones being set on the wrong frequency. One girl is so hot you can't stare at her too long because she is like the sun, but oh, does she warm you up. Then the other is a walking piece of Kryptonite to you."

Calming down abruptly and giving a reassuring smile, Clint laughed and said, "I guess you're right." He sounded remorseful as he held his head down and started walking again, this time slower.

"It's about time you came to your senses," Corbin said, hurrying to catch up.

After walking ahead of his friend for a while, Clint said with a sideways glance, "I know it's odd, but I just don't like Amber."

He was cut short with the look of utter terror that Corbin gave him at these words.

"It's true!" Clint said to make him stop. "I don't like girls just for their looks alone. Besides, it won't work out. I think she only likes me because I'm the only guy who won't turn into a slave around her. Like you always do when she comes around. She is too old for us anyway. What grade is she in anyhow?" he added sharply.

Corbin was staring at him. "I know more about being a young, vigorous man than you do. I'll just have to help you understand, that's all, and her grade is an A pulse because she sure makes mine race."

They didn't talk for some time as they walked on. Their steps took them further away from the sounds of the school and into the heart of the homes surrounding the area. There was something to say about living on the outskirts of San Francisco by Oakland. Every road and driveway were set on rolling hills that made the area a driver's nightmare. Also, the houses had to be built practically sideways to stay upright.

Clint and Corbin often didn't talk when they reached the largest and steepest incline on their path home. They didn't like to look too out of shape in case they were seen. When they got to the top and were almost at the street where they would go their separate ways, Clint started the conversation again.

"I will explain it to you. I won't hunt for Amber if you help me not be so stupid when Melanie comes around," he said crisply.

"I think that's a very fine idea, but you will need a lot of work, and I don't really need your help. I mean, she's already my woman. She just doesn't know she's my woman yet," Corbin said smugly.

Clint cast him a curious look with sparkling eyes. They were almost to the corner when something on the other side of the road caught Corbin's eye. Clint followed Corbin's gaze and found an old figure standing alone, motionless, at the end of it. It looked like a man covered in old rags. He was covered in so much dirt that even his face appeared to be a different color, almost red. He wore a hat that looked like it belonged to a farmer and a horribly grimy suit coat. The most disturbing thing was the way he watched them.

"Newcomers. He looks like he should be with the March Hare and the Dormouse," Corbin sneered. "Isn't that the Robbins house? I think I heard they called him Bill the Blunderer, that weird kid who has a crush on your sister. He's so gothic. He looks like a zombie who fears tanning beds, large books, people in suits who say big words, and animals with hair."

Clint didn't say anything. He kept watching the figure standing there alone, studying him. The expression on his face looked like he didn't have anything better to do but stand there and sway slightly in the breeze. There was something that made Clint worry about being watched like this.

"Doesn't your dad forbid Bill to talk to your sister?" Corbin continued, still not walking but examining the same pile of rags as Clint.

This brought Clint's mind back to his friend. Tearing his eyes away from the beggar to the ground below, he mumbled, "He's not my father. My father is dead, and that man's my stepfather."

"I'm sorry, forgot," Corbin apologized quickly.

"It's bad enough that everyone around school calls me Clint Holden," he said, shaking his head. "Holden."

"I know. Calm down," Corbin said weakly.

"My last name is Staeli, and it will always be Staeli. Just because some guy shows up and wants to replace my dad and expects me to love him for it. He takes my mother away from me, and I am supposed not to care. Or get along with him whenever he tries to do something with me."

Clint seemed to be outside of himself. He didn't realize he'd started walking again or appear to know what he was saying. He was so angry that he didn't realize Corbin wasn't walking beside him. He was almost to the corner when he heard something behind him. He froze on the spot and turned around quickly, the anger still simmering inside him. The dirty man from across the street was walking over to Corbin. Corbin's small eyes seemed to be moving so fast between him and the scary man that Clint was amazed he didn't throw up. Corbin's fat legs were moving fast to catch up to Clint; even when he dropped the illusion that he was in shape and started to breathe heavily, he wouldn't make it in time.

The man was walking strangely, like his back was bothering him. His soiled suitcoat and pants looked like they had never been cleaned, and the shoes were riddled with holes. Clint couldn't see anything around the man's middle due to the coat being buttoned up oddly in this heat. Realizing that he had to help his friend, Clint started to walk back to Corbin while trying to calm down.

He was almost to him when the homeless-looking man spoke with a cough, "I'm new here." His voice was high, like he had been sucking on a helium tank. "I heard something of a family called the Holden's." His focus turned to Clint. The man's face had so much dirt on it that he couldn't even make out what he looked like.

"Is one of you Holden's?" he asked excitedly.

Corbin looked sideways at Clint as he shuffled over. Corbin didn't say anything. His jaw seemed to be shut tight by fear.

"What do you want with them?" Clint asked bravely.

"I just need know if one of you are a Holden." The man had reached the curb of the street and stopped. His feet didn't move, but he squirmed oddly, unable to hold still.

There was something furious behind the man's eyes. The way he looked at them both or the fact that everyone was calling him Mr. Holden all day at school brought his feelings back to their surface. Clint's anger started swelling up inside him again. "No. My name is Staeli, and this is Corbin."

Clint was thinking fast. Why would a homeless man want to know about his family? He probably just wanted to ask his stepfather for a handout or something. Why should he even answer this man anyway? He was tired of answering everyone lately. He continued making a great effort to sound convincing when he went on, "We go to school with the Holden's. They're a family that are mostly fat, short, you know, slobbers a lot."

Corbin, still suffering from lockjaw, was able to give a reassuring nod with every word he said. The man didn't seem convinced. He even took a desperate, wavering step forward, leaving only three feet of space between them. Clint forced himself not to panic. The man was now close enough that Clint could smell him.

"You both are not Holdens, and you both know not where the Holdens are?" The man was now hunching over, looking down as if in deep thought.

"We told you our names, and that was more than we should. Now, get lost before we call the police," Corbin said, trying to be heroic, his shaky voice betraying him. He took Clint by the arm again and started dragging him off. Clint kept an eye on the peculiar man. Under all the filth, his strange eyes stared at them, and he began to speak to himself as if someone was right next to him. Clint tried to listen to as much as he could until he was out of earshot. "They are clever but speak the truth." The stranger paused, still giving them a stare that would ward off a charging rhino. "Yes, returning to post."

The man was walking backward, and the last words carried in the wind to Clint sounded like him singing a strange song softly. He had never heard any song like it. It gave him icy chills.

The man seemed to be stumbling his way back to where he was when they first saw him. Before he knew it, Corbin was off like a shot, pulling Clint as if he were on a leash. Clint's feet moved uncertainly as if he were on a ship during a storm. He tried to break Corbin's grip on him and move under his own power.

"That's the second time you've pulled me like a dog. What's up with that?" Clint complained, trying not to keep looking back.

"You may not have noticed, but I just saved your butt again; you're welcome," Corbin replied.

Reaching the corner, Clint asked, "You couldn't save Amber from a clothing sale! What do you think that guy wanted anyway, and what was he doing just standing there?"

Corbin stood next to him, and from the way he was looking back, Clint knew that he felt just as relieved as he did. Clint shifted his backpack's weight higher on his shoulders and sighed heavily.

"You know, I heard the Robbins were taking in some refugees. Something about the tax break they were getting. I hope yours don't all look like that," Corbin said in a low whisper.

Clint's head was buzzing. It was filled with the expression on the man's dirty face. The way he asked him his name made him feel awful. He still didn't want to look back, and he didn't think he could even if he had wanted to.

"Is he still there?" Corbin said before looking back. Clearing his throat, he said uneasily, "Yep, and I'm glad he asked for you and not me. He keeps looking up and down the street. Not at us anymore."

"I've had enough. I'm going home before someone pulls over and tells me something else is wrong with me today," Clint groaned while walking up the sidewalk, leaving his friend behind. Thinking twice about it, he called over his shoulder. "And Corbin, don't forget, I'll make you a deal. If you stop pulling me around, I'll work the wild card for you to Amber."

Still looking down the street, Corbin called back, "I need no help from the likes of you. I know what the ladies like. Besides, I'm going to help you with Melanie. I got it all worked out upstairs." He added the last words while pointing at his head.

"If you're so good and can help me with that, why not help me with my grades, country music, rashes, zits, and fix it so I don't have to go to Camp Happy next summer?" Clint moaned quietly.

Corbin was almost down the road and out of sight when he yelled back, "Hey if you have a girl, you don't need anything else, not even a Nobel Prize."

"A Nobel Prize," he thought. Corbin didn't mean anything by it, but those words seemed to cut him to the heart for some reason. Clint's feet carried him forward, dragging all his emotions with him. Every thought that came to him could not be discarded easily from the time of his father's death to this very moment. He never raised his head away from the grey sidewalk to see the blue sky with clouds.

One moment, he was eager to get home, and then, as soon as he arrived, he wished he was anywhere else. Clutching his backpack firmly, he somehow left his emotions on the street as he traded them for new ones. The past feelings were behind him, and automatically, new ones turned to the future.

The next horrible prospect would come at dinner. It was Monday, and that meant family night. Walking under the arch over his driveway and past the well-kept lawn, he was reminded of how different things were now. He missed his old house. He even had to share a room with his brother there. He'd thought he wanted his room, but it felt hollow now that he had one. The large windows and dark wood frames covered the outside, while the inside of the house reflected a comfortable atmosphere. Comfortable for those who Clint noticed made funny noises when they stood up. Older people seemed to want nicer things that he was told he couldn't play around with, and this house was full of them. It had fourteen bedrooms, eight bathrooms, six fireplaces, and enough closets that he kept losing his coats because he forgot which one he'd left his in. Moving from a small home into this mansion would be a dream come true for most kids, but as Clint looked around at the giant oak doors, the chandeliers through the windows, and the six-car garage, it felt less like home and more like a prison. Not even the arcade games that lined the walls in the television room gave him any comfort.

Straightening up, he put his hand on the door to open it but stopped. The feeling that he was being watched raised the hair on his neck. He saw nothing uncommon in the yard, the street, and the open park behind him. He couldn't see anyone peeking out of their windows. He stepped back a pace or two to see past the large bushes and trees that decorated the outside of the house to examine his closest neighbor's home, Margret Hutchings. She was a very old woman, but she would never admit it. She was tall, thin, and had thick white hair. She looked to him like a well-used Q-tip, which started to turn yellow at one end, and the other was broken off, revealing two spindly legs. She strategically placed one window to have an open view of their home. She often complained about Clint and his siblings being too loud or disturbing her dogs. One day, after they had lived there only a month, one of her dogs went missing. She branded him and his entire family as criminals that should be shot, drowned, stabbed, hung, and burned at the stake. At least those were the words she yelled at them from over the fence through a bullhorn. It turned out her dog was in her pantry, where he'd spent the past week eating everything. That didn't stop her hatred for them, and she even went so far as to blame him for sneaking into her house, claiming he locked her dog in there. She had married a wealthy man, and after he died, her sole purpose seemed to be to make Clint feel like an escaped criminal.

He couldn't see her bony, long fingers holding her curtain, allowing one of those bloodshot eyes to spy on his every movement. Breathing easier, he returned to the door when he thought of the hulking man who had stopped to talk to him and Corbin. One more examination of everything around him only revealed a chattering squirrel in the small, well-trimmed bush next to the door.

"Oh, shut up!" he called to the squirrel as he opened the large door to his house and felt worse than he had all day as he walked through it.

Fifteen

AM I GOING TO NEED A LAWYER?

He took off his bag as he walked across the foyer, allowing the door to shut by itself. To his right was John's office, and the lack of the computer humming and classical instrumental music meant his stepfather was still at work. Behind the closed doors lay an array of child-repellent items; large furniture, including a desk with several computers and a large piano, awards in every space where one could be placed. The only thing which any child would find remotely interesting was that all the digital pictures changed in their frames, showing a vast variety of extraordinary landscapes and art.

A slight shiver of relief that John was not home yet hit him as he walked under a larger chandelier hung low to give a warm light from the ceiling. Dropping his bag down at the foot of the large spiral staircase, he made his way to the kitchen.

Over the music in the kitchen came the sounds of his mother cooking. She was singing along with the music, banging her hands on the counter, and tapping pots and pans together in rhythm. He figured he should go and give her a kiss hello, as he usually did when he came home from school. If he didn't, she would know something was amiss.

His walking showed his depression as he went by several rooms and hallways until he reached the kitchen. Before he entered it, he fixed his face into a smile. The smell of roast meat and vegetables filled the room and almost caused him to forget all his problems. His mother was bent over, tending to the roast in the oven. With her head down, the chance for a quick getaway presented itself while she was preoccupied. Clint unstuck his throat and asked happily, "How was your day, Mom?"

"Why were you sent to the principal's office?" she asked sternly as she straightened up.

"Uh…" Clint was as shocked as if someone had just told him he had an incurable disease. His mother's secret gift was the fact that she could read his mind when he didn't want her to. Also, it was remarkable how she could look amused but also stern at the same time.

"I got a call from that old secretary right before you got here, and he said you would have a note from the principal's office for your father and me to sign." Clint's face started to resemble the look of a ship's crew that had just been told that shore leave was canceled for the next twenty years.

"So, let's have it, what is it?" she asked, resting her hands on her hips.

Thinking fast as he was backed into a corner, he said, "Why do you think it's bad, Mom? It could be good news."

She pursed her lips, breathing through her nose, making the nostrils flare wider. She filled her lungs, expanding her chest till he thought she was going to explode. Her high-heeled shoes clicked on the hard kitchen floor as she made her way around the center island and came face to face with him.

She stripped off her oven mitts and held a hand toward him, palm upward. Feeling like he was having his own civil war, Clint reached into his pocket and pulled out the letter. His mother's glare was strong enough to burn sand into glass. Clint felt his innocence fade while he unfolded it and set it into his mother's hand. She read it faster than Superman could before she turned on him.

"It says you disrupted class to get attention," she stated, returning her hands to her hips. All the family knew they were in trouble when she took that stance. It was her old west street fighter, gunslinger, ready to draw an invisible gun stance.

"It wasn't for attention! It was Corbin's fault! He asked me a question, and it just came out. I couldn't stop what I said, and I didn't know he would do his dolphin laugh. It was amazing that his seat was still dry when he stood up," he said defensively.

"I know you think you have been through the mill lately," his mother said sternly, "but you need to understand how good you have it right now."

Knowing what was coming, Clint was mistakenly starting to tune her out. But she raised a hand, sensing what he was about to do, and gently held his chin so they were nose to nose. Her face changed from one of anger to love.

"What do you have, Clint?" she asked sweetly.

"I have a home, a great school, food, clothes…" Clint droned on, sounding like Principal Miller. Then, adding excitedly, "Oh, and a note from the principal condemning me to death, written by a gorgon."

She was as still as an ancient tombstone while Clint tried to read the expression behind her eyes. With the silence lingering, he suddenly gave a wide smile.

"Clint, you have my love," she said softly. She bent over and hugged him. She hugged him in a way that made all the despair fall to the floor. His fake smile was replaced with one of relief.

Clint realized how bad his day was when all the darkness went away. Feeling a warmth in his chest burn from a tiny ember that grew until it filled him, he said, "I love you, Mom."

"I love you too, son, but we have to do something about this, and you are the one to do it," she said tenderly. She let him go and went back to work on the vegetables on the stove. The steam engulfed her long, red hair as she took the cover off a pot. It made her look like red, angry vapor was coming out of her ears. The feeling of the hug she had given him was slowly disappearing.

"Do what?" he asked.

"Why do you sound like you're being asked to donate a kidney? All you have to do is tell your father."

He knew she was being lenient right now, so he could learn something more important than just how to behave in class. This would force a time when he would have to talk to his stepfather. He had been avoiding these moments ever since the day he met John. Clint could still remember when his mother introduced him to John.

Proving again that his mother could read his mind anytime she wanted, she said sharply, "You will have to tell him tonight when we are at dinner."

"What!? Come on! There're things you don't know. She's a hard teacher. She makes me sit in the front row. Corbin laughed like Mickey Mouse, and that makes everyone else laugh. I didn't eat a good breakfast.

It was hot outside. The moon is closer than normal, causing a hormonal imbalance, and…"

"You're just deranged," she interrupted, chuckling.

"But, Mom," Clint said in desperation.

She gave him that same stare that told him this was over for now. There was nothing really to be frightened about and a parent had never hit him in his life, but sometimes he thought that being hit would be better than seeing his parents' disappointed looks or hear their sad voices. She looked at him meaningfully and said, "Now, straight up to your room and do your homework." Then she waved her hands at him to hurry him out of the kitchen.

"Yes, Mother," he said with the same joy as if he was told that he had to go and test fireproof underwear.

His mother was busying herself with dinner again as he started to walk back down the hallway. He picked up his bag, which felt heavier as he walked upstairs to his room. When he passed Tamara's room, her strange music was being played backward, faintly pounding its way out around her doorframe. The hardwood floor squeaked softly under his feet as he passed the bathroom. Looking around the hall told him that Kayla was not in her room but that his grandmother was.

His grandmother never came out of her room anymore. Clint had only seen her out of her room about ten times since they moved here. Mostly when she had a doctor's appointment or to complain about how no one living in that house wanted her still breathing. Her room was right next to his, and if he walked by too noisily, the door would crack open to reveal a glaring eye, a strong smell of prunes and denture cream, with gameshows playing in the background.

Thankfully, his homework didn't take long to finish. It was almost dinnertime when he heard the soft roar of a car working hard to pull up their steep driveway. Clint put the finishing touches on his paper about the Hundred-Year War as quickly as possible before getting up slowly and parting the curtain to see outside. The view from his window allowed him to see almost everything in front of the house. The car he heard belonged to his stepfather's coworker. Clint pushed his face against the glass, hoping to see the coworker's new girlfriend. He had only seen her once, and she was someone not to forget. The passenger car door opened as his stepfather got out but turned back and bent low to talk to the driver. Clint never really got to know his stepfather's best friends like Jamie and Cody. Clint thought they did it just to be friendly to John and to get a job out of him later.

He could see the curtain move in Mrs. Hutchings's spy window from the corner of his eye. She looked like a mummy without its wrapping. Clint thought as he snooped on them. John waved goodbye and entered the house while the car slowly drove down the other side of the driveway. Clint watched until the car was out of sight, blocked by trees and homes. He stood waiting for a long time, staring at the open field of trees and grass in front of the house. He had chosen this room to look out the window and see the wind in the trees and grass. Now that he had the room, though, it wasn't as great as he'd thought it would be. He could see families spending time throwing a football or a Frisbee. Couples sat spending time together with a meal or reading a book while others lay enjoying warm weather. It was always a cold reminder of the times he had spent with his father.

He stood, letting his mind wander as he watched a lone man walking in the park toward his house. Perhaps his future would be just like that solitary man walking. He would have no one around to worry about. No one cares about him. He would just take care of himself when he grew up. He was better off alone.

He watched the man walk around as if he didn't have a care in the world. If he were to be like that man, he would be better dressed, though. The man appeared to be trying to impersonate a pirate stunt double. He hoped that when he was older, he would be taller. That guy was almost his height now that he could see him a little better next to a tree.

"Clint, dinner's ready," came the sound of his mother on the home intercom. Instinctively, he jumped into action, walking toward the door before he even had time to think. Remembering the task he had to perform during dinner, he slowed. Returning to his desk, he picked up the note from the principal. Grabbing it, he rolled his eyes and saw someone standing outside on the sidewalk. The man wasn't moving now. In the last light of the setting sun, he wasn't sure about his features. At least it wasn't the same one he and Corbin had seen earlier. Clint shrugged as he headed to the door and started his last march down to dinner.

Clint went down the stairs and had his first up-close view of his stepfather that day. He was walking briskly from the front room past the stairs and into the hall with his brow furrowed, deep in thought. But he was carrying something odd this time. It looked like a portable, safe suitcase. It was not uncommon for John to bring home important papers, but nothing like this before. Clint followed him as quietly as he could so as not to attract any attention to himself. He was almost past the kitchen and into the dining room when John said, "Smells great, dear. Is everyone home and well?"

Clint was apparently the last to arrive, as his mother smiled and answered John while herding all the other kids into the dining room. When she saw him, her expression spoke volumes. Her eyes told him she expected him to conduct himself properly with John. He could feel his face start to redden and his lips go dry. He slowly looked to the floor, avoiding her eyes as he passed her to take his usual seat.

The dining room was far too elegant for Clint, and he missed the good old days when he could grab something, sit in front of the television, and eat. It was large and rectangular-shaped with the same electronic rotating picture frames. They only showed classic art pieces in this room, which made Clint feel claustrophobic. A long dining table sat in the center of the room, surrounded by graceful chairs with a thin line of lights over all their heads in a circle, illuminating the room over them. The room was bigger than they needed. Many leaves were taken out of the table for everyday use because John often invited important people for a catered dinner. He always told Clint that his place was upstairs and to keep quiet. John sat in the chair at the far end of the table with a sigh of relief. All his brothers and sisters sat at the sides while his mother always sat at the opposite end of the table from his stepfather. Clint was never too fond of the seating arrangement according to age.

Sixteen

THE GLASS IS OVERFLOWING

John always wanted a weekly report from all of them on Mondays. He started with Cody, who was to his left and went down around the table to Kayla, who sat to John's right. As Clint remembered this, a lifesaving idea came to him. He pulled the chair away from Kayla before she could claim it and quickly sat down before she could. Kayla gave him a questioning look, and he knew he would have to pay for taking her seat later. Everyone but Cody thought this was odd for a moment, but Clint didn't care. If he finished eating before the time came for him to talk, he would have a slim chance to get out before he had to speak to John. The delicious smell of the food grew as his mother brought in the last plate, and he suddenly felt ravenously hungry. His stomach's growl reminded him that he hadn't had his usual snack when he arrived home from school. When he sat down, he couldn't help but look at John. He couldn't make out his mood now. He seemed physically tired, but despite the dark gray circles under his eyes, he seemed more alive than he usually was. Did he just give him a soft smile?

"*That's going to change*," he thought.

Not being able to take looking at him anymore, Clint looked at Cody, who was still wearing his football jersey and pants. Today's practice must have been particularly good because he looked even more pleased with himself than usual. Clint didn't like Cody when he was like this. He always sat as far away from him as possible because Cody gave off a smell of sweat that would make even a pig lose its appetite. Also, there was the fact that he would have a better chance of getting a candy bar that fell from the sky and landed at a Weight Watchers camp than getting anything to eat around Cody when he was hungry. It wasn't until Clint was ten that he learned pizza was more than a crust or that potato chips were bigger than the size of his fingernails, thanks to his older brother.

Tamara sat next to Cody and almost toppled off her chair because of his aroma. It was that or the fact that one of her body piercings made it difficult for her to eat. She looked as if she had wandered into a baker's flour fight and was awarded the blackest wig in the world for winning. The first time he saw her, he thought she was from the Adams Family. At the far end of the table sat his mother. The room's light made her appear almost beaming with a new inner glow.

Grant was on her left, and Clint and Corbin agreed he was a two-eyed, young Mike Wazowski. Grant took his seat, flinching at the soft clinks of silverware on plates when everyone took out their napkins.

Kayla was sit-dancing silently in her chair, bobbing up and down with one foot, kicking one of the table legs repetitively, causing Clint's place settings to shake.

Quiet fell over everyone when John put his hands together, which was the traditional sign for them to say grace. Once the amen was said, war broke out over the entire table for each dish before them. As the saucers were being passed around the table, John addressed everyone as he filled his plate with potatoes. "Cody, will you start us off? What are your week's agenda and attainments?"

Cody went on about his practice that day, the dance that was coming up, and while it was ladies' choice, he had already been asked by seven girls if he would ask them to go. Tamara started her business as Clint was scooping up some gravy and spreading it on his potatoes. Her eyes were shining unkindly as she explained that she had already asked someone to dance. She also added hotly that any dance invitations given by anyone were just conforming to over-suppressing government leaders. Furthermore, from the songs she was listening to walking home from school when she saw two snails, a worm, and a stop sign that was upside down, the world was changed forever that week.

Clint force-fed himself at break-neck speed to escape the table as soon as possible. While Grant started talking about a new way to invent a small heat-seeking missile that would do away with the best fly swatters, Clint emptied his glass of milk, causing one eye to close from the pain. Grant also looked like he was going to wet himself when he explained that camping was the most significant cause of child disappearances. A look from his mother told him that was enough.

Everyone knew that Grant never did well in any physical activity. Since John and Robynn had married, she wanted to help show Grant in any way she could that there was such a thing as a world outside the house. She had signed him up with the local Cub Scout troop as soon as she could. This idea had been met with heavy resistance. With the upcoming campout trip, Grant kept telling the family of bear attacks and leaving missing child reports from the newspaper cut-outs wherever his parents would see them in the house.

This made Clint even more uncomfortable when Grant started to ramble off all the medications he would need for his two-day campout and asked for bear repellent and the money to stay in a hotel. The amazing thing was, his troop was going to the local park in the city for the day, and then, before night, they would drive a half-hour to a campground in the mountain that had a world-class hotel resort twenty minutes away.

Clint couldn't help but roll his eyes as he finished his corn. He glanced over to Kayla, who started talking about her experience correcting her teacher today when he had made a spelling error on the board.

Clint had just finished eating when she was done talking. "Can I be excused?" he asked John just before it was his turn to speak. He didn't look over at his mother, but he could tell from everyone else that her mouth must have puckered thin again.

"We haven't even gotten to our dessert yet, Clint," John said in surprise.

"I don't really want anything, I don't feel good," Clint said, still avoiding his mother's gaze. It was true. Right now, he wasn't feeling at all well. The fact that his mother didn't say anything meant that she wanted to let them work out things between them.

"No, no, I want to hear about your day. If you are concerned with how you are going to share it, we will give you more time. How about your mother and I go before you while you ponder? Would that be altogether satisfactory?"

Looking down at his empty plate, Clint felt his stomach hurt from eating so fast and knowing that every effort he had made to live another day had failed.

"Yes, sir," Clint said, with a burp that seemed full of apprehension.

"Fortuities then. Shall I tell them, dear, or would you care to ensue?" John asked across the table.

"Go on, dear, you tell them. I still cannot believe it myself. Also, I am sure Clint could use the time wisely to tell you about *his day*." Robynn said in excitement, emphasizing the words of *his day*.

John set his knife and fork down and finished chewing what was in his mouth before he wiped his lips with his napkin.

"Your mother and I are very proud of all of you, and since we have been married, you all are aware that I haven't been home much because of work." Clint thought he sounded cheerful about all this as he slumped in his chair.

"We are departing on a little trip," John said, and when he did, both Tamara and Grant yelled at once, asking where they were all going and what they should pack.

"No, no, no," John said, smiling. "We are not *all* going. It will just be your mother and me."

Grant and Tamara glared at their father at the same time in the same way. They were never left behind when their father left on business trips before. Seeing his stepbrother and stepsister not get what they wanted made Clint's spirits rise slightly. They were spoiled, and he loved letting them know when times presented themselves.

"Your mother and I are going on a cruise, and this isn't just any cruise. We will be leaving tomorrow morning and be back on Friday evening. We will be on the same vessel, bringing the Olympic torch to our country. The President will be in attendance, as well as most athletes and some of the most prominent people worldwide.

"Will the Zombie Safe Keepers be there?" Tamara asked eagerly. This was her favorite musical group. If you could call it music. They would sing some words in their songs, but you had to be already dead to understand them.

"I would not think so, Tamara," muttered John. He always sounded like he had a piece of food in his throat while he talked when eating. His voice was unsteady and low-pitched. It gave Clint the heebie-jeebies.

"No, these will be the world's leaders as well as some of the most intelligent scientists on the planet. They will all be coming to the peace summit while the Olympics are here." There was a note of pride in his voice and a proud glint in his eyes. Clint chuckled for a moment as he pictured John's eye twitching like a cat who had just been thrown over the fence of a military K9 training school.

"We will be absent most of the week, and your sister Jamie will be taking some time away from college studies to aid in our absenteeism."

"Not her!?" Cody shouted, spitting out some food.

"Yes, her!" his mother shot back as fast as a bullet. She always knew that her oldest two children didn't care very much for each other.

Cody and his mother stared at each other for a long time. This was a new tactic of hers, to just stare, but it was working wonders on Cody. Coming to his wife's aid, John started talking again. "Her arrival should be sometime this evening, and we did not come to this decision without deliberation. There is a probable opportunity that our refugee family's arrival could be soon."

There was a sudden silence at this new piece of information that seemed to make time stop as knives and forks clattered onto their plates. Everyone took a deep breath because they knew what was coming. John dropped all looks of eagerness as he looked at each of them in turn with a newfound energy of seriousness.

"I do not require a response on this subject," he said, an odd expression on his face. Was it anger or pity?

"We have great resources to use at our leisure, and these people have had everything taken from them. We are obligated to help through mutual cohabitation." Clint squirmed at these words.

"Gifts have been given to us, and if we do not share them….?" John sounded like he said it every day.

"You lose it." Everyone at the table finished saying it together.

"That is right," John stated proudly.

"We should return before they arrive, but we have left instructions with Jamie if they come prematurely. Subsequently, we will be attending the Presidential Dinner Friday night. This week will require your best behavior. Are we in agreement?" There was another general slow murmur of approval. John smiled slightly again and asked, "Did I miss anything, my love?"

"No, but I think it's Clint's turn," his mother said, her brown eyes narrowing.

Clint trembled, looking crestfallen. "Really?" he said hesitantly. "I thought I went already. My, how fast this time has gone. Great dinner, Mom." He gave a fake hearty laugh.

"Yes. I almost forgot I have something to talk with you about, Clint," John said as he started eating again.

Thinking that his mother had told John everything and that the jig was up, Clint decided to come clean. Clint dropped his voice, saying, "I had to go to the principal's office today."

Whatever his stepfather was going to talk to him about, it wasn't this. John started coughing on whatever he had just put in his mouth. His face started turning a red shade that would shame a rose.

Coughing still, he gagged out, "Why?"

"For disturbing the class," Clint said slowly.

"Why?" he said louder, coughing even more in disbelief.

"It just happened! I couldn't help myself. It was Corbin's fault."

"Clint!" John snapped, making all other chatter around the table go quiet as eating stopped.

"This has occurred far too often. Originally you were playing a game with your friends where all day you would only ask questions to all of your teachers and never give an answer. Only questions to everyone all day long. Then, you made a pin launcher out of pens and rubber bands that were strong enough to put a hole through the ceiling tiles at school. Wasn't it the last time because you took over the school's computer system? Then, you used your zeal and changed all the class agendas to study karate kittens and added new definitions to the menu items in the lunchroom. Something about adding other children's names and limbs to define the courses they were serving and, if that was not enough, a story at the end of the menu called "Lunchroom Ladies Gone Bad.""

Clint chuckled softly as he relived each of those moments, counting them off with his fingers. These stories of Clint's wrongdoings piqued Grant's interest. The rest of the kids' interests were piqued as well. It wasn't often they were told what the other kids had done wrong unless one of them was brave enough to go and listen to Grandma's door upstairs, where she was talking to herself about all the evil doings of the youth of this house.

"You must desist these actions and the course you are on. You require too much supervision for your age. It is only wise to fulfill your purpose and integrity. Your interests are too short-term."

Clint's felt his temper rising. He couldn't think why this man would take it upon himself to lecture him. *"He isn't even my father. Why doesn't he just lay off me?"* Clint thought.

His voice almost sounded rehearsed. Clint's face was growing redder and redder.

"When I was your age, I had to seek employment to help my family. Your task is to tend to the backyard, which is now so overgrown you can't see the forest for the weeds."

The thought that he was comparing his perfect Nobel Prize-winning life to Clint's made his anger spill out. Not knowing what he was doing, not aware of what he was saying, Clint found himself suddenly on his feet, shouting and brandishing a fork at John.

"What would you know about what I am going through? What do you know about how things are at my age? You don't even know me! You're not my dad." Clint could feel tears rolling down his cheeks, but he didn't know how they got there. His stepfather looked a little shocked at Clint. This only made him angrier, watching this man tell him off but unable to take a dose of it himself.

"Stay away from me!" Clint shouted, even though John hadn't moved from his chair. "You're not my father, and you never will be. My dad's dead. He's dead, and I don't need another one, so leave me alone." He started to march out of the room, not seeing how everyone's eyes were on him except Cody. He shrugged as soon as Clint rose from his chair and started eating wholeheartedly. His eyes were so wet that he didn't see his mother's worried expression as he stomped by her. He had no idea where he was going as he tore through the house. He passed the other set of stairs at the far side of the house, raced past the other rooms, and toward the backyard. Before he was out of earshot, he heard Cody ask someone, as if nothing had happened, "Can you pass the potatoes?"

Clint opened and slammed the back door so hard that it was a wonder the frame didn't break. Taking his first step into the backyard, more anger filled him because of all the work left for him. It was a long, narrow yard with random patches of flowers carved out with concrete blocks. Long, slender trees lined their property on their side of the fence. A small water fountain was set in stones that trickled merrily, with a large tree planted in the far-right corner and a tree house in its bulky limbs. The entire area showed signs of neglect and needed weeding.

Seventeen

TIME TO PAY THE FIDDLER

He followed the path of matted grass in the long overgrowth toward his treehouse. He peered around as he brushed the weeds aside with his shoes at the tree's base. In the dim light through the weeds and grass, he could see the top of his unused lawnmower as he climbed the wooden pegs up the tree. It was just one more thing that everyone else was telling him that he had to do. Why wasn't he good enough for anyone? Why did everyone keep telling him what to do and what he was not able or supposed to do?

When he reached the top of the wooden pegs, he lifted the gate of the treehouse and went in. The sun had set, and he couldn't see much without the house's light or stars. He didn't need any light to know where the table and chairs were. This was one place where he could be alone to sit and do his homework. When he suddenly felt the heat in his chest ebb away, it was replaced with a cold feeling. He didn't know why, and this cold feeling only made him feel worse.

"Real boys don't cry," he told himself. He raised his sleeves to rub his cheeks vigorously as if the tears were drops of acid burning him.

Then, the soft sound of the house door told him that someone was coming out after him. Hastily wiping away any sign of tears, Clint moved slowly to the window. In the light over the backdoor, he could see that it was his mother. In the growing darkness, she was choosing her steps carefully, and Clint could see that she had a somber look on her face.

Clint started counting his breaths to calm down when there was a knock on the bottom of the treehouse. He suddenly didn't feel like saying anything. He just sat there in silence. It seemed that his brain had stopped working, and all he could do was feel. His feelings even seemed to cause his tongue to swell as he failed to respond to his mother's knock. The hatch opened slowly, and his mother's hair came up. Then, the rest of her came in, and she slowly closed the door in silence behind her.

Clint tried not to look at her, but when she didn't sit or say anything, it was very difficult not to. She didn't move. She just stood there, not even seeming to breathe.

"How long are you going to be a slave to your hurt feelings?" his mom asked. She said it as if she was stating a fact and not looking for an answer. Clint didn't respond; he couldn't respond. He just sat there with his head down. "We had ice cream for dessert, and we are saving you some if you want it," she added lovingly.

"I don't want anything from anyone in there," Clint said soberly. He looked up and finally realized how much he must have been crying because of how cloudy his vision was. He lifted his knees to his chest, wrapped his arms around his legs, and rested his feet on the chair. He looked at his mother's face, which seemed to shimmer in his wet eyes. She didn't look angry anymore. She looked concerned. It was as if someone was tugging on his insides as she just watched him, saying nothing again. She seemed to be waiting for him to speak.

Not being able to stand the silence, all he could do was say what he knew he should. "I'm sorry." He started shaking even though it wasn't cold.

"I know," his mother said with a slight smile. "You are having a rough time."

Clint just nodded, not wanting to speak anymore. He didn't know what he wanted. He just knew that it hurt.

"You know when you are hurting, others around you hurt?" His mother was talking softly, but her words seemed to carry the weight of someone hitting him in the gut with a baseball bat.

"I know, Mom, I… I…" The lump in his throat caught and kept him from talking again. He was trying to think of why he was so angry before but could not figure it out. A new feeling of guilt crept up into his mouth.

"I know you didn't mean what you said during dinner. But others don't, and we have to give them a chance to get to know you," his mother said as she moved to sit in a small chair beside him. She lightly took his hand in hers, and oddly, the knot in his middle loosened a little, causing his legs to fall to the floor.

"You remind me of your father, but that doesn't mean John can't also be your friend."

"Then why isn't he here?" Clint said, his voice getting louder with a drop of anger as the knot started to tighten again. "Why isn't he here trying to get me to come back in there and have me sit down where he can chew me out again?"

"He didn't chew you out. I asked him for a moment to talk to you," his mother whispered lovingly. Then, adding with a wink, "Because I was afraid you would jump out of the tree and strangle him before you hit the ground."

Clint sighed and again let time pass between them in silence. The breeze in the tree softened the mood as they could hear a chipmunk or a squirrel chattering nearby. His stepfather didn't do anything wrong, nor could he have known what kind of day Clint had had. He was careful not to make any noise as he moved in his hard chair to face his mother.

"Mom, I know I haven't been taking this well," Clint said, still struggling to talk. It was easier yelling when he was angry at the dinner table, but now that it came to telling the truth and facing the facts, it was like being back in front of Mrs. Christenson's whiteboard.

His mother still waited, turning her warm brown eyes to his. "Mom, I just don't know what I am supposed to do… I miss Dad." He had to clear his throat, and he felt like he was going to cry again.

His mother nodded, leaned forward, and softly kissed his nose, squeezing his hand.

"I miss him too, but we have to move on with our lives and make the best of the time we have. Just like we did when he was here, he wouldn't want us to let time go by without doing all we can to live." Clint's heart was now somewhere in his throat as he twisted to look at his mother.

"I should go in there and talk to John, right? He's my stepfather, and his only fault is that he has great taste in women."

"No," his mother said patiently. "He wants to give you time." She said a little more cheerfully, "When we come back from our trip, we will take care of this. I won't ask you to do more than you should. I want you to see how happy you can be."

"I know, I know, Mom," Clint cut her off, dropping his voice. "You just love to say stuff like that, don't you?"

His mother looked breathless with interest when she said smartly, "That's why you are my son. So, I can say that over and over. Just remember who you are. You're my son and my friend, but you can also be the same to John. Just choose to be the best friend you can be, won't you?"

"Yes, mother. Will you tell that guy…" he stopped at the look his mother had just given him. "All right! Will you tell *John* that I'm sorry and I will talk with him when you guys get back?"

"I love you, Clint Holden," she said.

They both smiled as his mother stood up and hugged him. At first, Clint thought the floorboards were getting old and squeaking, but it was that squirrel chattering away again as if he was excited.

"Will you come inside now? There should be some ice cream for you, and I think everyone has left the dining room to do their chores," his mother asked softly.

Clint lowered his head in thought. He wanted to go back in but didn't want to be seen giving in too easily. To him, acting tough was a matter of pride, but he also had to be careful not to overdo it.

So, sounding exasperated he said, "All right, just give me a moment and I'll come in."

"Don't wait too long. You're like an annoying skin rash. You always show up in the wrong places, and you have to be closely monitored. So, don't stay out here too long."

His mother started her way down, and she called back up when she was almost to the house. "Clint?"

"Is it time for some rash ointment?" he asked as he was about to go down the trapdoor.

"No, dear. Leave your paper for us to sign on the kitchen counter. We will sign it for you on one condition."

"What would that be? Clean John's deer rifle and have me dress up like a buck and run around with a target on my butt?"

All she did was put her hands on her hips like she had done before. She said, "No, you will have to apologize to your teacher and take care of the lawn while we are gone. We will sign your paper if you promise to do both."

The night seemed to be closing in on him while he considered his options. There wasn't anything else he could do. "All right, your walking rash will do it, but I want some charms, garlic, and a lighter with some kindling before I have to go to Hogwarts tomorrow and try them. If none of them work, I will apologize." The sound of the backdoor opening and closing told him he was alone.

After a deep breath, he exhaled and, nodding to himself, admitted he felt better. With a little swagger, he made his way out and down back to the house. He had four or five days to think of what to do about his stepfather and one night and morning to come up with the best way to make it through all her flying monkeys and talk to his teacher.

When he opened the back door, something caught his eye, causing him to stop. That chittering squirrel was right above the door, clinging to the side of his house. Miss Hutching's dogs next door barked at any other small animals, but Clint didn't hear any of her dogs. Now that he thought about it, he hadn't heard them all day. He had not heard them at all since he got home from school, and that was odd.

Shrugging, he walked into the house, surprised to find no lights on in the kitchen or dining room. The soft glow from changing picture screens lit the rooms enough that he lost no time walking to the kitchen counter. He took out the slightly worn paper his parents had to sign. Flattening it out, he signed it quickly and took two hurried steps to his room. He didn't want to see anyone right now as the house felt dark and empty, and he remembered what he had done when he stormed out. Until he saw the bowl of ice cream on the counter left out for him. Suddenly, things didn't feel so bad.

Eighteen

DO NOT DISTURB

After finishing the ice cream, he started to make his way to get ready for bed. It would take a long time for his head to stop buzzing with thoughts of the day. The cascade of different emotions had left him feeling tired and weary. As he went up the stairs and marched down the hallway, he heard the sudden snap of a door behind him. His grandmother must have been spying on him as she must have been told or listened to what he had done. She always took it upon herself to monitor the house but did nothing about it other than muttering her protests under her breath. Forcing himself not to feel too apprehensive about his actions that night, he walked quickly on.

He felt safe as he entered his room, shutting the door behind him. All he could do was fall flat on his bed as his hands and feet felt heavier. The bed no sooner stopped creaking when a loud yell of "HA!" came. Just then, two little hands grabbed him from under the bed.

Clint let out a cry of shock that sounded like a giant lizard had just jumped on him as he fell to the floor with a bang. Pale-faced and screaming, he saw Kayla emerge from under his bed in a fit of silent giggles. He got increasingly irritated as he got up, rubbing his sore bottom and elbows.

"What are you doing here? You know you aren't supposed to be in my room unless you ask for permission!" Clint shouted, breathing heavily.

Kayla sat up on his bed smartly, "Well, if you want me to go?" She faced him as if he were a clown who'd just failed to make her laugh.

Clint opened his mouth and closed it three times, unable to find any words.

She bounced on his bed a few times before she climbed off it. "I just wanted to see how you were doing and if I could help you. But now I see that you're just like a little girl. I mean, you scream like one, and when you talk to a girl, you talk as good as Grant does."

"No, don't go," he said regretfully. He fell flat on his bed again while Kayla strode slowly back over to him.

She sat with one thigh on the bed and let her other leg hang over, folding her arms. Breathing heavily through her nose, she looked around the room.

"Why are you looking like that?" Clint scoffed.

"Like what?"

"Like you are an early Hollywood star waiting for someone to ask for your first autograph."

"You're sticking the fork in the toaster talking to me like that, you know," Kayla said, squinting at him. "Not to mention the clothes you left on the floor," she added, pushing her eyebrows together as she looked around the room again.

She stopped when she came to a picture of their family before their father had passed away next to his bed stand. Clint noticed that she was looking at it.

"I never liked how I looked in this picture," she said, picking it up.

Before she could look at it too long, Clint gently took it from her and set it back down in its place. He raised an eyebrow, suspicious.

"So, what really brought you in here?"

Kayla's smile twisted slightly as she grinned, showing some of her teeth. She sat for a moment, seemingly sizing him up. Until she said, "Well, after you gave us dinner and a show, Dad kept talking about what we are doing this week, and he's allowing all of you to go to the Halloween Dance this Fri—"

"What? Oh mannnnn," Clint interrupted.

He suddenly felt happy at the thought of going and knew who he wanted to go with. With everything else going on, he had completely forgotten about the dance. The happiness faded when he thought about who he wanted to go with and what if she said no. Would she ask him? What would she do when he sent her an invitation? Would he forget Corbin's name again?

"I take it this wasn't the best news to give you?" she asked, looking concerned.

"No, no. It's all right. I just thought I was going to be dead a minute ago, and now I have this to look forward to."

"Really, because you did that thing you do when you think hard and move your eyes around a lot, you did that. It made me worry your eyes were going to roll back in your head, and we were going to have to call a priest."

"You've been hanging around Tamara too much."

"Don't say her name," Kayla sighed as she stood up. "The last time I asked her who she was hanging out with after school, I made her come home late every day. She explained how you could take a hangman's rope and bury it, wait two hundred years, and if you take a root from a tree that grew over it, you could cure athlete's foot." She walked over to his window, shivering with discomfort.

"Really?" Clint asked, not wanting an answer.

"Yep, she said she tried it, but the hangman's weight must have been off because her feet just got worse. What's really scary is she said she would try again."

"More power to her," Clint moaned.

"On that happy note," Kayla said as she started to look out his lone window at the night sky, "I thought the news would cheer you up."

Clint started to bounce a little on his bed before he got to his feet, saying, "You'd think so. It's… it's complicated."

He searched around the room for something to change the subject to while she walked toward the window to look down. Clint slowly marched over to feed his fish. With the lights out in the room, his fish tank offered the only light save for what the window provided from outside.

"What do you think about Mom going with John on a cruise?" Clint asked, sounding like he was just doing it to end the awkward silence.

"Well, have you felt like something was coming?" she asked quietly, still looking out the window.

"What, like heartburn or gas?" Clint said quickly.

"No, silly," Kayla retorted animatedly and said thoughtfully, "Like earlier today, I was coming out of school and bumped into someone, making him drop a book. I picked it up and apologized, but the guy just looked at me for a long moment. Then he just told me to keep it, bowed, and walked away."

"Are you nuts!" Clint spat.

"It wasn't like that," Kayla cut him off before he could say anything more. "There wasn't anything in the book. It was a blank journal."

"Oh yes," Clint said mystically, "and we see how well that worked out in Harry Potter for Jenny."

"Never mind. We have enough going on this week," she said dismissively.

"Tell me about it," Clint said as if he were ordering his last meal.

Kayla turned her attention for the first time away from outside and towards Clint. "This is the first time we have been left alone. This is the first time Mom and Dad have both been gone at the same time. You know them," she said thoughtfully. "They must have been talking about it for months and waited to tell us at the last minute so we wouldn't get any bad ideas."

"We are not going to be alone or have freedom. We will be like a heresy kiss in an Abbey on the last day of fasting from food. Our presence will be just as uncomfortable, and we will be fought over and devoured at the end," Clint said as he returned to sit on his bed and started bouncing to ease the tension. "Jamie is coming."

"Jamie?!" Kayla laughed, looking shocked. "You know her. She will only come out of her room for food, the toilet, or if we lure her out with her phone on the end of a string."

Kayla looked uncharacteristically serious. "We have an opportunity here to prove ourselves to Mom and Dad. This is the first time that we will be able to show them that they don't have to worry about us so much. We will be okay with all the changes that have been going on."

Clint rolled his eyes, feeling she had now come to the point of her visit. She came away from the window and sat next to him on the bed. "Clint, I know it's hard, but you have to do better. You have to be a better example for me, you know." She patted him on the back and smiled.

He leaned forward, hunching over before saying, "All right, I will be a good boy." He changed his look of desperation to excitement, then punched her softly on the shoulder. "You know Mom already gave me that 'Be Good or Else' speech with a hint from the Responsibility one."

"Oh, that one where she asks you," she took on a new look as she imitated her mother's voice,   "Do you know who you are? Do you know I love you?"

"Yep, that one where I wish I had a mute button for her," Clint laughed.

Kayla took a moment and kissed him on his forehead. In the silence that followed, she walked back to the window where she was before and resumed considering the night.

"Was there something else?" Clint asked. "I thought if I agreed to what you wanted, you would leave me in peace," he said, adding a grimace.

"No, there's just some weird guy out on the sidewalk watching the house. He hasn't moved since I saw him. Hey!"

She yelled as Clint jumped out of his bed and almost knocked her over so he could look out the window. His force almost caused them to fall over, forcing them to hold on to each other, so neither fell.

Clint didn't care about her distress as he suddenly felt goosebumps. They both untangled themselves and shared a worried look at the stranger outside.

Feeling like breathing was challenging, they both tried to make out as much as they could about the man in the dim light from the streetlamp. Right where Clint had seen the figure before on the street curb was the same man he'd seen before dinner.

"What is he doing here?" Kayla asked dully.

Clint didn't respond for a moment and was about to tell Kayla about the person who stopped to talk to Corbin and himself when they were walking home from school. He opened his mouth but thought better about it when he remembered Kayla wanting him to be better this week. He wouldn't make a good impression if he just started telling her a story that made him sound paranoid.

"Probably just a landscaper who decided to wear what he works with and would like to try on our lawn for size. It can't be anything too bad. Put him out of your mind; besides, Mrs. Hutchings will call the police on anything that stands still long enough."

Kayla grinned broadly as she looked up at him. "Oh yes, anyone seeing that person would know that. How do you come up with that stuff? That's mean."

Before they could say anything else, someone turned on the light behind them. Startled, they both jumped. Turning fast, Clint saw his stepfather in the doorway with a hand still fixed on the light switch. Kayla also turned around so quickly that she whipped Clint in the face with her hair. John just stood there, not saying anything, with a humorous, confused look at their reactions.

"Excuse me, but the door was open slightly, and I wanted to talk with you before retiring. I didn't mean to alarm you both," John said.

Kayla fixed her hair as she responded with a dewy smile. "It's okay, Dad. Clint was pointing something out in the park."

"I know you would not want me to intrude in your room, Clint, but I went to tuck Kayla in when I discovered she wasn't in her room," John had a tone that sounded almost worried.

John looked as if he was trying hard to think of something to say to gain some trust from Clint and bridge the gap between them.

They shared a very uncomfortable silence where they exchanged odd looks before John started to walk toward the window. "Oh, what is it out there, hmm? Some spectacle unseated in the outer stratosphere? A culmination of the monarch butterflies mating in the park?"

Clint closed his eyes as John walked toward them, dreading what was coming. Clint felt him stand next to him and could picture him squinting through the glass and what his reaction would be when he saw the person outside. He would probably use some long words that only made sense to him and someone who'd memorized a thesaurus. No such strange words came. Clint opened one eye as his stepfather removed his glasses and polished them with his ugly green tie. Clint's mouth went dry as he waited for John to say something theatrical.

Kayla was the first to break the tension in the room. "He's gone!" she said in surprise as she pressed her face against the glass. Clint turned to see, and a new stillness descended on them all. All their eyes were darting from tree to lawn, mailbox, trashcan, to any place where a grown man could hide. Clint was completely winded as his mind was spinning.

"Who has gone?" John asked, still looking but only halfheartedly now.

"There was an, uh, interesting man who was watching the hou… I mean walking by. We were talking about him, wondering if he was from another country, and were wondering if it was someone who was coming to stay with us," Kayla said quickly.

Clint was amazed and half impressed at his sister's quick lie. "Yeah, he looked like he must be from India or something. He looked lost."

"Well, he's gone now, taking this quandary with him. Besides, we have an entire family staying with us, and they aren't from India. But it would have been nice to converse with someone from India. They have the most remarkable traditions and extraordinary study habits. Wondrous people," his stepfather added fondly.

"Now, you two, it's off to bed with you. You both have a promising day tomorrow," John said as he reached over Kayla and shut the window drapes. He softly exited the room, holding Kayla's shoulder to lead her out with him. At the door, he turned around with a sigh, "Clint, I am relieved you didn't go rigid when I came into your room. Please use this time to escape this mental and emotional quagmire you are in."

John stared at him awhile, wondering what he'd just said. His mind was still buzzing with the oddities of the day. Clint could only hastily nod and add a weak smile. Kayla waved to Clint while John closed the door behind them. With a click of the doorknob, they were gone. Clint stood still for a moment, alone with his thoughts. He changed quickly into his pajamas and got everything ready for school tomorrow. He said his prayers and crawled into his bed after turning off the light. Closing his eyes, he pleaded with himself to go to sleep quickly. Time went on, and as he rolled over again, trying to get comfortable. Frustrated, he opened his eyes and looked around. He came to the picture that Kayla had picked up earlier. The same picture with him sitting just below his father. Knowing he was too old for this, he reached out and took it off his side table, leaving a space free of dust where the frame had been. Turning over on his side, he lifted his blanket and held his family picture close to him as he fell asleep almost immediately.

As Clint fell deeper asleep and everyone else in the home headed off to bed, no one was left to see the jumble of raggedy clothes surrounding the person who had returned to watch the house.

Nineteen

YOU RISE, YOU SHINE

Morning came to the Holden's house without any cautious eyes, still monitoring it. Clint heard a rustle from somewhere downstairs, which meant that someone was awake. Trying to ignore it, he rolled over, moaning. Pulling his blanket over his head, he felt like his eyelids refused to open. Sharp pain in his chest told him that he had rolled onto the corner of his family picture frame.

Groaning again, he pushed the frame onto the floor and rubbed his chest hard. The pain seemed to lift the weights from his eyes. Waking up, he turned around and saw that his family picture had broken.

"Clint," Cody called from downstairs, "you better hurry. Mom and Dad are leaving."

Lost in his worry as his day unfolded, he sat up and snatched up the broken frame. The frame was cracked, with spider web lines on the glass. Holding it in his hands, he forced the frame into its correct position, willing it to mend itself. He struggled to get out of bed and summon the energy to prepare for the day. Setting the pieces down on his desk, he half-heartedly dressed when he heard a car door shutting and an engine starting. Reluctantly, he clambered to his window, fastening his pants. His mother and stepfather were getting into their car with almost everyone else outside to bid them farewell. Pulling his shirt over his nose, he saw Cody and his grandmother were the only ones not out.

John kissed all the kids and moved to the car's driver's side. His mother spent more time kissing, hugging, and fixing their hair. She gave a few choice words to each child before she climbed into her seat in the car. Before either got in, their eyes traveled to his window where he was standing. The look on his stepfather's face of worry was overcome with a large smile. Clint could read his lips as John said, "We will bring you something back. We love you."

His mother demonstrated the strange power of knowing Clint was there even before she had turned. She twisted slowly to look up at him. She gave no smile but just raised a steady hand toward him. Clint lifted his to wave but suddenly felt stupid and tried to run his hand through his hair instead. It didn't work as his hand stuck in his tangled hair, resembling a giant ball of lint. He only smiled and waved back with his elbow as he still couldn't free his hand. He watched them enter the car, shut the doors, drive down the driveway, and pass the park until they were gone.

"Clint, get a move on, or you will be late for school!" Cody's voice called again from the intercom by his door. He was still dazed and foggy-eyed as he opened his door to take his usual morning march to the bathroom. He heard Cody's heavy feet thundering down the hallway until he pushed past him wearing only his underwear. Cody yawned in Clint's face, blowing his unbrushed-teeth breath in his face. Clint's yelling was cut short when Cody shut the bathroom door behind him.

"Hey, why don't you use your bathroom downstairs?" Clint called to him.

Cody's drowsily voice sounded behind the door, "Cause Jamie's here. She came late last night. So now she's in the shower with her phone. Don't ask me how she does it." Clint rolled his eyes in disgust. Cody left Clint in a stupor as he started singing, *Dancing with Myself* in the bathroom.

Clint had a miraculous thought as Cody was not doing too badly staying in key. Corbin would have said he was off as fast as the top of a tissue box cover in a room full of elderly women watching a Titanic marathon. With his parents gone, he would use their bathroom. Everything in it was voice-activated. The shower heads all moved synchronized to music from speakers from the ceiling. The only bad part was all of John's shampoos had Rogaine in them. He didn't mind as he sang along to the music in the shower. He didn't stop dancing to the music as he brushed his teeth, looking at himself in the mirror, marveling that John also had a screen in the middle of the mirror showing the morning news. He was having a great morning until he was gathering everything into his school bag back in his room when the thought of the man from last night came to him.

He reached to pull open the curtain, but he hesitated for a moment. He willed that there would be no one out there. He looked right where the man was standing and opened the curtain. He rechecked time and time for any place a person might hide in daylight. He feared he would see him again, and then he was more afraid if he didn't. "Pull yourself together, Clint," he told himself. "The hard stuff is over. Time to have a day in paradise."

He finished getting ready and went downstairs for breakfast with a swagger in his step. He sat his bag next to the front door and walked into the kitchen to find all his brothers and sisters getting their breakfast ready. Cody was helping Grant get some cereal and was warning him about the Oreos and snacks he was trying to sneak into his bag that he was going to take camping.

"You can't take that stuff, Grant," Cody said excitedly. "You are going into the woods, and if you eat any candy a week beforehand, the bears will smell the little left on your breath or in your back molars and tear your whole jaw off. No matter how often you brush, they can smell that stuff ten miles away!" Cody was working very hard not to smile as all the blood drained from Grant's face, which turned as white as paper.

Tamara was sitting in the middle of the kitchen, eating her cereal with a preoccupied mind as she shoveled mouthfuls into her mouth. She was bent low over her bowl with her eyes moving at breakneck speed, reading the cereal box, which was upside down.

Kayla was standing on a stool, busying herself, making eggs over the stove. She was wearing her mother's cooking apron that went down past her feet. She was the first to notice him, and when she did, she greeted him with an enthusiastic smile.

"I have some eggs for you," Kayla said, sounding remarkably like her mother.

"Really, thanks."

"Why didn't you make eggs for me?" Cody whined. Kayla shot him a dangerous look that was uncannily similar to her mother's. It was so similar that Cody sheepishly backed down for a moment.

"Because Tamara will be out of here as soon as she can to see her boyfriend, even though Dad told her not to see him anymore. Grant won't be able to keep anything down the way his knees are shaking. We won't see Jamie until she needs help with her bags when she leaves or the phone bill comes, and I have never seen you devour five Hot Pockets as you did this morning anyway," Kayla said smartly.

Clint got a plate and couldn't help but watch Grant, who was trying to straighten his legs, but to no avail. When he went by Cody, he heard him say to himself softly, shaking his head, "Pizza isn't junk food. It's the health feast of heroes."

They were all eating when the doorbell rang, causing them to stop momentarily. "Is anyone going to get it?" Kayla asked as she was tending the eggs. Tamara's untamed, dyed black hair protruded over the cereal box.

"I will," Tamara said flirtatiously.

Clint looked at Kayla, who was watching Tamara with disgust. Shrugging his shoulders, Clint met Kayla's eyes and, without words, said he also shared her feelings. As Tamara left the kitchen, her high, black leather boots smacking the floor loudly, Kayla answered him, saying, "Paperboy."

"Oh, no," Clint said, louder than he wanted. He went back to looking at his plate while Kayla distributed some eggs on it, and he remembered all the times the paper boy came to the door rather than just leaving it on the doorstep.

Clint never even took the time to find out his name, nor did he care. This kid would do anything for a chance to see Tamara. She never passed up an opportunity to tease the boy. She loved making him think that he had a chance. Clint knew better. Mother Nature had an unwritten rule on who could date who by what they looked like, and this kid could only date something that looked like a semi-truck had run over it.

Clint could hear Tamara's fake laugh when she opened the door. Kayla was also smirking, telling Clint they were sharing the same thought.

"Grant, your ride is here with a black hearse!" Tamara called back to the kitchen. The little color left in Grant's skin drained out as he dragged his feet toward the front door. Cody was right behind him, looking just as happy as a lottery winner as he told Grant that when he was his age, he killed a grizzly bear with nothing but a spatula, but only after the bear had killed everyone else in the campground, to say nothing about the wolves and what they could do.

Clint decided to skip out on the upcoming drama as Grant made his slow march and Tamara returned to her breakfast. Thanking his sister for breakfast and taking care of his plate, he left them and started for the front door. He was reaching down to pick up his bag when someone whispered his name behind him.

Twenty

WHY DO SIBLINGS HAVE TO BE SO STRANGE?

"Pst, Clint." Turning around, he saw a head sticking up from downstairs. Clint could see that Jamie appeared after not thoroughly drying herself after showering that morning, but her eyes gleamed dramatically.

"Come here a sec, will ya?" Without waiting for a reply, her head shot out of sight with a swish of her hair. The thought crossed his mind that he could go to school without talking to her, but then it would give her a reason to tell his parents that he was causing problems. He picked up his bag and slung it over one shoulder before going downstairs. He followed the music to her room. The door was open, but feeling he should play it safe, he knocked on the door frame rather than just walking in.

"Come in, come in," Jamie called excitedly, "and shut the door." Clint closed the door behind him and was amazed to see that her room looked like her luggage had exploded, and his sister didn't care as she lay on her bed. Seeing her now reminded him how long it had been since he had seen her last. She had grown a little more and looked more like his mother. Her hair was longer, fuller, almost springy, and fit. She had received a scholarship for playing volleyball when she was in high school. This meant that she spent a great deal of time practicing, which would account for all the trophies she seemed to be hanging her laundry on.

"Sit down," she said, seeing him look around the room.

"I can't, sis," Clint said uncomfortably. "I have to go to school soon. He hoped he sounded offhand but still had a look of interest on his face. Also, he couldn't find a spot to sit.

"All right," she said unsteadily. "I wanted to ask you something since I have been away so long. I haven't seen Mom and Dad since the wedding."

"Yeah, what is it?" he asked impatiently.

She looked around the room briefly, then asked coolly, "How is the mood here between kids and parents?"

"What? If you want to know how I'm doing with John out of the blue, there's no way I will tell you."

She looked taken aback momentarily, still moving her eyes around the room. Her focus stopped on a picture frame that was next to her trophies. Clint could not make out who was in the picture as it was lying facedown.

"How are things with Mom and Dad? Are they in a good mood, or are they taking this trip because they need a break from all of you?" she asked with more strength, this time in her voice.

Eyeing her wearily, Clint said, "What's going on? Are you treating college with the same enthusiasm as living in a rest home?"

"No, no, my fall courses have been harder than what I had in the summer, but that's not it, well, it's…" She seemed to be eyeing him strangely, sizing him up to see if she should tell him something important. "It's nothing with my school," she said very fast, but something in how she said it made him feel like she wasn't telling him everything.

"What's going on, Jamie?" Clint asked eagerly, folding his arms.

"I'm not telling you!" Jamie shot back at him dangerously as she sat up on her bed. "Just tell me, what's the best way to bring something new to Mom and Dad? I used to talk to Mom first, and then she would open up and be more likely to listen to you when she was in a better mood. Then, when you would have Mom on your side, it would be two against one when we brought Dad into the mix." She sounded like she was talking to someone on the phone. Like he couldn't see her rolling her eyes and talked very excitedly.

"So, have things changed much?" she hissed, seeing that Clint would not answer her. Clint had learned by watching his older brother Cody that when someone older wanted something from you, you never gave it to them for free.

"I'm not telling you until you tell me what's going on," Clint said with an evil smile.

She watched him as if he had just uttered a terrible swear word. "You sound like Cody! Have I been away that long?"

"I am not helping you for nothing! You two took advantage of me as your younger brother one too many times for me not to learn a thing or two," Clint said bitterly.

Jamie pursed her lips the same way her mother did. "I only loved you, Clint. Everything I did was for you to…"

"Oh, shut it!" Clint thundered, seizing the moment. "You are the one who would have me suck on a tailpipe just to make you laugh."

"Like what? When?"

"When I was seven," Clint said flatly, holding up one finger. "I had that rash on my face from that fish Mom got—that was the last meal that came out of that restaurant—on my face. I was going to tell Mom, and you told me it was nothing to worry about, and before I went to school, you told me I had 'hemorrhoids' on my face. You said if I told Mom, it would only make Mom angry if she had to stay home from work to take care of me. So, I went to school telling everybody I have hemorrhoids on my face."

"That was nothing, Clint, besides…."

"Secondly, Clint interrupted, "it wasn't until I was ten that I found out what all those ultra-absorbent things you kept asking me to get you from the bathroom were!"

"I didn't like doing that, I…."

"Thirdly," Clint said, not giving her a second, "when I was a little younger, and my voice was cracking, you told me to swallow some bleach mixed with vinegar, gasoline, and cologne every morning to straighten me out and give the ladies something to talk about. If Mom hadn't been there to stop me…"

"All right, all right, you little emotional hypochondriac!" Jamie said, rising off her bed in anger.

"You know, you could choose to be better than I was to you," she said soberly.

"Oh, right," Clint said, staring up at her. "Besides, I have to get to school."

"Fine, go, you cheeky little hobgoblin!" Jamie snarled at him, waving her hands dangerously. "We'll finish this when you get back, and you had better help me out, or I'll make up some stuff to tell Mom and Dad about how much trouble you're making around here."

It took a moment for Clint to understand that his mouth had fallen open. "You wouldn't!" he said in anger.

Jamie didn't say anything but gave him a devilish smile. This weighed heavily on his mind before he could gather himself. "OK, OK, I'll play nice and help you," Clint said in defeat.

"Good, oatmeal for brains, and you better," Jamie said as she scraped up her phone and lay back on her bed. She waved with her free hand, trying to persuade him to leave the room, and before he was gone, she was talking to someone else.

Twenty-One

SEND IN THE CLOWNS

Clint blew a raspberry at her as he shut the door behind him. Feeling frustrated, he glanced at his watch; it told him he only had fifteen minutes to get to the street corner where he always met Corbin before school. He quickly ran up the stairs out of the house and down the driveway. He was almost on the sidewalk when that feeling of being watched came over him. His eyes widened as he took a hurried moment to look closely around for anything unusual. He walked slowly and listened intently for an expected rush of feet from across the street, but there was no one. It was customary to be chased by one of Mrs. Hutchings's dogs. Then, out of the corner of his eye, he saw Mrs. Hutchings move from her favorite spy window. His mad rush out of the house must have caught her off guard. She would probably be scamming all day on how she could get back at him for denying her the pleasure of watching him run from her dog as if the zombie apocalypse was behind him.

Rechecking the time, he jumped at the thought of being late. He started to run, feeling his bag banging back and forth on his back, holding one strap with one hand and pumping for more speed with the other. He raced down by the park, streets, and blocks, as he did almost every day.

Clint was rewarded for his hurry with the sight of Corbin pacing at the corner where he had seen him last.

"What kept you?" Corbin barked at him.

Clint wasn't expecting such a cold greeting when he came to a stop. He was breathing heavily and readjusting his school bag. "What do you mean?" he asked in a hurt voice.

Corbin eyed him up and down, and not waiting for Clint to catch his breath, he started to walk down the sloping sidewalk. He didn't even glance to see if Clint was following him when he began to talk. "I needed to get to school early today," Corbin said.

Still panting and working hard to walk next to Corbin, Clint managed to say after each gasping breath, "Why, you haven't been to school early or on time since the Christmas tree was still up."

"Well, I'm tired of trying to work hard to get good grades, valedictorian, you know, a world-class brown nose," Corbin said with a long sniff. It was odd, Clint thought because Corbin was looking out onto the hillside and didn't meet Clint's eyes when he said this. Clint looked over to see if anything was interesting on the side of the hill where Corbin was looking. The sidewalk was separated from this open area by a short wooden fence, and just past it was a field overgrown with weeds and small bushes holding the dirt together over the almost vertical surface. No houses were built on this side of the hill because it was so steep.

They both walked quickly down the sidewalk as the sun rose higher in the foggy sky, casting long shadows of the houses on the opposite side of the road. For some reason, there wasn't any traffic on the road that morning. That was odd in itself, Clint thought. There were always cars on the road with unhappy adults drinking coffee going to work or larger cars or vans full of kids being taken to school. Shaking it off, Clint thought there might be a detour for the road. Clint immediately cast it out of his mind, turning his attention back to Corbin.

"So, how bad was it last night?" Corbin asked. Clint replayed everything that had happened the night before, apart from the bit where he'd seen the man watching him from out on the street. Clint didn't like the idea of his best friend thinking he was getting jumpy and scared. It didn't take long to finish, and Corbin didn't interrupt him.

Clint asked, "How about you? What did your mother do when you gave her the letter from school?"

Corbin's head dropped a little more. His eyes now pointed at the sidewalk as if looking for money. "Well, uh, my mother started to tell me how I should uphold the family honor and be a good example to all those little people. I asked her what others? It's only her and me in that house. That's when she left the room to get a drink. Then she read the letter from Mr. Miller. When she was done reading it, she started to get that nervous tick where her chin twitched. After that, she was just an unpleasant person to be around. I mean, from how she talked, she was never in trouble. She never did anything wrong in her life when she was my age." Corbin gave a great sigh as he heaved his school bag higher on his shoulders, then gave another sharp sniff.

Corbin lifted his head, finding it difficult to relive the feelings that returned from retelling his story again. He put his hands in his pockets, which was hard for him as his school uniform pants were tight enough to cut off the blood circulating in his legs. Clint glared at him and knew that he wasn't going to tell him anymore. This meant that the subject of his father probably came up last night. Corbin's father looked exactly like his son, only older and with loads of facial hair in his ears and nose. Clint only found this out from the pictures that were around his house. Corbin never really talked about his father in what he would call normal conversation. Whenever the subject came up, he would change the rules and talk about something else, telling anyone his father was away on business.

They shared a long silence that made Clint feel very uncomfortable. Not wanting Corbin to keep thinking about what else happened last night, Clint tried to think of a question to change the subject.

"Are you going—" they both said at the same time. They looked at each other and knew what the other was trying to do. "Go on..." Clint encouraged.

"It's nothing, but something else happened last night when I was getting ready for bed. I looked out the window, and I thought I..."

Corbin stopped talking. He even stopped walking. Clint took one or two steps before he could not stop because of the slope of the sidewalk and the weight of his bag. He twisted back and was going to ask what he was doing, but when he saw Corbin's face, his question left him. Corbin looked sick with horror, and Clint couldn't ask him anything as he stared at him. Corbin's popping eyes were focused a little further down the road. Clint turned his head in confusion as he watched Corbin's mouth fall open in a silent scream as he started to shake. It looked like he was trying to point at something but could not remove his hands from his pockets. Clint, on the other hand, started to laugh at his friend, wondering what in the world he was doing. Clint turned to see what was down the street that was causing his friend to act so oddly, and he heard Corbin mumble the word, "Run."

Clint didn't recognize Corbin's voice because it was so full of tension and fear as he scrutinized a point down the street. Clint raised a hand to block the sun when he saw it. The same dirty-faced man who talked to them yesterday was hammering his short feet as fast as he could right at Clint.

Clint barely had a chance to take a great breath of air before his attacker was almost on top of him, his short, dirty arms thrown out in front of him to grab Clint. Horrified and panic-stricken, Clint couldn't think as the dirty man dove right at him with a massive howl like an enraged wolf. Acting on instinct, Clint turned and shoved Corbin with all his strength over the small wood fence, causing them to fall onto and down the steep slope.

The fence broke apart when Clint hit it. Their aggressor overshot and flew past them, barely missing them both. When Clint hit the ground, he felt the broken wood send a sharp jolt of pain into his hip. As he started feeling out of control and the earth spun, he heard Corbin give a long wheeze as the wind was knocked out of him. They both tumbled through the sparse grass downhill for a couple of feet. Clint's bag was swinging around dangerously before he could grab some dirt to pull himself to a halt and get his feet underneath him.

Coughing, not knowing what was happening, he steadied himself as he rose to his knees. Nothing was in focus yet when Corbin's rolling body slammed into him like a heavy log rolling down a mountain. For an instant, before he was hit, Clint caught a glimpse of his assailant. Perhaps it was his impaired senses, but the man seemed smaller than when he'd first charged them, and he was starting to descend the closer he came towards them. He was tearing off most of his odd clothes as he bounded down, closing the gap between them. They seemed too large for him now and oddly encumbered his descent. He was so impaired at one point at a particularly steep part that he fell flat on his face. He was so wrapped up in the clothes that he couldn't even get his arms out in front of him. Clint once again found his footing and, this time, grabbed Corbin, who had rolled right next to him. Steadying each other, Clint was sure that as the man arose, his face had changed because of the impact. It must have been because of the early sun shining behind the man, but as Clint tried desperately to breathe past the dust, the skin of the man's face was bright red.

The little red madman wailed in anger as he ripped through his shirt and rubbed his eyes frantically to see. Still unable to see, he tried to pursue them again, but his little feet were still entangled. The sound he gave at any other time would have been humorous as his shout of rage and triumph turned into one of a frightened bellowing animal as he fell again, wrapped like a burrito on the hard earth.

"Get up! He's coming!" Clint bellowed at Corbin, who was hunched over, heaving each breath as if he'd just emerged from underwater. The crashing noise of the man rolling down the hill with yelling that deepened pitch with each brutal hit on the ground came from behind them. Clint groaned as he hauled Corbin to his feet, and without waiting, he started bounding down the hill toward the houses below. Right beside him, running very unnaturally, was Corbin, clambering down the hill as fast as his fat legs would take him. The oddest thing was that he still had his hands firmly stuck in his pockets. He looked like an over-large hotdog trying to stay upright, bouncing down a mountainside.

Clint took giant strides, hopping over the steepest parts of the treeless rise, and was almost to the bottom of the hill that ended in a long white fence separating all the cookie-cutter homes' backyards. Looking around to see how far back their pursuer was, he saw Corbin's colorless face gasping for breath but muttering strange words that made no sense to himself. His pursuer had freed most of himself and was back on his feet, chasing them once again.

The thing chasing them seemed smaller and even uglier. It must have been about the same height as they were now, and its old clothes were almost gone completely. It had a leather vest on showing a deep red-skinned midriff and head, with long, red hair flowing behind him. His chase was still odd because his pants were now several sizes too large for him.

"What is that little circus freak?" Clint asked, seeing how the man's appearance had changed.

"That little sucker has horns on his head!" Clint called, suddenly realizing he'd kept his eyes off the ground too long as some uneven ground pulled him down. He fell and rolled again all the way down until he painfully hit the fence. The sky was still rolling in his mind as Corbin was still running, hitting the fence right by where he lay as fast as he could. Clint knew he was seeing things when the one thing that he took away from that image was that Corbin's hands were still firmly locked in his pockets.

With a bang, Corbin broke through the fence, his fat legs still pumping and his mouth open wide in a silent scream, leaving a trail of dust behind him. Clint was surprised at his friend's sudden ability as he clumsily got to his feet, fighting to stay upright as the dizziness held on. He rubbed the dust out of his eyes and used a fence beam to stabilize himself. Suppressing the urge to throw up, he squinted up the hill and saw four copies of his pursuer. He was halfway down the slope when something swooshed by Clint's head and hit the beam with a thud. His vision came to focus on a long knife sticking in the fence two inches from his face.

It brought him to his senses as he tore off as fast as his legs would take him, following Corbin's path. Corbin seemed to find his voice yelling at the top of his lungs, sounding something like a lead singer at a rock concert who was getting electrocuted on stage.

Corbin had run right into the owner's house, whose fence he had just demolished. He blew through the screen door while Clint passed a large swimming pool. Clint could hear screams from the house in front of him. Clint didn't care as sheer fear drove him on, not knowing where to go or what to do.

Flying through the broken screen door, Clint stopped just inside the house, panting, looking this way and that for any sign of which way Corbin had gone.

Wham… Wham! Two more daggers hit the wall just by Clint's shoulder. His fear seemed to push him hard in the back down the hall, passing a kitchen table full of a family of four who had stopped eating and were looking wide-eyed, goggling at him. He tried to ask for help, but all that came out was, "Psycho, circus clown burping, knives… after us." A howl and thud told Clint that Corbin had found his way to the front door and had just gone through it.

Running down through the house, Clint knocked down pictures, ran over the family's cat, and stumbled over some toys and a business suitcase. He felt a sudden push forward as if someone had shoved him in the back, just as he turned a corner and found the front door open. He flew through it and slammed it shut behind him. Clint saw Corbin running down the road, weaving in and out of traffic. Clint heard more screams, but they came from behind him this time. His feet throbbed as he went after Corbin, who was still screaming but at a much higher pitch and only between breaths. This part of town was much more compact and not as wealthy, but more people were in and around attending to the morning business. He ran past an old lady walking her dogs who had stopped to watch them or because her dogs had started to howl in concert with Corbin's scream like he was some sort of runaway fire engine.

Clint ran as fast as he could, closing the gap between them. Corbin's bulk started slowing his feet down, but not his screaming. He ran by slow-moving cars, past some old man in a robe getting his morning paper, some young woman walking her two kids, and one girl about his age who was going to school. Passing each of them, he gave hurried excuses as he received furtive looks from each. Saying things like, "My friend got stung by a bee." Or "Skunk! There is a skunk after us! That skunk is ten pounds back there," and last of all, "My buddy is chasing after his imaginary friend who keeps leaving him."

Finally catching up to him, Clint reached out and grabbed his shoulder. Corbin howled and screamed loud enough to make everyone they went by think that fire alarms were going off all at once.

"It's me, you idiot!" Clint puffed, pulling hard on Corbin's bag to slow him down. Corbin's face was frozen in a look as if someone had just told him Mrs. Christenson was going to live with him.

Clint pushed Corbin around, dismissing all the nasty looks from the early risers who had stopped what they were doing to watch them. A few onlookers also shrugged as if this sight was nothing new to them. He moved them both toward a patch of grass surrounded by bushes and trees in front of an elegant home with lawn ornaments stacked everywhere. Corbin seemed to have taken on all the attributes of a fire hydrant. He wasn't going to be moved but could erupt at any moment.

Chest heaving, Clint forced Corbin to bend down. It was very difficult as Corbin was stiff as a board, his eyes wide and unblinking, and his legs were still pumping up and down as if he were running in place. Clint struggled to keep Corbin in place and looked back over the bushes at the way they had come. Looking back, Clint could see up the block. Many of the people they had so unfortunately disrupted were returning to their daily lives. His eyes scrambled everywhere, searching for any movement, for a sign of whatever was chasing them. Thankfully, there was nothing.

"I, think, we, are, safe, for, now," Clint said still panting between every word. Corbin didn't say anything. All he did was look terrified at any sound around them, giving off loud, short screams and hyperventilating between shrieks resembling a tiny dog barking. They sat there concealed, catching their breath while Corbin seemed to turn from sheer white to a more reddish-purple color.

"What *was* that?" Clint asked, still panting slightly and looking over the bushes behind him again.

"You think I know? It was a cotton man who shrunk in a dryer, possessed by Randy Johnson wielding knives if you ask me," Corbin said, bellowing like a wounded whale.

Clint kept taking fleeting glances up the road, checking and rechecking for anything that would warn them of something after them. Every time Clint would turn sharply around, Corbin would tense up even more as if someone was about to light a fire under his backside.

Edging toward the deepest coverings the bushes could provide, Clint started to relax. He saw his hands shaking when he asked, "What do we do now?"

Corbin didn't say anything that Clint could understand, and it was all just mindless babbling until he started to suck his thumb. Clint leaned forward and pulled it out of his friend's mouth disapprovingly.

"Stop that! Come on, what are we going to do?" he shouted.

Corbin jolted awake as if Clint had just slapped him across the face. His eyes fell on Clint as if someone had flipped the circuit breaker back on in his head. He looked almost normal.

"Wha… what just happened? How did we get here?" he asked in dismay.

Not waiting for an answer, Corbin looked at his knees, seeing the dirt stains from where he had rolled down the hill. Then, his shoulder, where he had broken down the fence where white paint could still be seen on his shirt. His eyes traveled around their hiding place, and all at once, it was like all the weight of what had happened had just hit him. Laden down with emotion, he kept looking around, trying to find words to say something that would make sense of it all.

Clint leaned forward, balancing on his toes. "We have to get away from here and get some help."

"Help? From where? From what?" Corbin asked, holding the stitch in his side.

"We'll go to the police. They'll take care of it," Clint said, more to himself than to Corbin.

Corbin kept looking around and now started grunting. Clint took it as him disagreeing with him.

"Well, what else are we going to do?" Clint yelled. "We just can't let this go; that cough drop with horns just tried to schedule us for a halo fitting with wings and a harp or horns, tail, and pitchfork with a sixty-minute eternity workout program."

"How do you know that? He might have just been lost or something or someone who really needed a hug, and I don't know about you, but I don't want to face any more problems with school and my mother and the last thing…"

Clint never heard what Corbin was going to say next because something came over the bushes at them and said, "So you are the maggots who are stealing my papers!" Suddenly, Corbin let out a scream of fear that sounded like an opera singer was stuck by a pin. He jumped out of their hiding place and ran as fast as if a plane flying over had snagged his underwear with a hook and was now pulling him along four blocks.

Clint jumped and ran right behind Corbin, not looking at the old woman who had yelled at them with her wig hanging oddly off her head.

Clint ran once more as if the devil himself was behind him, not taking a moment to look back at the old woman in her nightgown brandishing her walking stick at them, bellowing, "DELINQUENTS," at them as they ran away.

They ran once more, fear of death driving their heels. Corbin was not screaming as loud this time as his feet carried him through more people goggling at him again. Clint didn't offer any explanations for their haste this time. He lost track of where they were going as he ran with Corbin's massive body leading the way. Corbin took them down a neighborhood road until he turned toward a new street that ended at their school. They slammed against the metal fence that surrounded the school's track. Corbin practically fell on it as if his mother was waiting with stretched arms for him at the end of a forty-mile marathon.

"What, do, you, want, to, do?" Clint asked, gasping for air again, holding Corbin with one hand and the fence with the other. "Just, forget, that this, ever, happened?"

Corbin was breathing so hard that his eyes looked like they would pop out. Clint felt suddenly heavier and fell on his side. He was going to turn and lean on the fence with his back, but when he did, he felt his bag hit the fence much earlier than it should.

"What?" Clint asked more to himself than Corbin.

Clint took off his backpack as he collapsed next to Corbin. He swung his bag onto his lap and moaned in pain as he stretched out.

"When are you going to get in shape?" Clint asked in desperation.

"Well, I didn't know that I would be running for my life this morning. I was under the assumption that I would have a good morning, with a nice walk toward my school, but if I'd known that there would have been a mad freak chasing me this morning, I would have scheduled a few more hours on the treadmill last night... but my personal trainer was busy, no protein shakes, and my schedule was too full with working out things with my moth..."

Corbin stopped talking as his eyes widened. He looked down at Clint's bag and swung it over his legs to lay it between them.

"What?" Clint asked, following Corbin's eyes to his bag.

His stare lingered on something that was sticking out of his bag. Clint swallowed hard and looked around to see if they were alone. Finding that they were, he reached down and pulled a two-foot-long dagger covered with odd signs and markings from his bag. Clint's insides felt like lead as he gripped the cool handle and held it out for them to examine.

Twenty-Two

WHO GOES TO SCHOOL JUST FOR AN EDUCATION?

Corbin pulled Clint's bag over to him and opened it. He removed Clint's history book, and Corbin stuck his finger through the knife hole as it fell open. The book's cover had a cut where the dagger penetrated half its pages.

"Wha, wha, wha, what, wh, wh, wh, why?" Corbin held the book to his chest for dear life, muttering odd words incomprehensible to anyone but a monkey.

"Shut up, and get a brown paper bag to breathe in!" Clint exclaimed, not being able to take his eye off the blade.

After a moment, he said, "We need to figure out what to do."

Just then, a bell rang from the school, warning them that there were only fifteen minutes left before the first classes started. Clint barely heard it as he was hypnotized by the dagger now turning over in his hands. Corbin, on the other hand, came to his senses by its sound.

"We have to get to class," Corbin said almost happily.

"What?" Clint asked in shock. Shaking his head, bellowing, "Something just tried to serve me up as lunchroom mystery meat. I'm shaking like a paint mixer. You are more worried about making it to class than me staying alive and in one piece; what kind of friend are you anyway?"

"A friend who knows when you need help and when to shut up and listen,"

Corbin spat back. "You're asking me to miss school, report some crazed, glow-in-the-dark, height-impaired, doggy door user with an extremely bad inferiority complex who hates kids and urgently needs Desitin." Corbin stood there looking resolved, trying to read Clint, who kept looking at the dagger. Then added, "And I mean Desitin all over, allll over!"

"If you're not mature enough to go to school, if you're so pitifully insecure and in such need of validation or some strange sense of gratification, then go to a policeman. But you'll just make things worse by not going to class, and I'll end up with another note to my mother," Corbin said, looking at his watch and noticing that they had a little over ten minutes before class started. "All I'm saying is, please let's do something after school, please. I'm tired of being at a crossroads with one road getting in trouble and the other getting in worse trouble with you."

Clint thought hard, scratching his sweaty head. Corbin clearly felt he had to lay it on thicker. "Your parents are just leaving to be with people who, just for the record, will say anything for one of our tax dollars. Do you want them to get a call and turn around because his son just ran into a... a—"

"A whatever," Clint finished for him in a relieved tone.

"Yeah," Corbin said tiredly. "Now, let's go," he said in barely more than a whisper, still out of breath.

He started to walk away but was suddenly stopped when Clint called out to him. "Wait; what am I going to do with this thing?" Clint was holding out the dagger to Corbin. "I can't take this into school."

"Mr. Harrison, the school officer?" Corbin screeched. "He couldn't even catch a woman to go on a date with him. He is too busy acting like a general as if the school were at war."

"Not him. He couldn't see anything past his uni-brow. I mean the metal detectors and searching," Clint bellowed, thrusting the dagger toward Corbin again.

From how Corbin looked, he was now thinking the same thing. "All right. All right, bury it out here by the fence, and we'll get it after school," Corbin said, looking around excitedly as if he'd just remembered they were outside.

Clint used the dagger's tip to make fast work of a hole. Once done, he quickly covered the dagger with the soft dirt and then took some small broken pieces of concrete that once held the fence to mark its place. When he'd finished, he jumped up to find that Corbin wasn't waiting for him and was almost around the school's main entrance.

He raced up the stairs to the open doors of the school and felt more at ease now that he was around others. His fellow students were giving him odd looks, and after comparing himself with those around him, he realized how dirty he was. He quickly tried brushing the dirt off him, but the more he tried, only brought more dirty looks toward him. Before going through the doors, he waited a moment, letting others pass him as he took one last look behind him. Not seeing anything abnormal, he let out a sigh of relief and went into school.

It might have been his dirty appearance, but he was selected to have his bag searched. Rolling his eyes, he opened his bag to be searched by a plump woman wearing too much makeup. She gave him a nasty look when she saw the cut in his backpack and how dirty he was. She sent him off with a nasty sneer, muttering something about kids who go bad.

All his classes went well, except he couldn't concentrate on the lessons. As hard as he tried, he couldn't stop thinking of what had happened that morning. That thing who almost killed him, the dagger that he had hidden, the person who watched the house; what was going on?

He wouldn't see Corbin until lunchtime. They always sat together with a group of friends in the center of the lunchroom. But when he got his food and sat down, Corbin wasn't there yet.

"Anyone seen Corbin?" he asked crisply to everyone around the table.

"Yeah, he was in science class right before this with me," said a girl sitting on the other side of the table. "Why do you ask? Didn't you come to school together?"

"Oh yeah," Clint said oddly. She looked at him as if he were in costume for The Pirates of Penzance for lunch. "You all right?" she asked, eyeing him in concern.

"Fine, just fine, why wouldn't I be fine, I'm fine, fine as can be, just fine, I'm fine," he said hastily, looking around for Corbin.

She still looked at him casually but must have decided he was being dumb on purpose because she went back to gossiping with her friend sitting next to her, resuming their conversation about who they would take to the Halloween dance. With five minutes left of lunch, there was still no sign of Corbin. Everyone around Clint kept asking him if he was all right, which only heightened his nerves. With time running out, Clint finished what he could eat and went to his locker to get his books for the last classes, convincing himself that he would see his friend in the last class of the day. He was about to go to his P.E. class when someone behind him called his name.

"You are Clint, right?"

"Fine, I am all right. Why does everyone keep asking me?" Clint said as he whipped around. He stopped short as if someone had hit him in the gut as his eyes fell on the one who was talking to him.

Feeling stupid, his eyes widened to take in Amber's entire frame, standing in her Cheerleader outfit, flanked by her usual honor guard of popular girls. He couldn't help but take in how beautiful she was from head to foot. That is until she opened her mouth. With a pompous look of overwhelming superiority, she started talking, showing her sharp, perfectly glinting teeth and nose in the air.

"What were you saying?" Amber said airily.

"Never mind, it's just another day in the jungle," Clint said quickly, trying not to look too distracted by how she looked at him.

She swished her platinum blonde hair out of habit when she wanted to talk to a boy. It didn't work on Clint, but many other nearby guys started to look over at her.

"So, I wanted to talk to you because, like, well, you know," she said with an airy laugh.

"I know, what?" Clint asked irritably, wishing that she would go away.

"Like, you are the thirtieth boy to invite me to the Halloween dance this Friday. I, like, need to let you know that I will let you know my decision on who will be going with me. So, you will just have to hold on and wait until I decide, OK?"

As she spoke, each word seemed harder and harder for her to say, especially the bigger ones.

"I did what again?" Clint asked, sounding more confused and shaking his head. He looked at all the girls behind Amber, who started bobbing their heads in disbelief that someone would speak to her like that.

Amber looked at him in incredible disappointment. With her mouth sounding dry, she turned around to the nearest cheerleader behind her, nearly cutting her head off with the swish of her hair. "Is this Clint or what?"

The girl she asked blinked hard with her long eyelashes that were heavy enough to keep her eyes shut longer than Sleeping Beauty listening to Michael Bolton on eternal repeat. She looked at Clint for support. Clint rolled his eyes as he nodded affirmatively, coming to her aid. Her eyes popped, and she nodded vigorously at Amber, who bore down on Clint as fast as if he were a pompom she had dropped.

"All right, sale shopper. Like I came down here where deodorant is in short supply and acne is a plague, to talk to you and help you in whatever change you thought you had. What Would help you is to like get up-to-date fashion, but why are you acting so stupid?"

It took all of Clint's energy not to snap back at her. He settled for the words, "I don't know what you're talking about, and there are not many who would."

With an exaggerated sigh, Amber held out her right hand and snapped her fingers. At once, another cheerleader pulled out several letters and, ruffling through them at breakneck speed, came to one and placed it in Amber's open hand. Amber took it and shook her long blonde hair. Again, with a look of despair at Clint, she began to read it.

"To Amber." Then she added a self-fulfilling chuckle. Clint suddenly looked like he was about to throw up right on Amber. "Will you go to the Halloween dance with me, Clint Holden, yada, yada, yada, you're wasting my time." Then, pursing her lips, she twisted her neck to give him a look like he was something foul-smelling.

Clint looked at her and wrung his hands, wishing she would disappear. Feeling that he shouldn't say what he really thought of her, the bell rang, letting him know he had to get to class.

"Sorry, Amber, I have no idea what you're talking about," Clint groaned, shutting his locker and getting ready to leave.

"Who do you think you are, little bottom-of-the-social-class boy, talking to me like that! You can't just take the spontaneity out of my moment, and you probably don't even have a credit card," Amber snorted. "I came down here where the people need to get a life and a stronger, whiter toothpaste to talk to you. I mean, I saw a girl wearing clogs for crying out loud. Like, I was just trying to be nice; there was not going to be even anything between you and me, okay? You know you thought you could be that rat who might make it through the maze and be seen with me. So please don't cry or start following me and draw this out. Oh, and don't think about asking me for a referral."

Clint couldn't take it anymore before he gave a warm smile and suddenly said seriously, "I know that this is hard for you, but you are a little ray of the dark side of the moon. I don't know if you got the right Clint, but please cancel whatever subscription you think I want because I don't like your issues because I don't want you to think I'm insulting you. I'm just defining your class. We good here, all done? All right!"

Clint started to walk away slowly, still facing her, oddly waving his hands with each word. "I know you really are a great person, and I know that because you keep telling everyone that. Now I'm going to class," Clint said, adding a genuine smile.

Amber stood there, not moving, while everyone else in the hall waited, not breathing. It took her some time to react as though her hard drive was rebooting. All of a sudden, she regained her swagger and said airily with frustration, "Right, so now, I will get back to you." At these words, she turned her back on him and motioned for all her followers to part as she tossed the letter out of her hand back to the young lady who'd given it to her.

She walked away in a manner that Clint was sure she had spent years practicing down the hall, causing a huge wake behind her.

Clint thought this was one of the strangest days he had ever had. All through his running laps in P.E., he wondered who would pounce on him next. The answer came when he was going to his last class. He was almost to the door when he saw Corbin coming toward him from the other side of the hall.

"Where have you been all day? Do you have any idea what I have been through worrying about you? You scared the pimples out of me," Clint called out angrily.

Corbin didn't say anything but shook his head hard, causing his chubby cheeks to wobble.

"You look the same as you did when you were running for your life this morning from the…"

Corbin grabbed Clint's head and turned it around to see someone standing over them in the doorway to their class.

Mrs. Christenson was holding a math book in one hand and was banging it against her other hand in a menacing way.

Smiling evilly, she said, "Gentlemen, I hope you learned your lesson yesterday."

Corbin gasped and swallowed hard, while Clint looked up with a quivering laugh and said, "Right, by the way, I think we ran into your child when we were coming to school this mor…"

Clint stared resolutely as Mrs. Christenson slammed the book in her hand in frustration so hard that Clint was amazed it didn't split in two. Corbin cringed under the glare from her eyes that would make babies cry. Corbin reached into his pocket, and in his shaking hand, he held out his signed letter to Mrs. Christenson. Clint almost threw his at her before grabbing Corbin's shoulder and moving them into class. Clint's eyes never left her until they both sat in their seats. It wasn't until he hit his hard seat that he remembered Melanie was in this class, and with a spasm of fear, he whipped quickly to see if she was at her desk. She was sitting forward with a small smile, and when she noticed him, she gave him a wink.

That warm feeling that started to grow in his rib cage didn't last long as he turned back and saw the teacher, who must have spent her spare time sucking the life out of small, cute animals, watching him. She was sitting at her desk with her bony hands clasped, waiting for the class to start, but it was her eyes, her eyes, that just watched Clint and Corbin. It was as if yesterday, after sending them away, she didn't expect them to return alive. Clint shrugged, thinking that between last night and what had happened that morning, he was lucky that he was alive. Hating the sight of his teacher, Clint felt Corbin looking at him. He saw Corbin's mouth silently, saying, "Be a good boy."

Clint let out a long, forced sigh and mouthed back, "OK," and then added, "Maybe she sent that thing to kill us. I wouldn't put it past her to have demons locked in her basement."

"Be good!" Corbin moaned audibly.

With the last bell ring, the class started and went on for what seemed like days, but when it finally ended, Corbin and he jumped up. They were the first two out of the class and into the hallway. Clint waited until they were safely in the mainstream of students struggling to get out of school as quickly as possible.

"Where have you been all day?" Clint asked in bewilderment as he hit Corbin in the shoulder with his math book.

Brushing and bumping into other kids going in every direction around them, Corbin said with his nose in the air, "I was unavoidably detained."

"What are you talking about?" Clint asked angrily. "Unavoidably detained?" Clint asked, mimicking Corbin's voice like an English manservant. "Who talks lik—"

"Excuse me?" Came another voice behind Clint.

Clint looked around and saw that it was Melanie. She hurried to walk next to him, and at the sight of her, Clint was suddenly distracted and stumbled a step or two. "Hey, hey there, Melanie," Clint said with a genuine smile.

Melanie started to hum lightly and shrugged, giving the impression that they should both know her thoughts.

"Melanie, what can he do for you? Whatever it is, I am sure that he would only be happy to do it to you," Corbin interjected with a hearty smile. Clint hit him again.

"I mean… do it with you," Corbin whimpered. Clint hit him a third time.

"You know what I mean, and if you don't, then I would be more than happy to try and explain this unsaid thing between you two a third time, as long as I don't get hit again." Clint didn't hit him this time as Melanie laughed. Then Corbin said softly, "I am just a breeding ground of good ideas that don't come out right."

"I wanted to talk to you about your invitation to the dance this Friday. Is that all right?" she asked kindly. Of all the things that Clint thought she would say, that was not it, as he was still wondering what was wrong with Corbin.

"The dance?" Clint asked, sounding stupid.

"Yes, I wanted to thank you for your invitation, and I will get back to you soon if I can," she said, concerned at Clint's uncertainty.

"Oh, yeah, sure thing," Clint muttered with more emotion than necessary.

"Great," Melanie said in her peaceful voice, making Clint's toes melt. She started walking away, and his head felt like someone was setting fireworks in it. She called over her shoulder, "I will see you soon, and thank you again for your invitation. Have a good day."

Clint watched her pass through the sea of students and teachers until she was out of sight.

Whack! Corbin walloped him in the arm. "Come on!"

"Ow," Clint said, still out of his mind.

"Thank you for your invitation," Corbin said, fluttering his eyes. Then he looked at Clint in disgust as if he knew he would be better off dead than to go through what Clint was.

Then, the thought came to him. "Hang on! I didn't send any invitations," Clint muttered.

"I think I hear my mom calling me from across town," Corbin said, although there was no way that he could hear anything over the hallway noise, least of all his mother from his house. Suddenly, he was gone in quick steps as he tried to blend into a group of babbling younger kids.

"It was you! Where did you go?" Clint called as he came out of his love-sick stupor, noticing that Corbin was gone. "So that's what you were doing all day!" Clint exclaimed, making out Corbin's head in the crowd.

"Corbin!" Clint yelled, causing curious looks from those around him. Clint's skinny frame aided him in catching up to Corbin, who was hampered by his weight. Faster than Corbin would have wanted, Clint was on top of him, literally. Clint had launched himself at Corbin when a gap appeared between a crowd of kids and held him fast.

"You did it, you did it! Don't deny it," Clint shouted, not caring about the continuing looks and even one yell from a teacher for him to let Corbin go.

"Yes, yes," Corbin said, looking like he was forcing his smile to stay in place, brushing himself off as he was covered in dirt and dust again.

"What are you doing to me?" Clint asked desperately, letting Corbin go and grabbing his head.

"You weren't going to do it," Corbin garbled, walking away. "I strongly suspected you needed cheering up after this morning and last night. So I signed your name and told the teachers selling the invitations that you were too shy to buy them yourself. So, I stepped in to save you."

"Save me? From what?"

"From yourself. You're a love-sick dope, and you have no place in a civilized society!" Corbin said, like a loving mother to her son, finally landing on the moon.

"How many did you send out?" Clint asked hesitantly, looking almost sick with anxiety.

"I don't know. I thought of every girl you said you liked and everyone I would have asked…"

"How many?" Clint asked again, sounding more alarmed.

"Why do you still look at the opposite sex as if you were going fishing? That you try one lure and line at a time, casting again and again," Corbin asked, jostling to get further away from Clint, reaching his locker. "You know," he said as he opened his locker as fast as he could, "it's more like when you go hunting. You can take your time for one good shot at what you want. Or if you keep going with "your" approach… that would work, and she would fall in love with you by the time both of your teeth fall out. Or, you can send out as many bullets as possible to see what you hit, spray, and pray. Then you can choose what you want to keep and what you want to…"

"HOW MANY?" Clint shouted so loudly that it made a lot of people look around at him in alarm.

Corbin was having a hard time keeping his face straight. He stopped dead and moaned, "Well, I don't know. I think about nine."

"NINE?"

"Or maybe it was nineteen," Corbin said, grabbing his books out of his locker and putting them in his bag as fast as a bullet.

"Nineteen?" Clint asked, looking like he was going to pass out.

"Yeah, I think maybe it was thirty-nine. So you should be very popular the next couple of days," Corbin said before starting down the hall to put as much space between them as possible.

"WHAT!" Clint called before slamming his locker shut and following Corbin, looking as wild as an animal on the hunt, calling, "Corbin? Oh, Corbin? Come here, Corbin!"

Corbin's walk quickened. When Clint caught up to him, he stopped calling for him. They walked silently out of the school's doors, not looking at each other. Clint wanted to protest more, but what awaited him outside filled his mind like an imminent lousy report card. Young trees were planted along the sidewalk, dotted here and there, and several bushes.

The way was almost clear since they were some of the first out of the school. Some kids were going to the parking lot, where those who could drive enjoyed standing around their cars and talking with friends. Some mournfully waited for their parents to pick them up, while others waited in line for school buses.

Clint walked briskly on an invisible line home that they always took. Clint took the lead and deviated from the line, suddenly walking by the fence and trees. He could feel the afternoon's heat and realized the sick feeling was not all from the heat. Corbin followed closely at Clint's heels, now and then opening his mouth to say something but saying nothing. This continued until they reached the dirt pile concealing the dagger. They looked at it as if they stood there long enough, the morning would turn around, and everything would return to normal. Face pale, hands shaking, Clint scraped off some of the dirt, hoping that the dagger wouldn't be there. It was hard for both to look inconspicuous together while Clint dug something up just outside the school grounds. Football and track practice was starting on the fields next to them. This made Clint even more nervous. What if they were seen? And, more importantly, how were they going to get home?

When Clint's fingers hit something hard, he froze. His sick feeling suddenly got worse as he again didn't know what to do. Nothing else was happening in his mind except the memory of almost being killed that morning.

"You know, Clint," Corbin said quietly, "I'm sorry I sent all those invitations out for you."

"I don't know what to do," Clint whimpered, almost crying.

"I know your relationships have as long a life span as fruit flies in a humidified room. If we don't make it home, I just wanted you to know that" Corbin squeaked.

Clint unearthed the dagger and held it close to him, hiding it from view from any players in the field behind them. Corbin came closer and stood right next to him. He was shoulder to shoulder; both eyes locked on the weapon. Corbin reached up, felt the blade's ornate markings, and oddly smiled for a moment before it was wiped off his face as quickly as Mrs. Christenson would give someone detention for laughing in her class.

"Well, there goes the neighborhood," Corbin said in a matter-of-fact tone as if that summed up all the answers. He even readjusted his backpack and was going to walk away.

"What are we going to do?" Clint coughed.

"What is it with you and asking that question today? Is that cursed, because as soon as that thing came into your life, get it, came INTO YOUR LIFE, you can't think of what you should do."

"All right," Clint shot back, "let's get out of here as fast as we can. We can't go home the same way we came. Remember there wasn't much traffic this morning the way we were going to school?" Clint asked, sounding brave.

Corbin thought hard, but when he said nothing, it was clear how badly that morning's events had affected him.

"Never mind," Clint said, smiling. "We'll head to your house first and stay around other people as much as possible. Then I'll make my way home the best I can after that, all right?"

"For once in my life, I would rather stay at school than go home," Corbin said as if he'd just swallowed some nasty medicine.

They were both so worried that they would meet something evil that they walked close to anyone going their way. They were so close that some thought that they needed to be separated at birth. The sky was a forget-me-not blue with darker rain clouds gliding high. Nothing foul met them as they made their odd way around to Corbin's home. When they came to his front door, they both shared a moment of glee without words.

"I think that we won't have anything else to worry about," Corbin said, panting a little from his fast walking.

Clint wasn't breathing hard as he positively shook his head. "Yeah, we have nothing to worry about. I don't want to blunder into any more trouble for the rest of the week. I'll call you when I get home."

Without waiting for a reply, Clint clasped Corbin's shoulder reassuringly. Setting off at a jog, he looked every way he could for any opportunity to conceal himself while trying to make his way home. The dagger was safely hidden in his bag, but it was all he could think about every time it bounced around. His luck held as still no harm came to him, but every shadow held horrible pictures in his imagination. That is until he was almost home, and seeing his house brought new hope. He quickened his pace, reaching his driveway. He leaned heavily on the stone pillar of their front gate, taking a long breath. It was all over, and he even found a smile on his face. Suddenly, something was right behind him, and he barked.

"AHHHHHHHHHHHHHHHH!" Clint didn't think; all he could do was run. He ran for the front door with all his might, screaming steadily all the way. He didn't look back, he couldn't look back.

Miss Hutching's favorite horrible white poodle was behind him, running flat out on all four manicured paws.

Clint ran, holding his hands straight out. He gripped the doorknob, and in two seconds, he was in his house, shut the door, locked it, up the stairs, and in his room looking down out of his window, watching that dumb dog prance back to her mistress, who he saw standing out on her front porch.

Miss Hutchins seemed to be dressed for a royal ball. She held out her bony arms to welcome her beloved animal back home after a successful mission, as if she had just won a battle that would bring a long war closer to an end.

With a long sigh, Clint took off his bag and lay flat on his bed. Closing his eyes, he started to laugh, unable to think of how stupid he had been.

Twenty-Three

THERE IS NOT ENOUGH HOSPITALITY IN THE WORLD FOR YOU GUYS

"Ding, Dong."

The sound of the doorbell cut through his laughter. Still laughing at himself, he went down the hall to the landing by the winding staircase to the front door.

"Is someone going to get that?" Clint called.

The lack of an answer told him he was the only one home from school. Of course, he thought, with Mom and Dad gone, everyone would take extra time exercising their freedom without supervision.

"Ding, Dong."

"All right, all right, I'm coming," Clint said, taking two steps at a time. He looked out of the peephole when he reached the front door. Clint saw in the strange, magnified glass a tall, apparently bald man with his head down, wearing a terrible striped, pink golfing cap.

Clint unlocked the door, thinking that this must be one of his stepfather's friends coming to ask for a game of golf. Opening the door, this thought was confirmed because, from head to toe, the man was wearing the worst-looking golfing clothes that Clint had ever seen. Right down to his padded loafers, long argyle moldy color socks, high water pants, and a long-sleeve sequence shirt with an astonishing sweater.

The man eyed him with his weathered face. "Is this the Holden residence?"

"Yes, but my father is busy right now. I can take a message for you, and I think the tryouts for Caddyshack are over."

"Clint Holden?" the man asked, looking over Clint's head into the house.

"Yeah," Clint said with a crack in his voice.

Wham!

Without warning, Clint was knocked on his back by the force of the door slammed into him by the man he was talking to. With one long stride, the man was right on top of Clint, standing over him, glancing around in every direction.

"Secure the area, no sound," the man called out, "and gather all those found with information."

As if they were conjured out of thin air, more people rushed in like quick blurs all around him, with the man standing over him giving them hand gestures to show which way they should go. The large man who was on him suddenly rose and shot off. Before Clint could move an eyelash, another man slumped right on top of him, pulling his arms and legs, stretching him out, and pinning him to the wood floor. As soon as the man was on him, a thick hand fell right on his mouth, and with the other hand, he held it up to his bearded mouth, silently telling Clint to be quiet.

Clint was pinned to the floor, and his limbs seemed to have the strength of a doll in comparison with his attacker. It felt like he had a giant beanbag on top of him, with the weight of a full-grown man. Clint started to cry for help behind the man's hand, but all that came out was a muffled moan. Eyes wide with fear, he saw the short man scanning his home. The man had very thick hair and had a very oddly shaped face. His face seemed old and almost like a potato. He was also wearing strange golf clothes that didn't match.

Panic took over, causing Clint to struggle harder and shout louder, but nothing helped. He couldn't hear any of those people now who were going through his home.

"Quit, boy," the bearded man said, leaning down, eyeing Clint past thick eyebrows.

The man had bad breath with a strange-sounding accent. He was also slightly taller than Clint but felt he weighed more than he should. With his free arm, the man reached into one pocket and took a piece of leather. Simultaneously, he moved one leg while still pinning Clint and shut the door quietly behind him.

"We aren't here tae harm yoo boy," the man said, now taking the leather strip and gagging Clint. Nothing Clint did even made the man move an inch, but Clint kept up the struggle. This man had him pinned like one of the dead bugs in the principal's office on display.

"We are here tae help yoo, just wait a tick and we will explain every thin'," his captor said.

Clint yelled again, but all that came out was a moan.

"Please, boy," his captor pleaded. Something in his voice sounded like sincerity, but Clint fought with all his strength.

Clint's arms and legs started to burn and hurt. He heard the quiet footsteps of those who searched his house start to return. His captor stopped looking around and fixed his gaze on one position toward the kitchen. Even being pinned down, Clint arched his neck to see what the dwarf-like man was looking at. His eyes hurt from the strain of looking up so hard as he saw a tall man standing at the base of the stairs. He was also dressed like the world's worst golfer. When Clint saw his face, he froze and even stopped struggling. The man had light blue skin and a long, sharp head. His long purple hair fell around his pointed ears as he lifted the golf cap off his head.

"Och yah, dat may seem a wee bit odd, but yoo will get use tae us. Once yoo doo, yoo will never want anyone else at da part'a," The man who was holding Clint said, arching his bushy eyebrows.

Clint couldn't take his eyes off the blue-skinned man. He couldn't see any paint smears on the man's hat or shirt collar. What would weirdos like this be doing here? The man just stood there, leaning on the wooden handrail and looking around, taking in Clint's house, observing the pictures on the wall with interest.

"Report," came a husky voice from somewhere in the kitchen.

"Clear up," the blue man called as he stood to attention.

"Clear back," sounded a woman's voice from somewhere else.

"Clear down." "Clear front." "All clear," came different voices from all over the house.

Then the man on top of him called out in a low tone, "Da butler is seecure."

"Regroup at entrance," the low, husky voice sounded out from the kitchen once more.

Clint couldn't hold his head up anymore and turned it down with his ear to the ground. He felt and heard more footsteps from all over, which got louder as they got closer. His neck and back started to hurt from the weight of the man on top of him, and the hardwood floor didn't help. All he could make out was the many different-sized shoes marching around as they formed a straight line next to him.

"Let's hear it," came the same voice from the kitchen, now sounding like it was coming closer. Even the short man on top of him jumped to attention with his chest out and arms back.

Clint, now free to move a little, looked up to see the blue-skinned man standing on the stairs was the first to speak, "Sir, one found upstairs, category, innocent by age." He had a low voice.

A strong woman reported, "Lower-level hold one, just of age sir but category innocent also by way of mind."

"How bad in mind?" the man standing in the hallway asked.

"When I checked, I heard her talk to someone, but when I opened the door slightly, she was talking to a small box that she was holding in her hand. She was alone, no one else in the room present for her to speak to. Clearly out of her mind," she added as an afterthought.

"I see. Continue," the man said from the hallway.

"Sir, this boy here seems tae be the only one here of competence," the short man who stood over him said proudly.

"Area intact?"

"Aye, sir, no hostiles," the short man answered.

There were footsteps again from the hallway coming closer. Clint couldn't tell if it was the man's steps on the wood or if his heart was beating so hard that it might jump out of his chest, but they seemed to carry a lot of authority. Clint closed his eyes when the footsteps stopped right over his head. Clint opened one eye to see the man standing over him, looking down at him with a kind smile slowly crossing his face.

"Hey, kid," the man said, smirking.

Clint couldn't say anything, nor did he know if he could. His feelings were suddenly mixed as he opened both his eyes. He was so afraid that he could feel his hands and feet starting to shake. As this man stared down at him, Clint couldn't help but think he had a kind face.

The man turned to face all those with him and ordered, "Maintain location for quite thirty. Keep protocol as we wait for local confirmation on the prize."

The man looked back down at Clint and, sounding kinder, said, "We won't hurt you, but we need to talk to Clint Staeli Holden. We must do so now. Do you understand me?" As he asked, he locked eyes with Clint in a commanding stair.

Clint suddenly remembered that he was no longer being held down. Stiffly moving his hands over his head to the leather strap, he removed the gag in his mouth. When he touched it, the man above him gave him a look that stopped him suddenly. Even though this man didn't have a gun on him, his stare was enough to make any person feel like they were looking down the long barrel of one.

"Do you understand me?" the man said once again with concern in his voice. Clint nodded.

"All right, we will allow you to remove the binding in your mouth if you give us your word that you will hear us, and we will give you our word that we will not harm you or those around you. Agreed?"

Clint thought for a few seconds. Who talked like that? Where were these people from? What did they want from him? He thought that if he said yes, he might be able to call down to Jamie for help. Or he might be able to make a break for it out the door. But if he didn't do anything, there were a lot of them, and he was all alone with no hope of getting out of this.

Moving very slowly, he nodded in agreement, feeling his neck ache, and before he could help himself, he sat up with the thought that only one thing was standing between him and the door. The short, dwarf-like man had held him down for so long. The leader reached down and gently removed the leather gag. Without thinking, Clint leaped to his feet, and in one swift movement, he jumped at the short man to push him out of the way, reaching for the door handle. It was a great plan, save for the fact that Clint put all his weight and strength behind him when he hit that short man, and it felt like hitting a concrete wall. Clint drove all the force of his shoulder into the man's mid-section. All the air came out of his lungs as he fell back and hit the floor again. He didn't even move a hair on the dwarf man's face.

"Ohhh," Clint moaned as his head fell back, hitting the hard floor in the same place again.

"You would break your word so easily?" the man standing over him asked in disbelief.

Clint found his breath while he reached up and rubbed the back of his head. Coughing, he got to his feet as fast as his aching body would allow.

Standing now, he locked eyes with the man who must have been the leader of this group and said in anger, "Of course, I would. What do you think I would do? Let you guys just come into my house and do whatever you want, and then you ask me to trust you because you gave me your word? Who let the crazy out? What is wrong with you people anyway? Why are you here? What kind of people are you?" Clint was backing away from the man slowly without realizing it. His voice came with more fear in each question.

"I mean, why is all this happening to me? Who are you people? What is going on?" Clint shouted as he backed into the short man who felt like he was built of bricks.

"You said Clint Holden was here. Where is he?" their leader said in a calm voice.

"What do you people want? Who are you?" Clint shouted louder now.

"Where?" the man repeated firmly but not loudly.

"I am Clint Holden!" Clint whimpered as he felt tears fall down his cheeks. He fell to his knees and squirmed up against the wall by the door, crying. All those around him just watched in concern. This was not what they had expected. The leader who had asked him where Clint was strode over to him quickly and knelt in front of him. His eyes were full of amazement, and all those behind him shuffled to whisper to one another as they stood still in a line. Their leader looked confused and in awe, as he said, "You? You are Clint Staeli Holden? But you are a boy!" he said, more to himself than to Clint.

The tension and strain built until his grandmother called from upstairs. "Keep it down! Lethal Weapon is on!" Then, she was gone with the sound of a cracked door shutting.

Crying, Clint breathed past his tears and panic. All the feelings of that morning's near-death experience and his home being broken into overcame him as he asked, "What are you going to do to me?"

Their leader smiled, rubbing his bald head thoughtfully. He was eye to eye with Clint and said authoritatively, "My name is Banks, and we are here for you, Clint Holden, and the Requiem."

Twenty-Four

FIRST IMPRESSIONS WERE THE MOST IMPORTANT

Banks helped Clint to his feet, and without warning, he took his sleeve and wiped away Clint's tears. Clint's mind was racing as emotion mingled with wild ideas rushed into his mind. What should he do? Where should he go? How did they know his name and where he lived? Who were these people? Looking around at all those in the lobby, Clint felt stupid and embarrassed for crying. Although his tears were gone, he was still sniffing. He straightened up, feeling his back throb with pain. He looked at the man who was giving all the orders.

"You must have many questions," Banks said, clasping Clint on the shoulder. "I will keep my word and see that no harm will be brought to you, but we must also know certain facts. Is that understood?"

Clint didn't know what to say or do when asked such a direct question. So, he just stood hunched over, not talking or moving. He thought of the nearest place to call someone for help or if he should even try.

"Since we are still here, and you are silent, we will take a moment to explain. Why don't I tell you something, and then you tell me something? Would that be satisfactory?" Banks asked, and when he spoke, there wasn't any frustration in his tone, but he talked normally as if everything was going according to plan.

Clint nodded slowly, and as he did, he looked at the one blocking the door. The hairy man crossed his arms, smiling widely as if daring Clint to try it again. Clint felt like someone else was moving around in his head. Banks moved to the stairs where the tall blue man stood in line. When Clint saw him this time, the man was not looking around the room at the pictures but was more interested in the wooden handrail that went up the stairs. Everyone in the line wore the worst golfing apparel Clint had ever seen. Terrible hats, some shoes had metal spikes while others were rubber, sweaters on a hot day, and shorts with long socks.

"My name is Banks, team leader and Knight of the Salvation Alliance. Then he indicated with his hand at the short man standing like a portable barrier between Clint and the door. "This is Hodge O'Neil, scout, recon, and second in command."

The man named Banks thrust a thumb out at the tall blue man standing on the stairs, "This is Tremayne, Turshon Druid." Tremayne, who must have been seven feet tall, nodded at Clint.

Banks started to walk down the line, pointing a finger or clasping each person on their shoulder as he went by, introducing them. Standing next to the blue man on the stairs in the reception area was a woman slightly shorter than the blue man but with many of the same features; she had the same slender, long face, long, sharp nose, and pointed ears. On the other hand, she had light purple skin and dark blue hair that reflected in the sunlight coming from the windows over the door, making it almost look black.

"This is Ohlwiler Stone, Carimint Druid," Banks said as if he was not surprised at how different those two people were. It is as if blue and purple people grow out of the ground or come in your mail. Ohlwiler smiled at Clint warmly and thrust her chin out at him in greeting.

Next to Ohwiler was another woman. Even in Clint's panic and fear, he couldn't help but notice that she was not much older than John and was very attractive.

"This is Ravin Gonion, and she is, well…" He stopped for a moment and looked around for the right words. Not finding the help he sought for, he said, "It is enough to know that she is hot."

Clint looked at Banks, wondering if he was trying to be funny. Clint smiled at this joke but quickly coughed into his hand when he saw that everyone around him was somber and that Banks meant no joke. Ravin didn't give any sign of welcome or greeting to Clint. She stood at attention, looking preoccupied with everything except Clint.

Next to Ravin was a huge and muscular man, like someone Clint would see in a football game. His clothes were positively bursting as they were so tight from his muscles and several sizes too small.

"This is Nix Warrant, our Paladin and aid," Banks said, still moving down the line. Nix smiled broadly at Clint and laughed softly and cheerfully with a wink.

Next to Nix down the line was another person like the first two, but his skin was dark, and he had a similar nose, ears, and long black hair in a ponytail. "This is Hobb Nortinson, our long archer." Hobb saluted Clint like he was a professional soldier.

"This is Transun Disctor," Banks said as he padded the back of a very petite woman who was even shorter than Clint. When introduced, she bowed deeply and smiled partly without showing her teeth to Clint.

"And last but not least, our mid-Archer Chiowood Quicklist." Chiowood smiled almost clumsily as if he didn't know what to do. He was the most normal-looking one of the lot, except for his clothes. He had red hair, freckles, a slightly overweight face, and a mid-section.

"This is our team," Banks said as he walked back over to Clint. "And we need to know how many people live here and if any adults are named Clint Holden. Now, can you tell us that?" Banks gave him a penetrating eye that would have melted butter.

Clint licked his dry lips and said, "There are nine here, and my stepfather's name is John." Thinking fast, he continued, "And he should be home any time now; he's a Major in the military, and when he gets here…."

"Hold on, Clint," Banks cut him short, "We know when you lie." Without warning or explanation, he grabbed Clint's neck. Clint suddenly panicked and tried to free himself, but the man was not choking him. Banks examined Clint as if he were looking for zits or a rash. Then he let go of his neck and moved Clint's face left and right. Clint was breathing fast, trying to block the man's hand from forcing his face. Clint slapped and hit Banks's arms as hard as he could, but he might as well have been hitting a flag pole. After Banks had checked behind Clint's ears, face, hair, and hands, he let him go.

"Hey!" Clint shouted in protest. Banks looked over to O'Neil as if surprised not to find any bugs on Clint.

"No change! It is like you reported; they can lie, and nothing happens to them. Wonders be odd and terrible," Banks said, now appearing deep in thought.

"What are you talking about?" Clint said, again looking at Banks and O'Neil as all the others were muttering to each other.

"No, I gave you some information. Now you tell me what I need to know. How many people live here, and if any adults are named Clint Holden? This time, no lies!" Banks said, and he sounded impatient and concerned for the first time.

"Nine are in my family here. My parents are away. My grandmother is upstairs, older sister downstairs, everyone else is at school except for Grant, who is camping," Clint said, with the same tone of impatience as Banks.

"How old are they, and what do they look like?" Banks asked quickly, pacing around the atrium.

"Oh no," Clint coughed, rubbing his neck, "I told you what you want; now it's my turn. Why are you here, and are you with that red rat that tried to kill me this morning?" Clint demanded.

Banks just said calmly, "Describe him to me."

"Describe him?" Clint gasped. "What? Is this an everyday thing for you? For me, murder doesn't come with my cornflakes. Someone tried to kill me this morning!"

Banks looked at each one of his parties.

"Were you with the one who tried to kill me?" Clint said with strength that superseded himself.

"Threat confirmed. This boy has had his nostrils opened," Banks said oddly, but everyone beside Clint seemed to react like the White House had lost their favorite puppy.

Everyone there looked at Banks, waiting for instructions, and O'Neil even took a step forward and said, "Sir, please?"

"Not yet. We must find out what we can and if this is the best way to confront before we continue," Banks said, moving his eyes back to Clint and holding up a hand for O'Neil to relax.

"But, Sir?" O'Neil pleaded once more.

Banks didn't pay any attention to O'Neil this time but said to Clint, "No, we are not with the group that tried to kill you, but I need to know about that entity that attacked you and what those other family members look like who are coming here." He paused briefly, adding, "It is for your safety and ours."

Clint described all his family and pointed to their pictures on the wall, showing each one. Banks and all the others listened intently. Banks asked when each should arrive and was satisfied before he demanded what happened that morning. Clint told him everything, and as he spoke, his head ached from talking so fast without breathing enough. The stress he had gone through that day didn't help. Banks gave Clint a forced smile when he was done, letting him know not to worry.

"Excuse me for a moment," Banks said quickly and turned to address all those who came in with him.

"Hostiles confirmed. The Fury is here, and they are after the Requiem as well. Disperse pattern, Tremayne take the back, Ohlwiler the front. Chiowood and Hobb the roof or best high position. When in position, set up every protection until we find the Requiem. Report every thirty, and The Reclamation doesn't seem to have taken place here, so be on the point for anything, and I mean everything."

Everything that Banks was saying seemed almost normal to them, except when he mentioned something about The Reclamation. When Banks talked about that, a spasm of concern rippled around the room.

"We know there is at least one imp, and one isn't enough. Opposition strength is unknown, so we will stay here until we know what we are facing and we have what we came for. The rest of you head back and pick up our supplies and be on the watch while O'Neil and I work out what is going on. Understood?"

"Sir, yes sir," all those who were with him said enthusiastically as one. They each hurried fast at this, leaving Banks and O'Neil alone with Clint.

"Hey, wait! You can't just…" Clint started to say, but they had all left.

Banks rubbed his bald head again, looking tired for the first time. "Is there a place we can sit and talk?" he asked Clint kindly.

Clint didn't answer right away. Some of his trust had worn off now that just the three of them were together. He gave them a nervous glance and wished that this was all a dream. Clint didn't know if he should trust these men or try to get rid of them as quickly as possible. They could be part of the group that was after him that morning. Banks seemed to know what he was thinking and patted him on the shoulder so heartily that Clint thought his spine might break.

"Let's talk, all right? Come with us, and we will try to prove our intentions." Banks pulled and steered Clint toward the kitchen. He sat Clint down on a stool while he sat beside him. O'Neil did his best to climb and sit on a stool, but he had difficulty because of his short legs.

"I know you have many questions. I will explain what I can," Banks said. It was odd for Clint to be talked to like a soldier instead of a child.

"We have a limited window, and the frame is uncertain. Our coordinates, enemy strength, and intent are all dark. So, we need new light primary intel," Banks said.

Clint sat unmoving for about a minute before he said, "I'm going with the answer 'D' almost always. One out of four chance isn't too bad."

This time, Banks was the one who didn't move until he said, "O'Neil."

"What the immediate officer her' is sayin' is we don' know where we are and who is with dat highly emotional imp this morn. We are her' tae find the Requiem before it gets boring and…" O'Neil stopped suddenly at an intense look from Banks.

"We are here looking for the Requiem," Banks continued as O'Neil started to look around the room excitedly. "Our historians tell us that it is foretold of a time when we would have it for our people or the Fury would bring about destruction."

Clint was listening closely, but it made no sense to him any more than when Mrs. Christenson asked him to work out an answer in front of the class. His heart was beating somewhere up in his neck, and his face must have had an idiotic look on it.

"I have no idea what you are talking about. There is a mental health facility next to the hospital," Clint said weakly.

"I think yoo made it a wee bit tae thick fur the booy," O'Neil said sounding more caring than Banks.

"I see," Banks said as he stood up and walked around to the other side of the kitchen island where Clint's mother was, just yesterday, making dinner.

"In our world about three to five hundred years ago, or maybe even a thousand years ago, there was a war that almost ended all life that we know of. Several versions of our history tell a different story, but we know that there was what we call The Reclamation." Banks started pacing around as he spoke.

"The Reclamation is the one thing that saved all life; we have seen that these people in this location do not have it," Banks looked at O'Neil in unbelief.

"The Reclamation is when yoo do something wrong," O'Neil said, taking on a tone like when Clint's mother would talk to him when he was sick in bed. "In our world, when someone does somethin' bad, lie, cheat, steal or anything bad like 'at, well, they change." O'Neil looked like he was casting his mind around for something that would make sense to explain what he was thinking. "They just look bad," O'Neil said, looking very proud of himself like he'd just given the world's best history report.

"How do they change?" Clint asked, thinking that this was the best story he had heard. These psychos were a lot of fun.

"They change into something evil. They do evil, so their looks reflect evil doings," Banks said, exasperated, struggling to make Clint understand. Banks was looking at the stove with excitement before he went on, "I know that this is an inadequate explanation, but after The Reclamation, there was a great transformation worldwide. Peace and prosperity came about for those who wanted to do good and even amongst those who did change and wanted to be good once more. The two sides separated the world after the wars and set a boundary. There hasn't been any major conflict for years, but there have been costly skirmishes." Banks looked like he was thinking about something else trailing off from the past. Clint felt strange seeing this man continue, even though he knew he was pretty mad.

"A war? Between who?" Clint asked before he could stop himself.

O'Neil cleared his throat, and Banks looked around, taking in the room until he saw Clint, who looked like he had fully come back to his senses and shaken his dazed, confused look.

"The war was set about between those who wanted freedom, that is us, and those who take away the freedom of choice. Those who wish the power of ruling are the Fury. We have some records that confirm all this information," Banks went on, but he seemed more tired this time.

"It also tells us about the Requiem. It would be best if you were not so concerned about our history. We have come a long way, and our duty is clear. The Requiem will bring all who live together or destroy all we know. The means of finding it is here, Clint, and we need it."

"I'm sorry, need what again?" Clint's brain sagged under the weight of all this information.

"Information on the Requiem; we are not leaving here without it," Banks said with authority.

Clint looked to O'Neil for help. He didn't find any when he saw O'Neil looking at the fridge in interest.

"I don't know what you are talking about. We are fresh out of rec rooms. We don't even have a rec room. So, you guys had best be off to the eighteenth hole on the green, and I will send you a postcard at the next terrorist group therapy session," Clint said, adding a quick, short smile.

Banks sat unmoving with a commanding stare. Until he looked over at O'Neil and asked in a strong tone, "He is not lying, is he?"

O'Neil was grinding his teeth and looked at Banks seriously. Before he answered, he reached down, took out a hip flask, and took one quick drink from it. Whatever was in that flask almost took all the air out of him, just the same way as when Clint had hit the ground when he ran into O'Neil. O'Neil spoke to Banks in a voice that seemed like he had just inhaled a load of helium and was shaking off the effects of the gas, "Nope he ant lying," O'Neil said going cross-eyed.

Banks took in a long, deep breath before saying, "Those in this will have to be protected so the order of deployment stands, O'Neil. We are going to have to set up a command center here, and for our inconvenient presence here," he said to Clint, "I apologize. We will not be here one minute longer than necessary to complete our mission."

Clint started getting suspicious and felt every moment as he started to get scared again. These two men actually believed what they were saying, and if they felt like they weren't going to get what they wanted, would they become dangerous?

The house seemed colder as it was quiet now for a moment. Neither O'Neil nor Banks spoke for what seemed like ages. They both seemed to be faced with the same thought that they weren't going to share.

Suddenly, Jamie's voice started to grow from the floor below. She sounded like she was still on the phone when Clint saw her foot appear in the hallway. Clint's heart leaped when he realized he could get help. He opened his mouth to call out, but when he saw Banks's thoughtful and worried face, he couldn't say anything. Clint's mouth fell half-open to say something, but nothing came out.

Clint's heart raced as he tried to find an excuse to explain these two odd men in the kitchen. Horrified, his mind went blank. Clint looked at Banks and O'Neil with new eyes, one a fully-grown man and the other a short, dwarf-like man who'd just drunk something, almost knocking him off his feet.

As Jamie walked into the kitchen and engaged in heavy conversation with whoever was on the other end of the phone, Clint opened his mouth again, and this time, he was able to say something with a shutter, "Jamie, I can explain. Jamie?"

Clint had stopped trying to talk because Jamie walked into the kitchen as if she were alone. All three of them were watching her, and O'Neil even moved out of her way so she could open the fridge. She didn't even bat an eyelash at any of them. O'Neil investigated the refrigerator as she opened it and even let out an audible "Oh" in amazement at what was behind those cold doors.

Jamie grabbed some soda and a sandwich with one hand, her other still holding the phone as if it were part of her body. She kept talking without pausing, in disbelief about another girl talking about her latest serve in a volleyball game and something about her missing the ball because a boy had given her a wolf whistle. After collecting her food, she retraced her steps and left the kitchen, not even looking at any of them. Her voice carried down to her room, balancing her food and phone in her hands. With a snap of her door from downstairs, she was gone, back into her room.

"It must be hard tae hae a mentally ill sister in the hoose," O'Neil said in pity. His voice was now returned to normal as the effects of the drink had worn off.

"Yep, that's what it is, hard," Clint replied. His feeling of apprehension was diminishing again.

"Look, I'm sorry. I can't help you, but I will get you to someone who can, all right," Clint said in a voice that he hoped was calming. He stood up and was walking to the phone in the kitchen when something sounded like it was coming down the hallway from the front doorway. It sounded like sharp, tiny claws running on the wooden floor coming toward them.

O'Neil straightened up, alert when he heard it. Clint moved his attention over to the corner of the kitchen to see what was making the noise with the phone in his hand. Whatever it was, it was heading right toward O'Neil and Banks.

Twenty-Five

KIDS THESE DAYS

The sound of the small animal's scurrying stopped right at O'Neil's feet. He moved one of his knurled hands and brought up the small animal.

"A squirrel?" Cling asked, forgetting that he was still holding the phone. O'Neil held the squirrel two inches from his rock-like nose, and then the squirrel began to squeak quickly. Clint froze in amazement as O'Neil was gabbing at the small animal.

"Are yoo sure?" O'Neil asked the squirrel hastily.

The squirrel replied in quick squeaks before it scurried up O'Neil's shoulder to rest. O'Neil turned fast to Banks with the squirrel holding on tight.

"It's on you! Get it!" Clint called out to O'Neil.

O'Neil didn't pay any attention to Clint but addressed Banks, who was ready and waiting for his report. "Sir, subject approaching the hoose, not fitting any description of the family. It looks like it is scurrying around cautiously. Ohlwiler is waiting for instructions," O'Neil added quickly.

Banks moved so fast that Clint dropped the phone in surprise, "Send Nuts back out and tell Ohlwiler to disarm and detain. I want answers," Banks said as he ran silently. He was heading down the kitchen toward the hallway and the front door. O'Neil let the squirrel run down his leg, and it followed behind Banks. Clint leaned, watching in disbelief as the squirrel practically flew past Banks and O'Neil, up the stairs and out of sight. Clint couldn't move for a moment as these people left his sight. He just stood there in a stupor. His mind refusing to work.

"Wait," Clint called after them as he unknowingly hung up the phone and followed them toward the front door. Banks ran and slid on his knees to a stop, slamming himself up against the front door with a thud. He waved to O'Neil to go into the office room and then gave him several signals with his hand, instructing him. O'Neil dove toward his stepfather's study and crawled into the room low and out of sight. Clint stood stupidly, awestruck at what these two men were doing. Banks looked around, checking the stairs, both rooms to his left and right, and when he saw Clint, he motioned his hand down, trying to tell him to do something. Clint stood there, not moving a hair. Banks coolly repeated the sign. Clint wrinkled his nose and huffed in unknowing protest as he folded his arms and leaned against the hallway wall. Then, when Banks gave him the same sign a third time, more urgently, Clint still did nothing. Banks mouthed silently, "Get down."

Clint smiled, exasperated, and said out loud, "OK." He didn't say it very loudly, but it had the same effect as a firework in the house as it cracked the silent atmosphere before he got to the floor. He felt like he was at school during a fire drill on what to do when there was smoke in the room. He lay on his stomach, almost laughing, waiting for one of them to yell, "Surprise!"

Banks, his back still to the door, slowly moved his head to the window on the right side to look out while remaining unseen from the outside. He moved fast, taking a quick look with one eye, and then pushed his head back out of view, safe behind the wooden frame.

Clint wished he could see what was happening outside and figured that rather than try and run by some of these crazy people to get out of the house, and he would wait and see what happened next. Seeing them in those weird outfits and watching one talk to a squirrel meant they were worth some of his time before he called them in. Banks stretched out his arm and held out three fingers, and when he did so, there was a strange noise from outside the front door. Then, when Banks had dropped one finger, there was the sound of something like wood and leaves being brushed against each other. Then, when Banks dropped his last finger, a loud sound, like small branches being cracked, followed the others.

Clint couldn't take it anymore and started to rise to one knee. "Ok. That's enough. I think you two, Happy Gilmores and Squirrel from Enchanted, should catch your boat to Shutter Island, alright?" Clint started to say but froze. Seconds after Banks dropped his last finger, he opened the door and dove out of the house at something just outside. Clint couldn't see it clearly, but whatever it was, he was tackled by Banks. All he could see was a shadow of something that was about his height.

Clint fell back on his butt in shock and started to move like a crab back against the wall. What if it was the little red man who tried to kill him this morning? What if all of this wasn't made up after all? The horrible feeling that all of this could be real came to Clint fast as Banks leaped into the house as quickly as he had jumped out of it. Now Banks was holding something over his shoulder, and as quietly as possible, he shut the door with his foot.

"Keep watching out there and let me know if anything saw us," Banks whispered to O'Neil. Clint grabbed his head as he saw O'Neil flat on the floor with only his head high enough for one eye to look out of the center window of his stepfather's office at the front of the house.

Banks then moved fast, holding what looked like a roll of tree branches into the kitchen. He walked right over to Clint, and when he got to the kitchen, he slammed the wrapped wood bundle onto the kitchen center counter.

"What are you doing!" Clint yelled as he clambered after him.

"I said keep it down!" His grandmother called again. "It's not every day you can watch a Lethal Weapon Marathon," with another snap of the door closing.

When Clint made it into the kitchen, the pile of wood looked like string clumsily wrapped around something. Clint looked bewildered as O'Neil called out from the other room, "Nae detection, we are clear."

"Check up and down on the innocent, O'Neil," Banks replied.

O'Neil ran flat as fast and quietly as he could behind Clint, going up the stairs.

"What just happened?" Clint asked, looking like he had just been told to move to the North Pole. Banks didn't say anything as he was holding down the pile of wood and getting something out from under his shirt. Clint looked over, realizing that Banks was between him and the phone in the kitchen.

O'Neil came down the stairs and then to the lower floor, pushing Clint out of the way, his short feet making hardly any noise going into the basement.

Then Clint saw something that made his blood go cold as he took small steps into the kitchen to the counter where Banks had just taken out a long knife. Clint saw that the pile of wood was moving, and a pair of shoes were on the far end of all the wood sticking out.

"Is someone in there?" Clint asked hesitantly. Why did he keep asking questions that he really didn't want to know the answer to? Something was wrapped around and around by wood branches so tight and strong they were instantly mummified by wood.

"What are you going to do with that?" Clint gasped, looking at the knife now.

"Stand back," Banks said, and then he took the knife and, with one fast swipe of his arm, started on the top end and finished on the other. The wood-like rope was still only for a moment, and then, all at once, the bindings were pushed away from the inside.

Clint yelped in shock as a muffled moan came from the cascade of wood. Then another sharp, short cry came, but this time from Corbin, whose head shot out of the tangled wood wrappings. Banks took his knife tip with the speed of a viper strike and pointed it right in Corbin's face with tremendous skill. He held it unwavering an inch from his eye.

"Who are you, and why do you come here?" Banks demanded. His voice was not loud, but it was one not to be questioned.

Corbin was held by fear in a silent scream, opened mouth, not moving his eyes away from the knife. He just lay paralyzed, not even breathing.

"Wait," Clint yelled, throwing his arms over his friend. Banks didn't put the knife away, but he did move it back far enough not to be so threatening.

"Do you know this boy? Is he safe? Can he be trusted?" Banks demanded; it didn't sound like a command to know, but the look he gave Clint said it was.

For a fraction of a second, Clint laughed at the thought of saying that he'd never seen Corbin before in his life, but luckily, he didn't. "This is my best friend; he was with me this morning. He is at risk as much as I am from what was after me. He needs your help, too. Please don't hurt him. He's just having a really bad day," Clint pleaded.

Without waiting, Banks put away the knife as O'Neil returned from downstairs. "Both their heids are out the winda but they seem as Jake as can be." Then he gave a reassuring nod toward Clint, seeing that he didn't understand what he just said. Now that the knife was gone, some life had returned to Corbin, and he could at least look around the room even though his mouth was still open. He was white as snow as he sat up a little higher on the counter with his eyes popping.

"O'Neil, he is friendly, but tell the others to keep vigilant," Banks commanded O'Neil, and then, with a fatherly expression as O'Neil left the room, Banks turned to Corbin. "Sorry about that, son, but we had to make sure."

"AHHHHHHHHHHHHHH," Corbin screamed as loud as he could, as if he'd been saving all his breath up for hours.

"He has been doing that a lot lately," Clint told Banks in response to his bewildered look. "He really is all right… most of the time," Clint added.

The kitchen was littered with pieces of wood in thin strands that had now become hard and fossilized. For the first time, a sheepish grin came across Banks's face. Clint was surprised and found something about this man that made him feel safer as he started to examine everything that had happened that day. The strange man who seemed to change sizes with the red face, the knives that almost had taken his life, the trouble after school, and now his best friend mummy wrapped by a tree.

Clint braced himself as these memories tripled in speed before him and then slowed, bringing him to one conclusion. Banks was examining Corbin, who was searching around as if he were looking for someone to jump out with a camera, calling out that he was part of a prank show for television. Corbin's gaze stopped on Clint while he searched for a simple explanation of someone playing a joke on them. Corbin saw Clint's face change from a look of interest to concern as he looked around at each one of them with a new understanding.

"You guys are for real, aren't you?" Clint asked tensely.

"Of course, we are real, whit do yoo think we are, a tale that didn't tally?" O'Neil barked impatiently from behind him.

"No, I mean you guys are telling the truth. You are not from here," Clint turned from O'Neil to see Banks's eyes like a mirror into his own.

"We are telling the truth. Why would we want to lie?" Banks said indifferently.

"Lie. Lie? You guys are, are real? This is all real!" Clint said, making wild gestures with his hands gripping his hair and then holding them over his mouth.

"Are yoo kidding, of course we are telling yoo the truth, and what did yoo take us fur some wild people on your viewing boxes?" O'Neil called back.

Banks leaned against the counter, giving Clint and Corbin a wry smile. Clint thought he looked like one of his parents when they asked him a question they knew Clint had an answer to. Corbin could only sit looking perplexed and out of place.

"Our origin is unimportant at this time. We need your help, Clint," Banks ordered.

Clint thought he saw O'Neil give Banks a surprised look as if he didn't agree with that kind of command for someone so young. Banks looked back at O'Neil and, without talking, warned him not to challenge his order. O'Neil was at a loss for words for a moment until he looked at Clint but talked to Banks. "With yer permission, sir?"

Banks nodded his approval and started gathering up the wood. Clint thought that Banks seemed frustrated with himself. Clint was momentarily confused about how O'Neil's and Banks' moods kept changing and how he couldn't keep up with it. Meanwhile, Corbin was still looking like he had just popped out of a cake meant for a party but ended up at a funeral, wondering what had gone wrong. O'Neil watched Clint, wondering how he should put what he wanted to say. Before he could say anything, Clint interjected, now that the awful truth was hitting him in the chest that this was all for real.

"Is Corbin going to be OK?" Clint asked as his hands started to shake.

"Way shouldn't the wee lad be? Uh, maybe noot so wee, is he?" O'Neil chirped. "He is a fine strappin' young laddie, and if he is your friend that speaks highly ay him. If he did make it out alive when an imp wis after him, that's not bad my boy, not bad at aw."

"IMP?" Is that what that thing was?" Corbin asked, sounding shocked. "Did you guys bring it? Is it loose? I'm allergic to imps! How many are here? Do they come in pairs? Imps are European, aren't they?" Corbin looked frantically around as he stood up on the counter, dancing like a woman frightened of a mouse.

Banks didn't show his surprise as he muttered, "Kids," under his breath, taking an armful of wood out through the back door as Corbin whimpered.

"It's all right, son, new one here will hurt yoo," O'Neil began, but when he saw the remaining wood pieces around on the floor he added shyly, "Uhyeah, about 'at, we are sorry about tying yoo up, but we thought yoo were, uh, someone else. Uh, somethin' else."

Corbin slowly stopped dancing but started to brush off all his clothes as if he were covered with invisible ants.

"Stop that!" Clint called as he came forward, grabbing Corbin's hands, "Why don't you start telling people about that rash thing?"

All three of them froze and shared a very awkward moment as they locked eyes.

Thankfully, Corbin's lips were the thing to move when he asked, "Is Mr. Potato Head speaking English?" Corbin asked, still confused. Clint pulled and helped Corbin down.

"Look here, booth ay yoo," O'Neil said firmly. "There are dangers here that yoo have never dreamed of things from our world 'at will not gonnae stop at nothing tae get the what da are after."

"We are wasting time," Banks ordered. Corbin and Clint jumped, not noticing that he had returned. It was amazing how quietly he moved, Clint thought. "The rest of the family will be here soon. We need to get the Requiem, then regroup until the portal opens in three days," Banks said, more to himself as he picked up the last of the wood off the floor and counter.

He gave a sharp look at Clint. "You said before you didn't know where the Requiem is." He set the wood pieces down on the counter and started pacing again as he spoke, "We will stay until it is found. The Fury knows your location is somewhere around here, but they might not know we are on site. We will guard and protect until the Requiem is found and—"

"Hold on!" Clint barked.

The reaction around the room was immediate at these words. Corbin, already scared out of his wits and with his drawers probably filled, jumped back, hitting the counter and bouncing off, hitting the floor with a loud thud. O'Neil looked like he was going to laugh for a moment, then stood straight as a board, arching his short back so his beard that came down to his chest quivered. Banks stopped pacing and eyed Clint in warning as if he had just done something very wrong.

"I don't have a requirement or whatever. My parents are out of town, and you are not staying here. So, you can do something with Magic Grow on my trees out front. Who cares? I want my life back to normal," Clint said in desperation. He felt the tears start to come from behind his eyes as weariness filled his chest from this new emotion. Everything suddenly felt lost. His heart and head were so out of touch with everything he held dear. It was as if someone had turned his world upside down.

"The only world you can change, kid, is yourself," Banks said as if to console him, but since Clint's face didn't change, Banks realized his comment hadn't helped. Then he turned to O'Neil in frustration, saying, "I don't expect them to understand. They are just children. We will stay here and protect them until we find the Requiem. I want guards around this house and fortifications for all essential people. Once done, sweep the house for the Requiem and have some of the men double back and probe the area for the opposition. O'Neil, you lead them after we brief these two."

"Sir!" O'Neil said in the affirmative.

"Now, you two," Banks said, looking at Clint and Corbin, who was still lying on the floor behind the counter for some reason.

"Corbin was it, where is he?" Banks asked.

Corbin's head slowly appeared as he rose, still holding Clint's hand like a shy child being introduced to a stranger.

"Corbin and Clint." Corbin shot up like a plant at being addressed by what sounded like a general. "First thing is first," Banks continued, eyeing Corbin oddly for a moment and then pacing again. "Is it uncommon for your family to be this late?"

Clint's head started to hurt as he was being spoken to like a soldier rather than someone his age. "No, not really, with my parents gone," he said weakly, his strength gone. With all these emotions turning in him, he noticed and felt that Corbin was still holding his hand. Feeling very silly, he jerked it away, looking like he had noticed a spider on his hand. This seemed to bring Corbin to his senses.

"We need your help if we are all going to live through this. Did you see anything else out there that was different this morning?" Banks asked.

Clint and Corbin looked at each other. Clint hoped Corbin would speak for a change to give him a break.

"No, not really, other than you guys," Corbin said after a long pause. "Which brings me to the question that must be asked. WHO ARE YOU GUYS?"

"Ok, this is what we have to do," Banks said determinedly, ignoring him. "We need to get everyone in the house at once to be safe. First, if that imp could find you, they can find your family.   Secondly,   we need to protect you or eliminate the threat but keep things as normal as possible to the outside world. Third, we need to find the Requiem even if you don't know where it is."

"Imp again? I can't help but notice nobody has told me if that was the thing that was trying to use a knife as a dipstick to check my oil. Is that what you call that thing that was after us this morning… and you are saying there are more of those things around?" Corbin asked fearfully as O'Neil returned on his way to the backyard.

"An imp," O'Neil interjected, pulling out his hip flask, "is a wee man who is one solid color with wee horns on tap o' his pointy wee head. They hae the ability tae grow in size or shrink tae a degree; they are the Fury's workhorse. They ain't very strong but can sure take a walloping. Does that sound like whit was stuck tae your shoes this morn?"

Both Clint and Corbin looked scared. "I think so. Hey, I still have it in my bag," Clint said, remembering what was in his bag in his bedroom. He ran off to get the dagger.

"Have what?" Banks asked.

"What's the Fury?" Corbin asked while Clint waved to Banks to hold on a moment as he ran out of the kitchen toward his room.

"The Fury is the organization of all those who the Reclamation changes. The Fury is their leadership, army, and government," Banks said quickly as he pulled something out of a pocket that looked like jerky.

"Changed," Corbin said in confusion. Banks tried to explain the Reclamation again to Corbin this time but to no avail. Banks explained everything he had told Clint about why they were there and looking for something called the Requiem. They were saved from another question from Corbin when Clint returned with the dagger. He sat it down gently on the kitchen island counter. It still felt odd in his hand and was completely out of place on the counter.

"This is one of the daggers thrown at us," Clint said, wondering if this was helping.

Banks looked at it for an instant, then picked it up, examined it, and handed it to O'Neil. "Show the team," O'Neil said nothing but stood to attention before he gathered the last of the wood and went off to the backyard.

"With luck, we will get what we need and not have a fight on our hands, but if we do, you both need to do exactly what I tell you when I tell you. Is that understood?"

"Yes, sir!" Corbin said happily, sounding like he'd just been given a free candy bar for changing his attitude. He smiled at Clint as if he were already part of the team. Clint looked at him, thinking his friend had accepted this too quickly. He was so eager and willing to go along with everything that Clint couldn't believe it.

"What is wrong with you?" Clint scoffed. "These aren't the kind that love thy neighbor. These are the kind that wake thy neighbors." To this, Corbin didn't reply. He just smiled momentarily at him and snapped him a salute.

"Why are you here anyway?" Clint asked Corbin in frustration at his friend's new joy of being a recruit.

"You didn't call me!" Corbin said. Clint hit his forehead in surprise, feeling dumb. "I'm sorry… I was distracted by some… unexpected guests," Clint said sarcastically.

Banks took a large bite of his jerky and chewed it quickly, seeming like he hadn't eaten for a while. Clint thought it was a good time to ask questions while his mouth was full. "Where did you get those clothes?"

Banks looked down at how he was dressed and then at Clint and Corbin, noticing the difference between their school uniforms of black trousers, white shirts with ties, and his golfing attire.

When he had finished chewing, he started to talk, not like a general but as a man who thought he owed them an explanation.

"We arrived three days ago. I do not know where we arrived, but there were long stretches of grass and some areas with flags in the center of them. Some areas of sand pits and pools of water around them. We thought it was an obstacle training course."

"Mountain Brooks Golf Course," Corbin said in surprise. "It's not too far from here, and I heard someone broke into their worker's shed. So that's where you got those clothes?"

"We found these in a box in what we thought was a barn that housed some horse carts," Banks said nonchalantly. "We buried anything else that would give us away, and early that morning, two men with clubs came along, hitting white balls at targets. We subdued them, and Nix transferred our tongue into your language."

"What?" Clint and Corbin asked at the same time.

"We knocked them out while Nix blessed us all so we can speak and understand your words." Neither of the boys knew what Banks was trying to say, and rather than press their luck, they didn't ask about it again. Banks took another large bite of jerky and, with his mouth full, said, "We have been looking for you since then, and we only have three days left before we need to be at the portal entrance by midnight to go home. We have until then to retrieve the Requiem and save our world."

Before anyone could say anything else, the Squirrel was back, its little claws scratching on the wood floor from the back door this time. Right behind him was O'Neil. "Sir," he said hurriedly, stopping just short of the kitchen and bracing his weight on the hallway door frame. "Sir, two of the family members are coming: one is the younger sister, who was described as Kayla, and the other has the features of Tamara."

"Let them pass, but make sure there is nothing following them. Nothing comes close to the house," Banks said fast with a mouth still full of jerky. He was hurrying to get to the front door again as quietly as possible when he called back, "Corbin, clean up any remnants of the wood. Leave no trace. Clint, you are with me."

Corbin jumped to action as if someone had just cracked a whip behind him. In contrast, Clint moved with the same purpose as if he was walking to the principal's office. He followed Banks, wishing he could go to bed as he looked, shocked, at how fast Corbin was working. He was working harder than Clint had ever seen him. He didn't even notice that having a squirrel running loose in the house was odd. O'Neil took the squirrel, and Clint watched him run out the back way.

"Almost killed by a mad imposter, sending out invitations like lottery tickets, best friend tied up like a hot pocket, squirrels telling people things, Corbin working hard, what's next for me?" Clint muttered sarcastically, wishing that this would end soon while he caught up to Banks.

The feeling in the house was tense as Banks got to the lobby, but this time, he didn't take his previous position at the door. He crept quickly into the study, waving for Clint to follow as he strategically watched out one of the windows toward the driveway. Clint followed slowly, checking his watch; typically, he would be working on his homework, and if his mother were here, she would have scolded him for breaking his daily schedule. Banks motioned for Clint to come and look with him out the window.

Clint sat down and peered out the window past the bushes and leaves of the trees. It wasn't tough to see what Banks wanted him to look at. At the far end of the sidewalk, past their yard, their property met Mrs. Hutchings's. At the stone fence that separated their property were two people. Clint squinted in the late afternoon light so he could see two outlines of girls coming slowly toward the house.

"Are those your sisters?" Banks asked as he retreated down out of view from the window.

Clint watched the two people moving, unable to make them out for a moment past a lamp post. It didn't help Clint that he felt Banks's eyes on him. First, there was a bush in the way, then the fence line, and another tree.

"I don't know, I think so," Clint said, not sounding like he cared much.

"We need to know so you are either sure or not. Are they your family?" Banks said reprovingly. Clint didn't like being told off. Most of the time, Clint would have said something to give Banks a hard time, but one look from Banks made Clint think twice before defying him.

"Uh, I think they are…" Clint said." That was Tamara's hairstyle next to another lamp that lined the way up to their driveway next to the mailbox. Then, someone smaller and with blonde hair took a moment next to the mailbox. Only Kayla would see that the mail was brought up with their parents gone.

"Yep, that's them."

"Are you sure?" Banks asked, staring at him intensely.

Clint took another long look out the window. His sister's heads were bobbing up the driveway now. Clint and Banks couldn't see them directly from their low view, and bushes were in the way.

"We need to know for certain," Banks repeated.

"It's definitely them," Clint said with a dubious look when a new thought entered his mind.

"Right," Banks said, getting to his feet and grinning generously.

"We will need time to explain all this to your family, so please bring them into the room where we talked before. We will give you a moment, and then let us know when we can come in. Is that sufficient?" Banks asked.

Not wanting another disapproving look from Banks, Clint nodded in agreement as he suppressed his stubbornness and urged to be indignant toward authority. He went toward the door as the voices of his two sisters arguing came to him. Kayla talked to Tamara as if she were the reason for the delay in coming home so late. For once, Clint appreciated hearing that he was not the only troublemaker in the house.

As he stood at the door, a new thought seemed to press through all others. What was he going to say? How was he going to say it? The doorknob turned, and he grabbed it impulsively, not letting it turn.

Not knowing what he was doing, the doorknob suddenly finished turning despite his grip. *"Don't let them in,"* he thought. *"You have to save them. What will* they *do to them?"* The door creaked open normally as a pink hand pushed it open. The little voice in his head told him, *"Now, do it now, RUN."*

It was time; if he was going to do something, it had to be now, but he didn't do it.

"No," came Tamara's voice with the open door, "I was talking to him, not kissing him. You should even know the difference between those two things. Besides, stay away from me and what I do. It's none of your biz!" Tamara shouted as she came into the house.

"You two were talking mouth to mouth if you ask me," Kayla retorted. "And if that's not kissing, that is the most disgusting conversation with tongues I have ever seen. It was like two blind people trying to read lips by touching them together and one repeating the words of the encyclopedia while the other was trying to repeat them. I'm going to tell Mom and Dad about this." Kayla indicated a small red book under her arm. Kayla entered the house as aggrieved and agitated as a mother would while picking up their child from prison.

"I am keeping track of everything that is going on while Mom and Dad are away, and I am keeping a section, especially for you, marked undead boyfriend lip activity," Kayla said importantly, tapping the book under her arm again.

In two steps, Clint slammed the door with one hand and locked it with the other before his sisters could turn around.

"Clint, what the—" Wham! Tamara was cut off from saying anything else as Clint was so emotionally overcome that he wrapped both Tamara and Kayla in a bone-crushing hug. He buried his head between them, holding them tightly. He was thankful to be alive for the first time today and didn't want ever to let go.

"Uh, Clint? You all right?" Kayla asked as if this were one of the most disgusting things she had ever had to ask her brother. Clint held on with a firm grip until Tamara started slapping him, yelling, "Get off me! Get off me," smacking every inch of him that she could reach.

"Ouch," Clint cried as he hit the floor, once again wishing they had put carpet by the front door.

"What are you doing disgusto?" Tamara demanded as she straightened her black dress and quickly checked her many earrings and jewelry. "You scared the life out of me with your sudden love-sick emotion. You are turning out to be just like your older brother, one big hormone."

"We have to go. We need to get out of here now!" Clint pleaded as he got up and pushed them both, trying to make them move back toward the door. With all his might, he could only move them a couple of inches. "Move, please!" he cried.

"What is up with you? Did you hit your head again, or *should* you hit your head again?" Tamara called in disgust.

"Come on, Clint, everything is going to be all right. Just tell us what is wrong. What happened to you?" Kayla asked lovingly, rubbing his back as high as her short arm could reach while securing her book still under it.

From the hallway came the sound of those tiny feet against the wood floor. Clint's eyes snapped wide open as the sound moved behind him, and to his disbelief, he felt something pull aside his pant leg. The weight went quickly up his body.

Clint screamed as the tiny animal ran up past his hip. Instinctively, he pushed off from his two sisters and started to dance as the squirrel's feet began to tickle him as it made its way up his shirt. Both Kayla and Tamara were looking at him in bewilderment. From the look in their eyes, they knew he had gone entirely out of his mind. Clint danced, feeling the little claws penetrate his clothes and tickle his body until it went over his shoulder blade. Nuts finally came to a halt and rested on his left shoulder.

Kayla and Tamara screamed so loud that they made Clint's ears ring. Tamara made a mad dance as if someone was shooting at her feet. Kayla was so afraid she had dropped her motherly manner and couldn't even talk clearly. All she kept trying to say was "rat, rat, rat". What came out was "Lat, at, yat, rat," as she pointed at Clint's shoulder.

They both ran screaming down the hall, Kayla holding her book with both arms close to her chest, Tamara hot on her heels, waving her hands high over her head as she dropped all her books. Clint followed, tripping on them with the squirrel screaming squeakily in fear as well, hanging on as best as it could, digging those ticklish claws into his skin.

"Wait," Clint cried, following his sister's shouts as they echoed down the hallway.

"Hey, girls," Corbin said cheerfully, paying no notice to their crazed action as he was sweeping up the kitchen floor, blocking the way to the backyard. The girls were undeterred from yelling and incomparable babble Tamara was giving as they turned fast into the dining room. They separated, one running along the right side of the table, the other the left side. They met on the far end of the table, slamming hard into one another. Clint entered the room with the squirrel still firmly attached but no longer screaming as the two girls were holding on to one another tightly.

"No, listen! You don't understand, he is not a lat, I mean rat, there is a lot here you don't understand," Clint tried to explain but no one was paying any attention to him. There was a hurried rush of footsteps and a call from Corbin cheerfully explaining that they were in the dining room. O'Neil was suddenly at his side, panting as if he had just appeared by Clint like magic, holding the wall to retain his balance.

"There yoo are, come here yoo bad boy," he called out with a smile and with all the gentleness of a mother bird moving an egg. He took the squirrel and sat him on his shoulder. The muffled whimpers and sniffles brought O'Neil's attention to Clint's sisters holding each other on the far side of the room.

"Oh, uhh, I am sorry," he apologized, looking like a rough old basset hound and nodding with love toward the squirrel. "But sometimes me Nuts here get the better ay me."

Kayla and Tamara's eyes rolled up in the back of their heads as they fainted. They hit the ground together in a heap, and Clint covered his eyes while Corbin walked in and asked, "What's wrong with them?"

"Noo idea." O'Neil shrugged as he and Corbin left the room. While O'Neil was talking to his squirrel about how strange girls were, leaving Clint alone to sort out his two sisters lying on the floor.

Twenty-Six

YOU WOULD NEVER READ THAT IN SOMEONE'S RESUME.

It took some time for Clint's sisters to come around. When he finally got them to wake up, Clint wished he'd left them passed out on the floor. He didn't know what was worse, Tamara screaming "rabies, rabies!" or Kayla trying to get to the phone to call their parents and pest control, a priest, the national guard, the veterinarian, and even Mrs. Hutchings's dogs.

It took him a long time to make them stop yelling and even longer to get them to listen to him as he tried to explain what all these strangers were doing in their house. He struggled to tell them anything because he was still trying to wrap his mind around it himself. Right before he would give up, Banks came to his aid. He went into the room, followed closely by Corbin and O'Neil. O'Neil came in with his chin lowered, looking sheepish without his squirrel. He explained as best as he could about the Requiem and that others here would kill them all for it. Kayla didn't believe it until Clint told them what had happened that morning. O'Neil showed them the dagger while Clint held out his book bag and history book with a hole in it. Tamara was still skeptical and mocked them at every chance until Ohwiler came in.

When Ohwiler walked in, she let out a small squeak, and after recovering herself, she said, "Nice paint job. Did you want to look like a flavored popsicle stick?" Clint gave a heavy sigh and closed his eyes. He didn't see Ohwiler look for approval from Banks for his next action. When it was silently given with a nod, Ohwiler held out a pinecone to Tamara, and in the blink of an eye, they watched her make it grow into what was unmistakably a tiny, three-inch tree that had Tamara's face reflected in the side of the wood with leaves for hair. Silent, wonder-filled Tamara, Kyla, Clint, and Corbin. It seemed now that all four of them were facing the same problem that Clint and Corbin had had since that morning. There were so many questions, with so little time and no sure answer to what they would do next.

"How did she do that with the tree? How can I learn that?" Tamara asked. Clint thought it was amazing that his sister, who would only bend over to pick up a coin because it had a picture of someone dead on it, would change so abruptly at what she'd just seen.

"We will answer whatever questions we can for you, of course. But we have questions as well that are critical, even more important, I dare say, than how Druids work," Banks said from the head of the table, calling everyone's attention back to him.

Luckily, they had stopped talking momentarily because Tremayne had just entered the room.

"Sir."

"Yes?" Banks asked without looking at him. Oddly, Banks was looking at Clint.

"Sir, our supplies are here, sir," Tremayne said as his green eyes roamed around the room, admiring the pictures changing. When they fell on Tamara and Kayla, he lifted one heavy eyebrow at how they were gapping at him with both mouths open.

It was Banks who brought everyone's mind back from wandering. "O'Neil, get our supplies distributed, rotate the guard, and take thirty for rest, confirm defenses are up. Then report back. We still have two other family members out there somewhere." O'Neil got to his feet abruptly, saying, "Sir!" before leaving the room.

"Where are your two brothers?" Banks asked.

Kayla was the first to answer, "Well, Cody should be getting out of football practice any time now, but he might go straight to work. He has a job at the gas station just a few blocks away, and Grant is camping."

"Locations?" Banks asked quickly.

Kayla looked over at Tamara for help, but she shook her head. Her stiff black hair hardly moved as she shrugged her shoulders in a negative response.

"I don't remember. You're the one who keeps such good tabs on people in this family, whether they look like they are kissing or not. How should I know where he is?" Tamara spat.

"Well, since he's your brother, I thought you might care enough to remember where he is?" Kayla answered back smartly, getting to her feet. She was so short that this hardly made a difference. "And I am still telling Mom about what you did with that boy's lips," she added with a smirk.

"Oh yeah, like I am going to keep track of everyone just in case some freaks with horrible taste in fashion come. Besides, it's not like you will ever make out with anyone," Tamara blurted, getting to her feet.

"Silence!" Banks ordered. His voice was not loud but carried the weight of authority that hit everyone's hearts in the room. The room went as quiet as if someone just announced a death in the family.

"Who knows their locations?" Banks asked solemnly.

"Cody would know where Grant is. He talked with the scoutmaster that picked him up," Kayla said eagerly, as if she wanted to make up for getting out of hand earlier.

"We do not have much time. It will be dark soon," Banks said as he got to his feet. It was odd, but everyone, including Clint, stood when he did.

"We will give you time to rest, and then we will retrieve the one called Cody. Who will go with us as our guide?" Banks asked, looking around first to Corbin, Clint, and Tamara.

Kyla raised her hand as if she were in her class when the teacher asked a question. Banks gave her a warm smile and said, "Any others?"

Clint felt strange about what was going on. Then, to his amazement, he saw Corbin raise his hand. "What are you doing? You don't ever volunteer. Not even for that kissing booth for last Valentine's Day dance last year when Betty Hayward was in line and the guy who was doing it was on break," Clint exclaimed as the very thought was too horrible even to contemplate and left a bad taste in his mouth.

Sounding hurt, Corbin looked at his raised hand and said to his friend, "I want to help. I will call my mom and tell her I will be sleeping over here for the next couple of days. Believe me, it will be better for me after the note I got from the principal the other day. Every time she looks at me since then, it's like she's worried I'll tell her I'm a drug mule or something."

Shrugging, Clint said, "Well, I might as well be one too then." Then slowly he raised his hand. Tamara looked around the room and raised her own. "I am not doing it to help you guys. I just want to learn what I can and get you on your way," she said.

It was a good speech even by her standards and everyone smiled, everyone except Banks. He stared at Tamara as if he had never seen her before.

"What of the girl downstairs? What can we do about her?" Banks asked, still looking without blinking at Tamara. Everyone lowered their hands, and Tamara did it with haste of defiance, almost looking like she regretted raising it with the look Banks was giving her.

Clint had been thinking about her, "I say we don't do anything. With any luck, she will do what she does best and stay down there minding her own business, and you guys will be gone before she knows what is going on."

Banks looked like he was thinking about that idea for a moment as he continued to watch Tamara. She was starting to shrink under his glare as the sun began to set over the mountain and trees, giving the day the last light it would see from the sky, as the clouds were almost over them now.

"All right, we will leave Jamie out of this for now until we must," Banks said soberly, still peering across the table at Tamara. "Unless something changes. And what about the old woman upstairs?"

"Well, she has to have her meals brought up to her, and we have to make sure she is well taken care of with her medication. Someone should check on her periodically to spend time with her; they could read or just talk to her about her past," Kayla said, hinting with a smirk at Tamara.

Clint and Corbin both let out a slight snicker of amusement from the looks that were being exchanged between Kayla and Tamara. "And who is going to do all that for you?" Tamara said, gritting her teeth.

"May I have a moment to talk to Tamara alone?" Banks said in a soft voice as he leaned forward with fists on the table. Clint was taken by surprise for a moment. He had been alone with this man, but he had spent most of the early evening with him. To ask to be alone with his sister when he had just earned her trust about an hour ago was something else entirely. He was even more surprised that Corbin and Kayla both got out of their chairs as if someone had just stuck a porcupine under them and were already almost out of the dining room before Clint got up.

Banks must have noticed the look on Clint's face because before he left the dining room, he put a firm hand very softly on Clint's shoulder. "It will be all right. I just want to talk to her. I won't shut the door. Please go get some food and change into something you don't mind getting dirty." He was addressing Clint, but his eyes never left Tamara. "Please go now and tell the others."

Clint was going to ask to stay, but when he looked into Banks's brown eyes, he forgot all about his concerns. Banks gave him that same grin that he had when he'd first spoken to Clint. Clint walked on and was halfway into the kitchen before he remembered why he wanted to stay.

"Clint, you better have a look at this," Kayla called from somewhere in the front of the house.

He walked down the hall and found Corbin, O'Neil, and Kayla all in the television room watching the six o'clock news.

"Oh good, Clint, you had better watch this," Kayla said as she turned up the volume as O'Neil watched in astonishment. He looked like he was itching to ask a question but waited when he saw the looks of concern on everyone else's faces. He stroked his beard as the newsreader opened with a breaking news report.

CHAPTER

Twenty-Seven

WHO SAID THERE'S NOTHING GOOD ON TV?

"**G**ood evening, and this is Nicole Wilsonland for your Channel Ten News at six. Shockingly, we have for you tonight the story of the police officer who was assaulted. A sergeant reported that this officer was sent to investigate a disturbance of Halloween juveniles. After some altercation where shots had been fired, he had not been heard from until the following morning when police, who have been stretched to breaking point, verified what happened to their lost man. Now we take you on location with Ned Sanguster."

The television screen left the good-looking woman behind her news desk and went to a remote-looking farm with a short, handsome man with black hair with, a touch of gray, and a matching color mustache. Beside him were two odd-looking farmers who looked very pale but excited to be on the news. They kept trying to smarten themselves by readjusting their clothes and hair, but sadly, they only revealed their farmer's tans.

"Buenas Noches, Nicole!" The man greeted the newsreader with a beautiful smile. "As you can see behind me, there is Officer Cooper's police vehicle that has been left here since his altercation. Officer Cooper was not able to give comment, but we have two eyewitnesses who, oddly enough, were found locked in the back seat of the officer's vehicle until the next morning."

Ned's smile widened as he raised his free hand to hide a snicker while lowering his microphone for a moment.

"What can you tell us, Mr. and Mrs. Bernard?" Ned asked as he held out the microphone for them both. Mr. Bernard snatched it out of Ned's hand, and with a smile showing how many teeth he was missing, he started to talk excitedly.

"Well, me and the misses was about to go to bed and we was haven some difference of opinion on who was to use de TV remote when it happened, cuss all the tarnation." With a long look of personal satisfaction and wide, wild eyes, he said, "The aliens came."

Ned had to pull Mr. Bernard's hand back over to him so he could speak into the microphone, "Excuse me, did you say aliens?"

Mr. Bernard, looking like a wounded hippo with suspenders, yanked the microphone back as the cameraman had trouble figuring out who to focus on as the picture bobbed around.

As the microphone was being fought over, Mrs. Bernard said pompously, "Thet's right."

"Shut up, ma, I is da one who is doing da talk'n," Mr. Bernard bellowed once he had control of the microphone. "People jest reckon your jest plan stooped ma, now where was I, Oh yessuh, the aliens." Mr. and Mrs. Bernard looked more enthusiastic than ever while Ned had to turn away from the scene, being so overwhelmed with silent giggles.

"They came af'er the miss's first when she was a going out to our outhouse right out thar," Mr. Bernard pointed without looking away from the camera, hitting Mrs. Bernard in the forehead causing her to fall to the ground and out of sight of the camera.

"They were a-comin' from all sides an' when she came a runnin' into the house a bellerin'. I came from the farm, that's when we phoned the po-lice. Then they came for me and me pride and joy, love of me life, my cow. Had to kill her so they couldn't probe her like they wanted to da to da wif an' me. Took the po-lice a fur piece to get here, I kin tell you that, so me an' da misses were frighten them little—" Whatever Mr. Bernard called them was bleeped out, and that's when Mrs. Bernard reappeared, and she seemed to be missing her wig when she started moving her arms as if she were warming up to fight in a major heavy-weight brawl.

Mr. Bernard was practically jiggling with excitement as he kept talking, "We was able ta hold them little, bleep, bleep, off for some time till officer Cooper came, but he wasn't much help thou, as a mater oh fact we taught he was one of them, dawgone it." Mr. Bernard took a step forward, looked as serious as his unshaven, mostly bald head would allow, and swallowed before he said, only a foot away from the camera, "They can do that you knows, take on the form of others."

Ned gently pulled Mr. Bernard back a step, and, re-gaining his child-like manner, Mr. Bernard went on, "Officer Cooper told us to stay in his vehicle until he got back, but he never did come back. Shut my mouth! We was sho'nuff in there for a long time, I tell you what, we was first afraid of the trunk monkey but when it came time ta use the outhouse again we didn't knows about, what did you call them Ned? Auto-matic deoor locks. They ain't like the little pin that push and den pull, you hit a button in this hyar car and it does it all by its self! I tell you what. We didn't knows about dat. Someone should have told us when you get in a car dat is a button to unlock dat door, I tell you what."

Ned reappeared as the camera panned out away from Mr. and Mrs. Bernard. There were tears of laughter in Ned's eyes and down his cheeks as he reached for the microphone, saying, "Mucho gracias, but we need to take a short break," but Mr. Bernard shoved his hand away while Mrs. Bernard's bony arms shot out as she fought to get a hold of it to talk for once. She never stopped looking at the camera with a tooth grin. "I ant done yet, they gots ta knows about them lights in our field over yonner and the prob'en."

But whatever Mr. Bernard was going to say was cut off when they went to a commercial.

"How do they do that, with the picture from a single glass?" O'Neil asked, "When we was looking fur yoo, I saw one down the street in a window."

"It's called a television," Kayla said smartly as there was an ad going on about child safety in a new car seat.

"It plays movies or shows that are recorded somewhere else and shows them here on the television for entertainment or information," Kayla continued before she was cut off.

"Where is this place that they are showing?" Banks asked from behind Clint, causing him to jump. Banks was right next to him without him knowing it.

"How long have you been standing there?" Clint asked, still breathing hard, holding his chest, leaning on the sofa.

"Long enough," Banks said, looking weary. "Can you get us to that location?" he asked Kayla.

Kayla thought for a moment, "Let's see if they say where it is when the commercial is over."

They were now showing an advertisement on toilet paper when they looked back at the screen, but it was blocked by O'Neil, whose face was now inches from it with his tongue hanging out.

"Hey, down front, move," Corbin called as the news returned with Nicole once again. O'Neil moved to the side as she started to speak.

"Thank you for staying with us as we now return to our harrowing story, which comes to a close as the missing police officer is found. We now rejoin Ned Sanguster, who is live with us out at the scene of Officer Cooper's recovery, Ned." Nicole was gone and once again the screen was showing the farm area, now not with the patrol unit and an old broken-down farmhouse in the background but a farmer's field where there appeared to be a clearing where all the trees, weeds, and grass were pushed down.

"Here is the terrible area where the fallen officer was found," Ned said nobly. The Bernard's were not in the picture but in the background noise the camera was still picking up strange comments like, "I is a-gonna be a star, I was on the TV, I was on the TV, if only Maribel my prize hog was still alive." With the Bernards not in front of the camera. Ned was able to keep a straight face even though his eyes were still watering, and the lines of his tears were still apparent from his laughter.

"The officer was somehow incapacitated and here for hours alone with only his training and nerves of steel to save his life. The police left this terrible area and took all those who are, uh," he looked away from the camera, "comparable witnesses to be questioned. Officer Cooper has been admitted to St. Suadalupe's Hospital and is expected to make a full recovery. Let us hope that no more of our protectors will fall. We have just been cleared to come to this site after it has been searched by a special unit from out of state. This is Ned Sanguster reporting to you live from the Bernard farm just a few miles from Callaway's Bar, adios."

"Thank you, Ned," Nicole Wilsonland said as she was back on. "Now we will have a report on the recent local changes. After thousands of refugees have come to our area, there has been a surprising number of people disappearing. In the past twenty-four hours alone, there have been thirty-two people found missing from around a single area alone. If you see anything suspicious or have any information as to the whereabouts of these people, please call your local law enforcement agency or dial nine, one, one. Authorities strongly urge our community to remain calm and guarantee that Swat and National Guard are on their highest alert of readiness for your family's protection." She finished and sorted through the paperwork that was resting on the desk before her.

"Now we have an update of you on our president's journey with many Olympic champions on the cruise ship Majestic. Later, we will have the president's comments on the growing tension of religion and rumors of world conflict."

"I have seen enough," Banks said.

Kyla took the remote and turned off the television. It seemed only then that O'Neil came back into his right frame of mind. "What happen tae the people in the box?" he said, looking around the room as if he was waiting for them to come out of the walls or the ceiling.

Twenty-Eight
THE OTHER SIDES OF THE COIN

"Please get some food and dress for a recon search and retrieval. We have thirty before you go," Banks said as he left the room.

"What?" Clint asked, not understanding what Banks meant. He followed Banks as he walked toward the kitchen but before he could ask anything else Tamara caught his eye. She was sitting on the stairs with her head down. She was crying softly, holding her head in her hands with her black hair hanging down over her face.

"What happened to you?" Clint asked as he changed direction from following Banks to walking slowly towards his sister. She sat a few steps up the wooden spiral stairs. Clint suddenly felt angry as he was now only two steps down from where she sat, still moaning softly.

"What did he do to you?" he asked angrily. He turned to rush down the stairs to tell Banks off and call the police when Tamara sat up and grabbed his arm. When she looked up, Clint saw her raccoon eyes, makeup running, and very oddly, she smiled. It was the first time he had ever seen his sister smile like that. He had seen her smile before, but it was always from someone else's misery or when she tried to drive off people of authority with that small bag that she carried with her that she said had dirt from a graveyard in it.

"What is it?" Clint asked, looking at her in bewilderment, wishing that she would let him go. She looked at him like she had never done before. She reached up with her other hand and wiped her nose and mouth while holding off her last sniffle. "He just talked to me, and Clint I'm, I'm sorry for everything I have done wrong to you. Please, please forgive me, please," she croaked.

"What?" Clint asked in astonishment. Out of all the things he'd expected her to say, this wasn't it.

Before he could ask something else, she grabbed his arm harder as if she were holding onto a ledge for her life. "Please forgive me. Please," and before he said anything, she buried her face in his elbow and began to cry again, pleading softly, "Please, please."

"I, I forgive you, all right," Clint said quickly, trying to free himself. Not knowing what else to do, he gently rubbed her black hair, feeling like he was just asked to pet Mrs. Hutchings's dog after it had just lifted its leg next to him. After rubbing her head twice, he wished he hadn't done it because she just howled louder. She reached out and hugged him below the waist, holding him fast, making him feel very uncomfortable. She almost made him fall as he grabbed the railing for support, and after a moment, he patted her on the head and said, "I have to go now, sis, they need me, all right?" She started to let him go slowly. Clint reached down and pulled his sister's arms off him. She didn't look up as she started to make her way up the stairs very slowly, as if she were sick. With a click of the door closing, she was gone into her room.

Clint stood for a moment until he turned around and saw Corbin at the bottom of the stairs, looking dumbstruck. "Was that Tamara?" Corbin asked, looking like he had just won a million dollars.

"How should I know? Nothing's right today," Clint said, looking crestfallen.

"It looked like her, but normally she would have done something like hit you, I thought," Corbin said in surprise as he leaned on the handrail.

"I know. This day definitely ranks about a nine on my weird-o-meter," Clint said as he and Corbin went into the kitchen for food while Kayla busied herself for a moment writing in her red book. Although none of them said it, they were all wondering what was going to happen next.

Twenty-Nine

THAT THING THAT WENT BUMP IN THE NIGHT.

THAT WAS ME

Clint, Corbin, and Kayla ate for thirty minutes while talking about all that day's oddities. Corbin had called his mother explaining that he was going to spend the night and through all her moans of dismay wishing that he would be a saint, she consented. Kayla then tried to call Cody at the gas station but was unsuccessful.

"It's no big deal," she said to calm Corbin, who started to panic, thinking the worst. "It's amazing that he even has a job. He doesn't do anything there that anyone would call work and one time, I overheard Mom tell Dad that the only reason they kept him there was a lot of students or football fans would show up to see him. He is probably talking to some girl who only likes him because he scored two touchdowns in his last game. Honestly!" Kayla said as she slammed the phone down, still unable to reach Cody for the fourth time.

"Where are all the other house crashers?" Clint said, looking around.

"They must be out in the back or something," Corbin said through a mouth full of cookies. "It's not like they are taking a nice stroll through the park waving to all the people driving by."

"I don't know, this is California," Kayla said, giving a soft smile. "They could run for governor. It might be good for them." They all laughed at this and spent the rest of their time talking about all the questions they wished that they could have answered. Kayla was wondering how a Druid could make things grow.

Corbin groaned, saying, "You wouldn't want to know that if you had seen it firsthand like I did." He said he was very eager to talk to O'Neil to ask if he could learn to talk to animals. Clint was curious about what untold wonders they still hadn't seen yet.

O'Neil came in with the warning that they had five minutes left. They each went into their rooms and changed, with Corbin joining Clint. Corbin, being much larger than Clint, couldn't find any clothes to borrow, so they went into Clint's parents' room to see if there was anything they could find that would fit him that was dark. He had to settle for Clint's stepfather's old silk pajamas that were mostly black. He had to roll up the sleeves and legs, so they would fit properly but that didn't help the swishing sound he made when he walked around.

"This is like the best night game ever, isn't it?" Corbin said enthusiastically.

"I hope we just get there and get back, and if you have to run in those things, please just don't do it next to me. You sound like you have a loose fan belt walking around in those things. I wish we could drive," Clint said soberly.

They both came downstairs, and, not wanting to do anything too bad, they waited in the kitchen to be joined by Kayla, who walked in wearing her old gymnastic outfit, which comprised of tight leggings and a leotard that also covered her arms. When Clint and Corbin saw her, they both started laughing.

"What?" she protested. "It's the darkest thing I have, all right!"

It was lucky because O'Neil returned from the backyard with two others that Clint knew to be Chiowood and Hobb. They were dressed very differently. They had abandoned their golfing clothes and had dressed themselves in what must be something from where they came. O'Neil was wearing what looked like brown pants and a heavy black shirt that was buttoned up the front, but over that was a large square patch of the same material that buttoned over that to cover his front.

Hobb was wearing similar pants but had a dark green shirt that was covered in long pieces of cloth with greenery on them that made him look like a walking bush. It was something like what Clint thought a person in the Special Forces would wear. His top was folded back, giving him the appearance of a two-legged shrubbery with a head poking out of the top.

Chiowood looked the most normal of the three. He had on black pants, with a white shirt and a long black cloak that seemed to shimmer in the lights of the kitchen.

"Here we gow," O'Neil said smartly. He talked as if he were a new bus driver taking them all to school for the first time and felt like he had to explain the rules.

"Corbin, yoo are going with Chiowood here. He will be covering our right side, Kayla yoo are tae accompany Hobb here," he waved a hand to Hobb, who was standing to his left side.

"And Clint, yoo will be with me going down the center. Transun will be our back up an' will be following us in just ou' of site, all right," O'Neil finished, rubbed his hands together, revealing that he wore thick brown gloves that looked like tough leather.

This seemed to be overkill, Clint thought, to just get his brother and tell him to come home. One look from Kayla should be enough, but remembering what had happened to Corbin and him that morning was enough to appreciate not going alone. They didn't say anything or give any sign that they understood, nor did it seem apparent that O'Neil needed any confirmation.

"Banks has talked tae Tamara tae make sure that your Grain Mammy should be taken care ay tonight and that yer sister Jamie should not get suspicious. The rest of our group will stay here too watch ower the house," O'Neil went on. "If there are any problems, come run'n here as fast as yoo can. Alrigh'?"

Kayla raised her hand. "Yes," O'Neil answered. "Did you say Tamara was going to stay and take care of everything?" she asked in disbelief.

"Yeh, anything else?" O'Neil said flatly as if that was not a proper question. O'Neil didn't waste any time as Kayla raised her eyebrows.

"Tamara taking care of someone else, that's a first," Kayla said bristly.

"All right, we will meet yoo out front in two. I need tae report tae Banks," and he started to walk out to the back with Hobb and Chiowood following.

"Move out," he called over his shoulder.

Clint, Kayla, and Corbin thought for a moment, and then, realizing what O'Neil meant, they left the kitchen quickly. Clint and Kayla exchanged worried looks as they opened the front door while Corbin seemed to be having the time of his life. The night was dark without a star in the sky and the lights from the homes of their neighbors were oddly misty. The air was not cool but felt like it came from a steam line that turned the normal cool night air into a warm, muggy night. Also, the light from the lamp posts was dimmed by some sort of haze. Here and there were signs of life as a light in a window went dark as someone walked in front of it.

"Boy, it's humid tonight," Corbin said gleefully to Clint.

"What are you trying to do? Make light conversation?" Clint asked, looking at him as if he just asked if he were pregnant.

Corbin took the hint as they stood waiting in silence until Corbin started to laugh.

"What?" Kayla asked.

"Look at yourselves," Corbin huffed. Clint looked down and suddenly felt stupid, thinking what they must have looked like to an unknowing person passing by. They were all in odd clothes, standing out in front of their house on a school night. Clint looked anxiously at himself in his black turtleneck and black pants, with his black church shoes. All three started to laugh, not being able to stop.

"I wonder what would happen if Mrs. Hutchings found out what was going on over here," Kayla chuckled.

"She probably knows more about what is going on than we do. As she only lives to spy on us and jeopardize our lives," Kayla said through a snicker.

"That has been going around since this morning," Corbin groaned.

"Mrs. Hutchings must be behind everything," Clint sniffled past a laugh.

"Hey Hutchings, watch this!" Corbin said a little louder than normal as he started to dance. Clint and Kayla started laughing, and Clint joined him while Kayla clapped to an imaginary rhythm that they were moving to.

At first, they didn't hear a new sound coming from the corner of their house. It sounded like a bird chirping. Clint and Kayla didn't give it a second thought, but Corbin stopped laughing and moved to give the new sound his full attention. He moved into the night, motioning for Kayla and Clint to follow him as he stalked toward the bird sound.

Clint felt stupid as Kayla followed Corbin, hunched low, hovering over the grass, each step quiet and quick. Kayla and Corbin looked each way as if there were horrors in store, just waiting to pounce as soon as one of them started walking. On the other hand, Clint was walking upright, his hands in his pockets as if it were just another night.

When they got to the end of the house where the rock path started and wound toward the backyard, Clint couldn't see anything until three lumps moved from the edge of the fence, coming towards them. It made him feel oddly tense and slightly startled. Kayla wasn't making a sound while Corbin swished and swooshed his way, following her. They went right behind the three hunched figures and followed them down the yard, staying close to the fence to remain hidden.

When they got to the corner of their fence, O'Neil checked them and motioned to Chiowood to go over. He went over it as if he were rolling over a simple chair. They all followed suit. Only Corbin had trouble scaling the high fence. He tried three times to get over and failed, each time grunting louder and louder. Finally giving up, he just ran around through the gate to join them, not concerned about making noise as he went swishing all the way.

O'Neil gave a silent thumbs up and waited for them to reciprocate. All in their party gave the same sign, staying as quiet as possible before O'Neil set off across the street. He hid by a tree and waved each over in turn to cross. Once gathered, O'Neil waved to each pair to proceed. Both Chiowood and Hobb shot off into the night, followed by Corbin and Kayla. They moved close together, low to the ground, until they were swallowed by the night.

O'Neil looked at Clint and waited with an apprehensive air. It took Clint a moment to understand that he wanted to know which way they should go. Coming to grips with what he had to deal with, he pointed in the right direction down the street. O'Neil nodded and moved quickly, scurrying close to the ground like a rat. O'Neil went off straight away, choosing a path that clung to the darkest parts of houses and streets, with Clint right behind, mimicking his movements.

Clint felt like a cat, keeping away from areas with a lot of noise and never crossing the path of light. O'Neil broke the silence only once and asked Clint softly, "How much further?" while concealed under a large bush next to a modest home. As they lay underneath its branches, Clint saw O'Neil barely breathing hard, while Clint felt like a dog jogging behind his master with his tongue out, panting.

"About ten blocks," Clint panted briskly.

"A Bloock?" O'Neil whispered. "How fare is that?"

"Uhh," Clint moaned. Not knowing how to explain it, he shrugged and smiled, still trying to catch his breath.

"O'Neil nodded and held out his hand, showing all five fingers. After a confused look from Clint, O'Neil mouthed, "Take five." Clint nodded and rested his head, trying to keep his breathing as quiet as possible.

"Can I ask you something?" Clint asked quietly past his heaving breaths. O'Neil also nodded in affirmation while his head kept turning around in all directions. They shared a pleasant feeling of tension under the bush in the sea of night, like they had just crossed an invisible line into enemy territory.

"How are you able to talk to animals?" Clint asked as he started to breathe normally. O'Neil was keen to see anything that might be lurking around when he answered.

"I can't speak tae animals. Just me secound, Nuts."

O'Neil was silent after that explanation, which told Clint that it was enough. Either that was supposed to be enough, or Clint was not supposed to ask anymore. It was difficult for Clint not to give in to the temptation to ask another question as they shared the silence. Clint was about to ask again, but O'Neil tapped Clint with his foot, indicating that they should move. They both started toward the gas station.

They moved fast now and didn't stop until they came to a point where the gas station could be seen just down the road. It was placed at an intersection where the only lights around were from the large blinking sign high in the air, which showed the company's logo. There was one vehicle getting gas on the far-right side of the parking lot, illuminated by the light billowing out from the station's windows and several large high lights over the parking lot. O'Neil moved down closer to an old plastic fence right next to the station. It was amazing, Clint thought, that they had gotten this far and had not been seen by anything or anyone. O'Neil held out a hand for a moment and indicated that Clint should wait where he lay. Then he set off, making as much noise as a spider would until he reached the end of the fence next to the sidewalk. Once there, he looked around and waved for Clint to follow. Clint shuffled his way along until he was with O'Neil.

O'Neil pointed two fingers to his eyes and then pointed to the far side of the street where a large bus was parked. It took Clint some time to see what O'Neil wanted him to see. Under the parked bus by the front wheel were four shadows that were a little darker than the rest. Clint finally recognized them as his sister or Corbin with their escort. Clint and O'Neil waited for some time, as quiet as mice.

A car went by with its front headlights blazing. Clint, now in the groove of things, panicked as O'Neil pulled him to the other side of the fence, just missing the light by inches. As soon as the car went by, O'Neil went back out of the light of the gas station and returned to their cover behind the fence.

Something caught O'Neil's eye at the far end of the station, and he sat back to communicate with Clint. O'Neil held his hand flat out to Clint and then pointed his finger, telling him to wait and stay put. Just then, the lone car that had been filling up with gas started its engine and began to drive away. O'Neil appeared not to be used to this new sound and needed to be calmed down by Clint when he almost leaped over the fence to fight whatever was causing that horrible noise. The car drove away, and O'Neil, regaining his composure, indicated that he would go to the station. Clint gave a thumbs up and lay down next to the fence to hide better. O'Neil reached around the fence and gave the same hold sign toward the bus and then to the far end of the station. He sat back and took off a belt that held all his weapons and lay it down next to Clint making sure that he didn't make any noise. Now that Clint could see it freely, it had many different types of weapons on it that he had never seen before. O'Neil then gave a reassuring nod to Clint and was gone before Clint could even blink.

Thirty

FILL HER UP, CHECK THE TIRES, AND PUT SOME AIR IN ME PLEASE

Clint moved himself along the ground as quickly as he could to watch O'Neil. O'Neil carefully made his way toward the front door of the gas station. Clint could feel the thick grass pull on his shirt as he lifted his head up to see through a gap in the fence. He watched O'Neil first walk into the door with a bang and then open it before he swaggered in. Once opened, Clint heard a soft dinging sound and dreary music come into the still night. Once O'Neil was in, Clint lost sight of him. He lay back down but couldn't stay still. Anxiously, he got up in a crouched position, putting all his weight on his toes as if he were going to jump from behind the fence where only his head was visible around the corner. Deep layers of worry built upon each other every moment that he was waiting.

He started to bounce on his toes to ease the pain when a new noise began to grow from behind him. It was emerging from the same direction they had come. Clint turned as it reminded him of the soft popping firecrackers from a distance. All the lights from down the road blinked out as if a gigantic blanket was rolled out over the neighborhood. The blackout washed over the lights to the gas station and continued further down as far as Clint could see.

Not knowing what to do, the excitement of the thrill of sneaking around was gone in a heartbeat and replaced with a terrible feeling of fear that was now milling around in his chest. Clint could see O'Neil run out and motion for everyone to come toward him.

Clint ran as fast as he could toward O'Neil, feeling the stiffness in his legs loosen, his vision bouncing up and down as he watched out of the corner of his eye Hobb and Chiowood leading Kayla and Corbin out from their hiding places.

"Hobb, Chiowood, get the kids out ay here it's going tae get hoot," O'Neil said vigorously. Then he looked around at Clint with an air of impatience. "Get in there and get that pompous wind bag out, we have tae go, we have tae…" O'Neil stopped talking abruptly.

"What? It's just a blackout. The power to the lights is out. They will come back on in just a moment," Corbin said uncaringly. Clint saw that some of the fun in Corbin's eyes were gone now and was replaced with weariness. Hobb and everyone else didn't wait for any other explanation as they took off around the gas station.

O'Neil grabbed Clint by the scruff of his neck and practically threw him toward the door of the gas station as he yelled, "Git inside, noo." He half-ran, half-fell toward the glass door with O'Neil right behind him. Clint hit the door with so much force that it swung and slammed against a display of oil, the containers scattering across the floor.

"It's only a blackout. It's not like the neighborhood is going to blow up or anything!" Clint shouted in protest at O'Neil. Cody's large frame was right behind the service counter.

"If you could hit like that in the field, you could be worth something," Cody said as he smiled stupidly in the dark at Clint.

His smile was gone as quickly as it arrived. "Now clean up this mess and go home." Another bang announced O'Neil had just come in. With a click, a set of emergency lights on each wall came on in the gas station.

Clint tried to straighten up as he rubbed his sore shoulder when O'Neil suddenly turned around and looked back out the front at something unseen.

"Git down," O'Neil yelled as he grabbed Clint's back, forcing him to the ground. Clint hit his head on the counter with a soft thud as he fell. Another sound followed the sound of flesh, bone, and wood connecting when he hit his head as time seemed to slow down, everything happening in slow motion. Clint felt shocking pain in his head, his hands slamming on the hard floor to break his fall. Cody gave an odd sound of disbelief and laughter at a sharp, crashing sound of glass breaking. Glass shattered, and there was a 'whoosh!' right where Clint's head had been. Then, the loud thud of a single arrow hitting the wall, barely missing Clint's right ear, which covered up Cody, swearing as he slid down to the floor.

The pain was right above Clint's right eye and temple as a thin line of blood started to run down his nose and mouth from where he'd hit the counter. O'Neil grabbed Clint's shirt and dragged him behind the first aisle row in the middle of the gas station for cover. As he did so, two more sounds of glass breaking, and then two arrows hit where his body just was. Clint's vision was blurry as white lights were popping wherever he looked. Time still seemed slow for him as he could hear O'Neil laughing and giving a loud howl of excitement. On the other hand, Cody was screaming as loud as he could, yelling, "NO!" over and over again as arrows kept streaming in. Suddenly, with the sound of breaking glass came a soft light that followed what looked like a laser bolt shooting through the gas station, erupting with sparks when it hit a wall. There were so many arrows coming that Clint couldn't count as they were hitting all around them, showering them with broken glass, as oil and everything that could be knocked off the shelves came raining down on the ground about them. Several electrical bolts melted and burned everything they hit.

"Whew, they got good shooters, they almost hit yoo," O'Neil said excitedly. He was bellowing everything he said as if he were cheering on his team at a home game. The arrows kept coming as O'Neil pulled Clint closer to him, and then, after a ripping sound, Clint felt his head being wrapped tightly right where he had hit the shelf.

"Stay down, yoo fool and shut yer heid," O'Neil called out to Cody. "Maybe next time someone comes in and tells yoo tae come with them tae save yer life, yoo will listen tae them rather than make fun ay them."

More arrows were coming without end, so many that things were starting to fall from the ceiling now as the tiles were being broken up and unpowered lights shattered. Clint's vision was now coming back to him as the white stars were growing dimmer, but the calls for help and yells didn't decrease as each arrow struck something, either shattering it or hitting the wall and floor with a horrible thud. The last of the emergency lights was struck by an energy bolt, showering Cody with sparks and causing him to dance in his crouched position.

"Git down, keep yer heid down!" O'Neil called in between his cackles of laughter as he finished bandaging Clint's head.

"Clint," O'Neil called, grabbing his shirt while he lay flat on the ground like broken glass and candy showered all over his head. "Clint, where is me belt with me weapons on it, boy?"

Clint's heart fell as fast as if his marriage proposal had been rejected. Holding his head to think, he saw it in his mind lying on the ground next to the fence where he'd left it. Ashamed to tell O'Neil that he had left it behind, a new thought came to his brain, the thought of Banks. Banks wouldn't say he'd forgotten it. This gave Clint new bravery, and for the first time in his life, he wanted to do better.

"I will get it for you," Clint said as he started to crawl toward the front door. "No booy, are yoo crazy?" O'Neil cried as he grabbed Clint's shoe and pulled him back to cover as another bolt of fiery light whooshed by, hitting the floor where he had just been. It burned a hole in the floor with a hiss, and the light of its impact caused Clint to shield his eyes.

"Those archers are tae good boy. They will cut yoo in two," O'Neil shouted. "We'll have tae use something else."

"I can do it!" Clint said as he opened his eyes and winced, feeling the pain in his forehead renewed.

"Don't die, boy! This an't the time ta meet the man with the trump. What else can we dae?" O'Neil called as he picked up a mirror that could be attached to a car to watch children in the back seat. It was one of the many items that scattered the floor, knocked off the shelf by the onslaught of arrows and fire pouring in on them. O'Neil raised the mirror over his head for an instant. He angled it so he could see over the aisle toward the front as arrows seemed to be hitting everything around them. Clint shivered in fear as the arrows seemed to be hitting everywhere, as if nothing was to be spared.

"I make out thirty ta fortay shooters and one dark archer," he said as a dark energy bolt hit the mirror, shattering it in his hand making him pull it back, breathing fast. "Ain they like us only as target practice."

Clint was thinking fast and wished Cody would shut up and stop screaming. He shuffled across the floor to get right against O'Neil and away from the arrows that were almost right on top of him. He moved through the debris on his belly and elbows. Sitting up, an arrow hit one of the oil bottles that were scattered on the floor from when he entered.

Seeing it gave him an idea, as he picked up one close to him. "We can try something that I saw in a movie!" Clint said, still with a twinge of fear.

He reached up and grabbed a cigarette lighter off a display case and a couple of bandanas. As quickly as he could, he attached the silver metal cigarette lighter to the oil can with the bandana. As he pulled it as tight as he dared, he tied a knot around the lighter, and taking up a fragment of glass, he stabbed a small hole in the plastic oil can. He lit the lighter and, gave it to O'Neil and screamed, "Throw it!"

Without waiting for an explanation, O'Neil took it in his hand and twisted around, getting to one knee just low enough to stay safe. He threw it hard enough. Clint thought that it would make it into the road beyond the pumps. Clint twisted, looking through a crack between the metal shelves, and saw it hit a fragment of the window that was still loosely hanging in its frame, causing it to spin and land in the middle of the parking lot pump area. It took only a moment for the tiny flame to ignite the oil which was bleeding out of the bottle. There wasn't an explosion, but the oil burned hot and fast, causing smoke to fill the front of the gas station. Clint was hoping for something more than just a puny Fourth of July show from the oil can. Slowly, the arrows stopped as O'Neil grabbed yet another mirror and held it up.

"Cody," Clint yelled, "can you shut up now? Stay low and get over here as fast as you can." Suddenly, Cody's head poked around the corner of the counter. Clint could see he looked like he had been electrocuted and bombed. His face was wet and dirty. His hair was a mess from holding his head down. He was also covered with debris, bits and pieces of everything that was around him. He seemed to be frozen with fear as Clint waved him over. Cody shook his head and let out a small squeak of fear when an off-balanced Twinkie fell next to him on the counter as he dropped back out of sight.

"You got anything else over there, boy, coz now they will be coming," O'Neil said soberly as an arrow went right through the shelf by his head. "These things will stunt yer growth if the end of one hits ya."

Clint looked around for anything that could be used to help them as the onslaught of arrows began again. There was a candy bar, an instant camera, and even some feminine products, but nothing that would help them as the smoke was now depleting, and the oil had almost completely burned up. Clint was out of ideas when Cody said softly, "The alcohol, over there."

Clint looked over to see only Cody's hand was on the counter as the rest of him stayed low. He was pointing to the far end of the shelf in the refrigerated area.

"RIGHT!" Clint shouted as he understood when another dark bolt cut through the metal. It burned through and past his left side between his stomach and arm that he had been leaning on. It only burned his clothes and blackened his skin, he discovered, after he finished screaming and inspected it. He moved fearfully, as low as he could, feeling bits and pieces of glass cut into his hands and knees. Reaching the end of the shelves, he couldn't open the glass refrigerator doors without exposing himself to harm. He tried twice but the arrows kept coming, one shattering the glass to the door he was reaching for. Frustrated, he sat back down where he was safe.

"Try one of those sticks that hold ya up after ya drink too much," O'Neil said, pointing to some walking sticks on the end of the aisle parallel to the one they were cowering behind. Clint grabbed a walking cane with a curved end. Thankfully, as soon as he had moved, an arrow flew by right where his hand was. Clint took the end of the walking cane, holding it by the foot, and used the curved part to push open one of the sliding glass refrigerator doors. He started pulling cans and bottles alike out of the fridge. Some shattered when they hit the ground, filling his nostrils and stinging them with the smell of the drink. Then he rolled the ones that were unbroken down to O'Neil.

"Tear pieces of those cloths on the other end of the aisle up there, the size of the bandage you gave me," Clint called out, coughing from the smell of smoke, beer, and alcohol. He groaned as he moved back to O'Neil, sliding across as many bottles and cans as he could in front of him as he slithered on his belly again.

"Whit do I dae with these?" O'Neil cried out, holding some pieces of cloth out to him. Clint took one in one hand and opened a bottle labeled 'whisky'. As soon as he twisted off the cap, he shoved part of the cloth down, leaving most of the cloth hanging out.

"Get me another lighter," Clint called as part of the ceiling panel fell on him. He covered his head; it felt like the whole world was falling around him.

"A whit?" O'Neil asked.

Clint screamed again as he felt something cold touch his hand that was over his head. It felt like metal and as Clint tried to open his eyes with everything showering around him, he saw the outstretched arm of Cody holding a lighter.

Clint smiled and took it from him. "Whitever yoo two are goin' tae dae boys, yoo hurry up and dae it,'cause they are goin' tae be comin'," he said, looking in the mirror he was holding up.

Clint tried to strike the lighter, but it wouldn't light. Again and again, he tried and as he did, he looked up into the mirror that O'Neil was holding and saw in the last bits of smoke the shadowy outline of figures coming closer toward them. Even in the small mirror and through the smoke, Clint could make out they were holding weapons, ready and waiting for them.

"Come on!" Clint urged the lighter.

A swish, a spark, and suddenly, there was the soft light of a tiny flame in Clint's hand. He held it under the cloth from the bottle and was shocked at how fast it caught fire. In disbelief, he almost dropped it. The fright left as he felt the thrill of holding the lit bottle in his hand. With all his might, Clint threw it the same way as O'Neil had. The round bottle rolled in the air, and with a crash, it hit the parking lot just beyond the sidewalk outside of the building. Clint, Cody, and O'Neil lifted their heads to see a whoosh of flame erupt.

In horror, Clint could see green skin around the newly ignited fire of those who were closer than he thought. With cries of pain, Clint could see their dark outlines run away as O'Neil let a whoop of laughter and Cody prepared other bottles ready to light and throw.

"What about the phone?" Clint asked as he turned around to lie on his back and took up another bottle. It was difficult work as he looked at the cuts on his hands from the broken glass.

"They are out," Cody said incredulously. He lit another bottle and, while he was flat on the ground, he threw it, craning his neck to ensure his aim was true.

"What about the back door?" Cody asked as the light from the fire grew when another bottle crashed.

"No, they will be watching 'at," O'Neil said as he got to his short legs and poked his head just for a second over to see the fire.

"What are we going to do?" Clint enquired and reached down to check his pocket, hoping that he'd remembered his cell phone. With the feeling of an empty pocket under his sore hand, he could see his pants that he'd changed out of and remembered that he'd left his phone in them, now in his room at home.

"We need tae extend our area," O'Neil said impressively. "Moove up!" he called as he grabbed a bottle in each hand and started to move fast, feet slipping on things on the ground as he ran toward the front of the gas station keeping low. The arrows had thinned but were still coming and more accurately now.

Cody's eyebrows contracted in amazement at the bravery of this man, and without being told, he also grabbed all the bottles and cans he could and followed him. Clint's head hurting, he stayed low and pushed what was left of their alcoholic ammo and grabbed as many lighters and rags as his sore cut hands could. Before he got to the end of the rack, he heard three more crashes of glass being broken and saw O'Neil and Cody throwing them as far as they could still while trying to keep under cover behind racks and displays. As Clint peeked around the corner of the aisle, fire reflecting in his eyes, he couldn't see any of their attackers, but saw spots of fire in different areas all over the gas station's parking lot. O'Neil moved right up to the front of the store window's frame and threw more bottles until they were all gone, and the entire area was a ball of fire.

Cody and Clint moved, still staying low, to get to O'Neil. All the glass in the front of the gas station was broken except one panel that was in the far corner of the station behind some newspaper dispensers. It helped with the growing heat now rushing into the store to have a little cover.

"So that's it?" Clint asked with the merest hint of excitement.

"Och, I am afraid not," O'Neil growled. "They went tae a lot of trouble tae get this far."

"What else can we do?" Cody asked desperately.

"Will the fire lite the pumps?" Clint asked, quivering as an arrow glanced off the glass, cracking it.

"No, there is a safety valve that prevents…" Cody suddenly stopped talking. Clint pulled his eyes away from the flames and noticed his older brother shaking.

"They are probably waiting fur the fire tae die out or they are coming tae us from the back way or waiting fur us tae make our move. They have us, and they know it," O'Neil said as he slugged Cody's shoulder. "At was a good fight, ah, boys!"

Before Clint could answer, the light from the flames suddenly dulled considerably. He turned his head so fast it made his neck hurt. He could see that the fire in the very center of the burning area was dissipating. A clear path was starting to form from the far end of the flames where the bus was and laying its way toward them, devoid of flames. Even O'Neil's grin that he had from the first shot till now was falling. The arrows slowed and stopped coming altogether.

"How… how can they do that?" Cody asked slowly. "Who are these guys?"

"Later," Clint said as he forced himself deeper into the corner for cover, looking around through the glass, O'Neil's eyes searching to see what was coming for them, peering over the newspaper and magazine containers. Then it appeared on the very edge of the firelight, standing resolutely, moving so slowly that it might as well have been standing still.

It was a black shape, darker than the night, hunched over wearing a large cloak, limping its way where the flames had died before it. It hobbled, ghost-like, hovering toward them, the fire retreating in his wake.

"What is that?" Clint shouted, full of fear.

"It's gonnae hurt, whatever it is," O'Neil said seriously as he grabbed the cane off the floor that they had used to get the bottles from the fridge. Clint and Cody watched O'Neil brandish the cane as if it were a sword, testing its strength and swishing it around in the air before them.

Then a voice, an unpleasant voice that seemed to cut the final flame wall down between fantasy and reality, came from the thing pushing the fire away with a mere wisp of his hand under his cloak. It said, "Give it to us."

When it said that, even O'Neil's stance faltered for a moment. None of them could look away from it as it came closer. "Stay pit and when I yell run, make yer way back tae the hoose, don't stop fur anything. Just make certain Clint makes it and dinnae worry about what might happen tae me," O'Neil said out of the corner of his mouth so low that only they could hear it.

The hunched-over dark mass limped its way towards them. It was much taller than O'Neil but seemed weaker as it couldn't walk straight and even seemed to stumble once or twice. It grew closer and closer, and as it did, Clint felt the air get colder and could even see his breath. O'Neil suddenly made his move, and for a second, it had trouble raising itself just two or three inches over the curb to the sidewalk right in front of them. O'Neil lunged right at it with a cry of an eagle diving for its prey as he shot out, using the broken window frame to push himself right at the figure. He flew straight at it at an amazing speed with the cane high over his head to bring it down on the dark figure with all his strength.

Whatever happened next was over in a second. The figure under the dark cloak just moved one arm and hit O'Neil with a flash of white light as if it had just dismissed an absentminded thought. It hit O'Neil with a sound like a rock hitting ice. Horrifically, the hit caused O'Neil to fly back as if he were no more than a pillow. His body shattered the metal frame of the front door, causing it to chime for the last time. Dismayed, Clint and Cody watched, unable to move, hunched and hiding.

O'Neil's attack didn't even cause the dark figure to slow or become more off-balance. It moved closer, right toward Clint and Cody, until the glass was the only thing that separated them. Cody had pushed Clint behind him and practically sat on him in protection. Clint struggled, looking beyond the clouds of breath now visible from their mouths as he was pushed against the wall and fridge. Clint watched transfixed as it raised its white bony finger out under the cover of thick cloth, and as soon as it touched the glass, it shattered into a million pieces. After the glass had all fallen, Clint looked up and saw its entirely white hand reaching slowly closer to them.

Sirens and lights cracked the night, causing the figure to stop inches from Cody's heart, which Clint could feel pounding through his back. At least three police cars flew up the road and came to a screeching stop, flooding the open gas station with their headlights. Clint covered his eyes from the shining light and heard the sirens stop and car doors opening.

"Put your hands on your head and get on the ground now!" An officer called.

The hooded figure turned from Clint and Cody to face the officers now. In its shadow, Clint could see six officers, two to each car, standing behind open doors shielding them, as they each held a gun pointing right at the dark figure.

"Get down now!" the officer ordered once again.

The figure didn't move. It just stood there, until Cody found his lips again and cried out, "We are in here, help us!"

"Move away from the building, or we will respond with force," the officer commanded again.

Amazed, Clint watched as the cloaked monster limped away from Clint and Cody and stumbled slightly as it dropped off the sidewalk on the parking lot's pavement. Clint started breathing easier until something grabbed his arm, causing him to scream. It was O'Neil. Blood was trickling down his shoulder. "Move! We have tae get out of here," he whispered.

When Clint screamed, there was a shout from one of the officers, "Drop him!" There was a click and the sound of electricity as Clint pulled his eyes from O'Neil to see an officer running out to the figure in the shine of the headlights. They had just tried to shock the hooded figure. From what Clint could see, there was no reaction at all, no indication that it had any effect on it whatsoever.

"Now, they have him," Cody said happily.

"We have tae go now while it is distracted. It will kill them all an' then us," O'Neil said as he spit blood onto the floor, pulling on Clint's sleeve to make him move.

Clint started to move until that cold voice caused him to be still, "You have no honor," the cold figure said, raising its hand again toward them. O'Neil practically picked up Clint and Cody to make them move, but no one could look away as they watched.

"Take him down!" An officer called as every gun that was pointed opened fire. Clint didn't wait for anything else but moved as fast as he could on his belly and elbows toward the back of the store, following O'Neil.

"My ears!" Clint shouted, covering his ears as shotgun rounds were being fired now. Cody tripped on Clint's shoes, weaving around the rubble and debris as both followed O'Neil.

"We need to talk to the police," Cody called as the gunshots ceased.

O'Neil led them to the rear of the gas station and leaned painfully next to the restrooms.

"What the—" an officer said, causing Cody and Clint to turn to look back. To their horror, the dark figure was still standing.

"Check it, Morgan," another officer ordered.

"We need to get upfront and have that shoulder and head looked at," Cody said, taking a step forward and gently taking O'Neil's good arm as if to take some of his weight.

O'Neil pulled his arm back and groaned, "All they have done is postpone ar date with six mates hold'n us by the handles each as loveone split ar belongings."

Clint could see the single outline of an officer moving forward in front of the headlights. His ears seemed to prickle with fear as he heard the clicks of the officers reloading their guns.

The single officer who was feet away from their dark target stopped. From under the cloak's hood came a large stream of breath that rose like a kettle full of boiling water had just been removed from under it.

"What is that sound?" Cody asked breathlessly. It was the sound of the figure breathing excitedly as it raised its slender white hand high and pointed it at the officer who was coming closer to it. Clint watched the officer convulse as if he had been hit by a lightning bolt and go rigid before he started shaking. Even from far away, Clint could see the officer's breath as if he were in subzero temperatures, struggling for every bit of air. He dropped his weapon as he fell to his knees, grasping and pulling at his chest and throat. In the headlights, Clint could see ice starting at the officer's mouth and spreading around his face.

"He's being frozen from the inside out," Clint said, not knowing that he had done so out loud.

Without command, the rest of the police opened fire. Clint and Cody fell to the floor as the shots were sporadic, almost hitting them this time. The shouts came between the torrent of discharged weapons calling for their fallen comrade, their voices full of fear at the sight of one of their own taken down by the point of a finger, now just turned into an ice sculpture frozen to the pavement.

"Let's get out of here!" Cody yelled as he went for the back door. O'Neil grabbed his hand, stopping Cody from pushing it open.

"They will be waiting foor us," he called, whipping the blood from his head with his beard. The sounds of shots from the officers slowly stopped and were replaced with coughs and cries for help. Until each one of them fell. Clint was lost, not knowing if he was alive, watching the black shape point its finger toward each of its targets until they were all motionless on the ground.

"What are we going to do?" Cody asked O'Neil as he slapped Clint, bringing him back to his senses. O'Neil didn't say anything but fell back against the wall in pain. He raised his good arm and, not looking, pointed at a fire extinguisher. "Can that be used fur anything?" O'Neil coughed. Clint started to shake as Cody pulled the fire extinguisher from the wall and, pulling the pin, sprayed the front of the gas station. He knew at that moment that they were dead. Clint saw the cloud seem to linger around the figure until…

"Stay where you are!" came the sound from a loudspeaker, and a new light shone brightly from the sky as the screaming sound of a helicopter flew over the gas station. The figure bent low away from the light for the first time as the helicopter kept it on him, circled around, and then hovered over the gas station sign.

"Help me," O'Neil whimpered in pain as he slid down the wall. Cody grabbed his good arm and Clint the other. He was heavier than he looked as he pointed back to the front.

The smoke dissipated, and in the few seconds their eyes were off their attacker, he had vanished. The light from above was searching all around now as more sirens could be heard from a long distance away.

"Let's goo, now it's good," O'Neil said pulling heavily on Clint and Cody's shirts as he tried to move weakly. They made their way to the front of the station, looking all around for anything else that would cause them harm, O'Neil gritting his teeth in pain with each step.

"We made it," Cody said in relief as they came out into the parking lot. All three started to laugh as the light from the helicopter worked its way toward them. Their laughter grew until something grabbed Cody's leg, causing him to scream. Cody jumped and started to dance in place, dropping O'Neil and taking Clint down with him.

"Don't hoard all the fun," Transun said, looking up at them. She was in a cloak that made her almost invisible, blending into the shadows lying flat on the pavement.

"It's about time you showed up. I was missing the presence ay a good woman. Where have yoo bin?" O'Neil asked painfully.

"Met a few people!" she said, getting up fast and quietly grabbing him. With amazing strength started to move them away toward the side of the gas station and out of the headlights of the abandoned police cars.

"Who are you people?" Cody asked, stretching his back.

"First things first, where is your little brother at?" Transun said as she pushed even harder to make all three of them move faster. There was an air of emergency as the sirens were getting louder and closer. She took O'Neil to the edge of the parking lot, just dodging the light from above. As they went by, the frozen officers' Clint could see their skin was drained of any color and was now white, cracked, frozen, sealing them forever in a position of their last moments of life.

"Is he in trouble, too?" Cody asked quickly.

"Just answer, boy!" O'Neil ordered. "Why da ya have tae make things sae difficult? All dis could have been avoided if you would just hav listened tae me, dunderheid!"

"He is at Camp Square Lakes over in the red woods next to the coast," Cody, mesmerized at the way he had just been addressed and everything that had just happened.

"Come on, we have to get out of sight before others get here," Transun pleaded, pushing harder. Clint understood now as he let Transun pull O'Neil and grabbed Cody to stop for a moment. He could see the first signs of the police cars lights were almost on top of them.

"You have to stay and explain all this," Clint said, running over and retrieving O'Neil's weapon belt. "Tell them anything," he pleaded as he returned by his side. He lifted them over his shoulder as he watched O'Neil being carried around the corner and out of sight. Clint hurried to follow them, but O'Neil still called back to Cody, "Say whatever you have to and get back to the house as soon as possible. We will explain everything there. Go now."

"Wha, when, why, hospital, popsicle, pincushion, sale," Cody was saying in disbelief, pointing at everything around him.

"Do yoo always argue and not follow advice when yoo are told? After whit jist happened I thought yoo would listen a wee bit more," O'Neil said from nowhere.

Clint turned the corner, following O'Neil and Transon, just as the lights of the police car were now visible and only seconds away.

"How am I going to explain this?" Cody called back. "How can anyone explain this? I mean, where is Olaf?"

"Do as I say, boy, and don't go home alone, and don't go straight home in case yoo ur followed, you Bampot!" O'Neil called back before anything more that could have been said would have been drowned out by the sirens, the light of the helicopter now focused on Cody.

Clint could only guess what Cody was going through as he ran as best as he could, following the strange sight of O'Neil leaning on Transon who was still camouflaged, appearing almost see-through.

"Put your hands on your head and get on the ground," a woman's voice commanded Cody from somewhere behind Clint.

"I work here!" were the last words Clint heard as he ran, catching up to O'Neil and helping him under the other arm as before. As soon as he arrived, Transon swung her cloak over all three of them. It concealed them from the helicopter light searching above them and more police cars closing off the area. The three of them limped back the way they came, departing into the night.

Thirty-One

I'll Tell You Mine If You Tell Me Yours

The trip home felt like it took forever, Clint thought with each sore step. Transon led them along another route that would be difficult for anyone to follow. The further they went, the weaker O'Neil seemed to get. He wasn't bleeding out of his mouth anymore, but every time Clint readjusted his weight, O'Neil would breathe in sharply in pain. Clint thought that he must have had some broken ribs.

"Can't we stop and rest for a moment?" Clint asked as they paused for a moment while Transon checked around a dark corner.

"We can't stop for any reason. If we are set upon, I will leave O'Neil and see you safely home if we must," Transon said as she urged them on, still taking on the greater part of O'Neil's weight. Clint almost stopped where he was in shock. He felt disgusted that she would let O'Neil fend for himself in his condition and run after what he'd just done.

He didn't have the strength to protest as he took all he had to keep going. At other corners or dark alleys, Transun told him that she had met the others when they were on their way back to the house. They had to fight a little to get away from the gas station as well, but they were all right and had lost those who were following them before they got to the house. It took her longer to get to the gas station because she had to pass those who were after Kayla, Corbin, Hobb, and Chiowood.

It seemed like it was almost morning when his home was finally close enough for him to see. They were almost to the driveway when all the lights came on from the blackout. They moved as quickly as they could up to the door, and Clint had to admit that their house had never looked so good as he pushed it open with a groan, his shoulder and arm killing him from holding up O'Neil.

As soon as the door opened, several sets of arms pulled O'Neil off and wrapped him up in hugs. Nix was the one who took O'Neil and went straight into the office. He was able to pick O'Neil up with ease as if he had picked up Clint. Clint saw Nix push everything off his stepfather's desk and set O'Neil down softly.

"Report," Banks asked out of nowhere. Clint looked up, finding himself in Banks's arms. He was the one who was helping to hold him up after O'Neil was taken from him.

"Sir," Transun said, "the other is at a location called Square Lakes Campground. It is in the redwoods next to the coast." She took off O'Neil's weapons belt that she had hanging over her shoulder. She then filled Banks in briefly on what happened at the gas station. Now that Clint saw her in the light, she was one of the most muscular women he had ever seen.

Kayla lovingly came and held him around his waist. Clint was so transfixed on Transun's camouflaged cloak that he hadn't noticed her until she asked, sounding worried, "Are you alright?" Clint looked down and saw her dirty face.

"I'm good, but that gas station is beat up, though," and nodded, allowing her to release him. She let out a snake-like hiss when she saw his head. It was only then that he remembered that he was still wearing the bandage O'Neil had tied on him when he hit his head. Clint heard Corbin's flat, distant voice coming from the couch he was lying down on in the television room. Before Clint could go and see his friend, he was cut off when Banks moved in front of him.

"See Nix when he has a moment," he ordered, tapping his own head in the same spot where Clint was injured and then hurrying off down the hall at a brisk pace. "Kayla, can you show us roughly where your brother

Grant should be with the information that we now have?" Banks asked, indicating that he wanted her to follow him.

"Wait," Clint called down the hall, causing Kayla to stop. "What about what just happened?" Banks stopped for only a moment, and without looking back at Clint, he said, "We have to act quickly to get to your other brother while there is time. Since they attempted to acquire Cody, they will also try for Grant, if they haven't got him already." Then Banks was gone.

"It's all right," Kayla said to Clint. Then, as she looked around with eyes full of terror, she choked out, "Cody?"

"He's all right. I will tell you everything when we can talk."

"All right," Kayla said as she walked down the hall. Oddly, she didn't look away from Clint as he waited, suddenly feeling very tired and heavy.

Being alone for a moment, he let out a deep breath and went to the office where Nix was working over O'Neil. O'Neil was so short that as he was lying flat on his back, his legs barely hung over the edge of the desk.

"Nix says, I will be all right. I jist need a day off tae rest," O'Neil said squeakily.

"Thank you," Clint said, struggling with his grin. "Thank you for everything."

"Jist give me a drink aw the good stuff an we will call it even," O'Neil said wearily.

Nix stepped over between them. "Sorry, but I must take care of him." He gripped Clint by the shoulders and moved him out of the room, but when he had stopped moving him, he didn't let go. Nix held him fast as his eyes wandered over Clint.

"Hold on one moment," he said as he patted Clint with one arm as he let him go. Clint noticed that Nix sounded like he was from New York. Nix reached into a pouch that hung from his belt and pulled something out as he pulled Clint to face up toward him. Nix took off the bandage and eyed the cut on his head while opening a tin that had something in it that smelled like gasoline. It was a blue gel liquid, and before Nix explained what he was going to do, he rubbed it liberally in the cut on his forehead.

"Hey, that stings," Clint shouted, trying to pull away. Nix held his head and rubbed it over it for only ten seconds. The pain seemed to leave his head as soon as Nix put his hands down. Clint tried to raise his hand to feel his head, but Nix slapped it away as he forced opened Clint's eyes wide to examine him.

"Do I need stitches?" Clint asked, worried for the first time about his cut and what Nix was doing. Clint suddenly felt like a piece of meat in Nix's large hands as he then forced open Clint's mouth to look down his throat.

Nix looked confused for a moment. "I don't know what stitches are, but just keep the top of your head dry for an hour, then wash this off, all right?" Then Nix gently slapped Clint across the cheek and went back to work on O'Neil, not giving Clint a chance to say anything. Clint exercised his sore face now that he was let go and was a little hurt at not getting a good response back. He quickly felt his head with a shaking hand, sure that he would have a large gash on his head. To his amazement, there was nothing left of the opened wound or anything to cause him pain. He only felt dry blood and the wet blue liquid that was still there. He couldn't even feel a bump.

"How did you do that?" Clint shouted into the other room as he examined himself in the reflection off the glass of a picture of his brother by the stairs.

Nix swiftly asked, "Can you shut the door?" Clint felt his head over and over, amazed at it, and confirmed that his head was still there in the first place. He felt his chin and nose, where he saw on his hand remnants of dried blood as he shut the door, wishing he could get more out of Nix.

Clint made his way over to the television room and saw Kayla and Corbin looking tired, but other than the need for a shower, they were not hurt. Corbin was lying on the sofa as if he had just run a seventy-mile marathon. While Kayla looked tired, examining her clothes, and telling herself how to get the stains out of them. Both were watching the television, which was not on.

"What happened to you guys?" Clint asked as he sat down with his back against the wall between a pinball machine and a large shelf with all the stereo and controls for the room. When his hands touched his legs, they smarted, and he wished that Nix could have worked on his cut hand and not just on his head.

Kayla explained that all four of them had run for it as soon as the trouble started, not toward the house but more down to the central part of town, hoping that they would run into more people. Hobb and Chiowood stopped at certain places and fired some arrows behind them, but they never really saw anything following. So they turned and went toward the house until they saw the imp.

"It was a different one this time," Corbin said, interrupting Kayla, "It was a green one, and for some reason, it sounded like a pig, but the funny thing was I could understand it."

"Was anyone hurt?" Clint asked. He didn't sound worried. He felt numb for some reason; he couldn't sound worried even if he wanted to.

"Hobb got a dagger in the leg, but Nix fixed him up in about a second when we got here," Corbin said, sitting up excitedly. "He is what they call a paladin. He can heal people with a touch." Corbin looked more alive at that moment than he had all evening. After no one said anything for a moment, he laid back down again, wincing a little from being so sore.

Kayla broke the silence, saying, "Hobb didn't even complain that he was in pain until we were almost here. He kept turning and shooting as we ran on back at something. We only saw it once, and when we were about halfway there, he shot an arrow, and it hit the imp."

"Yeah, we know because there was a pig squeal sound that you could have heard if you were with Grant," Corbin said, laughing, "It was one of the funniest things I have ever heard."

"Then we made it home all right. What about you?" she asked as Corbin grunted and squealed like a pig between laughs.

Clint told them both what had happened and relayed every detail, but it was hard to keep going with the thought of what was still out there looking for them. Kayla and Corbin listened closely to every word that Clint told them and were shocked that they'd made it out alive. Just when Clint was telling them that Cody was talking with the police, Banks came in. He held up a hand to stop Clint from talking.

"Sorry to interrupt but I wanted you to know that I have sent out Ohlwiler and Tremayne out to get Grant. In the meantime, I suggest you get some rest. You will have a long day tomorrow."

"What do you mean, what are we doing tomorrow?" Kayla asked, not able to help herself and unable to hide the defiant fear in her voice.

"You will all have to continue with your daily routine as much as possible. If you did otherwise, it would give away that we are here and bring more attention to yourselves than needed," Banks said as he started to leave.

"Wait," Kayla pleaded as she got to her feet. Clint could see that her outfit was torn now that she moved. Probably from cowering under tree branches and bushes. "We can't go. We have to help you find the, the whatever."

Banks came back into view, and for a moment, he looked like he was irritated but still responded in his steely voice, "You are kids, and I am sorry to inconvenience you and your home, but since we don't know what the Requiem really is or what it looks like, there isn't much you can do to help us. What you can do to help us is do whatever you normally do. The Fury knew about Cody, and they might know about Grant. It is reasonable to assume they know this location. The best thing to do is be ready and vigilant."

"We want to help," Kayla said halfheartedly, looking downcast.

"Then rest; you must go on tomorrow like tonight didn't happen," Banks said, leaving the room without giving any chance for the conversation to continue.

"What is up with him and kids?" Corbin asked, not lifting his head.

"Don't know," Kayla said, still standing, looking at the spot where Banks had been.

"It's not that he doesn't like kids," Clint said. Both Kayla and Corbin turned around to look at him.

"Why do you say that?" Kayla asked.

Clint smirked as he got to his feet. "He just doesn't like you two," he said, leaving them to change for the night. As he went up the spiral staircase, Kayla and Corbin jokingly pointed out reasons why they were each so unlikeable.

Thirty-Two
NOW THAT'S A CAMP FIRE STORY!

The night revealed every insect alive hovering over Grant's head. He had already bathed himself in insect repellent but kept reapplying layer over layer when another insect would buzz over him. Short and skinny with a prominent upper lip showing his large front teeth, he was the most popular target for the camp bullies. It seemed to escalate as soon as he got in the car and took his pills to prevent motion sickness. That's when the other children started to make fun of him, and now everyone's conversation seemed to be directed at him. From first going to the outhouse and having it pushed over while he was in it to being shot with paintballs, blow darts, and a slingshot, it was a wonder he was still alive. The other children wasted no time laughing at him whenever the leaders were not around, but for the first time that night, as everyone sat around the campfire, Grant felt safe sitting next to an adult.

Everyone was roasting marshmallows as each person, in turn, told scary stories of past camping events. Each story always ended in a near-death experience, running from a madman with a chainsaw or aliens taking away every camper one by one. It was now a young man's turn who sat two places down from Grant. He was telling them all about a time that a bear nearly ate him as it tore open their camping trailer, having eaten everyone else but still thirsting for young blood.

It was then that Grant's fourteenth marshmallow caught on fire. He pulled it away from the flame and attempted to blow it out as best as he could, but with his asthma, it took several tries.

"Geez, Holden," a rather large boy who was sitting on the other side of the fire called out to him, "can't you do anything without hurting yourself or almost setting yourself on fire?"

There was a gale of laughter from all the kids that went around the campfire. This was the most popular kid, and he wasted no time showing everyone he had the best camping equipment.

"Boys, boys," the man sitting beside Grant said gruffly. This man was Grant's only relief from the rudeness and teasing. He looked down at Grant and gave him a wide smile as all the young laughter died away. He even went as far as get him another marshmallow and place it on the end of Grant's stick so he could try again.

"Whose turn is it now for a story?" another man asked on the far side of the bonfire.

The man sitting next to Grant spoke up. "I believe it's my turn," he said with a smile as the firelight reflected off his white teeth. Grant looked and saw him in his scout uniform, this man with his many merit badges, almost like a kid again with the anticipation to tell them all a story. The man took his stick out of the fire and sat it down on the log so that the point that was in the fire would not touch the ground.

A new sound from a distance caused them all to pause; it sounded like a pig squealing. They all looked around into the dark that danced just out of reach of the firelight. The only sound they could hear now was from the stream trickling smoothly right next to their camp and the waves crashing from the ocean far away against the shore.

"What was that?" a boy asked.

The man beside Grant leaned forward so his face was in the light of the fire, a look of concern on his face. He told an elaborate story of children who came upon a witch in the woods, which ended with all but one being boiled, as he ended and threw something in the fire that made an explosion that sent every kid falling back of their log in a hail of screams.

They all started laughing as they got back up onto their log seats. Grant straightened his glasses and found his can of bug spray as he sat back on his log. He was determined not to look too scared, so he brushed himself off and sat up as everyone commented on how stupid each other looked. They all were settling back down when Grant had a horrible thought. If they continued telling stories in the same pattern, it would be his turn now to tell one. Completely forgetting that he was just drawn into a story that almost made him wet himself, he felt a new rush of fear that made his face turn ashen, not wanting to talk in front of all these people.

There was a sound of something crashing from a distance away like a massive tree cracking as it fell. Grant looked into the firelight as the man sitting next to him had slowly stopped laughing.

"Great story, sir," one of the kids said. "Yeah, that was all kinds of good," said another boy. "What was that you put in the fire?" another asked.

"Ah, that is a secret," he said, looking like he hoped someone would ask him that question. "If you become good scouts, you'll learn what—"

He stopped talking. As a matter of fact, he wasn't even there. Grant was sitting right next to him, and all he saw was the man's feet flying in the air as if someone had tied a bungee cord around the man's waist and tied the other end of it to a boulder and pushed it off a cliff.

The murmur and laughter slowly stopped as everyone looked over to where he had been sitting. Grant looked across the flames towards the only other adult who was supposed to be there, and when he got to his feet, he found that the place that the man had been sitting in was empty. There were kids on either side of where they sat, but the men were gone.

"What happened to them?" a younger boy than Grant stuttered.

"They are just playing a stupid joke on us," the boy who was the most popular and biggest bully said smugly as he got to his feet, the firelight showing how much taller and heavier the boy was than the rest.

"Ok, come out, you guys," he called as Grant looked on and was thankful he wasn't the only one who looked scared. They were all searching as they stood around the fire for some sign of what was going on, something that would give them comfort, but as they all found, they were alone. Every sound pricked their ears, telling them the night only held the water's movement in the stream and the insects buzzing around, but even those were fading. It was as if every bug stopped humming and buzzing one by one until they had all ceased, and the boys were left in absolute quiet. Not even the wind in the trees was there anymore. All they could hear were their own breaths and the water beating the rocks of the stream over the crackle of the fire.

A very tall boy to Grant's far-right took a long stick out of the fire and held it out so the burning wood illuminated with its flame what was outside of their circle. As he held the stick out, nothing was behind the boys except their tents, and Grant felt his hands sweating as he reached into a pocket to get his inhaler. The tall boy went around, shining light from his torch until the light revealed the feet of a man who was next to Grant. Grant cowered right behind the tall boy, and he swallowed, moving the light, driving back the dark, showing first a man's legs, then waist, then his torso, then the light showed something new that was not the man. It showed a large animal paw. The paw was covered in gray fur and was right by the man's armpit. The tall boy gasped, startled, and stepped back, tripping on Grant, causing him to raise the torch as high as he could, which cast the light over the entire animal. It was a gigantic gray wolf, at least as tall as Grant but ten times heavier, its jaws wrapped around the man's throat.

Every boy backed away closer to the fire until they were practically in it as the popular boy also took a long stick and shone the light in the opposite direction to find the other leader who was on that side also lying on the ground with another large black wolf holding him by the throat.

As the light hit both the wolves, they growled and dragged the men an inch or two away from the firelight. A new sound above the boy's sharp intakes of breath and small squeaks of fear called out to them. It was the sound of footsteps coming their way from the direction of the stream, snapping twigs, and fallen branches. The sound of feet on leaves and snapping twigs grew louder and was coming toward them. Then, just outside of the light, with every boy looking that way, the sounds of the footsteps stopped just outside of view, but they could see the dark silhouette of a man standing by the closest redwood tree. They could hear the man breathing, and then he spoke calmly, almost humorously and joyfully.

"They are not yet dead," he said to them. Grant started to feel his back burning from the fire that he was almost standing in, trying to keep as far away as possible from the sight of two wolves and the stranger.

"If you want these men to live and your own lives spared, I need one thing from you," the man said, making everyone jump.

"And why should we listen to you?" came the popular boy's voice from across the fire. "It's just you with two mutts. We can take you!" he called, taking another branch out of the fire and brandishing it as if he wanted a fight to the death.

The figure in the shadows held out a hand that Grant could see in the light of the fire. It made him jump back even closer to the bonfire and burn himself. He stumbled over the other two boys he was holding on to. Thankfully, he wasn't the only one because the figure's hand had unmistakably dark, green-colored skin. The dark green hand hung in the light for only an instant and snapped two fingers. As soon as that sound echoed in all their sensitive ears, a new sound came. Growls and snarls from around them made them spin their heads in every direction. All together, like a terrible dance routine, several wolves' heads came into the firelight, not making a sound other than from their jaws that were borne, showing each and every fang they had, with their ears back. Their bodies were low to the ground, ready to spring at the boys at any moment, and the fur on their backs was standing up in anger.

Everyone around the fire jostled and moved around to get away from the wolf that was closest to them but only found another wolf hunched low before them or another boy in that spot cowering in fear. The hand that was still in the light faded in and out of the shadows when a boy moved, blocking the firelight. The hand snapped once more, catching all their attention as if he had just fired a shot from a gun in the air. This brought the wolves to a halt as the boys sniveled and whined in fear.

"What do you want?" the popular boy asked, almost crying, holding back the tears, sounding more like a frightened rat than a boy. They all waited for the shadow to say something, holding on to each other. They waited with the hot breath of the wolves before them and the heat of the fire behind them.

"I want the one named Holden!" the shadow said.

Every eye turned to Grant as they froze in disbelief at what the shadow figure had said. It was as if everyone's heart stopped in an instant.

"He is the one you want!" said the fat, popular boy who sounded so brave before the wolves came. All the other boys looked at the popular one as if he had just lost his mind and couldn't believe what had just happened.

The green hand in the light returned, flinched, and pointed right at Grant. Every wolf moved to come right in front of him. It was as if his legs forgot how to work as the eyes of the wolves reflecting flame and ash now only reflected Grant as they all shuffled into position, teeth bared, jaws snapping at each other as they moved in for the kill.

"Slam, rip, bang!". There was the sound of something moving very fast right at them, and for an instant, the wolves turned around to see what was coming. It was then that Grant ran out of sheer panic. It was not bravery but the terror that drove his legs as his lungs only filled partway as his breath wheezed and whined from his asthma. As he took two steps, the slamming sound was right on top of them as. Grant saw an enormous tree trunk slam down right in front of him and another swing up to his left and slam down on the ground behind him. Grant stayed on his feet, dodging around another tree trunk that dropped right in his path. He started to run by it when the trunk that nearly fell on him lifted once more off the ground. Grant looked up to see that they were the legs of a giant tree as high as the redwoods, but where the center of the tree was was not just wood but a person with its arms and legs in the wood tree controlling its movement.

Grant ran down toward the stream, and in the firelight behind him, he saw looking sideways, all the boys scatter as the tree-like giant practically jumped and landed right over the fire, and with its massive tree limbs that were the size of a car swung around the boys, hitting wolves, and tossing them aside and lifting them, throwing them like they were pieces of paper. The wolves were howling and shrieking from pain and the last thing Grant saw was the person in the tree embedded in the bark, controlling the tree's movements, fighting to save the boys. The person in the tree had a green-skinned face, and it saw him running but turned its concentration away as a wolf jumped over the fire, trying to strike at the man and not the tree.

Making haste, Grant took feeble glances behind him as he ran as fast as his wobbly legs and odd footing would let him. The way down to the stream was not kind to him. The shrieks, wails, and howls from the wolf's attack on the man in the tree assaulted his ears. He stumbled twice, almost falling over rock or roots. Suddenly, he fell hard on the ground, hurting his legs and hands, not knowing what had happened. Crying in pain, he scrambled to keep moving until he reached the small stream, where he stopped. He stood paralyzed, giving all the strength he had to control his breathing. His lungs ached with pain, not being able to fill them full of the oxygen he needed to keep going. He looked back to the camp and could only hear the squeaking of the tree moving over the creek ridge he had just come down. It sounded like old wood moving in the wind each time a breeze would push it.

"The boy is not here. Find him. Hunt him. Go!" a voice cried into the night. Panic-stricken, Grant jumped into the freezing water. It stung his legs like a thousand tiny needles pricking him in every pore. His breathing was getting more labored as he started to cry, moving in the rushing water that was now up to his thighs. He held his hands high, trying to keep dry and out of the cold as something else was crashing down the way he had come. The stream wasn't very deep but cold enough to slow anyone down.

Whatever crashed behind him hit the water with a splash as soon as he left the other side. He felt the tears from his eyes run down his cheeks as he scampered into the night on all fours to climb up the other side of the embankment. Using exposed tree roots and rocks, he propelled his feet and hands to climb up as fast as he could. A loose rock gave way in his hand, causing him to slide down an inch. Instinctively, he turned back to see what had plunged into the water behind him and saw in the moonlight the lifeless body of a wolf being dragged down the river. He ran panic-stricken without direction or thought other than what was behind him and the soft cry for his mother coming from his lips as he kept gasping for air.

The tree branches did not diminish his way because of their height, but the undergrowth heavily impaired him. He had never run this hard in his life. He was never physically active, and his tiny body couldn't go much further. He fell once more and then again and again as his strength was giving out. His eyes were getting accustomed to the dark, but it was the trees that mainly hampered his vision. Then, with his glasses askew, he saw an old, gnarled tree stump half-weathered and corroded that he could hide in.

Behind him came a growl and howl of what unmistakably was a wolf coming closer. With his chest feeling like a knife stabbing him with short, sharp breaths, he walked and crawled toward the tree, not bothering to wipe his tears and snot until he grabbed the side of the tree.

Climbing inside, he started to grab his inhaler from his pocket, and with his shaking hand, he lifted it to his lips and clicked it. It was like someone had taken the gag out of his mouth as his lungs gratefully expanded, letting him breathe. He took great gasps of the cold air and swallowed them down. His legs now numb with cold, he fell in the cavity of the wood trunk, concealing himself as best as he could. Listening hard, Grant could hear the patter of other feet and the heavy breath of the wolves now all around him. Their paws hit the dirt, leaves, and brush with little thuds. Grant rubbed his chest, trying to slow his breathing down, and took another shot from his inhaler. Returning it to his pocket, he froze, holding to the tree tight as the sound of the wolves' pattering paws slowed and stopped right where he was hiding. Try as he might not make a noise, he couldn't stop the tears that flowed from his eyes behind his glasses in two steady streams. The pain from his frozen, wet legs was getting worse.

Abruptly, the sound of movement to his right came to him, and then the sound of a long nose sniffing the air was close. Grant pushed his back even harder into the wood, fear overwhelming him as the sound of a clawed paw against wood came from outside the tree that he was hiding in. The sniffing of a nose came closer and was almost on top of him.

Then, there was a deeper growl of an animal that Grant had not heard yet. It was not from the wolf right on top of him but just outside, where he was hidden, a couple of feet away. Then the growls of the wolves sounded, as the one above Grant jumped away off the tree, hitting the soft earth with a dull sound. Grant couldn't help himself as he moved to see what was going on. He angled his head to see out of the side opening of the tree. There in the misty light of the night was the unmistakable outline of a giant bear, its shaggy, dark fur rippling with each movement as it charged toward him. Grant saw on top of the giant bear's back a person holding a long wooden staff in one hand, bent low and holding the bear's fur with the other.

The wolves formed a half-circle around the newcomer and without warning charged the new threat. With a roar that split the night, the bear opened its enormous mouth as the first wolf lunged right at it. Wham! One swipe from the bear's large claw sent the wolf hurtling off course. The wolf tumbled and rolled for a moment but regained its footing.

Three more wolves circled the bear and snapped at it just out of range of the bear's jaws and swipes of its gigantic arms. The wolf who was first struck joined its pack; with maws open, growling, they surrounded the bear. The bear's head was turning this way and that, trying to keep each one of the wolves' insight. The person on top of the bear bent low as close to the animal as it could be, with the staff held out high over them, ready to strike.

The wolf that was right behind the bear jumped first, but the person on the bear was ready. The rider pulled on the bear, causing it to rise onto its back two feet, roaring, and as the rider hung on, they swung the staff, hitting the wolf in the face, crushing its snout. The wolf's body fell to the ground, but before Grant could see what had happened to that one, the other two from the sides moved in. One jumped high, and the other lunged low. The one that jumped high was met by the right claw of the bear, knocking it back, and before it hit the dirt, it was dead. The other drove its long teeth into the bear's leg. The bear roared in pain and fell back on all fours. The rider kicked out hard, causing its boot to connect with the wolf's face. The wolf let go and shook its head in pain. The bear swung around and swiped at the wolf but too late, the wolf jumped back just out of the way. Then the other wolf with the limp jumped when the bear's back was to it, this time not aiming for the bear but for the rider. The wolf met the end of the rider's staff, and with a terrific yell, the rider struck the wolf's body, causing it to fly over her and hit the other wolf. When they connected, they both yelped in pain. The bear lunged at them both so fast that the fight was over in the blink of an eye. With two great swipes with the bear's long claws, the wolves stopped howling and moving. The last wolf limped away into the night, bellowing with each step it took with its right front leg until Grant couldn't hear it anymore.

The bear circled, searching, breathing heavily. Grant could see the breath coming from the animal's mouth and nose in the night air. When it stopped searching, the rider got off the bear and patted it lovingly, looking around into the night. Grant made out the slender form of a woman as she turned her head, looking around at the ground.

"Grant?" she called.

Grant didn't move. He froze and watched this woman as she searched the night for him. The bear sat down and started to lick its injured leg.

Grant retreated down into the tree again to the same place where he was out of sight minutes before.

"Grant, we are here to take you home to your family," she called again. Grant still didn't make a sound or move out of the tree. His eyes had not yet run dry from the tears that were still coming.

"Can you smell him?" the woman asked quietly. The bear gave a threatening huff, and then he could hear the sound of the bear making its way toward him. Grant could feel another asthma attack coming on but dared not move as his chest grew tighter. The sound of the bear sucking in sharp intakes of air through its nose was sickening to him. The bear stopped just outside of the tree, and Grant could hear someone's feet climb the tree, and then a slender head looked down right at him.

"Grant?" she asked softly. "Grant Holden?"

Grant still didn't make a sound but cowered down lower to get further away from the woman. His breathing was jagged as he held his hands close to his stinging chest, crying harder, still without making a sound.

The woman moved her weight around, leaning over the hole, and held down one slender hand. "Come on, Grant, I will take you home."

Grant saw it, and without thinking, unable to stop crying, he coughed out, "I want my mother." As he couldn't hold back the noise of his crying any longer, he wailed like an infant needing the love of a parent.

She held her hand out further and said lovingly, "I do not know where your mother is, but I can take you to the rest of your family, who is safe at home waiting for you."

Grant, sniffing hard and hands shaking, reached back into his pocket and, took out his inhaler and used it. The woman didn't move back but stayed where she was with her hand, ready to help him. Grant reached out, quivering from the cold, his legs hurting from being wet, but paused only an inch away from her hand.

"It's all right," she said softly without moving yet. "I won't let anything happen to you; I promise."

Grant looked at her hand and took it, and as soon as he did, his crying stopped as she pulled him slowly out of the tree and hugged him as he hugged her. "It's going to be all right," she said. "Everything will be all right." She picked him up and carried him toward the bear, sat him on it, climbed on herself, and with a couple of words to the bear, they were off. Grant, numb from cold, fear, and overwhelming emotion, rode into the night away from the camp toward his house and family.

Thirty-Three
HOME IS WHERE THE HEART WAS

It was well past eleven o'clock when Cody showed up at home. He was a little shaky, but all right. From the way he told it, it was amazing that he got home at all. It seemed the police wanted to keep him overnight or send him to a counselor to help him cope with his traumatic experience.

"I told them that they were a bunch of kids from Lipten High, you know, our high school rivalry," he said talking to Kayla, Corbin, Clint, and Tamara. They all sat in their stepfather's office; O'Neil had settled himself on the couch in the television room where they could hear him watching their collection of Disney movies.

It seems the police questioned Cody repeatedly about how the kids came in, took all the alcohol they could, lit them on fire, threw them around, and started shooting arrows at him.

"They bought all that but when they started asking how the police got frozen alive, I said I didn't know. I told them I just wanted to get home and walk a little bit so they gave me a lift and let me go three blocks down from the house. I climbed into a friend's window who I knew was away and snuck through their house and came up here. It was lucky the officer I was left with was a fan because I was probably going to be there all night! I also need to answer more questions later, they said. Also, there was some guy in a suit who just stood there and watched me the whole time not saying anything. Freak!"

"Any news about Grant?" he asked, taking a long drink of water. His mouth was dry from talking so much.

"Nothing yet, Banks said that they sent two of the druids," Kayla trilled.

It was then that all those who were there started to talk about everything they knew had happened in the past two days. It wasn't until they started talking about the Requiem that they didn't know any answers to their questions. "They don't even know what it is or where it is?" Cody said, amazed.

"Nope," Tamara said calmly. "But if they went to this much trouble, it has to be important."

"That reminds me," Cody said, looking at Tamara in a new light. "What's got into you? You are normally never out of your room unless you are glazed in black and looking for dead bugs to wear."

Tamara didn't say anything but looked at him frowning. With every eye on her, she squeaked out as she went pale, "I want to change."

"I like it," Corbin said shyly.

This made all eyes turn to him now. It was like a tennis match, with everyone looking back and forth between Corbin, Cody, and Tamara. Banks came into the room abruptly holding what looked like a crow under one arm.

"We have word, your brother is fine, Ohlwiler and Tremayne just got him out safely and are on their way here," he said without smiling.

All the family sighed and exchanged hugs of joy, knowing that everyone was going to be all right for now. It was like everyone in their family had been under the knife since that afternoon and was about to be put on death row. Clint, for one, was amazed that they had all made it out in one piece. Banks started to leave but was called back when Cody yelled, "Banks, can you spare a second? I wanted to know about this Requiem."

Banks peered back at him while O'Neil let out a loud laugh from something funny that he saw on television. "I cannot at this moment. It is my watch. You should get some rest and get ready for Grant when he gets here, then get some sleep, and above all else, don't get complacent," Banks said as he opened the front door and let the crow go that he was holding. Then he went out following the crow, leaving the door open allowing Ravin to come through looking tired. Cody watched her wide-eyed as she slumped down toward the kitchen, and they heard the back door open and close.

"Come on, Cody," Clint said as he hit Cody in the shoulder. "You have to be careful with her," and looking at Corbin, he lifted his fingers, giving quotation mark signs to what he said next. "She's hot."

They all laughed at Cody's face because he was the only one who didn't know what they were going on about. They all questioned if she was a druid or something like Nix who could heal others. Each thought streamed of wonders of these fantasy guests and what their abilities were.

It wasn't until midnight that something new caught their attention. The front door opened as Banks started the procession with Grant, who was covered in a blanket made of leaves, followed closely by Ohlwiler and Tremayne, who both looked very tired as they shut the door behind them. Kayla was the first to see them. She stood up quickly and ran to Grant, followed by Tamara. They both ran with their arms open to greet their brother but were met by Banks, who stepped between them.

"I know you want to see him, but I must talk to him before you do." Banks said, letting Ohlwiler and Tremayne pass. Kayla and Tamara stopped and looked uncertainly at Banks. It took a moment for Tamara to get used to the idea that she had to wait to talk to her brother. "As soon as we are done, we will send him to you," Banks said, smiling warmly at Grant but displaying a serious look at Kayla and everyone else when he said amicably, "Please rest!" With that, he vanished around the corner taking Grant out to the backyard.

The very last thing that Clint wanted was rest. Feeling impatient, he slammed his hand down on the table he was sitting next to, got up, and walked past Kayla and Tamara. He walked into the television room where O'Neil was almost dancing as he lay on the couch listening to the music from the Disney movie that had just started, "The Game Plan." As Clint sat down, he heard the familiar footsteps of Kayla, who was behind him.

"O'Neil, could I have a word?" Clint asked cautiously. O'Neil didn't say anything as his eyes seemed glued to the screen. Clint picked up the remote and turned the movie off. O'Neil's response was so funny that Clint wished he'd turned it off sooner.

"Wh, what, movie, happened..." O'Neil was looking for the right words to say as he looked all around, and finally, his eyes found Clint. It took him a moment for him to focus Clint into view.

"OOH, Clint laddie, did yoo kill the box?" he said, still glaring at Clint with cloudy eyes.

"I wanted to talk to you," Clint said.

O'Neil looked from the television, and with obvious displeasure, he nodded, "All right, but not tae much mind yoo, tired and sore." He stretched as if every movement caused him pain.

Clint was willing to bet that he just wanted to get back to watching his movie as he sat down on the loveseat and moved it to face O'Neil. Kayla sat down in the corner of the room on a reading chair that his stepfather sat in while he read his morning paper. Out of the corner of Clint's eye, he could see her sit and pull out a red leather-bound book, and with the speed of light, she started writing in it.

"I wanted to know about that thing that was after us," Clint asked airily.

O'Neil looked around as much as his tired frame would allow as he pulled out his hip flask, opening it and holding it over his hairy face while only a drop or two of the liquid fell out. Whatever was in there, even in its insignificant amount, was enough to make O'Neil cough and go cross-eyed. His voice was oddly husky as he said, "' At thin' was what we call a Spell Binder and an icy one at that." O'Neil seemed that was supposed to be enough.

"What is a Spell Binder?" Clint asked impatiently.

It would be a lie for Clint to say that he didn't see that his questions were annoying O'Neil. O'Neil looked around, checking who was about. He must have been satisfied as he began to speak very quickly, no longer looking annoyed and his voice had returned to normal.

"I cannae tell yoo tae much. Banks gave us orders not tae tell yoo lot tae much and what is going on in our world."

"Why?" Clint shrugged. All his frustrations and worry came out, making him sound louder than he wanted.

"Shh, boy," O'Neil said, looking around once more.

"There is a lot in our world that is different than this one," O'Neil went on.

"But there's a lot we have in common, but everything is different. The people are different, our houses are different, our way of life is different. I could tell yoo some stuff, but me lips is dry. Do yoo have any spirits around?" O'Neil looked at Clint like a small child asking for some candy.

Clint didn't say anything, not wanting to waste any time, as he moved briskly toward the kitchen, opened the fridge, and grabbed a can of pop without looking at what it was.

"Thank yoo, laddie," O'Neil said as Clint handed it to him. O'Neil looked at the cold can oddly, not understanding what to do with it. Mercifully, Clint took it out of his hand and, flipping the top, he opened it impatiently, wanting O'Neil to keep talking.

O'Neil looked at the can as the carbonation and fizz sounded. His eyes boggled, lighting up with excitement as he pulled the can under his nose and inhaled, giving Clint a wink.

As soon as he opened his mouth and poured some in, he immediately went pink, coughed, and spluttered, wheezing like an old car trying to start. Clint panicked, thinking that he'd killed O'Neil as he jumped forward and patted him on the back. O'Neil doubled up, gasping for air as he started to talk like a balloon, letting all the air out, "What is 'at stuff?"

"It's a Pepsi. Are you alright?" Clint asked in bewilderment, checking the can again.

"All right?" O'Neil asked, still struggling to speak.

"That's almost as good as a lass with supple lips, laddie!"

Then, taking another drink, he squealed, "Almost as good. Depends on which one of her lips is better, the top or de bottom but when they swim together to save min', oh, oh, ohhhh."

"You don't seem all right to me," Clint said, smelling the can of Pepsi, checking it. When the words left his lips, the thought followed that none of what was going on was all right to normal people.

O'Neil looked at Clint's face and noticed that he must have been acting strangely. He cleared his throat, trying to compose himself.

He looked misty-eyed at the can of Pepsi as he held it up as if it were the Holy Grail. "Thins are different 'ere. Like our animals are much larger than the ones yoo have here. We got some that I havn' seen 'ere, what did yoo call them again in that show I just watched, uh uh? Meet the Robinsons and Jurassic Pork. Dinosaurs yeah, wah we have plenty ay them, and we don't have only ay these stuff things that you couldn't imagine. There is another stubborn cork in the bottle. Yoo guys don't have any magic or classes. Yoo all just ur, ur, normal." O'Neil looked away from the Pepsi can at Clint as if he might have said something offensive.

"Really?" Clint asked in disbelief. It was like a dream come true. As Clint's mind boggled at all the action going on, he believed O'Neil without question. He could see his world in every detail. The trees, homes, beautiful landscapes, and people are able to do amazing things.

O'Neil must have read Clint's mind and said lowly, "But yoo don't have the evil that comes with it." O'Neil's look of love left his face and changed to a look of somberness and almost regret. He rubbed his thumbs across his drink and said, "I think that's why Banks doesn't want us saying tae much."

"What do you mean?" Clint asked, wanting to hear more.

"Well, our world is large, but those who are members say the Salvations Alliance, tak'—"

"The what?" Clint interrupted, still excited.

"Och 'at, the Salvations Alliance is our government, our military with all da big shots who don't buy a round tae much. Unless it's those religious folk, who—"

"You guys have a religion?" Clint asked in bewilderment, sitting up close on the edge of his seat. As O'Neil tried to gather his thoughts again, Clint could hear Kayla's scratches of her pen as she wrote in her book, but Clint didn't pay her any attention.

"Stop interrupting me, laddie!" O'Neil said weakly.

"Yoo see, there is the Fury, and we are the Salvation. We fight against those who would force their will on us. We fight tae worship and be free. The Fury fight fur moaney, gods and the fight tae enslave and take what isnae theres. Hundreds of years ago, there was the great reclamation People who were evil didn't look like yoo and me, they changed, and it tore families apart when something like yer father or wee brother would git up in the morn and be green. It could happen tae anyone who would dae somethin' wrong."

Clint didn't understand every word but also didn't want to be told off for interrupting again. So he tried to remember his questions for later.

"' En there was the first Great War!" O'Neil went on now looking back at the Pepsi can as if it were his long-lost child.

"The changed, and those who stayed the same were all mixed together, yoo see. So, they all fought as some were still changing while others just didn't know what was goin' on. No one won, but everyone went intae hiding, fur years they stayed underground and when they came out, our world was differen'. There were aw these different people and different animals around. Those bad ones who changed had fled to their lands, and those who were good formed the Salvations Alliance."

O'Neil paused for a moment, taking another drink of Pepsi, which sent him into another struggle for his breath. When he spoke again, it was like hearing a teenager with a cracking voice.

"Those who had changed gathered together and started tae fight us again, they called themselves the Fury and said it was the will ay the Gods that they take back what was theirs." O'Neil looked around to see if they were alone still.

"This was all many years ago; no one really knows how long ago it was, and there is still a great deal ay the land don' ay know about either. We do have something from the past, and they tell us that someday the Requiem will be found and save us." Then O'Neil turned his loving eyes from the Pepsi can and looked very seriously at Clint, "or destroy us."

"But what was that thing that was after us? That Spell Binder… where did that come from?"

"Och, yeah that," O'Neil said looking serious again.

"The Fury arenae like yoo and I. There are many different kinds just as there are as many kinds as us. They move up in rank and wealth by killin' dar superiors. Only the strongest survive, so da say. There are some so bad and strong that they even live around the gods. Those who are that bad are called the counted. They are those who have lived fur so long that they might have even been there since the beginning ay things fur us." O'Neil looked worried for a moment.

Clint sat back in his chair, his head spinning, and for the first time, he started to feel tired as O'Neil looked like he was lost in thought. Their world sounded to Clint a lot like the Garden of Eden, but they had thrown out the snake, and it was trying to get back in.

"How did you get into this?" Clint asked, still wanting to know more but didn't know what.

O'Neil jumped at his voice. "Ooh, yeah…" O'Neil started to explain everything that had happened to him when he found Banks, the night he had ran from some of the Fury when they had escaped mysteriously.

"And you and he didn't know how you got away or what killed all those waiting for you?" Clint asked, his brain hurting with the thought of all the odd things from that other world, like trolls, goblins, and orcs.

"Noo, we don't know. But Banks has been lucky ever since I met him. He was lucky I found him and that we got help from some others around us."

"Others?" Clint asked.

"Yeah, paladins an' such."

Clint didn't need to ask this time. O'Neil took another drink that almost made him pass out as his head fell on the arm of the couch, and, seeing that Clint was going to ask again, he started to explain once more.

"Yoo see some of us in the Salvations Alliance come with gifts and training like old Nix's over there for patching me up. He can heal, Druids wurk with nurture and some like Ohlwiler can command plaints well enough. While others like Tremayne are good with animals, but trust me, son, there are too many fur me tay explain here, and I dinnae know them all me self."

"It is just different than here. We have different animals and people who can do all sorts ay things that yoo lot cannae do here, like, well, magic and stuff, yoo know. And that stuff with the druids I was telling yoo about it has something tae do with their sweat." O'Neil suddenly looked tired.

Clint wanted to ask one more question and, being unable to stop himself, he heard the words come out of his mouth, "What about having a second? You said that's how you can talk to your squirrel."

O'Neil twisted himself to be able to talk to Clint but rest his head. He seemed to be tired but eager to talk. Clint thought that he had had a lot of practice telling stories.

"When we get tae a certain age some can hae a special relationship with just one animal, it's like we're connected. He knows what I am feeling and thinking, and I knows what he is feeling and thinking. Most from our world have one, but some don't."

O'Neil stopped talking suddenly as he heard footsteps coming from the kitchen. O'Neil looked worried and said in a hurry, "That's enough tae be getting' along with boy, thank yoo fur the drink now I have said enough, along with yoo now."

O'Neil laid his head back down as Clint saw Banks and Grant come into the front room. Clint wanted to hear more, but O'Neil's expression told him that he had said too much, and he wasn't going to say any more while others were around. Clint moved, defeated, from his chair toward the office.

"Short quart," O'Neil called to Clint as he wiggled himself comfortably on the couch. "Can yoo call the people ta pop in da box for me again before yoo remove yoor questions tae the other room?"

Clint resumed the movie for O'Neil and followed Banks, who had taken Grant into the office where Kayla must have just entered.

Banks stood at attention, seemingly holding Grant up. Grant looked weaker and feebler than usual as Banks rested his hands on his shoulders. Clint quietly snuck in so as not to interrupt what everyone was saying and saw Banks looked just as tired as Grant. As Clint sat down on a corner of the office desk, Clint shook his head to make certain because Grant looked more out of place at that moment than Banks. Grant seemed to be jumpy and turned his head at any noise.

"It is late, but I know none of you will sleep until you are all briefed. Tamara, report on what you told your grandmother and sister, please."

Surprisingly, Clint saw Tamara stand tall at once and speak like she was a soldier. "They know you are here but think you are the foreign family that has come to stay with us," she said proudly. Her proud attitude, on the other hand, didn't spread to everyone else in the room. They all looked at her like she was a stranger off the street. Especially Cody, whose eyes looked like they were going to fall out of his head and drop into his open mouth. Grant wasn't looking at her. He seemed to be in some type of shock. His blood-red eyes now barely left the floor, his expression vacant.

"What situation do you have tomorrow?" Banks asked like he was reading everything off an agenda sheet in a business office.

"We all have school," Kayla stated. She sounded like she was a little firmer than normal when she said it and looked past Tamara.

"How can all of you proceed to school and return with the best chance of safety?" Banks asked.

"I can drive my father's car, drop everyone off, and pick them up," Cody said, sounding like the very thought of the idea scared him.

Banks didn't look exactly sure what this meant but agreed almost at once. "We will be watching all of you as much as we can, although I feel if one of us was with you, it would arouse suspicion. Also, Kayla, we need to cover up everything that happened today, so no one is any the wiser that you and your family are anything but normal. Understand?"

It looked like everyone wanted to say something, but Banks never gave them the chance as he smiled and left the room. A protracted pause where no one said anything, after Banks left, was shared until Kayla got up and moved Grant to a chair. She sat him down and laid a blanket over him. Kayla went to talk to Cody for a moment while Tamara walked over to Grant and hugged him. Grant started to cry as soon as she wrapped her arms around him as if he had just learned how to. Kayla came back with Cody and said, smiling, "We think we have an idea of what to tell everyone about Cody's work and why Grant is home, but we need to hear what happened first."

Everyone looked at Grant, and for the first time since he was home, he was able to talk. He explained what had happened to him as best as he could. What was odd was he talked better as he went on. As if telling the story made living with what had just happened easier for him. When he finished, he asked everything he could about what was going on at home. It took some time to have him stop asking questions and listen as they all explained once more, starting with Clint. From how the day had started and was now ending to how they were all sitting in the same room together. It was almost one in the morning when they were done talking. Everyone was exhausted and hungry as if they had just relived everything that day all over again. Cody went into the kitchen to make sandwiches for everyone while Clint and Kayla talked about how it might be better if they all slept in the same room that night. Tamara and Grant were both quietly hugging one another almost the entire time and didn't say much.

After eating and Clint finally convincing O'Neil to turn down the volume on the TV, they all lay down to go to sleep, spread around the office in sleeping bags.

It took a long time for Clint's mind to stop thinking about what had happened that day as he lay down in the far corner of the office, resting his head on his pillow. Images of the dagger, the trip in the dark to the gas station, the wolves Grant had faced, and that Spell Binder. That terrible hood that hid its face and its long white fingers of death with just the tips barely visible under that cloak.

Clint's mind was still rolling over the memories when he started hearing everyone else's snores as they all fell asleep all around him. Cody was by far the noisiest in the room. He fell asleep as soon as his head hit the pillow and began snoring. Clint rolled over and couldn't help but wonder what the next day would bring. The only light in the office was from the wall rotating portraits. All of them changed, save one above his head, which was an ordinary poster of their family. As his eyes closed, he could still see each family member in that unchanging picture. He wondered if their family would make it with everything that was changing around them, just like that picture and all those around it.

He lay seeing it in his mind until he rolled over and saw the night gather in the darkness next to the door. Suddenly, the Spell Binder stood in the corner of the room and limped toward him. Clint felt his insides go cold as he tried to yell, but all that came out was his cold breath in a vapor cloud. He sat up fast as the sound of its black robes dragged on the floor, bringing it closer to him. It dragged one leg horribly, inching its way closer as Clint's limbs refused to move from fatigue and fear. He managed to push his back into the corner next to the bookshelf. The point of the Spell Binder's hood turned on him and moved slowly in his direction.

"Clint Holden," it rasped out as it walked lamely, coming closer and closer.

Clint held out his hands to shield himself from the Spell Binder, still being unable to say a word. All he was able to do was moan and whimper out of shock and the growing cold that was consuming him. The Spell Binder limped and dragged its carcass until it stood before him. It took its time to straighten its horrible frame and brought its hood down lower on Clint.

"Clint Holden," it breathed out, sounding like a demon.

Nowhere to go, Clint only crouched in the corner with arms shaking and faced his death. The horrible figure bent down over him. With one slow move, it held out its left white hand, and under it, Clint could see two paper white fingers coming to him from under the cloak. He tried to yell, he tried to scream, but nothing came out as those white ghost-like fingers moved closer and closed on Clint's fourth finger of his right hand.

As if Clint's finger was made of a toothpick, the Spell Binder froze it in an instant and broke it off with a terrifying snap. Clint screamed.

Shocked, Clint lifted his head from his pillow, cold with sweat and tangled up in his sleeping bag. Gasping for air, he looked around and saw that there was nothing in the room with him other than his family. He brought up his hand and saw all five of his fingers unharmed. It had been a dream, a horrible life-like dream. No one else was awake, and looking at his watch told him that it was only four in the morning. Shaken and still scared, he crawled back into his sleeping bag, burying himself down as far as he could go in it, and started a silent cry. He was crying himself to sleep, trying to get as warm as possible to get away from the cold feeling that was still in his chest. That cold feeling that he felt when his finger was snapped off in his dream. That cold feeling that he felt when he knew he was going to die.

Thirty-Four

THE BEST KNOCK-KNOCK JOKE ENDS WITH A HIT OVER THE HEAD

Clint heard hurried footsteps, and excited whispers woke him up. He couldn't remember the dream he had had, but he still felt very scared, as if it had really happened. He pulled his head out of his sleeping bag like a frightened turtle. glancing around with his messed-up hair to see where all the noise was coming from. Clint could make out Banks by the front door, also looking like he had just woken up himself, gazing around, signaling at least two others that were close by him. Clint couldn't see who they were because the desk impaired his vision, blocking his line of sight so he could only see the boots on their feet.

Clint sat up fast, seeing that Cody was also up, and when their eyes met, Cody held up a finger to his lips, telling him to be quiet. Cody was by the office door, standing looking in the crack between where the door was attached to the frame, the rest of the open door concealing him from view. Then he pointed with the same finger that he held to his lips toward the door and then motioned for Clint to stay down. Clint nodded vigorously and laid his head down as Banks unsheathed a long sword from his belt side. There was a soft count from someone upstairs as Banks put his free hand on the doorknob when the sound of whoever was counting called down softly, "One."

As his eyes slowly focused, Clint could see Banks tighten his hand on the knob as the count of "Two" was called down. Someone or something must be coming to the door, Clint gathered.

That must be Ravin, Transun, or Ohlwiler because it was a girl's voice that was up at the top of the stairs, he thought, as they said just a little louder, "Three."

Banks threw open the door and lunged out, bringing the long sword over his head down. Clint sat bolt upright with his chest heaving in shock. There was a thud and the sound of feet moving fast. Banks was moving back into the house, back hunched, dragging something large behind him. The desk was in the way, not letting Clint see exactly what it was as Banks shut the door quickly and looked up, "Anyone see?" he asked whoever was upstairs.

"Clear," the woman called from above as Clint got to his feet, and despite Cody's continued waves for Clint to lay down, he walked briskly toward the fallen figure unconscious on the floor by the doorway. Banks was now moving fast to secure the person's hands behind their back with a piece of leather he pulled from his pocket when he called out, "All clear." More footsteps came, some from upstairs while others were from around the doorway. Two other figures that Clint had not noticed until now appeared next to the door as he walked into the lobby, and the woman who upstairs came down. The television was back on, showing a new movie for O'Neil as he let out a high laugh.

Moving closer to the person on the floor, Banks jumped over the body and pushed Clint back. "Careful!" he cried. "He might be faking; stay back till I know for certain."

Banks had pushed Clint back to the wall, moved over to the body once more, and tied the person's feet. Whoever it was wore jeans, a normal T-shirt, and black bowl-cut hair. After Banks had tied him up with remarkable speed he stepped back and for some reason kicked the body on the ground hard in the leg. Just then, there was a shriek as Tamara shot past Clint toward the body out cold on the floor. When she turned him over, Clint could see why she had screamed.

It was the paperboy. "Is he dead?" Tamara shrieked again like an angry cat.

"No, just knocked out." Banks said confidently. "Do you know this boy?"

"Yes, he is the paperboy," she said, flustered as she lifted his head and examined it. Clint could see a large bump starting to rise on the very top of that bowl-cut head. Unable to stop himself, Clint started to laugh. It started as a soft snicker until it grew into a full belly laugh. This probably wasn't the best thing to happen to Tamara first thing in the morning because, in a fraction of a second, she was no longer the new Tamara after Banks had talked to her, but the old mean one again. Clint could see it in her face as she got up so quickly that she forgot that the boy's head was resting on her knee, and when she raised, the boy's head hit the ground hard with a sickening thud as if someone had just dropped a melon.

"That will cause another lump," Clint said, still laughing. Now Cody was laughing heartily with him as Banks shook his head and muttered, "Kids," as he sat down on the stairs, wiping his face and sheathing his sword. Tamara stepped on the paperboy on her way to go toe-to-toe with Clint. The laughing had woken everyone else up as Clint could hear their yawns and movement behind him as Cody kept laughing on and on.

Tamara was seething and looked like she was about to hit Clint, but right before she was on top of him, Banks cleared his throat. Tamara stopped at once and looked back to Banks, who didn't even meet her eyes with his own.

Tamara glanced at Clint and looked at her hands. Suddenly, she said, "Sorry," and without another word, she turned and ran up the stairs past Banks, who avoided her gaze as he leaned to give her room, and then she was gone.

Cody was helping everyone else get up as Clint watched Banks, who was still wiping off his face. Clint could see that Banks looked very tired and pale, like he hadn't slept or eaten much the past few days. Clint could not stop himself from asking after he finished laughing when he got to the foot of the stairs.

"What did you say to her the other day?" he demanded.

Banks stopped cleaning himself and sized up Clint as he put his handkerchief away. "I told her what she needed to hear. I told her the truth about how she looked and what she was doing. She didn't see herself that way at the time, but she was ready to hear it. I will tell you when you are ready to hear about yourself." Banks got to his feet. "Now get ready for what you have to do today and change out of those silly pajamas." Then he went out toward the back door, not allowing Clint to say another word.

Time flew by as everyone hastily made themselves ready, with constant distractions at every turn. The first came when Cody went to use the bathroom on the main floor and found a tree growing in the toilet. It also didn't help Cody when Corbin asked him what he'd eaten that caused it. The subsequent discovery was when Kayla, who was getting toast for breakfast, looked out the back window to see someone out in the backyard cooking over a small fire. Cody was the one who went out and explained the existence of modern-day ovens and refrigerators. As they watched him through the window, it looked like Cody had great difficulty trying to make them understand. He made them promise to clean up the yard and find another place for the tree in the bathroom. The best part was that while that was going on, Grant was trying to explain the revolution of indoor plumbing to them by shouting out the back door. This was also compounded with shouts from their grandmother, telling everyone that all the kids would do their best to remember to lift the lid.

It seemed Grant couldn't bring himself to get too close to their protectors and didn't want to leave the house. Grant gave up shouting when Mrs. Hutchings's dog next door started to bark. Grant retreated from the doorway and ran for his life. It seemed that any dog, no matter the size, would now give him cause to change his pants.

Once Clint had finished getting ready, he was to find out the effect of caffeine on a Dwarf who'd had thirty-three and a half cans of Pepsi during the night and had been watching movies without blinking once. Everyone else finished getting ready and had to wait for Kayla to gather her books so they could leave.

As they gathered in the hallway to the garage, a silent alarm was raised when someone on the second floor reported four people were watching the house.

"L, I, O?" Banks called, asking as he pushed by all of the kids, making his way toward the front door as he had done with each alarm.

"Front, across the street way, they are scouting and appear to be trained. No indication of being hostile, just observing." Now that it was silent and his interest peaked, Clint could tell that it was Hobb who was reporting from upstairs.

Chiowood appeared out of the kitchen in a soft jog and took up a guarding position between the kids and the door while Banks lay flat on the ground, rising just enough to peer out in the street. No one moved or even breathed for what seemed like an eternity.

"What is L, I, O?" Kayla asked in a whisper to Chiowood.

"Location, Intention, and Outfit," Chiowood whispered back over his shoulder, not taking his eyes off the Banks, and even raised his hands to hover over the hilt of a small axe without a blade that hung from his belt.

"Hobb," Banks said, barely audible, "I want demon darts for all four."

"Sir," Hobb replied, and Clint could hear the soft sounds of his feet retreating. Chiowood let his guard down and relaxed when he heard this.

"Demon dart?" Grant said, more in fear than asking a question.

"Go have a look-see," came the voice of Tremayne from the corner of the dining room."

"It still could be dangerous," Chiowood called back down the hall to Tremayne.

"The only danger would be ah standing next tae what your aiming at Chio," Tremayne laughed back. "They would be safe to take their eyes for a walk tae see. Might even teach 'em somethen so we don' have another pap' boy problem. Nix is in 'ere still sorten that one out and if this keeps up, we will be full up soon unconscious, lopsided biscuit eaters."

Chiowood's body language told them that he disagreed, but he bowed low, waving his hand and inviting them to pass. Cody was the first to burst up as Banks stood up and nodded his approval to let them watch. It was a mad dash for all of them to get to the best window to look out. Clint settled to be on all fours to see squishing his face against the glass in the same place Banks had next to the door, with almost everyone above him watching intently.

Clint saw three men dressed in suits and a sharply dressed woman standing beside two cars in the road in front of their house.

"Hey, hey, that is the guy who was there last night?" Cody yelled, and as he stood in excitement, he caused everyone around him to fall over and lose their balance.

"Cody," they all shouted in protest.

"Keep it down!" Grandma yelled again as they all untangled themselves and looked out the window again.

Nothing seemed to be happening until there was a soft call from upstairs. "Hobb is ready," Transun said softly. "On your order."

Banks was walking down the hall when he said, "Do it."

Clint and Corbin eagerly watched and saw all four of those spying on the house, one by one slapping their necks and then fall to the ground.

"Wow," everyone whistled together.

"What will happen to them?" Kayla asked, sounding worried.

"Just watch," Chiowood said grudgingly, standing at attention in the hallway.

Each of the four who had fallen got to their feet and looked around momentarily. After what looked like a quick conversation, they got back into their two cars and drove off.

"What just happened?" Tamara asked as she left the window in the office.

"It's the demon dart," Chiowood said as he reached into a pouch on his belt. They all pushed their heads together as they looked at what he held out in his hand. It was no larger than a bee and seemed to also move like one, only it wasn't alive. It looked as if it were made of wood and leaf, yet was almost life-like.

"Demon dart?" Corbin asked in wonder. His eyes were popping.

"Yeah, Tremayne mixed this batch up for us," Chiowood explained for the first time sounding civil and all right with what was going on that morning. "When they hit, they sting a bit, but after a moment, you forget about an hour or two of what was going on."

"I could use one of those," Cody said, not thinking.

"On what?" Kayla asked, sounding like their mother.

"Chiowood," Banks called from the dining room. Chiowood snapped to attention, returning the dart. "Get them moving," Banks ordered.

It was a worried and concerned group that went into the garage while Cody got into his stepfather's Jaguar and got ready to start it up. Banks came into the garage as they were all getting into the car.

"We are bringing the paperboy and ask you to drop him off where someone will find him but where no one will see you or know that you had anything to do with him. We will have Nuts check in on you when he can at different parts of the day. We will also have one or two of us close to your schools in case anything happens. You all go straight there and come straight back, understood?"

"Yes," Cody said, and then, thinking fast, he continued, "There is a dance tomorrow for most of us."

"Sorry, but that is impossible," Banks said without hesitating. There was a calamity of moans and displeasure from everyone in the car who was going to go.

"Look," Banks said normally, but it carried the sound that brought everyone to silence.

"We are here to protect you and find the Requiem, but for those of you who haven't thought of it yet, the Fury is here, and when and if we find the Requiem and go back, there is a question for you and us. Will the Fury just leave as well and not do any harm to you?"

No one said anything, as the weight of what Banks said dumbfounded them with fear. "They are not going to leave us alone, are they?" Kayla asked.

"Would you?" Banks asked as Nix and Transun threw the paperboy's unctuous body into the back of the car over their legs. They handled him with all the care of a bag of garbage being thrown out.

Clint thought for a moment; he knew the answer and said it with the same pain he'd felt when his finger was frozen and broken off in his dream. "No, they won't."

"We are going to have to stop them or convince them that you have nothing they want," Banks said as he stood up. "We will care for your grandmother and sister here while we do a delicate search. Don't worry, we won't disturb anything."

While Nix came up next to him and said soberly, "The paperboy has been given a mild sedative, and he will wake up in an hour or so. Hopefully, he won't remember too well what happened to him." Nix smirked as he went back into the house as if he was enjoying himself.

Banks started to turn to follow Nix, but Tamara called out to him and stopped him. "How are you going to do all that with the Fury?" She called as she moved over to the window and stuck her head out.

"I am going to keep things simple," Banks said as if he were explaining one and one make two with a smile. "I am going to kill the one who wants to kill me. If I can't change their mind first." His smile widened as he hit the top of the car with his fist and walked back into the house.

They sat in the car befuddled, staring at where Banks was standing as if his spirit was still there, and it was going to tell them more. When nothing came to them, Cody said mockingly, "So, there is nothing to worry about."

"That is the dumbest thing I have heard today," Grant said dully as he took another shot from his inhaler.

Thirty-Five

SCHOOL IS JUST NOT THE SAME WITHOUT SOMEONE TRYING TO KILL YOU

The garage door opened, revealing the dull light of a cloudy sky that looked as if it couldn't decide whether it was going to rain or not. They started to drive very slowly, with Cody behind the wheel, white-knuckled, searching every direction for anything that might harm them. He was not looking for any of the Fury that might come, but he was more concerned about the car than his own life.

"The Fury would be a dream come true to deal with compared to Dad if anything happens to his car while he is away," Cody said when Kayla asked why they were going so slow and if he saw anything while he was looking around.

They drove on as a light drizzle started to fall. It was just enough to start the windshield wipers going. Kayla was in the back talking with Grant, going over the plan of his explanation of what happened the night before.

"Let me hear it one more time, Grant?" Kayla said smartly.

Grant, still numb but jumping anytime he thought he heard a dog bark as if he were drunk with sleep, suddenly woken up. "We have been through this a hundred times, and you already called and left a message to my scout leader to let them know I am home," he sniffed in annoyance. Kayla gave him a look that told him to start talking, or by the time he filled out his Will, it would be too late for him.

"All right, but the law would be on my side for harassment," Grant said as he droned on.

Grant didn't even move a muscle as he started to talk. "We were sitting by the fire when I saw one of the leaders throw something funny into the fire, so I went to the bathroom. When I came back, everyone was high and out of their minds. So, I came home."

He ended with another sniff, and it was amazing how he could put so little emotion into what he was saying. Kayla nodded, "Right, that should cover everything for you, and that might even get those kids to stop bullying you."

"Here is a good spot for the Mr. Love paper cut," Cody said, and it was amazing, Clint thought, that they could drive any slower as they pulled over to the curb. Everyone checked once again to see if anyone was around as they tossed the paperboy out on the curb and made a speedy getaway, the Jaguar idling down the road with all the haste of a snail. They only went on for a few feet when the car stopped and reversed back to the body. The rear door opened, allowing a hand to deliver today's paper on his body, with a note in Kayla's neat handwriting attached saying, "To anyone who finds me. I am a mentally handicapped boy, please help me. P.S. I am friendly."

Nothing met them on the way to school as their eyes moved around nonstop as if evil were at every turn. They dropped Kayla and Grant off at their elementary school front door and made it to their school just as most kids were going inside. Cody found a parking spot that was far away from most other cars. They all took an extra moment together as if they wanted to go over something, but no one wanted to start a conversation. Clint was the first to just smile and get out, leaving everyone still sitting dumbstruck.

The start of school was easy enough without any major problems unless you count that no one had done any of their homework the night before. The fact that this was the second day that Clint and Corbin both had other things on their minds and didn't pay much attention to what was going on in their classes did not help them either. It wasn't until lunchtime that the fun started for Clint.

He had gotten his food, and with everyone around talking loudly in the cafeteria, Clint went to his usual seat, where he always ate. He sat down when the same red-haired girl who was sitting on the other side of the table noticed him. She looked like she wanted to talk to him.

"Did you find him?" she asked as she put some food in her mouth.

"Find him? Find him, him, find who, him who?" Clint said, much louder than normal, looking around and trying to look smooth.

She held up a hand for him to wait as she finished what she was chewing in her mouth.

"Corbin, did you find Corbin?"

"Corbin? Why, where is he? Is something wrong?" Clint asked, frightened and out of his mind. He looked left and right. He got to his feet, knocking his tray and causing the food to dance dangerously on the corner, almost falling to the floor.

Suddenly, a hand fell on his shoulder, making Clint snap his neck over so hard that it hurt. It was Corbin looking at him in concern; unfortunately, the lack of conversation around him meant that everyone was looking at them. Swallowing, Clint knew that this time, everyone looking at him was not a good thing. Smiling weakly at them all, Clint sat back down as the red-haired girl said, "So you did find Corbin; yesterday, you were looking for him." She gave him a worried look as she scooted her seat further away from him.

"What's wrong with you, I mean, other than the usual?" Corbin whispered into Clint's ear as he sat down, setting his food tray on the table. Clint's eyes moved around, seeing everyone close to him still looking at him.

"Would you sit down? There aren't any paparazzi here for you! Everyone is still looking." Clint felt Corbin hit him hard in the leg, making him sit down, but not as smooth as he tried to be as he missed his chair and, with a loud thud, hit the floor painfully. Clint felt everyone's attention come back to him as he felt the pain in his hip start to throb where he hit the floor.

"Would you sit down, you idiot? You are embarrassing me!" Corbin breathed out through his teeth, not moving his lips. Corbin extended a hand down to Clint, who took it. He looked around at everyone who was watching him, feeling his cheeks turning red.

"Some moron spilled their drink," Clint said as he started to sit down. "Who spilled their drink here? You could hurt someone!" Corbin yelled out to everyone who could hear him as Clint finally sat safely down, smiling stupidly.

It took only seconds for everyone to return to their conversations and lunches. Clint could see through the windows in the ceiling the storm was gaining strength as the rain fell harder without giving a glimpse of hope of letting up as lightning flashed overhead.

The red-haired girl had given up on trying to talk to Clint and went back to busying herself with her friend next to her, talking very fast about the dance and who they might go with. She seemed to think that Clint was being stupid on purpose.

Clint and Corbin started to eat their lunches, and the attention was gone from Clint enough that Corbin thought it was safe for them to talk. Corbin leaned over and, speaking low enough that only Clint could hear him, he said, "Now that you have finished acting drunk, I need to tell you that you need to watch out. Amber has a bounty on your head and is looking for you."

"What does she want with me?" Clint said as he wondered what else would happen to him.

"I don't see her here; so far so good, right?" Corbin said while craning his neck, looking around over the heads of those around them.

"Yeah, right, the princess of preening herself. She wouldn't be caught dead eating in the lowly lunchroom with peasants like us."

"Who you calling a peasant?" Corbin said through a mouth full of pizza with all the glory of an infant trying solid food for the first time.

"Why do you want to not see her? If she were looking for me," Corbin said as he whipped some sauce from his lips, "she would never have to look for another man again."

Clint almost looked like he was going to throw up, "She's the devil," he stuttered.

"Hey guys," someone called, slapping their backs, causing Corbin to gag on a mouth full of food and Clint to jump so hard that his knee hit the bottom of the lunch table, making everyone's lunch bounce on their trays. It was Cody, as he pushed both to move aside so he could sit between them, pulling away from another student behind them, causing them to fall.

It was probably from the pain in his knee or the fact that everyone around was looking at them once more that made Clint say angrily, "What are you doing here, Cody?"

Cody slapped Corbin on the back a couple more times as he was gagging even more on his last bite. "You, OK?" he asked Corbin as his face now was turning from greenback to his normal color. Corbin was coughing but nodded to Cody, letting him know he was alright.

"Why aren't you in class?" Clint asked, rubbing his sore knee.

Cody smiled as he spoke low enough so he couldn't be overheard. "I got out of class because I need to tell you that my practice after school is canceled, and I will see you by the car as soon as your classes are over." He stood up and said to those around them, "I know it's hard, but you can only take one girl to the dance."

"Why do you sound like a bad undercover cop?" Corbin asked, looking disgusted.

Cody ignored him as he bent over and whispered once more, "Also, I heard that there was something on the news this morning about a local family near here that had been killed as they ate breakfast. They took fingerprints at the scene and are looking for those who were seen running away when it happened."

Clint and Corbin looked at one another in shock. "What are we going to do?" Clint said low enough that no one could hear him, but Corbin read his lips. "I don't know," Corbin mouthed back. "Why do you keep asking that?"

"See you two after school," Cody said loudly as he started to walk away and left the cafeteria as heads turned following him. Most heads, except for Corbin and Clint, were preoccupied with their meals and just sat there looking down depressingly. Clint rubbed his head where he got hit the night before. It didn't hurt in that one spot, but his head sure did with everything that was going on. Corbin was looking around for a moment as if an answer was going to come to him if he just looked hard enough and found it.

"They are going to connect that something is going on with my family sooner or later, with everything with that family that was murdered, you and I running down the street away from where they were killed, Cody's bad day at work, and Grant's escape from that pound puppy trainer in the forest. How can things get worse?"

There was a tap on Clint's shoulder, and being deep in thought, he didn't jump but turned slowly around. This time, it was a girl who was standing behind him. Clint didn't recognize her, but she looked like she had eaten a double portion of unattractive cereal. Clint felt suddenly tired and didn't say anything while Corbin gave a small scream of fright at the sight of her.

"Clint Holden," she said with a smile that showed off her braces and the headset wrapped around her wild and tangled hair.

"Yeah?" he asked as Corbin was so overcome with the giggles he hid his head in his arms.

"I wanted to talk to you about your invitation to the dance this Friday and what we were going to be doing," she said; it wasn't a question. It didn't help that those thin steel rods in her mouth made her slur her every word and spit on him.

"Oh, that," Clint said, smiling at her while giving Corbin a dirty look he didn't see as he had his head down in his pizza and lunch tray. As Clint turned to face her, he kicked Corbin under the table, which only made Corbin snort as he laughed. Clint let out a heavy sigh before saying, "My invitation for you to the dance? Uh, well, I am sorry I, I…"

"He would be happy to go with you," Corbin said as he turned with remarkable speed and somehow was no longer laughing.

"What?" Clint shouted, at a loss for words. Clint's mind stopped working from what he was hearing and his best friend's ability to turn from a laughing clown to someone who could change his attitude to a law attorney with a straight stone face.

"I'm sorry I, I, I, can't, can't go with, with you," Clint stuttered in shock. He looked back and forth between the two. The contrast he saw was her look of disappointment and Corbin's look of glee.

"It's not because of you," Clint softened the blow, trying to save himself. "I have to stay home and take care of my grandmother; it's not because of what you look like, not that you look bad or anything, or that you would look bad; I am not saying that you would look bad, or that you even look bad now." Her disappointed look started to change as she was getting upset. She put her hands on her hips while two of her friends with similar facial qualities stepped in on either side of her. "I would love to go with you; I mean, who wouldn't want to go with you? Any boy, uh, man, would love you, I mean love to, die, uh, dance, I mean." Her eyes were ice.

"Go with you. I think…" he finished, adding a quick smile. The smile faded as quickly as it came until it appeared with a genuine one when a new thought came to him.

"Corbin could go with you," he said, partly pleading. "You are not going with anyone yet, are you, uh, Corbin."

Corbin turned and took a bite out of his pizza, turning back with his mouth full, and said something that sounded like a no. Then, as he smiled, allowing some of the food to fall out of his mouth and on the floor as he chewed noisily, smacking his lips together, he asked, "What was your name again?"

"Stacy," she grunted as she gripped her hands firmly on her hips, looking at him like he was a cockroach. Stacy looked to her left and right friends and winked at one. "Take his name for processing," she told one of them.

"What is your name once more?" the largest of the three girls demanded from Corbin as she took out a pad of paper and a pen accusingly.

"Uh, Corbin. At least I think it is today," he noted with all the nobility past a mouth full of food.

She sneered as she wrote down Corbin's name and then swiftly struck a line through his name, portraying she'd just happily cut his throat as Stacy and her other friend started to walk away.

Before the young lady with the pad went away, she shot at Corbin, "You will meet with an accident before the day is over. Sharp objects will fall around you. Light will fall as a Hulk will chase you." Then her eyes widened malevolently, adding, "And no one will go with you to the dance." She raised both her hands like she was casting a spell and said madly, "It is done, and the curse is on you."

Corbin watched on his face expressionless as he said, "Uh, thank you."

The girl waved her hands at Corbin in some odd manner as if she were trying to shoo a large insect, whispering, "Shame on you." Then, walking away with Corbin and Clint, watching all three go away proudly until Stacy hit her foot on someone else's chair leg, causing her to stumble slightly but not to fall.

As soon as she was gone, Clint hit Corbin on the shoulder as hard as he could in his cramped space. "What are you doing? You sent an invitation to her from me. What were you thinking?" Clint yelled while not caring to keep his voice down. Corbin was laughing so hard he couldn't sit still in his seat.

"Well, I thought if everyone else said no, she would say yes." It was remarkable how he was able to laugh squeakily between each word.

"How did you pick her name out of the rabbit's hat?" Clint called as he pounded his head on the table. Corbin was laughing so hard he was choking on each word, "I saw her on a documentary of a safari special in my science class."

Clint hit him again, which made his laughter turn into a kind of whimper of laugh and mown. "OK, OK, I asked Zack yesterday who was one of the smartest girls in the school and one that he liked. So now you see the winning combination of Zack's dream for the dance and brains."

"I wouldn't keep talking about her like that!" Clint warned as he tried to eat once more and not laugh at his friend, who was still snickering stupidly. "With our luck, they are going be to be right about you. You are most likely to meet with a terrible accident today, and you aren't going to the dance either." Corbin suddenly stopped laughing and looked at Clint in mocking outrage.

"Oh no, you don't mean?" he looked all around, even under the table, "That today is going to be my last day, and I won't be able to take Stacy out to the dance? No, not the, THE CURSSSSSE!"

Clint gave him a dirty look and got up, taking his tray with him. He didn't feel like eating anymore. He threw his food away and while he placed his tray to be washed Corbin appeared behind him. He shoved what was left of his food in his mouth, so he could follow Clint. Corbin started to say something, but Clint couldn't understand him as he moved out of everyone's path to put their trays away. He looked out over his fellow students, seeing all of them in their school uniforms eating and having a typical day. Clint took a deep sigh, thinking of how his life had changed in just one day when something funny struck him. In one of the corners where some of the gothic kids hung out, he didn't see his sister or her boyfriend.

"Clint, are you listening to me?" Corbin asked. "Corbin, I don't see Tamara," Clint said horrified. Clint ran over to the corner, passing and bumping into most of the kids without giving them an apology. "Have any of you seen Tamara?" he gasped to her friends.

They all looked at him as if he were an outsider lost and in the wrong room. A tall girl in a young man's arms, both leaning against the wall, held out her hands to all those around as if she had something to say. She had most of her hair forward and sticking up as if she had put her wig on backward and upside down with enough hairspray to stop a bullet.

"Who is asking?" she asked indignantly.

Clint looked at her closely, seeing that she looked like she had just woken up, and the only makeup she had put on was something a bank robber would use.

"I am her brother. Where is she?" he said desperately. The group of kids that he was talking to exchanged a look that said they could care less. Clint didn't waste any more time with them and jogged at a steady pace out of the lunchroom.

Clint heard Corbin moaning, "Where are you going? I eat too fast for this," as he followed him through the school to where Tamara's locker was. Not caring about the many people looking at him oddly because of their haste, he found that she wasn't at her locker either. Frustration and fear were closing in on him as he tried to think about where she could be.

"Haven't you been listening to me?" Corbin gasped, holding his stomach. "Why don't you listen to me for a moment?" he said as Clint tried to run past him, but Corbin grabbed onto him, bringing him to a stop. "Maybe she's at her boyfriend's locker?" Clint said as Corbin brought his feet to a halt.

"That is what I was trying to tell you before. You almost made me throw up trying to follow you," Corbin said as he slumped over on the lockers. "Her boyfriend isn't here today; she told us last night while you were talking with O'Neil that she was going to break up with him and that she wasn't going to the dance. I saw her this morning. She was fine when I saw her."

Clint forced himself to calm down as his mind still swept him around, seeing his sister being taken away by the Spell Binder. Corbin patted Clint on the back as if it were from a brother. Clint felt then that he was almost crying when Corbin said, "I know I haven't been helping you today. I guess I have been just having a hard time with what has been going on. It's like a video game just became real, but I can't go running down the street to warn people."

"I know," Clint said mournfully as he put his hand on Corbin's back. It wasn't until they noticed and remembered that they weren't alone in the hallway that they both pulled back their hands off each other as if they had been electrically shocked.

"Uh, let's get ready for class before the bell rings," Clint said as he straightened up. "We do have one thing going for us," Corbin said with all the dignity of a soldier in the Alamo. "They are not going to come get us in school."

"Why is that?"

"Too many witnesses and even they wouldn't survive the stuff we get served for lunch, and they wouldn't dare come around Amber today."

They both walked to their lockers, and it was really nice not to be around too many students as there were not many in the hallways. Clint started opening his locker while Corbin waited patiently with his eyes peeled, looking up and down the hallway. All of a sudden, Corbin's mouth fell open, and a look of shock erupted on his pudgy face. Clint looked at Corbin's boyish features fall away while he was looking at something at the far end of the hallway. Before Clint could turn around to see what it was, Corbin said one word in an undertone, "Amber." Clint spun around to see Amber and her popular army right behind her, emerging from the dark corner of the hall and heading right for him.

"Uh oh," Clint said as Amber's arm shot toward his face. Clint flinched, thinking that she was going to slap him. Opening one eye, he saw that she had stopped short of hitting him and leaned her hand next to his head to hold his locker door open. Clint froze until she slammed it shut for him, causing him to shut his eyes tighter. She stood before him seething, nostrils flaring as she breathed heavily in anger. There was a slight pause before Clint opened his eyes to see Amber's perfect face and Corbin twiddling his thumbs behind him, looking up at the ceiling.

"Clint Holden," Amber said feverishly.

Clint gulped before his voice cracked, "Amber, I know an invitation was sent to you by, well, me, and I know that you were coming to talk to me about it. I mean, why else would you talk to me?"

"Shut up," Amber ordered. "Like, all the others I needed to talk to came to me. Not like rude you, who made me come down here to tell you. I could have just sent a text if you were like a real human who I would have a phone number for. I mean, because of this, you are lowering my street cred."

Amber took a moment to compose herself before she started talking again. This time, she sounded as if she were reading every word off a piece of paper: "Clint, I have to tell you by due consideration from all the invitations I received and the many hours of deliberation on each invitation I have to…"

"Wait!" Clint shouted, shaking his head. Corbin turned around and saw a cheerleader standing quietly behind them, holding a paper, revealing that she was indeed reading every word she was saying.

"I can't go with you!" Silence filled the hall as everyone froze in astonishment. Save for Amber, who kept reading until what Clint said started to sink in. For a single moment, Clint thought that the conversation was going to be over, but it took a long time for the eruption of understanding to hit Amber. Her face went blank, and she stood shaking as all her beautiful henchmen cowered in disbelief. They started to inch away from the volcano of emotion.

Her face began to turn malicious. She looked at him as if suddenly he were the only thing between her and life itself. Clint suddenly got that smile that only lasted a second, backing away flat against the locker before she said tensely, "You, you are telling me that you, you, wouldn't go, with, me."

This gave way for everyone else in the hall to mutter, "Oooohhhhh."

Clint watched in terror as a tear started in Amber's right eye.

"Uh, yeah. I think," Clint said ambiguously.

A piercing scream filled the city as Amber went rigid. Clint closed his eyes again and covered his ringing ears. He thought a bomb had just exploded in front of him.

Opening one eye, Clint looked at Corbin for help. Corbin tried to gain his balance but being thrown back by the force before he simply gulped, looking like he'd come to school without clothes.

Once Amber's reverberating cry finally subsided, everyone's attention and senses returned to normal, and Clint opened his other eye. He thought that perhaps, as the people in the hallway had started to move that, Amber would come to her senses. But from the look, she was giving him a sick feeling that covered him as if he were a target for a nuclear weapon test. She started to fill her lungs as her chest expanded. Any second, she was going to blow as she was about to decapitate him. Shockingly, she let out a long sigh as her friends took a step forward as if to support her.

"What did you say?" Amber asked calmly.

"Uhh," is all Clint could let out.

"What do you mean you won't go with me?" she snapped, breathing heavily once more.

Clint looked yearningly, silently reaching for Corbin to help him. Corbin slapped his hand away, crouched low with his fingers in his ears, and ducked down, holding his head.

Clint opened his mouth, but nothing came out as Amber moved slowly up to him, looking like she had to have his cooperation or all life on this planet would end.

She stopped two inches from his face. From her grinding teeth to her widening mad eyes, she waited for what must have been a minute. She seemed to be like a viper ready to strike, and with a stab of horror, she yelled ferociously, "You will go with me and no one else, Clint Holden!" Abruptly, she turned away, stretching out her arms, parting the way of people before her. She seemed to be an insulted queen in a fashion show march until she came to the last of her friends. She turned to her and ordered her to, "Explain it to him."

Breathing quickly, she walked down the hall, parting people like Moses through the Red Sea. As all her girls followed, talking fast in disbelief, giving Clint looks of skepticism.

The one girl who was ordered to stay behind was giving him a penetrating glare as she walked towards him.

"Amber will be going to the dance with you, and if you do not accept this once-in-a-lifetime chance, she will go with one of the many others who would die for that opportunity. You will pick her up for the dance promptly on time and you will provide a dinner befitting her requirements. You will be allowed to spend time with her at the dance, but she does reserve the right to do what is best for her. If you do anything wrong or do not follow her wishes, well, let's just say it would be best if you did what you should," she said strongly with a look of disgust at the thought that he would say anything that would be disappointing to her lord.

She turned to leave but stopped halfway and reared back on him, "One more thing from Amber." Without warning or any notice of what she was going to do, she sprung forward and kissed him. Clint felt her soft lips on his as his entire body turned to mush. He didn't know it, but his eyes closed by themselves until she leaned back. He felt her breath on his cheek as she whispered, "Thank you for your invitation."

SMACK! His eyes shot open as pain brought him back to life. She had hit him sharply across the face. "That is so you don't forget to rise to Amber's high expectations."

Clint looked on in complete disbelief at what had just happened to him as the warning bell that class was about to start sounding. He rubbed his hand over his cheek that now throbbed slightly as Corbin looked at him with his mouth open, while other kids around him were snickering and laughing.

Clint was staring dumbfounded at Corbin, unable to comprehend what had just happened. Corbin mirrored his shocked appearance before he shook his head and slapped Clint on the back, causing him to close his mouth, finally saying, "Well, I'm off to class."

"What?" Clint gasped, still rubbing his cheek.

Corbin took five steps before calling back. "Let me know if something else is going to happen to you. I don't want to miss a thing."

Corbin started down the hall and turned in the same direction Amber went. Clint couldn't move until he saw that Corbin had also come to his senses as he reappeared, going down the opposite hallway to avoid another encounter with Amber. The hallway emptied quickly as another kid who was running to class bumped into him, causing him to regain his senses.

He barely made it to gym class on time as they were running and rope climbing today. Clint did everything physically, but his mind was worlds away. He was only on his second lap around the basketball court before he felt his mind must have turned into jello. Trying hard not to think changed for him as he was climbing the rope and was almost to the top when he saw through the skylight a small animal looking down at him while drops of rain were crashing against it.

"Nuts?" he asked. He tried to swing around to get a better look, but he slipped down the rope suddenly, almost to the bottom. Ignoring all the catcalls, he tried to see Nuts again, but he was gone. The rest of the class went badly, as he was getting some of the worst scores and running times that he'd ever had. It didn't help that everyone was looking at him oddly as he thought that everyone must have found out what was waiting for him when he got home.

It wasn't until he was changed after class that he saw he had smudged lipstick on his lips. He struggled but continued until his last class when a familiar fluttering of panic came over him. He found himself almost sick with worry remembering that he hadn't done his homework, wondering how he could get out of his last class. Nothing came to mind. As he followed the sea of students, he saw Corbin was waiting for him in front of Mrs. Christenson's class.

Seeing Corbin seemed to fill him with new life until he saw him up close. Corbin looked like he had just eaten something alive and was almost throwing up.

"Are you going to be sick?" Clint asked, crinkling his nose.

"Just do what I do," Corbin moaned forcing himself to be brave walking into the class. Fighting the insane urge to just run away, he followed him into the class. He was thankful he did, as he was rewarded with a smile from Melanie. A warm feeling washed away the cold one that had been lingering in him as a tiny ember of pride grew in his chest. He walked to his desk with confidence until he sat down and saw his teacher crush any good feelings he had. She sat behind her desk with a dreadful smirk on her pointed face.

"Psst," Corbin called.

"What?" Clint moaned.

"If you want to keep breathing, just do what I do in here, OK?" Corbin said right before the bell rang out, indicating the start of class. Class started like it did every day, by giving every student a feeling that their only future was to try and get a job as driftwood. It was when Mrs. Christenson asked a question about their homework that Corbin moved quickly out of the corner of Clint's eye. Normally, Clint and Corbin would have shrunk down to the floor in their chairs, trying hard not to catch Mrs. Christenson's eye. To Clint's amazement, Corbin had raised his hand high in the air and indicated that Clint should do the same. Not thinking, Clint flashed his hand into the air as well. As soon as he did, he started to lower it, but Corbin kept flinching, indicating to Clint not to drop his hand as he even grunted softly, holding his hand higher.

Mrs. Christenson paced in the front of the class searching to find her first victim to answer her question. To Clint's bewilderment, she walked right by his desk and didn't call on him or Corbin. He looked over in wonderment that every time she asked a question, they would repeat, throwing their hands into the air and never get called on. Corbin even started to overdo it, getting more enthusiastic with each question, and almost toppled out of his seat once after raising his hand so quickly. Mrs. Christenson continued ignoring them until the bell rang that ended their school day. Corbin and Clint shot out of their seats and once more were among the first out of the class.

"How did you do that?" Clint asked, not bothering to check if they were alone or being overheard in the hallway.

"It was easy! I bribed another kid to tell her that we studied all night to answer any question she had and even ask ones that she might not know the answer to," Corbin said smartly as they hurried down the hall.

"That was the best idea you have ever had. How did you come up with that one?" Clint asked, admiring his friend's newfound talent.

"Not now, we have to get out of here. Cody will be waiting for us," Corbin said as he got to his locker, and with blinding speed, he entered in his combination and took out the books he would need to do his homework. Clint followed, watching him eagerly as he did the same. Corbin didn't wait for him as he made his way out of the school, darting by many students as the announcements were being called over the intercom. Corbin didn't say anything until they could see their car in the parking lot. Huge raindrops were falling everywhere when Clint caught up to Corbin.

"It only cost me five dollars to bribe the kid to prolong our lives through class, but have you thought of anything to live with what you just lived through? Was that kiss better than your stuffed animals, or have you…?"

"Clint?" a voice called behind him.

When Clint looked around, he saw Melanie darting toward him. "Now what?" Clint thought desperately.

"Speaking of things you picture, in place of your stuffed animals," Corbin snickered turning away so only Clint could hear him. Clint turned round in panic, looking for Cody, who had not shown up yet. He could see that Tamara was in the back seat waiting for them as Corbin slapped him on the back and said, "I'm getting out of the open where I can be picked off by a sniper and watch this one from behind glass safely with Tamara if you don't mind."

"Hey, Clint," Melanie called as she drew her breath harder, telling him that she must have run most of the way to find him. She was wet and was holding her bag over her head, keeping her face slightly drier than the rest of her.

"Uh, Hi, Melanie," Clint said, wishing he sounded braver than he did. He felt stupid and wanted to talk to her, but he also needed to go so he wouldn't hold anyone up from getting home. Some of Cody's friends were coming over, following Cody's hurried pace to join the rest of the family and get out of the rain in the car. Most of them were calling out to him very loudly about the car Cody was getting into, making Melanie wait to be heard. Their muttering made it a much more awkward moment as he tried to talk to Melanie and make this fast.

"So, how was your day?" she asked loudly, cutting over the noise of rain and catcalls from Cody's friends.

"All right," Clint lied, wishing someone would just tell him what to say and do to get out of this situation as best as he could. One of Cody's friends who was just as popular in the football field saw him and called out, "Hey Clint!"

Clint rolled his eyes, wondering why in the world this boy would be talking to him. Feeling this boy only wanted to talk to him because Cody was in such a hurry, he felt a smile cross his face as he turned his attention back toward Melanie.

"You should be inside, out of the rain," Clint said, wiping the rain off his eyebrows. Melanie shook her long, wonderful hair that made Clint's knees weaken. "I am all right," she said, smiling. "I wanted to talk to you."

"Oh," Clint said dazedly.

Unfortunately, Cody's noisy friend called out loudly again, "Cody, did Clint tell you that he is going to the dance with Amber?" After the storm carried his words through the parking lot, the sound of wolf howls and grunts followed. The smile on Melanie's face faded and was gone as if the rain had washed it off. "I should go in out of the rain," she said tensely as if she had something in her throat.

"No, I am not going with her!" Clint yelled out pleadingly as his heart sank.

"Clint, you hound dog!" called all of Cody's friends as Clint reached out for Melanie's shoulder.

"Clint," Cody called. His voice caused him to stop as he came up short of stopping her. "We have to go!" he ordered.

Clint looked on, not caring about the rain, as he watched Melanie run back to the school. As soon as she vanished into the crowd of students, Clint turned around and walked to the car while Cody's friends didn't let up on him.

"How did you do it?" one of them asked while the others kept making catcalls, wolf whistles, and muttering that he was making school history or that his manhood was no longer in question. At this point, Cody dove into the car as quickly as he could, now that his friends' attention was on Clint. Clint thought if Grant were here, he would have dropped dead with all the wolf whistles he was getting. Clint didn't say anything as he got into the car and determinedly avoided Cody's friends' eyes. He sat down, forcing Corbin to scoot over. Cody apologized to his friends, telling them that he had to go, and before they could say anything else to him, he shut his door, and they sped off as fast as their car would go without touching the gas pedal until they picked up Kayla and Grant.

Kayla got into the front seat and said hello to everyone, bringing an end to the silence that Clint didn't notice was already there. No one answered Kayla as if they'd all agreed not to talk before they picked her up, as Grant got in as well, just as white as he was last night from the rain and lack of sleep.

"Have you ever had a bad idea that you dismiss at once because it was terrible?" Corbin asked Clint. "Well, this was one of those ideas that I should have dismissed." He swallowed hard and said sadly, "I am sorry I sent out all those invitations. If I'd have known everything that we would be going through I wouldn't, I wouldn't have," Corbin was searching for the right words, his eyes glittering painfully.

Clint felt slightly hurt, but it was gone as soon as it came. "It's all right," he said as he repressed the emotion to just panic. "You didn't know what was going to happen; besides, we aren't going to the dance. So, we will just ride out these next two days and hopefully be done with everything."

Corbin looked worried as Clint kept saying those words over and over in his mind, hoping that it would keep Melanie out of his thoughts as he repeated, "Ride out the next two days, ride out the next two days." The car hummed with the heater on and windshield wipers working hard so they could see in the rain, with cars passing them until they pulled into their driveway in the shadow of their home. Everyone was relieved to see that everything on the outside looked perfectly familiar and well.

Thirty-Six

Do You Have an Appointment?

They pulled into the garage safely out of the pouring rain that was now falling without mercy on everything that was not covered. When the car came to a halt, there was a long whistle of liberation and an even deeper sigh of thanks from Cody. They all sat, waiting to see who was going to get out first. Cody started to get out and was walking by his father's motorcycles, boat, and Jamie's old beat-up car when the garage door automatically started closing. He looked back at the sad, tired group following him as they got out of the car. As soon as the garage door was closed the door to the house which Cody was about to go through flew open. Chiowood burst through it, bow charged with a glowing bolt tight aimed right at Cody.

"It's me!" Cody yelled as Chiowood shunted Cody sideways, causing him to fall off the concrete stairs. Chiowood jumped over him, hitting the floor in a crouch. Hobb followed, worming around him as they both checked everywhere with the point of an electric arrow. To Clint's bewilderment, they kept saying "Clear!" over every section of the garage while everyone else except him lay flat on the ground.

It was a tribute to Clint's sour mood that he didn't get down or even out of the way when Chiowood and Hobb were ferreting around, blustering about him.

"All clear," they both called together. There were repeated calls of all clear throughout the house from everyone else inside. Clint wanted to be done with everything now that his home was not going to be the place of relief that he wanted.

As he made his way into the house with everyone, he only longed to go up into his room and get away from all the problems. He found in his way Banks, standing in the hallway looking relieved.

"Status?" Banks asked, concerned.

"What do you care?" Clint said, pushing by him irritably. He surprised himself at how angry he sounded as he walked away. He didn't even remember saying to Banks, "If you want a report, ask Cody. I don't feel like giving one. I have homework to do."

Clint didn't know what happened behind him but there was a call from Ravin, "Sir?"

Banks replied, "It's all right, let it go." Clint wished he had made it up the stairs before he had to hear anything else. He was almost in his room when his grandmother's door squeaked silently, telling Clint that she had opened the door to watch him.

"Isn't the TV enough to watch right now?" Clint barked at her door. The door shut hard enough that it shook the door frame, followed by her turning up the volume enough that Mrs. Hutchings's dogs would start howling.

His exasperation and anger grew in his chest as he slammed the bedroom door shut behind him. He fell on his bed, not bothering to take off his backpack. He lay there waiting for what would surely come. He knew that Kayla would be the one who would want to come and talk to him. Even that thought was irritating. He just wanted to be done with the whole lot of them. His back was aching from his pack, causing him to roll over. He watched the rain hitting his window, washing everything in his view, and the storm only grew in strength with the wind blowing hard.

He saw a shock of lightning and was counting the seconds to see how far away it must have struck when he heard a soft knock on the door. Clint rolled over and reluctantly called, "Come in, Kayla."

The door opened slowly, and to his amazement, it wasn't Kayla. It was Tamara who was looking bewildered, almost frightened, back at him. She looked around as if she were scared to even come this far. Clint was dumbstruck as Tamara came into the room and shut the door behind her. Her eyes roamed around, and she didn't even stop when she glanced at Clint. This was the first time she had ever been in Clint's room. Clint didn't know what to say. It was like having Mrs. Christenson suddenly develop a conscience and want to talk to him.

"Can I sit down?" she asked cautiously.

Clint took off his bag and sat up as he looked at the chair at his work desk. Tamara went over and filled the seat facing Clint. She sat leaning forward, looking a little lost as she watched him. She emptied all the air in her lungs and said, "I don't know what to say, but I do know what you are going through."

"What?" Clint said in shock.

This was nothing like his sister he had known a week ago. As a matter of fact, he was looking at her again in the soft light coming from the window because neither of them had turned on his bedroom light, and Clint noticed that she was not wearing any of her body or facial rings. She only had one pair of earrings, plain and pretty. A set that he thought must have been his mother's. She had done her hair differently and didn't have black makeup on like she always did. Clint didn't know why he hadn't recognized this change in her when they were in the car. But he remembered how he felt and that he didn't even look at her when they were riding together. She didn't even have on her dark leather boots and gloves she usually wore.

"I wanted to talk to you about the change I've made in myself," Tamara explained while Clint looked on blankly.

"I talked to Banks, and he said something that I will never forget." Tamara stood up, searching for words as she started to pace.

"He asked why I covered up so much of my looks with makeup. Why did I do things that I knew were wrong, things that made other people irritated and even hurt? I didn't know fully that I was doing that. I wanted to look that way because the people I was with wanted to look like that. I didn't want to be like the rest of my family. I thought you were a bunch of goody-two-shoes, preppies. I didn't know that my wanting to be different was hurting the ones I loved by pushing them away," she said briskly. It looked like what she was saying now was causing her pain.

"I just wanted to stand out. What I didn't know was that I was hurting, but I'd changed in a way that would never let me do what I wanted in the future. I didn't even know what I wanted to do later in my life. I was just getting by with what I wanted then. I just wanted to get by and there and take it easy. I let my grades go, I let my family go, I let myself go." She looked like she was going to be sick as Clint watched her, slightly surprised.

"I learned things that people had been telling me forever were true. I never knew what I was doing was really causing others to hurt. I didn't even want to love all of you. Until I learned that I could lose you like I almost did."

Clint shook his head, not understanding what she was saying. Tamara looked frustrated, as if she were not saying what she wanted. "Banks said that if we were in his world, I would have been changed and no longer a member of the family, not by force but by my choices. Everything I did that was wrong, I thought was fun; I thought I was getting away with. I thought it wouldn't hurt anyone if they didn't know or if I didn't get caught. Banks showed me that I was hurting someone. I was hurting myself, and if I was from where they came from, I would have been like… like those things that are after us." She said the last words as if they were the thing that caused her the most pain.

"I did some stupid things, Clint," she said as if everything she was saying was a terrible effort. "I went around school today and did something different. I went around smiling and said hi to everyone I knew, and Clint," she was now smiling at him, "they smiled and said hi back!" She was positively beaming now, "I learned that every girl is beautiful in her own way! I learned that what I was wearing made people judge me, and then I would get even angrier at everyone for judging me."

Clint watched her apprehensively, still not knowing what she was getting at. He watched her pace around the room, panting with excitement now.

"I want you to know that you can't change the people you are around, but when you change, it changes the people around you," she said finally.

She stopped, coming to a standstill in front of him. "I want you to know that you don't have to be angry. If you think of everyone else and put yourself second, you will learn who you are, and then you will learn who they are and how people truly feel about you." She bent over and took his hand.

"Clint, I know you don't like what is going on, but I do want you to know that whatever it is, I am here for you, and whatever this family goes through, we can get through it together."

Clint watched her hang her head low into his hand as she held it tight. Funny thing was, he was no longer angry, but he was thankful for the first time that she was his sister. Not just a stepsister but a real sister. They hugged each other for a long time, long enough that neither kept track. A knock at the door from Corbin brought them apart as he opened it a crack.

"Sorry to interrupt," Corbin said in a wheezy growl. He must have run up the stairs. "Clint, you need to see this," he huffed, still trying to catch his breath.

Tamara and Clint got up and started as Corbin went before them down to the television room. Clint grabbed Tamara's shoulder and when she had turned around to face him, he said, "Thanks." Tamara looked at him in a new light that seemed to shine from her.

She smiled and replied, "We had better get going, and you are welcome." Then, they both marched down to find Kayla, Corbin, Grant, and Cody watching the news. As soon as Clint and Tamara came in, Kayla turned up the sound.

On the television, a young man was standing in the rain with a large umbrella over his head, in a suburban-looking street. Clint had walked into a conversation of the news report that must have been going on for a moment or two.

"I know that this tragic scene of pain and wounded neighborhood would strike terror in the lives of any family, but despite reassurances from the police, the case of this family's murder is no closer to being solved. It has just been released that the DNA tests have been inconclusive, and the fingerprints that were found in the home were smudged, or they have nothing on record that matches their findings. Everyone is strongly encouraged to stay indoors and report anything unusual."

Clint looked over at Corbin, who was taking a deep breath of relief. So did Clint, but with everything else going on he didn't feel that much of a weight was taken off his shoulders.

"Halloween is still a go for everyone as the police force is stepping up patrols and guards to keep everyone safe tomorrow. This is Dallam Mark, signing off."

"Well, that's good news," Kayla said, looking nervous. "That was close."

"Close? Good news? It was lucky that Clint and I were moving so fast that we never left a firm fingerprint on a wall as we crashed through them," Corbin said as if he'd just finished a long, hard test.

"The rain is probably a good thing too. It would make anything outside harder to track," Clint said, not giving it any more thought than that.

They watched Kayla turn off the television as the news lady on the screen was talking about more disappearances, showing pictures of those missing. Tamara waved to Clint that she wanted to say one more thing to him as she went into the office. As Clint went in, he overheard Cody yelling at Ohlwiler. From the sound of it, Cody was trying to explain that a toilet is not the place to plant a tree. Clint smiled as he walked into the office, thinking what it must have been like to need to use the bathroom and find a tree obstructing your way. Then to have to explain what a toilet is really used for, as he looked out of the windows in the office. It only revealed that rain was still coming, and the dark gray sky surrounded every home that he could see.

When Clint came into the room, Tamara shut the door behind him as she started talking desperately. "I wanted you to know that I am breaking up with my boyfriend too."

"Ok, but why are you telling me?" Clint said, not understanding or letting her say anything else.

"Well, I was going to tell him at school today, but he wasn't there. I have tried to call him, but he is not answering. I am telling you this because I was told later today that you are going to the dance tomorrow with Amber."

"Whew, wait, wait, wait, I am not going to the dance with her," Clint said sharply, holding up his hands, urging her to understand.

"Because if you are planning to sneak out to go to the dance with her Highness…" Tamara spat, sounding angry for the first time. It was one thing to be corrected by Tamara, but for her to start telling him that he should know better was something else.

It took a moment to calm her down to a point where Clint could explain everything that had happened to him that day and how he was caught up with Corbin's sending invitations out for him. She listened closely, and when he was done, she said that she believed him. When they left, she went straight into the television room and hit Corbin over the head as she started to tell him off.

Clint really did like the change in his sister, as she was hitting Corbin's shoulder so hard her blows were causing him to fall to the floor.

The rest of the time was spent doing their homework without a word from their house guests. Neither did they try to see them until the sky was growing darker out the windows, and everyone started emerging out of their rooms after their homework was finished. Clint and Corbin had just finished the lengthy task of programming their calculators for their math assignment when they left Clint's room. It was then that Clint heard a strange voice coming from the bathroom upstairs. It was a very odd sound and took him a while to identify that it was the sound of a growling voice singing along to a song. Clint and Corbin both followed the sound to the bathroom and the steam coming from under the door.

"Is that O'Neil singing?" Corbin asked in disbelief.

"I think so," Clint smiled weakly. "It sounds like he is singing to Van Halen." They both started to laugh uncontrollably as Kayla and Tamara came out of their rooms to listen to the odd musical talent now singing louder from the bathroom. All four of them laughed themselves silly until the sound of the water died and a minute later O'Neil stood in the open doorway steam, surrounding him, wearing only a towel wrapped around his waist. His hair looked like he had been electrocuted as it stood out at every odd angle as he was humming what he was singing until he saw all four of them paralyzed with laughter on the floor.

"What ur yoo all laughing at?" he asked, holding his shirt and other clothes in his right hand and his left holding the towel covering him.

"Oh, nothing," Kayla said, snickering out of her nose.

"Just your singing!" Tamara said, which sent them all into another wave of laughter.

"Mah singing?" O'Neil said blankly at them. Then something clicked in his mind as he straightened up, looking frustrated.

"Fur yoor information, I was singing in there 'cause there is no lock on the door that I could see. Besides, I had tae come in here 'cause Ohlwiler just took the tree out ay here, and she is on watch out back, so I couldn't go and clean mah self-up out there." Then, with pronounced distrust, O'Neil swept by them all, holding his head up high and clinging to what was left of his dignity as he walked down the hall, only stopping once he was in front of grandma's door.

Turning to the crack in the door, he suavely said, "One day yoo will wish for a love that can no be filled, and then my lips will kiss yoor stooping time until yoor breath brings the stars tae fall." He bowed. The door snapped shut with the sound of someone fainting hitting the floor. O'Neil jumped, kicking his heels together, humming to himself as he went down the stairs.

The wonders kept coming through the evening. After they had picked themselves off of the floor and walked to the stairs that spiraled down, they were stunned to find a tree growing in the front lobby right next to the stairs that went all the way up to the ceiling. It was growing out of the wood floor and had grown over the wooden handrail of the stairs. The trunk looked as if it had been growing there for years as the leaves branched out, filling the entire room. Everyone stood dumbstruck, not saying a word until Corbin said simply, "Cool."

Cody came around the corner and looked at the tree, then at them, then the tree again, then to them. He started to babble words like "tree, boundary, why me, why, Jumanji." Finally, he shouted, "What is a tree doing in the house? I told them to get it out of the bathroom! I didn't mean to plant it in our floor!"

Everyone was shocked but Corbin, who said that there should be one in every home next to the fireplace. A closer look at the tree revealed that their faces had been sculpted in the bark all around the tree. This lightened the mood slightly as Cody paced around the base of the tree, crying about how they were going to get it out of the house.

"Looks good to me," Nix said, admiring the work of the druids as he walked into the office.

"Get it out of here!" Cody yelled. "What are we going to tell Dad?"

Nix looked perfectly calmly at him as he replied, "Tell your parents that there wasn't any decent room in the backyard after they finished working and changing it."

"No, no, no, no, "Cody cried as everyone ran for the back door. The difference between each person's expression was outstanding. Kayla was wide-eyed with amazement, like her dreams had come true. Clint was shocked, knowing that he was going to get blamed for this. Corbin was leaning back, muttering, "Cool" over and over again. Tamara wasn't saying anything but examining every inch of the yard until she just sat down in the kitchen, watching everyone else. Cody was partly in tears, pulling on his hair as they all looked through the back windows to see the changes in the backyard.

No longer was there tall wild grass with weeds everywhere. Every tree that hadn't been trimmed was now sculpted perfectly. Even in the rain, they could see the lawn grown to a perfect height, new and old trees spaced ornately, and each grown as if someone had taken years cultivating and nurturing them.

Tremayne came in after he saw all of them looking out the window. "Is there something amiss?" he said, sounding very proper.

"Yes!" Cody yelled as he paced back and forth between the refrigerator and kitchen island, pulling his hair. He couldn't say anything else as he whimpered, pointing out to the backyard and back to the tree by the front door. Tremayne looked out and, seeing nothing that was wrong to him, looked silently back at Cody as if pitting him as a mentally ill patient. Cody actually pulled out some of his hair as he groaned in frustration.

Thirty-Seven

I JUST CLEANED THAT!

Night was falling, coming fast as the dark clouds fooled the clocks, making them appear an hour slow. Cody kept moaning in frustration and pointed to the backyard and to the tree that was now overhanging the front stairs.

"You have gone barmy about the life we replaced. What got you all cheesed off?" Tremayne asked as comprehension dawned dully on his lips. It wasn't much of a change; he moved his mouth very little when he spoke.

"You don't put a tree in the middle of someone's house, and do you think that no one will notice that our backyard is now going to be the next site for the presidential luncheon? When it was set up for a redneck dinner party before you got here?" Cody yelled hoarsely, pounding his fists on the counter with each word.

"We havn cocked up anything 'ere. An what does a person's neck color have tae do wif one's culture of life outside and inside of their home. Now we ant ere to drop a cleaner but save yeah new what's the hard lines?" Tremayne said in confusion.

They were spared Cody panicking further by the back door opening quickly. Banks poked his head in and said deeply, "We have confirmed incoming!" Coming into the kitchen, he shut the back door behind him quietly. "Tremayne, take two kids with you and hide downstairs. Cover Jamie, just in case. The rest of you upstairs and hide, now!" he ordered.

Tremayne grabbed Grant and Cody, who were the two closest to him, and without question, picked up Grant and pushed Cody down the stairs.

"What do you mean incoming?" Cody huffed between shoves from Tremayne.

"We are going to avoid contact!" he barked as he briskly moved, not answering Cody.

Banks started pushing Kayla and Tamara, urging, "You have to move. Now! Go upstairs!"

"Why don't you just fight them like you have been doing against everything that has come to the door?" Clint asked as Kayla was being shoved into him.

"This time, we know it's them. Now move! You have fifty-two seconds to hide and hope they don't find any of us here. I hope they will search and pass by!" Banks yelled as he picked Kayla up and took her down the hall. Tamara led the way, running up the stairs to the first room they could go into. Banks turned off all the lights as he moved by the switches. Clint was leaving the upstairs landing when he saw the front doorknob turn.

Banks made a shushing sound as he pushed Clint into Tamara's room and said quietly, "Hide! Don't move unless you are found." Clint opened his mouth to say something, but Banks cut him off, still holding Kayla under one arm, "HIDE!" he pleaded as he shut the door without a sound. Clint could hear his footsteps running down the hallway toward his parents' room.

Tamara looked around and ran into the closet. She waved for Clint to come to hide with her, but Clint wanted to hear what was going on as he held up his hand, telling her to wait while he pressed his ear to the door to the hallway. She waved frantically for Clint to follow, but even through the bedroom door, he could hear the front door open over the sound of the storm.

The sound of the front door shutting filled his ears, alert for any sound. Then, there was the sound of heavy footsteps on the wood floor. Clint moved slowly to the closet, where Tamara was moving piles of clothes to get as far back as possible. Clint kicked something with his foot as he moved toward the closet. Whatever he kicked slid on the floor, hitting the bed with a soft tap. Was it just him, or did the heavy footsteps downstairs stop for a fraction of a second?

Looking down and silently cursing, Clint picked up Tamara's cell phone that he'd so foolishly hit and threw it on the bed without a sound. Why didn't he look where he was going? As he got into the closet with his sister, he burrowed under the clothes, concealing him from view while Tamara shut the closet door, carefully not making any noise. They watched out of the open slots in each closet door as Clint's heart pounded in his ears, the heavy footsteps fading slightly downstairs, entering the kitchen. Tamara started to shake as they couldn't hear anything but each other breathing. Was there just one down there, or were there ten? Where are they looking for just him or his whole family? What would they do if they didn't find anything?

Hundreds of questions filled his mind as they waited for a whisper or sound. Fear started to fill him as he thought of the rest of his family. Would they be all right? What if they were found? What if…?

Clunk, clunk. Clint stopped breathing as the heavy footsteps were now coming up the stairs. With each step it took, Clint could hear its heavy foot hit the wood as it slowly approached them. He could hear the floorboards creak under its weight as it must be on the landing now. Tamara held him closer as they caught its movement on the carpet down the hall. Tamara started to cry as Clint could hear it breathing and sniffing the air like a giant dog while he followed its movements, looking at the wall. It was outside of their door now as. Clint could hear what sounded like cloth or skin brushing against the door as it jiggled in its frame.

Clint looked through his Venetian blind at Tamara's door and moved as if something was leaning on it from the outside. The only light source was from Tamara's window, which showed brighter than his from the street lap outside. Also, a single nightlight by her bed shimmered, reflecting on the rest of her room, which was black down to the carpet.

Clint was looking for anything he could use for a weapon around the room, like one of the lamps by Tamara's bed or one of her gothic figurines, when the doorknob shook and then started to turn.

With a slight moan, the door opened, revealing a dark hallway beyond. It was like the storm had cut all power and most of the light through the house as the shadow of a tall image stood in her doorway. Whatever it was, Clint couldn't even see its entire head as it was taller than the door frame, at least to the ceiling. There was a flash of lightning again from outside, illuminating it for an instant. Clint saw a large green hand damp from the rain that looked big enough to grip a basketball and crush it easily. In its other hand, it gripped what looked like a giant, crude wooden club, balancing it on one shoulder.

It waited in the hallway, facing the door frame. Clint heard it sniffing the air and the drops of water falling from it hitting the floor. As it stood in the dark hallway, Tamara and Clint didn't move or even breathe. Whatever it was in the hallway took one gigantic step inside Tamara's room, ducking down to bring its head in. Tamara started to take sharper, panicked breaths. She pulled a sleeve of a shirt that was hanging up and bit it, holding it in her mouth to muffle her sound. Clint watched in awe as it moved deeper into the room in the dim light penetrating through the stormy window. Clint saw one of its wet feet was bare and must have been at least a meter long, with dark hair covering its skin in small patches on top of the foot. It took another step as it reared its large head, searching around for them, still sniffing.

Its muscular frame moved slowly, with its huge club raised, scratching the ceiling. It quickly checked the other side of Tamara's bed, ready to strike if something was there. It had almost no coverings over its skin, just some odd bits of cloth around its waist. It had what looked like tattoos on its arms, chest, and back. It also had a thick neck that stretched to see around the bed and then around Tamara's chairs, chest of drawers, and other furniture, taking an occasional sniff in the air.

Clint finally saw its face as it turned toward the closet when a lightning bolt illuminated the room. It was sniffing faster now, moving excitedly towards them. Its face was also green, with two large teeth growing from its bottom jaw. It had an upturned nose and a prominent overlapping bottom jaw like a barracuda. Its eyes were small and deep-set with prominent, bushy eyebrows. Thick black hair was pulled back in dreadlocks. It came closer and closer to them with each heavy step, making things in the room shake. It reached out with its club-free hand and touched the far-left closet door.

Tamara and Clint moved as far down as they could to the other side of the closet without making any noise. Clint felt fear and amazement coursing through him. Tamara started shaking as her breath became unsteady and separated as a large green hand hit the door again. This time, the closet door on her end sprang open slightly. Past all the clothes Clint had pulled on top of himself, he could see its fingers open the door the rest of the way. It sniffed some more and reached in toward them. It stopped short of Clint's arm and grabbed one of Tamara's undershirts. It pulled on it, breaking the hanger it was on with remarkable ease, and brought it up to its nose, taking one long sniff. It opened its large mouth and laughed softly, threw the undershirt over its club-free shoulder, and started to turn to the door where it had come into the room.

Clint moved just his head to keep the intruder visible through his small window space past the clothes and spy the opening in the closet door. The thing moved heavily but gingerly toward the door, and when it was out, it checked both ways down the hall and stepped out into the hallway.

Suddenly, a song cracked through the air from somewhere in the room. It was from Tamara's cell phone. Tamara shot bolt upright in a panic to see her phone on her bed ringing.

"It's Bill!" she whimpered in terror so low that Clint could barely hear her.

Wham! The intruder had leaped from the doorway across the room and slammed his club over Tamara's bed, shattering it into pieces. Tamara screamed as the creature lifted its heavy club and turned those small eyes toward the closet. It released a war cry that sounded like a lion charging to kill. It shifted its weight onto its back foot and started to charge right at the closet door; the club held high once more, mouth open, yelling, coming right at Clint and Tamara.

Slam! Banks shot from the open door, connecting with the creature only a foot away from breaking through the closet. Banks bared his shoulder into the massive green intruder and, with his legs pumping, drove him to the far side of the room. With both of their strength moving them, they were out of control as they whirled toward the window.

With an almighty cry from both of them, they shattered the window and plummeted down one story as they clung to one other, fighting and punching until they hit the moist earth with a squelching noise like a plunger in a plugged drain. Their war cries stopped as Banks hit the ground first, the green man landing next to him. Clint flung the closet door open and hurried to the broken window, looking down as the rainwater poured off the roof on top of his head and down to Banks and the intruder sprawled on his front lawn.

Clint watched as Banks rolled over on his back, unsheathing a long sword and holding it up in a defensive stance, while the intruder adjusted his grip on the club to hold it on the very end and swung it along the ground while not getting to its feet. The blow hit Banks's feet, causing him to fall sideways back onto the ground, splashing mud and water everywhere as he moaned in pain. The green intruder swung the club high in the air as it got to its knees and hit the ground like a hammer meant to drive a nail through the earth. His strike came down right at Banks' head. Banks pushed with his legs sliding down the sloping hill of their front yard, causing the club to miss him by inches and the force of the blow driving the weapon down into the grass.

O'Neil was suddenly by Clint's side, watching Banks and the intruder get to their feet and face one another.

"Orc!" O'Neil shouted as he pulled out a short metal handle, and as he brought it to the ready, a blue axe blade composed of flames erupted from it. The Orc howled again, giving Banks a taunting swing with the club, and held its arms wide, showing its bare chest. Banks stood firm and held out a hand as if he were telling the Orc that he wanted a timeout. At that moment, there was a sharp sound of a bow shooting. A glowing fire arrow hit the Orc in the right thigh, causing it to fall to one knee. Just then, O'Neil dove off the roof, planning to land on the Orc, but the Orc, with only one good leg, started to slide down the slippery slope, causing O'Neil to miss and fall face-first into the mud.

"We need intel, pursue and capture!" Banks called while Chiowood came out from a bush, firing a shot that hit the Orc high in the right shoulder. Tiny sparks erupted with the hit, causing the Orc to falter briefly as it rolled and kept moving. Banks slid down after the Orc, who was hobbling across the street without hesitating. It was so powerful that even with one leg, it moved as fast as Clint would at his fastest speed. Moaning in pain, O'Neil called up from below, his face covered in mud, "Secure the house! Clint, come with us. We need a guide."

"Me?" Clint said so low that only he and Tamara could hear him.

Thirty-Eight

AND THEY'RE OFF!

Tamara was pushing him, which was the only reason his legs would move and keep moving as he flew down the stairs and out the front door into the rain, running as fast as he could. O'Neil was driving hard and fast after Banks, about thirty yards ahead of him. Clint jumped over the uneven earth. O'Neil pulled a bow from his back, and a single light arrow came to life in it.

They ran one after the other, following the Orc through the park. Clint started to get soaked to the bone as he ran as fast as his legs would take him past trees, garbage cans, and bushes. He couldn't see the Orc but could make out Banks, who was leading the way, practically flying with speed. They were leaving the park as the Orc took them down the street to the more broken-down part of town away from Clint's school. This neighborhood bore the mark of families with less income as the houses were smaller and the yards cluttered and unorganized.

Clint jumped a small fence and cut across the yard, catching up to O'Neil, whose lungs were heaving and ankles hurting from running on slick services as the rain was still pouring down. As Clint started to pass O'Neil, who was breathing like Corbin would have sounded, another thought entered his mind as he ran, catching up to Banks, who'd just withdrawn something shiny from his belt. Clint noticed a car coming and people outside hurrying to get out of the rain or on their front porches watching in their direction. For the first time, both worlds were exposed to one another as he ran faster as if his body thought if he could catch up, he could separate these worlds again.

Banks was slowing for some reason, not closing on the Orc, who Clint could see now running through a brick wall. Banks followed, quickly jumping over the rubble that the Orc crashed through. They were running in and through backyards, the Orc crashing through everything in its path with ease despite limping on one leg, Banks still hot on his heels, Clint only a step or two behind him. First, they went through another stone wall, then a jungle gym, a pool, an apartment complex, and over a car, the Orc tearing through it all, knocking down everything that got in its way. People watched in amazement as this thing destroyed their homes and yards. The Orc had just taken them into a parking lot between two apartments when Banks slowed and took aim with what he had taken from his belt. He threw two daggers that sliced through the rain, hitting the Orc square in the back. It howled in agony but didn't even slow its pace. Clint went after him now with everything he had left in him.

Suddenly, Banks stopped as the Orc took them down a long alley connected to the parking lot. There was another snap from a bow as the Orc wailed again, turning and throwing itself into the solid wall to their right. With a crash, it broke through it, causing the mortar and concrete to fall all around it, leaving a large hole it just ran through. As soon as the path was clear, Clint saw O'Neil at the other end of the alleyway, hunched over, gasping for air but still moving his bow in his hands. Banks and Clint tore down the alley, moving fast, and leaped into the gap the Orc made in the wall. Banks went in first, and as Clint followed, squinting his eyes from the concrete dust, Banks suddenly pushed Clint aside. Before Clint could see anything, he was falling forward as a large marble table flew past his head.

Banks dove but got hit slightly in the arm as the table crashed into the alleyway behind them. After the table shattered, O'Neil poked his head in, looking amazed that it had missed him. They were in a furniture store that was apparently very expensive and only had the nicest things. The store's light was strong, making Clint squint as he watched the Orc crash through, tossing furniture aside as it ran toward the front. The store did have nice things before they got there, Clint thought as he got to his feet again. Banks flew after their target while the store's customers watched in shock and took cover. With another crash, the Orc jumped through the front store display window, showering the street with glass.

Banks was still behind him as O'Neil bounded by Clint, with all of them emerging into the open street. The Orc was running down the road toward the right, where another open park and stores were on the opposite side of the street. Banks, Clint, and O'Neil ran together past cars and people. They were only thirty feet behind the Orc when they reached the park. Suddenly, Banks skidded to a halt, splashing water everywhere, the Orc disappearing in the rain and dark as it crisscrossed in and out of the trees and was suddenly gone.

Banks reached out, grabbing O'Neil and Clint. "What, we have him!" Clint coughed as he held his sides.

"It's a trap!" O'Neil yelled as he pushed Clint to the ground. A dozen arrows shot right over him. They all were on the ground scrambling for cover as the small wisps of air were cut by the sound of the arrowheads and shafts over them.

"He wasn't running, he was leadin' us tae them," O'Neil called while his face was in a puddle of rainwater.

"We can't stay here. Clint, get us out," Banks ordered as he grabbed onto Clint's shirt and pulled him behind a large tree.

"Where?" Clint pleaded as a dark lightning bolt hit the tree behind which he had just taken refuge.

"We need a place with kids! Young kids," Banks informed him as he ducked under a park bench as the arrows sped all around him, sounding like bullets. "Hurry, they are trying to outflank us."

O'Neil shot off more plasma arrows, exposing himself only for a moment. Clint's mind raced; the last time he had been here was when his mother brought him shopping for school clothes. Then it hit him. There was a hospital that was not too far from here. He had been there once after accidentally stepping on a nail and had to get a shot.

"That way," Clint shouted as he pointed back the way they had come.

"Cover fire, O'Neil," Banks called, holding his wounded arm where the table had hit him. "Clint, take point!"

Clint was sore and tired without one place on him that was dry. Pushing all that aside, he took off running the way he had come, arrows whizzing behind him and a single dark energy arrow landing right in front of him. It hit a parked car and burned right through it. He ran down the sidewalk as he could hear the splashing sounds of O'Neil and Banks running steps behind him.

"Don't run straight, kid, zig, zag! Serpentine, serpentine, zig, zag!" Banks yelled.

Clint ran to the other side of the street, arrows flying all around him. It was challenging to try and change direction with the wet ground. He was speeding toward the furniture store, where people came out to see what had happened. To Clint's horror, one or two of them went down, being hit by arrows that came from behind him as he chased by. He shook his head with his arms pumping hard for speed, the rain dripping in his eyes. People around them who were out walking in the storm or getting out of their cars to see what was going on screamed and took cover as more arrows flew at him.

"Go, kid, go, go, don't stop!" Banks called, as Clint jumped here and there around cars, lampposts, mailboxes, and people; anything that he could use for cover as he kept his feet moving, working through his pain, not looking back at what surely was still after them. He was just around the corner when pain erupted in his left arm, causing him to scream in anguish. An arrow nicked him in the left forearm. If it had been a couple more inches to the right, it would have pierced his heart. As soon as he turned the corner, he held his forearm out and saw blood dripping from it, even in the rain. The hospital lights shining in the downpour were just ahead. Clint braced himself on a lamppost momentarily, gathering his breath in pain. His arm was burning as he held it tightly with his other hand. Banks and O'Neil came around the street's side out of the line of fire.

"In there!" Clint pointed to the hospital's emergency room entrance with his good arm.

"We have to get in there without being noticed and find a place to hide. How can we do that?" Banks asked as he ran on, waving for Clint to keep running.

Clint didn't feel like he could move another step until an arrow hit the lamppost that he was leaning on, the arrow shaft poking out of the solid metal frame. He lifted his heavy legs as O'Neil ran, pulling him toward the hospital. Thankfully, there was no one around the entrance as Banks was the first to move into view of the light from the glass doors. Clint saw some wheelchairs just inside through the glass door as he finally got under the cover of the hangover of the hospital doors.

"Wait one second," Clint said as he walked in and grabbed a wheelchair. He came out with it as O'Neil and Banks took cover behind vending machines and a newspaper dispenser.

"O'Neil, get in and put all your weapons on your lap," Clint huffed as he turned to look back where they had come.

O'Neil didn't hesitate as yet another arrow hit the vending machine, causing the light to go out. They were still piling on every bow, dagger, and sword as they walked through the automatic doors. Banks pushed O'Neil on with Clint following him. The smell of the hospital hit Clint like a smack in the face. The first person they saw was an old man in another wheelchair just around the corner leading to the emergency room. He was asleep and had a hospital blanket, and just like a magician, Banks took the bottom part of the blanket and, with a fast whip of his wrists, took it off without moving a single hair on the old man.

"Nice wark," O'Neil said as Banks covered his lap and everything he had on his legs up to his neck. Clint moved the wheelchair and O'Neil down the corridor. Several people stared at them and were rewarded with a hearty wave from O'Neil as if he were on a parade float. Clint's quick thought that they might blend into a hospital was immediately dismissed when he looked down at himself and Banks. They were covered in soaked, muddy, blood-stained clothes, and Banks was wearing his very thick, heavy clothes, resembling someone who had just stepped out of a fantasy movie.

THAT WON'T HELP A BROKEN HEART

"Where are the youngest kids?" Banks asked Clint hurriedly as a hospital worker came up to them.

"Can I help you?" The middle-aged women asked, eyeing them like they were lost.

"No, thank you," Clint said as he pushed O'Neil down the hall, moving faster and faster until he saw a map next to the elevators. "The nursery is up on level three," he said, pointing, and as soon as he said it, the lights went out, and emergency lights kicked on.

"We need to use the stairs," Clint said, opening the door and looking wildly around once more.

"They are still coming," Banks warned as he gathered up the weapons while O'Neil got to his feet and all ran up the stairs, leaving the wheelchair behind. Clint's sneakers made odd squishing noises as he ran up each step. When they got to the door, Clint went to open it.

"Stoop!" O'Neil barked as he took the doorknob for himself. He opened it slightly so that he could peek in. Clint looked at Banks's shoulder where he had gotten hit with the table. His thick shirt was stained with blood that ran down to his hand. The slight cut on his forearm didn't seem all that bad all of a sudden as O'Neil whispered that everything was clear and went through the door, keeping low. Clint followed but didn't sneak in. He walked through, trying to look normal.

There was a security door, and a nurse behind the counter was apparently looking at paperwork as Banks closed the door behind him. The room had four rows of comfortable sitting chairs and some flowers. The rain lashed against the windows lining the side wall opposite where the nurse was.

"Distract her, Clint. O'Neil, open the door," Banks ordered as he crept down low so that he couldn't be seen from the nurse's point of view.

Clint went to talk to her, but as he walked up, he couldn't think of one thing to talk to her about. She had very dark hair and wore scrubs that were a little too tight for her large body. She let her half-moon-shaped glasses slide down her nose as she looked up at him, letting her chins wobble.

"What can we do for… dear me," she broke off, suddenly shocked, her wide-open mouth revealing a lot of dental work. "What happened to you?" she gasped, clutching her enormous chest and getting up on her wobbly ankles. The chair she sat in clung to her momentarily, then dropped to the ground with a thud.

"I, uh, I just came to see why the power was out," he said smoothly, giving her a weak smile. He leaned over on the shelf with his good arm in pain.

"Dear me, you poor little thing. You need to get down to the emergency room." She sounded beside herself with worry. She bustled over, rubbing her dark hands together. She hit a button, unlocking the door. O'Neil started looking at it as he lay flat on the ground. His eyes grew to seven times their original size as he scurried out of the way back along the wall like a frightened mouse. Banks cowered back, working hard not to be squashed by O'Neil. The door swung open, barely missing his head as the nurse hurried toward Clint.

"Look at you," she said as she grabbed him and held him close to her chest, much to Clint's objections, which he couldn't say that loud from being suffocated by her all-too-tightening grip on his head. "We will have to get you fixed up, you poor thing you. Caught in the storm, were you? Got hurt when the main power went out? Never you mind now, we will take care of you right now. Don't you mind," she said, not giving him a chance to say anything or breathe for that matter, as her headlock didn't stop as she pulled him back through the security door.

Clint heard a sound from somewhere outside, even over the nurse's arm, that muffled everything. She turned, not letting go of his head, and looked back toward the window.

"Now, what in blue blazes was that sound? Did you see anything, dearie? I thought I saw something just for a moment outside the window, but that is plain old silly. We are so high, and what would be doing that in this weather?"

Clint pushed and pulled and finally was able to extricate his head from the nurse's Kung Fu grip, gasping for air as if she had been holding his head underwater. They were in the hallway that was dimly lit up and down, with many doors and ordinary pictures lining the walls. Besides, some walls were cut-offs where a computer desk could be seen, and one or two nurses were talking behind them. Clint could hear some of their conversation about how the main power should be back on by now and what was taking so long—the nurse, who was as strong as an ox, grabbed his arm. "Now come this way, you poor boy and we will fix you right up, that arm just looks so terrible. How you ever got that nasty cut is beyond me." She was pulling him down the hall, and as she did, Clint saw that the security door hadn't shut all the way. A small tip of a piece of wood was at the very bottom of the door, holding it open. "I have seen some young folk come in here with cuts like that, but it was mostly just from a fight or something, but you are much too nice a boy to be caught up in that sort of thing."

This nurse wouldn't quit, and her grip on Clint's arm hurt more than anything else that had been done to him that night. Out of the corner of his eye, he saw it just as they were passing her desk where she was sitting when he first came in. For an instant, something red outside the window flashed and was gone. "Wait, did you see?" he asked, forcing her to stop.

Crash! The outside window, second from the center, was shattered as the nurse howled in fright, grabbing Clint once more, causing all the air to rush out of him. Before Clint was blinded by her arms, he saw a small figure crash into the second row of chairs. He had red-skinned hands and a horned head.

"Get down!" Banks yelled.

He and O'Neil must have just come into the hallway behind them. Clint couldn't hear the door shut because the nurse was screaming so loud, holding him tightly, twirling in a circle. With two more smashed windows, two more imps came in from the outside.

"Move!" O'Neil commanded, grabbing Clint. Clint felt like a wishbone being held tightly by the nurse and O'Neil yanking his arm. His nurse started yelling random words so fast that Clint couldn't understand her. She let his head go a second time, and now Clint could hear something that sounded like a cat meowing in excitement and a pig squealing in reply.

Unable to help himself, Clint looked out to the sitting lobby, now covered in broken glass; most of the chairs had been knocked over from where the imps had landed, and rain was pouring in. Three imps were getting to their feet in the center of the room, the red one grabbing something from his belt. It was the same thing that had attacked Clint and Corbin the other morning. A blue-skinned, shorter one was to the right of the room, and a taller green one was to the left. Just as O'Neil pulled him to the floor, Clint heard them talk like a cat and a pig to the red one. How could they be talking like animals, and yet he could understand that they were cursing the fact that they were all thrown up here going through different windows?

"Keep going!" Banks yelled as O'Neil was still pushing Clint down the hall. The nurse was crawling on all fours, muttering fast. "I hate terrorists, and when did this neighborhood go so bad?"

Other nurses were running to them, but Banks called out, "Get out of here!" just as something heavy hit the security door.

They scrambled on their hands and knees down the hall. Clint was clueless about where to go, what to do, or why they were there. Banks kept calling to them, "Move, keep moving, and stay down."

"This was not in my job description, and this ain't no fire drill," the nurse yammered, almost crushing Clint. "Little colored tick tacks jumpen' through windows." While O'Neil crawled on, he muttered, "I like a healthy-sized woman." He was going to say more but was cut short when the security door burst open as something hurled through it, setting off an alarm.

Clint turned into a workstation where some nurses were talking earlier. O'Neil and the babbling nurse followed him around the corner. Banks dove on top of them as an arrow barely missed his feet and shrieked by. The pig and cat were shouting at one another, and the sound of their tiny feet pounded as they were rushing in pursuit. Banks rolled off them and pushed his back against a desk with a computer on it. O'Neil pulled out his short bow and threw it over the nurse whose mouth still was running fast to Banks. Clint squeezed out of the pile to move further away on his back as O'Neil grabbed the nurse asking her, "How doo we git oot ah here?"

Banks got to his feet and fired a light arrow down the hall. A cat howled and meowed in pain in response. As soon as he fired, Banks hit the cold linoleum floor as an arrow hit the computer screen right over his head, showering them all in sparks.

"I knew I should have listened to Leroy," the nurse babbled, pointing down another hall. "He has his own security company, but did I drive for him? Noooooo. I wanted to help people. I miss my nine-millimeter under my pillow."

O'Neil got to his feet and pulled off a pouch from his belt that held daggers. He threw them to Banks and grabbed the heavy nurse while Clint was already on his way toward the hall where the nurse had pointed. Running again with only the emergency lighting showing the way, his body aching in pain and cold slipping shoes on the floor, he heard Banks shooting the bow to keep the imps back. But as Clint looked behind him, even Banks was moving now, with so many arrows and daggers coming around the corner where they just were.

O'Neil was pleading for the women to be quiet, but Clint didn't think that she could hear him over her mouth. "Shut up, you hairy little desk jockey! I used to be a bouncer at Rudy's bar, but I had to follow Mike, my third ex-husband's advice who said that I might do better by picking a career in helping people. Well, we see how much good that is doing me now!"

"How much further?" Banks yelled from behind them as he was running now, stopping at corners notching another plasma arrow in his bow.

"Stay in ya rooms! Stay in ya rooms," O'Neil called to the patients who were coming out to see what the noise was. Clint and the nurse were in the lead turning this way and that down the labyrinth of the hospital halls.

Clint could still hear the imps coming as it sounded like the one that talked like a pig was in the lead, guiding the other two. Banks' shooting hadn't stopped them. A sharp snap sounded over their heads as all the lights came back on, stinging Clint's eyes, momentarily blinding him. Bumping into a wall not slowing as he blinked fast the nurse grabbed him as she told him to stop. They had reached some elevators and a different flight of stairs. Clint and the nurse were frantically pushing all the elevator buttons as fast as they could, O'Neil and Banks went back two feet to the last turn they took, both readying their short bow and more daggers for when the imps came around into view.

"As soon as I get into this elevator, I am going to go home and get my gun, then no little red, blue, or green Halloween people are going to be safe," the nurse was now yelling, still pummeling the buttons repetitively when Banks and O'Neil started to shoot down the hallway. With the frantic shouts from the nurse and the war in the hall, it was a wonder that Clint heard a ding as the elevator arrow light lit up. The doors opened revealing a male nurse waiting in it. Oddly soft elevator music played as the male nurse opened his mouth to speak but was cut short by the female nurse yelling at him, "What in the name of my aunt Debbie's makeup case took you so long, skinny? We been pushing them buttons since the war came. Now move you skinny behind over son, we got incoming."

"Come on!" Clint yelled, holding the door as he got in himself. O'Neil yelled at Banks to get moving as they ran for the elevator door. Even before they were entirely in, Clint hit the button to close the door.

"What is going on?" the male nurse asked.

To which the female nurse started to explain, sounding like a bug buzzing. "This ant the time and place, sugar. We got three angry munchkins out there and they seem to have a very high opinion of this young man. So, you going to keep asking questions or move your skinny butt over?" she shouted, pushing him out of the way.

O'Neil and Banks got in as everyone lined the walls while the doors were closing. Clint hit every floor that was going down. Before the doors fully closed a single dagger came into the elevator with a whoosh and hit the male nurse right in the chest. As the lift started down there was a cry of anger from the imp that sounded like a cat. The male nurse fell to his knees but before O'Neil could catch him in his arms, he was dead.

O'Neil gently laid him down on the elevator floor moaning, "The dagger has pierced his heart."

"What is his name?" Banks asked as he helped the man to lie down and with a gentle hand closed the man's lifeless eyes.

Clint took the man's name tag and saw the name "Austin Bryson." He read it out with a heavy heart while the female nurse was crying softly and for the first time, she wasn't talking.

The elevator chimed as they reached the floor below. The elevator they were in had two doors, one for those who worked in the hospital and the other for visitors. When the elevator came to a stop the back doors opened first. An old man stood waiting in a wheelchair. All he said when he saw them was, "I'll take the next one."

The doors shut again until they got to the basement floor where the employee elevator doors opened this time. "We have tae get out ay here noow!" O'Neil said with great displeasure as he swept by everyone out the door. He went into what looked like the laundry floor of the hospital. Clint moved also but when he noticed Banks was still looking back at him, he paused. The sweat from the humidity on the floor was terrible as Clint noticed that Banks was not moving to follow them but moving the dead man to lay better on the ground.

"We need tae go before they follow and more die," O'Neil said kindly.

Banks got to his feet standing beside the woman as the elevator started to close. Clint held out a hand to keep the doors open, still waiting and wondering.

"We were never here, and when we go, they will leave everyone here alone!" Banks said with a glower to the nurse who was with them as she was holding the dead man's head in her lap. She didn't stop sobbing but nodded heavily. It took another moment for Banks to move until the door started to close. He jumped out, causing the doors to rebuff open but started marching out, not wanting to look back.

They were busy trying not to be seen until they emerged back into the night and rain after climbing through a window of a vacant room. The rain was harder now but it might only have felt that way to Clint as they had come out of everything alive so far. As soon as they had emerged, O'Neil ran around to check what he could see. The one good thing that came from their escape was that they'd come out on the far side of the parking lot placing them next to a tall wall with small trees and bushes. The night was quiet except for the rain when O'Neil returned nodding his head and waved them on to follow him. Clint wanted to talk for a moment but thought better of it as he ran slowly after O'Neil and Banks into the deeper part of the fragmented bushes and trees.

They ran slowly but it was hard work after all they had been through. They kept out of sight, moving only when others were not around or there was a gap in the cars going by on the roads or people on the sidewalk. He looked around at O'Neil in surprise when they stopped for a moment. O'Neil asked in silence which way they should go. Clint checked the area and pointed up the road and instead of taking a long route O'Neil brought them determinately toward Clint's home and didn't take a long way. Nor was there any effort to make sure they were not followed as sirens sounded behind them.

After only about an hour, they made it back to the park that was in front of Clint's home. Nothing had ever looked as good as when they crossed the road to the driveway up to Clint's home. O'Neil was in the lead and as soon as his foot touched the grass he waited, staring into the dark towards the corner of the house.

The bush that was next to the house where O'Neil was looking at moved hauntingly toward them. O'Neil waved as Chiowood's head came out of the leaves.

"Everything is secure and squared away, no harm and traces fixed as best we could," Chiowood said, looking all three of them up and down worriedly.

It was a tribute to how tired he was that Clint didn't look up at his house to check and see how bad the damage was. The grass bearing the scars of the short battle in his front yard was gone. Holding his hand over his head to keep the cold rain from falling in his eyes, he saw the house as good as new. There wasn't a trace of anything on the ground. It was all fixed seamlessly in no time at all from the time they had left. He was about to ask how they'd fixed everything when Chiowood suddenly jumped back an inch and drew out a large wooden arrow and brought it up higher to his eye. O'Neil fell down, avoiding the aim of Chiowoods bow with a long arrow fixed in it.

"Someone is watching!" Chiowood shouted impatiently.

Banks didn't hit the ground, but he did force Clint to do so, which wasn't so bad since he couldn't get any wetter even if he jumped into a lake, as Chiowood looked down his arrow. For some reason, he didn't point it down toward the park. He was aiming it to the right, toward Mrs. Hutchings's house. The arrow was shot before he could turn his head to see what Chiowood was aiming at.

Clint got up fast, eyeing where the arrow had gone. Chiowood hadn't shot it at anything following them and not even at a person but at the favorite spy window of Mrs. Hutchings. Even with the rain falling steadily, Clint could see the arrow that had pierced the glass right where she always parted the curtain. Amazingly the glass didn't shatter; the arrow had just cut a small hole into it. The curtain that she parted so often to watch the outside world flew up as she pulled it off the wall and fell out of the way. The arrow didn't hit her, but Clint was down on bended knee as he saw Mrs. Hutchings's demon of a dog hanging on the far wall, the arrow hooked under its collar as the dog's legs frantically swiped in the air to get a hold of something while its body hovering terribly like a live picture, without a frame.

The next second held the moans and yelps from her dog, Mrs. Hutchings's screaming about an attempted murder and O'Neil rolling on the ground laughing as loud as the thunder.

"Exceptionally fine shot!" Banks said kindly as he walked uncaringly toward the door with everyone else in tow. "After you've had your fun, demon dart her," Banks ordered opening the front door.

Just like the evening before, when they came in a cascade of hugs and questions came to them. Banks and O'Neil explained everything to the others while Clint changed his wet clothes that felt like they were about ten pounds heavier than what they should be.

Everyone was talking when he came downstairs after he examined Tamara's room. Everything was as it should be. Later that night he found out that nothing had happened when he was gone except the druids mending the wood and house. It was a horrible tale when it came to the time to tell everyone that a man was killed at the hospital, and even more were injured when they were running down the street to get away from those who were following them. They shared a grim silence in the group when they learned someone else was killed, but it turned around abruptly when the subject came to Mrs. Hutchings's dog being hung up like a picture on the wall by an arrow. It wasn't until Corbin asked what they should do next that everyone's attention turned to Banks.

Forty

LIFE GOES ON WHILE THE WORLD IS FALLING

The entire house was worn out. This time Banks addressed all of them without being coaxed or asked. "I acknowledge since our arrival your lives have been affected, and for that, I apologize." He held his head low and set one foot on a stair as he thought for a moment, then said, "While you were away today, we searched this home and area for anything containing an essence of magic, for anything that could be the Requiem." He rubbed the bridge of his nose sighing deeply, "All we found is that the picture in the office does seem to resonate with where we are from." Banks waved toward the office toward Hobb, who was leaning close examining the picture Banks was talking about.

Noticing that Banks had addressed him and that he had everyone's attention, he jumped clumsily off balance and began to see what was behind the picture.

"That's it?" Corbin said stupidly as if a family picture was the last thing, he thought would be worth all this trouble. "I thought you guys would appreciate toilet paper more than something like that."

Clint had to agree with Corbin as Banks looked at him inquiringly. "You mean this is nothing special?" Banks asked Clint. He asked it to sound typical, but Clint could see the pleading in his eyes.

"It's nothing of real importance," Clint said, and seeing how it made everyone's expressions change, he added quickly, "I just don't know what you're after, I don't think that this would cause a life-altering change for a world."

Banks looked for a moment like he was in deep thought but wasn't given a chance to do anything else as Cody raised his hand.

"Dad has a safe behind that," Cody said going into the office. "I saw him once open it after he thought I had left the room."

Everyone followed him in as Cody led them to the grand piano next to the unlit fireplace. "He had it rigged like Batman," Cody said waving his hands over the piano keys. "He played the first couple of bars of the song Children by that Robert Diles guy."

"Robert Miles," Kayla corrected.

"How do we open it?" Banks asked.

Everyone exchanged hopeful looks at each other and all centered on Kayla.

"Me!?" she shouted.

"Yes, you," Cody, Tamara, and Corbin said together.

"I don't know how to play that," Kayla sneered, sounding like her mother. "Are you sure he didn't play something like Chopsticks? And I don't think it's right for all of you to just look at me to take care of things. I'm the youngest one here, for crying out loud!"

"You see, you are mature!" Cody shot back, "If all of you expected me or Jamie to do it, we would swear at you."

"So, can it be opened?" Banks asked seriously, stopping the joking.

"The picture? I think so," Cody said rubbing the back of his neck. "But the safe behind it, no. Who knows what kind of lock that would have, and the combination would require an IQ of about two billion. You would have to wait for Dad."

"We could call and ask him," Clint said quickly.

"Oh, yeah right," Tamara spat. "Hey Dad," she said mockingly. "We are having a great time here. Grant has earned his appreciation for the animal's merit badge, Cody just got promoted from gas pumper to pin cushion, we have been banned from the hospital and could we get into your work safe for a party we are having. Oh and P.S. we found a guy to replace our freezer."

"What do you think, O'Neil?" Banks asked hopefully. O'Neil looked to be lost in thought as he was the one keeping a look out toward the front.

He kept parting the curtain of a window checking every few seconds what was going on outside.

O'Neil didn't say anything but looked sorrowfully at Banks. "You can speak freely," Banks said encouragingly.

O'Neil, checked outside once more and nodded to Chiowood who was by him to take over for him as he stood up in his short stature. "Well sir, yoo see it's like this, we don't know what we are after and how we all got here and I cannae say more than that. Aw we know is that some high rankin' woman told yoo that these would lead us on the way tae find…"

O'Neil stopped talking at once with the deadly stare that Banks was giving him. O'Neil was shrinking under the piercing eyes and said suddenly, "Let's get back tae these toilet pepper thin', that sounds interestin'! How does it work?" he said eagerly.

"What is he talking about?" Cody asked, looking back at Banks suspiciously.

There was an unnatural silence around the room as everyone turned to Banks. From the look of things, Banks and O'Neil were the only two in the group that knew what they were not telling everyone else. Banks shook his head and took one hand and rubbed his bald head. He breathed in deeply and let it out slowly before he said, with difficulty, "I can't tell you about that and even then, there isn't a lot that I do know. You have all done well when given an order not to question me, but now that you know this much, I think you are entitled to know more."

Banks stopped leaning over the piano and stood up straight to face all of them. "There is a branch of our government that has been set aside just for historical reasons. They answer to our military and our heads of counsel. They are led by a woman whom I have never heard of before, but her position has been kept a secret except for the highest in rank. It was under her jurisdiction that we were sent here. It was on her orders I was sent to go and retrieve the stones that were lost that brought us here and opened the portal. She is the one who said this would lead us to the Requiem." Banks looked at every one of them in turn. Still looking into their faces, he pulled something out of his wet pocket. It looked like a torn piece of thin paper to Clint as Banks brought it up to his eyes and read soberly, "she is the one who gave me this, it's very old writing."

Clint eagerly came forward and leaning in read aloud," "Find Clint Holden at Lugrum Court eight fifty-two, Cody, Jamie, Kayla, Grant, Mel... Wait why does it have all these other names?"

"We know some of them," Corbin said in wonder.

"What's that thing at the end that says that the Requiem will be found by them?" Tamara said.

Even though Banks just explained as much as he knew or as much as he wanted them to know Clint was more confused than ever. So was everyone else by the look of things and not one of them could explain what was going on or what was going to happen next.

"Can I see that?" Kayla asked holding out her hand, but Banks pulled his back surprisingly.

"I am sorry, I cannot, I promised that I would never let this out of my possession to the woman who gave it to me even for a second. It is my burden and I have told you more than you need to know." Once again, he looked at each one of them, and for some reason, his eyes lingered longer on Tamara.

"It's getten late, sir," O'Neil said. "Whit are yer orders, sir?"

Banks looked around at him and for the first time that night, a smile cracked his mouth at the sight of the small dwarf who somehow was the tallest one in the room. Then Chiowood and Hobb stood to attention and one by one all those who came with him started to stand.

Without dropping his smile, he ordered, "Nix, check out Clint's arm and my shoulder. Everyone else either get some sleep or rotate your watch; be on your toes, they know where we are now, and we can't leave until we find a way to eliminate our opposition or convince them that these kids don't have what they want. Hobb, get the others and I want two Light Bringers on the roof concealed and ready by tomorrow."

"Tomorrow," Hobb croaked, in disbelief.

"If not sooner," Banks ordered and waved him out of the room. Hobb walked slow muttering to himself. "Even one Light Bringer in twenty-four with the complex rotator cuff, How?"

As soon as he left the room Banks focused on Kayla. "We will have to find a way to protect you at school and get you back safely as well. We will be sending out a patrol tonight to that farm location to check things there and we will need your help for both those things. The Fury know enough to find us here and set a trap or know that you live somewhere in this area; either way, they know a lot about you guys, so they might try to get you at school."

"Wait, they could be attacking any moment!?" Tamara screamed, looking at the front door.

"I do not think so," Banks stated, reassuring her by shaking his head. "They sent a scout and could have come here while we fought at the hospital. So, they might not have enough strength to engage us head-on because of insufficient forces. More than likely, they wanted intel."

"We could just miss a day of school," Corbin suggested a little too happily and to change the subject.

"Negative," Banks ordered. "If all of you don't go to school then that would arouse too much suspicion. We have enough of that at this time as it is with everything else going on. We had to demon dart more of those men this afternoon. Everyone be prepared for anything and don't drop your guard. Try to keep everything as normal as possible."

Corbin looked hurt as if he was afraid to have even said anything or that he was hoping for a compliment.

Banks seemed not to notice or care if he had hurt Corbin's feelings. "All of you will go to school but we will have to have help and watch all of you much closer. I want a patrol sent out tonight to see if we can find anything of the Fury. They are out there and if we can hit them first then we will have the upper hand. We have until tomorrow night at midnight before we go home. "Questions?"

As the storm was still splattering the windows and walls, it seemed that no one had any questions. Everyone started going upstairs or back to what they were doing. O'Neil began barking out orders for who would go with him on the patrol, and in a single minute, Clint and all his family with Corbin were alone except for Kayla, who went with Banks to talk. They didn't know what they should do until Cody turned around.

"All right everyone let's get some food," he said as he checked his watch. "It's almost nine, so let's get dinner and take care of Grandma and Jamie before they come out. Also, we will have to follow up on our excuse that we were watching a movie with checking how high we could get the volume, and that was the noise they heard when Banks crashed through Tamara's window." Cody fidgeted a little and then said, more to himself as he couldn't take his eyes off the floor, "then let's call it a night before someone really calls Mom and Dad, all right."

Unlike with Banks, there wasn't any command or sign of a disciplinary soldier movement as they all started to walk to the kitchen. Fortunately, there wasn't anything else that happened that night despite all of them jumping at every noise or flinching whenever someone came into the kitchen. Clint kept leaping to his feet when the back door opened while he was trying to eat a slice of pizza that Cody and Kayla prepared. Corbin stopped a stressed Hobb as he walked through the kitchen holding some interesting wood pieces that looked detailed enough to be from a car engine.

They all started to yawn, and their eyelids grew heavy as they finished eating until they were full. Clint took a moment to check outside as he put his plate in the dishwasher. He looked out the back window. It was raining, dropping softly off the leaves of the trees. He couldn't see any sign of life outside except for a soft light that was glowing in the window of the treehouse that was still the only thing that looked untouched by the druids.

"I know," Cody whispered in Clint's ear. He had walked over without Clint knowing it and was looking right behind his head. "I asked if they wanted to stay indoors with us but Banks said," Cody deepened his voice to sound like Banks, "that would not be appropriate, beside we need to stay on our toes and not in comfort." Cody smiled proudly so quickly it was as if someone had conjured it on his face. Even though Cody was proud of their new friend's lifestyle, it made Clint feel restless.

"Cody, I know you wish you could sleep outside, eat what you kill, and never bathe… Well, you already don't do that enough, but why does Banks not like kids?" Clint asked.

"I don't know, grasshopper," Cody said lovingly. "But what was that you started reading and came to a stop on that page. Wasn't that the name of…"

"I'm tired," Clint said quickly. "Let's go to bed before someone orders pizza and we get it for free and have to hide the body." With his smile firmly fixed Cody went away toward the front room. Now that he was ready to go to sleep Clint had a new worry. As he got ready for bed he showered and changed to go back to his sleeping bag, always minding the cut on his arm. Clint's head was vibrant with concern about having another dream-like he had the night before and he didn't really like the thought of getting his arm fixed right before going to sleep. As he was coming down the stairs to join the others who were all talking to one another someone grabbed his shoulder and said, "there you are, got you!"

Clint jumped and yelled, which sent everyone into a panic as if a bomb was falling on them. It was Nix who, at the first sign of concern and turmoil shouted, "It's all right, false alarm. Couldn't resist."

Suddenly heads were coming out of the front room to check on who made the noise. Nix gave them reassurances that everything was all right and muttered to Clint as he bent low crouching down by Clint's ear, "let's go and fix your arm." Nix guided him back into the kitchen which with no one else in there felt cold and lonely. Nix pulled a stool over and patted it with one hand indicating that Clint should sit. Clint lifted himself using his good arm and with a look of concern that would have been the same if it was from a barber who was going to give him a haircut, Nix rolled up his sleeves.

"Why so jumpy?" Nix asked as he helped pull up Clint's pajama sleeve, showing his injury on his forearm. Clint, feeling tired and not really in the mood, hummed for a moment.

"Just a lot going on in my life," Clint said trying to gamble his way out of talking. He was trying to sound convincing, just as if his mother was asking him something that he didn't want to talk about.

Nix picked up Clint's arm and examined it. He pulled out the same stuff that he had used on his forehead before. Not wanting to be asked another question, Clint decided to ask one before Nix could. "What is that stuff? It smells like gasoline."

Nix's focus wasn't taken away from Clint's arm as he replied nonchalantly, "it is a nectar that the Druids can make combined with some other things I can do to make it a powerful healer. But that is not your real problem, is it?"

"What?" Clint asked in confusion as Nix spread the healer on his arm. It stung only for a moment.

Nix shrugged and hummed a soft tune rather than answering the question. Clint thought that was an odd response to a direct question. He sat waiting with Nix working on his arm as Clint wished for something else to distract him from his painful wound. After a few moments, Clint couldn't take it anymore as that humming was all that he could hear.

"Do I act like there is something else wrong with me?" Clint moaned.

"I just think that there is more truth in you than what you want others to see, but you wouldn't be trying to hide something."

"What are you talking about?" Clint sighed, sounding very tired now.

Nix pinched Clint's arm hard all of a sudden causing Clint to almost fall off his chair. "Hey watch it, that hurt," Clint cried.

It started to burn again as Nix lifted his arm to examine his shoulder without giving even a look of an apology. "Sorry, just need to make sure there is nothing else wrong with your arm like I have seen sometimes when an arrow is poisoned. But you could handle that couldn't you."

Clint was starting to get very annoyed at all this. "Are you just fixing my arm or examining my mind as well?" he asked as his cut gave him another painful jolt as Nix gripped it hard.

"Is there something else wrong with you that needs to be examined?" Nix replied commonly.

"Why do you care and why are you asking me?" Clint said painfully as he pulled his arm back quickly. "Look let's abandon the arm, all right? I will be fine, OK?"

Clint was getting to his feet and took one step away when Nix said calmly, "that's good! I knew you would be."

Clint stopped as if Nix had just kicked him. Turning, he examined Nix up and down. What Nix just said made all the pain grow and erupt. His anger rose but Clint didn't know why.

"Why did you say that?" Clint pretested.

Nix rolled his powerful shoulders as he looked from Clint to the jar that he put on the counter. "I think you just like being mad at other people," he said, shrugging.

Clint stood rooted to the spot as Nix bent forward, leaning his heavy frame on the counter looking at Clint. "Everyone has been too soft on you, you don't need help, you are just fine on your own."

Clint's hands started trembling as an awful voice came out of his mouth that he didn't have any control over. He didn't sound like himself as Nix smirked at him. "What do you know about me?"

Nix just raised his head very briskly and ignored him. Clint didn't move, "Don't just stand there and blow me off. What else do you have on your mind about me? It's not like I had enough going on before you guys came. It's not just like I saw someone die like my… My?" Clint started to grind his teeth, facing Nix menacingly as he got angrier by the minute.

Nix let time go waiting, listening as he was now looking at his fingernails.

"What do you want from me?" Clint barked. Nix didn't say anything as he went on biting a hangnail. Clint might as well have chewed out the refrigerator to get the same response Nix was giving him. Clint started yelling, "you don't know what it's like. Losing your dad, moving, getting a new family, home, starting school having all those kids look at you weird, and trying to talk to…"

During this Nix shined his nails by rubbing them on his shirt and bit off another hangnail with his teeth, letting Clint's angry voice wash over him like it was no more than a breeze. Clint started to pace a little closer to which Nix asked, "do you get hangnails?"

"What do you want from me?" Clint demanded once more, sticking out his chest in anger. Nix said nothing as he moved his eyes around the room like he was looking for whoever was talking to him, and he couldn't see Clint.

Clint waved his hands stupidly in front of Nix's face, "Hello, anyone home?"

Nix jumped a little and looked at Clint as if he had just seen him for the first time, "do you want something from me?" Nix asked in a low growl.

"Why are you being a pain and not leaving me alone?" Clint spurted and without even waiting a moment Nix said quickly, "I could ask you the same thing," as he smiled broadly.

Clint thought for a moment; was he causing problems enough for Nix to notice it? Nix stood smiling slightly, showing a few of his white teeth, and with his eyes beckoned Clint to keep talking with a twinkle in them.

"What, what do you mean?" Clint asked now with no anger in his voice but something that sounded like apprehension. Nix walked around and rapped Clint hard on the back as he said calmly, "It's my job to heal. Not just problems with the body, but also of the heart. I know there is something deeper in you that you are letting hurt you. I see that you believe that it gives you energy and strength but unless you let out the rage and become calm you can be destroyed by it."

"What is that supposed to mean?" Clint asked, feeling better as he fought the anger in the back of his mind.

"What is bothering you?" Nix asked, sounding like a concerned father. The way he sounded sent a shiver down Clint's spine. "Don't tell me, but I want you to think of it," Nix said quickly as he rested a large hand on Clint's shoulder. "When you do think of it, I want you to decide what you are going to do with it because just letting it get the better of you is only letting it get the better of your life and life is too precious to let go."

Nix leaned over, and at first, it freaked Clint out that Nix held him with one massive arm in a small hug. He wanted to get away, but then it felt like something warmed him from the inside. It was like he had just drunk something warm, like hot chocolate. As soon as the feeling started, it diminished when Nix let him go and prodded him in the back. "Now, off to bed and remember what I told you."

Clint walked stupidly not of his own accord, but Nix was so strong that a simple push from him made Clint scuffle to keep his balance. With every step he took, Clint's bewilderment deepened as Nix went toward the back door not giving Clint another glimpse.

Clint was walking to the front room when O'Neil's voice came from nowhere, "Nix is an odd one isnae he?" Clint would have been shocked but what was left of the warm glow that was in the pit of his stomach that made everything easier to cope with had left him. O'Neil was sitting on the stairs wearing more clothes that were needed, as if he were going skiing, and had on the same heavy cloak that Chiowood had on when they went to the gas station only it was his size.

"Don't try tae figure it aw out at once boy, Nix is someone who will give yoo a wee bit at a time. Tae say nuthen that he is a wee bit off his heid," O'Neil groaned as he got to his feet. He sounded a little sore after everything that he'd had to go through so far that day.

Clint was at a loss of what to say while O'Neil made his way to the front door and opened it. He paused once before leaving and winked at Clint, "See yoo after me patrol."

Clint couldn't say anything as he was still battling the mixed feelings of being tired, angry, and loved all at once. Summing it up, he just decided that he felt stupid as he watched O'Neil shut the door. Clint stood for a moment until his legs took him over to the front room where everyone was lying down. Only Cody was still awake lying in his sleeping bag and this time he moved it to be next to Clint.

"What's up?" Cody asked tiredly.

"I don't know," Clint said sounding diminished.

"I know what you mean," Cody said heaving a deep sigh. "This has been a week where I am tired of saying, 'What the weird'. Speaking of weird, Tamara was telling me that she hasn't been able to get a hold of her boyfriend. You know, that one guy that Dad doesn't want her to talk to. She has been trying to talk to him and call him back since he was the master of bad timing when his call brought down the hammer in her room. He hasn't been to school and isn't answering the phone. She asked if she could go and see him, but Banks told her no, that it would be too dangerous."

Clint got into his sleeping bag and arranged his pillow and even though he was so tired he was keen to hear more. "Why does she want to get in touch with that guy so much? The guy's voice is too high for me, he sounds like a Pokemon who had a helium happy meal."

"That is just it," Cody said laying his head down on his own pillow. "They were going to go to the dance tomorrow and as far as that bum knows they are still going. She wants to keep her word." Cody gave him a furtive look.

Cody yawned, as Clint said, "She has changed, and she doesn't want to lie or cause any problems." Cody turned and looked at Tamara who was asleep by the piano.

Cody finished by giving Clint a sly grin and surprisingly dropped his head on his pillow and was instantly asleep. Clint looked with disgust at Cody who was snoring loudly, leaving Clint the only one awake. Before he closed his eyes, he said a silent prayer that he would sleep throughout the night without any bad dreams. He didn't know how tired he was until he felt like he was falling through his pillow and the floor. As he started to feel his consciousness leave him, the soft rain that was tapping on the windows was the only other noise giving him peace.

CHAPTER

Forty-One

LET THE COOL OUT

"**H**EY," Cody yelled in Clint's ear, sounding like James Brown. Clint found himself bolt upright in his sleeping bag as he watched the front door open. Remarkably awake and alert Clint saw sunlight cut through the thick clouds and shine into the house. It was morning as Clint watched O'Neil return from his patrol followed closely by Transun, Ravin, and Tremayne. They looked as if they had all been the subjects of bad jokes and victims of a surprise water balloon attack that they had lost. Clint and Cody were the only two of their family who were awake.

O'Neil paused and let all those with him pass as he manned the door. Clint, now fully awake, watched them inquisitively for any hint about what they had found. Even though Clint only moved his hand behind him to hold up his weight, it was enough to get O'Neil's attention. Catching Clint's eyes O'Neil shook his weary head negatively. O'Neil shut the door and gave Clint a sharp salute with a smile before he disappeared through the kitchen.

Clint got to his feet silently, so as not to disturb anyone as Cody rolled up his sleeping bag, scratching himself. Clint instinctively followed O'Neil toward the backyard stretching and yawning. He forgot that he was still in his pajamas until the cool morning air reminded him as he opened the back door. He squinted as the yard revealed the early morning sun was just starting to shine. The grass under his bare feet was wet from the rain and the morning held dark clouds showing a hint of redness with thunder sounding from afar. Clint had gone into his backyard hundreds of times but the feeling and look of the area were as different as if someone had taken a junkyard and changed it into beachfront property.

He walked gingerly afraid of the lack of protection on his feet. Amazement filled his sluggish morning mind as there wasn't anything in the soft grass that hurt him as he walked slowly to the treehouse. He had just walked under its leaves when suddenly something moved beside him, under the ground. He jumped as the grass looked like it was moving by itself.

"It's alive!" Clint yelled as he started to dance oddly as the movement under the lawn to his right started to shift and grow into a large lump. His yell didn't just make the lawn move but one or two bushes next to the tall tree started to wave angrily all of a sudden. Clint only had time enough to lift his head from the lawn to see the bush fly up out of the ground as Banks lay holding a bow and a light arrow aimed right at him, breathing fast.

"Wait, wait, it's me," Clint cried holding his hands out in front of him. It took Banks a moment to lower his bow as his arrow disappeared. Clint clutched his chest and leaned on the tree as Banks laid his head back down, relieved from his panic attack. Clint turned to look quickly back at the rolling grass. He saw Ohlwiler was in a hole under the lawn smiling at him.

Clint was gasping for breath muttering, "what, why would you be hiding like that and jump out at people?"

"Hold your heid boy," O'Neil called as he came from the other side of the tree. The bushes and trees that had so abruptly come to life relaxed as Clint saw arms and weapons lower and conceal themselves once more. "It's all right, yoo just woke up Banks that's all and he is a bit grumpy in the morn. He was on watch fur most ay the night. Yoo can come up now."

O'Neil waved at Clint to come up closer as Ohlwiler emerged and folded over the grass, covering up the hole like a green carpet perfectly fitted over a trap door. He escorted Clint closer to where Banks lay holding his tired head in his hands.

"Why are you guys down on the ground and not up in the treehouse?" Clint asked as he saw that he had woken up Banks who seemed to be trying to come around from a deep sleep.

"And what is up with that grass carpet trick and everyone else hiding in the new trees and bushes?" he asked as Ohlwiler stopped walking next to him.

"Sir, my apologies for the naffy morn call," Ohlwiler started to say, but Banks told him it was all right with a weak hand wave. Ohlwiler, feeling out of place, turned his attention to Clint, "Tremayne set that up for me and, as he put it, 'the grass is a bit of totty, and if any chap was coming a looken for us, he would have witnessed coming at um anti-clockwise.'" Ohwiler gave him a curt nod and a smart smirk. Clint and O'Neil shared a moment as they looked at one another, knowing that neither one had understood what was said.

Clint was still shaking off the odd sensation of the ground underneath his feet being as unstable as if there was a constant earthquake when O'Neil brought his attention back, causing him to jump again, "We don't go intae the treehouse 'cause if anyone were going to come to a looken fur us they would look fur us in the treehouse and nae on the ground."

"What is it, Clint?" Banks asked sounding frustrated out of fatigue as he struggled to even move an inch. As he started to yawn Clint could see that even though he didn't have hair on the top of his head there was grayish stubble on his chin and neck. Others were moving around behind the tree now as Nix and Ravin also were getting up.

All of them shared a look of exhaustion when Banks ordered, "change the watch." As most of them were leaving O'Neil and Banks started shaking off the tiredness that was still clinging to them heavily by readjusting their gear and positions about them. Clint knew from his older brother that it would be best to wait to talk until they were awake enough to understand what he was saying. Banks stretched and got to his feet and appeared to have forgotten how to stand as he leaned heavily on the tree.

"What is it, Clint?" Banks asked, still sounding tired.

Clint didn't waste any time but there was a fluctuation in his voice that implied he was still not too sure of himself. "I wanted to ask you why we went to the hospital last night?"

"Coz yoo said there were young kids there," O'Neil muttered as he took out something that looked like an apple but was the size of a softball.

Examining the enormous apple as O'Neil started to bite into it with a loud crunch, Clint said, "But why would that make any difference? They still came after us and they even killed someone."

"Coz kids who ur young cannae be given direct harm tae by those who are so evil like that Spell Binder," O'Neil muttered with a mouth full of apple that was now making his beard wet with juice. Clint still didn't understand what all of this meant, and Banks seemed to see that, but he was not the one who kept talking. On the other hand, he stretched and looked around in the gloomy sky and motioned for O'Neil to keep talking.

"Yoo see boy, when something goes that bad and evil there isnae much that will stop them, and with a Spell Binder they can use their power ower others tae destroy them. If a person did naething wrong all their life they couldn't harm them with their power. It would have tae be up close and personal if yoo know what I mean. But if a person did a lot ay things wrong, they wouldn't be protected unless they went back an' tried tae fix them. And kids, well kids are innocent. If there were no young kids in that building the Spell Binder would have leveled the entire feel good."

Clint didn't understand most of what O'Neil was saying, not just because of his accent and the fact that he might as well be hearing how the moon's gravitational pull causes waves, which affect the mating habits of penguins. But O'Neil also still had his mouth full of the apple, and when he had finished talking, he took another large bite and started chewing it noisily.

"I know you don't comprehend everything that is going on here," Banks coughed, sounding as if he had just come back from a basketball game and had shouted himself hoarse all night. "My apologies for whatever inconvenience we have caused to you and your family but no matter what and how today goes we will be gone today at midnight. Now is there anything else personally that you wish to discuss? Because we need to go and make ready plans for today on your safety with the others."

Banks looked at Clint with a hardened stare, but it wasn't hatred for Clint. It seemed more of like concern, but Clint had known from his older siblings when they were holding something back. He knew from long experience the best thing was to keep him talking.

Clint faked going back to the house and asked, "Why don't you like kids?"

Banks didn't react, but O'Neil did. He started coughing as he inhaled a large piece of apple that he was now gagging on.

Banks eyed him wearily in a steely gaze. O'Neil was slamming his back against the tree as the large portion of apple came out as he gasped for air. He immediately tried to say something, but Banks held up a hand to stop him. Which was a good thing because O'Neil was turning a rather becoming shade of pink moaning that he now felt sorry for that troll when they first met.

"There are enough things here that you do not understand, nor should you know. I do not consider it best to answer you. So please go and make ready for the day and we will hear no more of this. That is much more important than what you are concerned with." Banks said this not in anger but there was a note of something else in his voice.

"Are you patronizing me?" Clint asked, not backing down and matching his tone of voice.

Banks didn't say anything. He acted like he didn't even hear Clint.

"What aren't you telling us?" Clint asked, and he sounded serious for the first time that morning. Banks again didn't say anything as he gathered his gear and ignored Clint. O'Neil stood sheepishly, looking down at the ground.

Clint started to walk away as he was thinking about what Banks had and hadn't said. Why did he put it like that? Why didn't he just lie or play it off? He was sounding like he was from a bad movie remake depicting life in the seventeen hundreds. There was no doubt that there was something more that Banks knew.

"Prepare yourself," Banks called after him, breaking into his thoughts. Hearing his voice caused Clint to stop.

"If we don't do this right, it could be your last day." Banks' attitude was enough to scare Clint. The words were not loud or harsh, but they carried weight as if someone had just hit him in the gut with a semi-truck. He started walking and didn't realize that he'd reached the back door until he walked into it. He felt numb all over as he stepped inside and found the rest of his family eating cereal for breakfast. There was a genuine glumness around the room as everyone seemed unwilling to talk. Clint didn't break the mood but only added to it as he went and got a bowl, filled it with cereal and milk, and started eating quietly like the rest of his family. To his shock, Jamie came upstairs, her cell phone nowhere in sight.

Every eye was on her, especially Cody's whose hand had stopped part way to his mouth letting the milk drip off, hitting his shirt. Jamie didn't seem to notice as she looked like she had been up partying all night long. Her hair looked more like a wild tumbleweed that someone had glued to her head and her clothes appeared as if they were two sizes too large. Clint noticed that she had on Cody's football jerseys and shorts. No one broke her walk of the death march to the fridge until she missed the handle with her hand and turned on the ice maker, causing ice to hit the floor with small thuds.

"You on something, Jamie,'cause those are my clothes?" Cody inquired finally, putting down his spoon in his bowl.

Jamie looked around bringing Cody into focus and moaned, "I don't want to get my clothes dirty because I don't want to wash them. So, I borrowed some of yours."

"But you have tons of clothes downstairs that you have brought, and you have been having me wash your clothes for you since you got here!" Kayla shot back at her angrily, slamming her bowl down as she just finished draining the last dregs of milk from it.

Jamie was finally able to find the handle of the fridge and opened it taking out the milk, "I know," she said, "but all my clothes that I brought were dirty and needed to be washed, that's why I brought them."

"You mean you didn't bring any clean clothes for yourself?" Corbin asked excitedly.

This was the first time that everyone's eyes left Jamie and now traveled over to Corbin whose smile slowly faded like it had been drawn there with ink and then someone had poured water on it.

"What, I can hope, can't I?" he said in his defense.

Clint started laughing with his face down into his bowl as everyone else became very interested in their own cereal. Everyone except Kayla, whose shocked face Clint noticed out of the corner of his eye, was focused on something behind him. Clint turned and saw O'Neil coming to the back door through the window. As he was about to go in, Clint threw caution to the wind and started waving his hands.

"So, I do need to know when you guys get back from school today," Jamie said as she took a cereal box off the counter and started pouring it into her bowl so fast it spilled all over the floor.

O'Neil caught Clint's hands at the last moment when he grabbed the doorknob and saw Clint and then Jamie through the window. With a shocked face, he dropped to the ground as Jamie looked up at Clint.

"What's wrong with you, Clint? Are you testing out some new deodorant or something? What was that sound from the back door?" Jamie asked as her wild hair lifted to look at him and investigate the backyard.

"Nothing," Clint replied, quickly dropping his hands.

"Probably one of the Fournier's living with us, what was their family called again?" Jamie asked as she took a spoon out and started eating, causing more cereal to fall and scatter on the floor.

A moment of shock hit everyone in the room. Not one of them knew the name of the family that was going to come to live with them, and with everything else going on, Clint had forgotten completely about them, and from the look of things, so did everyone else. They all looked for one another to answer, and they all made up names and, regrettably, said them simultaneously. They each shouted a different name, causing Jamie to stop for a moment. She eyed them all suspiciously in turn.

"All right, I see what you are all doing," she said, putting her bowl down. She now looked furious at all of them as Corbin said in despair, "You know what's going on?"

"Yes, I do!" she shouted, pushing away the hair that was blocking her eyes. "You are trying to make me look bad to Mom and Dad, aren't you?"

They all were in a stupor again, not knowing what to say. This only seemed to fuel the fire as Jamie picked up her bowl again, spilling more milk on the counter and floor.

"Well, you all might think you are smart in your little scam to get me in trouble, but now all you have done is get yourself right in it. I will tell Mom and Dad that you all snuck out on me when I told you to stay home." Jamie looked now as if she had just said something that would have made her a million dollars.

From the unchanged faces, she went on with her assumption that she had everything figured out and went on with her ranting. "You are all going to get it now! Tell me when you leave school before I make up something else to tell Mom and Dad!"

"Uh, three… the same time as we have all week," Cody said in shock.

"That is better, you bunch of pig's droppings, and you better come straight home and get my laundry done. Then some of you can do your dance thing." She eyed them all viciously as she took her food down the hall and then downstairs to barricade herself in her bedroom again.

"That was a close one," Kayla breathed as she sat easier on her stool. The back door opened as O'Neil came in with a small squeak and slam of the door closing behind him.

"We have been avoiding 'er since we got 'ere. She's enough tae scare the last drop off a pint," O'Neil finished as he rested his head on the counter. It wasn't that hard for him to lean down on it.

"You are telling me," Cody said, also breathing a sigh of relief. "I had to grow up with that."

"Me condolences, lad," said O'Neil, giving Cody a serious look. Suddenly, O'Neil laughed his great barking laugh that sounded like an explosion. It took him a while to stop, but it was enough to change everyone's feelings around the room. They were genuinely lighter, and smiles were back on their faces.

"Now, on a mere business note, we need tae come together on this morning's missions. I mean, other than thinking ay ways tae hae yer sister git some brains tae match 'er looks." O'Neil chuckled at his own words, making most of them laugh. Not at his joke but how his laugh carried.

"We are going tae have yoo drive tae school again but this time Ravin is going tae watch yoo in one school and Chiowood will be going tae keep an eye on the other until yoo ur done then yoo lot come straight home. All right?"

"How are they going to watch us while we are in class? Won't we have plenty of warning if they come after us?" Tamara asked as she, too, had finished her breakfast.

"Och, there are other ways fur them tae get at yoo lot than just sending an Orc or imps. They have worse things than 'at."

"Like what?" Corbin asked interestedly.

O'Neil looked around once more. His eyes were full of worry, like when he started telling Clint something that he probably didn't want to tell them and was checking to make sure everything was all clear.

"I am not saying much coz yoo lot probably havnae heard of the stuff that is from oor world but it is at which will wet yer sheets at night. It aw depends on what they were able tae brin' with them." O'Neil wasn't sounding happy anymore but fearful.

Kayla looked around to change the subject and decided to ask, "How are Chiowood and Ravin going to check on us in school? They will stand out a little."

O'Neil cheered right up, his smile fixed back on his hairy face. "Ah, they can go almost anywhere they want, they can hide under a single flack ay snow in a desert and not be found."

They all looked at each other, not understanding what he meant.

"Yoo know it's the same ting at goes together like a shoe and dat microwave," O'Neil said encouragingly as if this settled the matter. "Now if yoo don't min' I get some leave time this morn and have me movies tae watch un games to play at mot-oh-cycle one been calling me all night. So yoo lot had better git a move on and don't worry. We got yoo taken care of really good like."

O'Neil started to walk out of the kitchen, kicking everyone off the stools they were sitting on as he left. He was walking with a little hop in his step toward the television room and arcades.

"He's right," Kayla stated as she started to clean. "We don't have much time." She hurried and finished gathering the last of the mess that Jamie had made as everyone else finished their food and started getting ready for the day.

Clint and Corbin were the first two ready as they came downstairs, not noticing the large tree that was looking fine in the lobby. They saw O'Neil jumping up and down on the motorcycle arcade game. They stopped to watch him as he was shouting and hollering, making his racer pop a wheelie. He wasn't doing too badly until Corbin's high-pitched laughter caught his attention. O'Neil noticed them and composed himself quickly as if he were a butler caught by his master.

"It's foon!" O'Neil protested as he started playing again as if they hadn't interrupted him. It didn't take long for everyone else to get ready.

They did have one moment of excitement as Transun reported someone was coming to the front door. There was an even more incredible rush to prepare for every possible threat that might come from the front of the house.

Banks was asking Transun, "Do we have Light Bringers?"

Transun suddenly looked like a wounded bulldog. "They have one up that is still a bit outside, and when I asked Hobb about the other one, he just started crying."

"It's that paperboy thing," Banks stated, looking out the window.

It was remarkable that Banks could recognize him as he was wearing a crude outfit that was made up of hockey pads and what appeared like a birdcage bottomed out and sat as a helmet, equipped to protect him.

Much to Corbin and O'Neil's dismay, they let the paperboy go without harm. They did enjoy watching him shiver and shake as he walked up to the door, threw the paper, and sprinted back the way he came. He ran well until, weighed down with equipment, he fell and rolled down the driveway. This sent O'Neil and Corbin rolling on the floor with laughter. It took another moment to gather everything and everyone in the hallway before they got into the car.

"How are you feeling?" Corbin asked as if he were pumping himself up before a game.

"Just itching to get this day over with coach," Clint said, as he thought that the sooner things started, the sooner it would be all over.

Waiting for the rest of his family, Clint glanced out into the backyard for another moment. A gentle breeze blew, and everything it met swayed. The light of the morning still held the area in a dull, gloomy haze that was slowly starting to drizzle in soft rain around the house.

Clint heard the soft thud of someone coming down the stairs, which made him tug his eyes away from the outside. Clint saw Kayla coming down the stairs with Nix. She struggled to explain the story of the frog prince to Nix as everyone else walked into the garage. Cody hurried in as Ravin and Transun were waiting for him. He opened the trunk with a click of his keys and started talking, not noticing Transun and Ravin's apprehensive looks.

"When we get to the school, I will open the trunk to let you out," he explained.

He then gave them a watch and gave a crude explanation of what the hands meant and when they would be let out of school.

"Look at that," Kayla said proudly. She was watching Cody with admiration as he spoke.

"Look at what?" Corbin retorted. "It looks like Cody might as well be campaigning for government office and explaining it to three-year-olds."

Ravin and Transun smiled but clearly didn't understand what was being explained. As Clint walked by Kayla, he overheard her say nervously, "Nix, he had a spell on him, and when he was kissed, he was free and became a prince."

"But he only knew how to be a frog. How could he lead a country? I would rather be a frog. Why would he want to be kissed anyway? At one moment, your entire life is all about what is buzzing around you, and then you have a nation to run," Nix said, annoyed, shaking his head.

"He was once human and wanted to be turned back," Kayla said flimsily. "It's just a story, a fairytale."

"Fairies don't have tales, just tempers," Nix said, huffing, folding his arms, and telling Kayla the conversation was over.

Clint got in the car, followed by Corbin and Tamara. The trunk snapped shut, shaking everyone momentarily as everyone else entered and closed their doors. No one said anything as they started out. The only sound was from Grant's inhaler, which he used now whenever he saw or heard a dog bark.

They moved slowly again as the car headed for school. All eyes wandered in every direction, searching for anything out of place. Tamara, Corbin, and Clint shared an anxious moment as they drove by Bill's house. Clint saw her eyes follow the house as they passed it and remembered that she had not heard from him. Just up the street was where the first attack had taken place. Clint could see the concern in Tamara's new, clear, loving eyes. They would have taken an alternate route to their schools, but Cody's inability to hit the gas pedal meant they had to drive straight there or be late.

"It will be alright. This isn't the first time that Bill the blund I mean that Bill has missed a couple of days of school," Clint said over-enthusiastically.

Tamara gave him a soft smile, "I asked that funny boy Zack at school who will tell you anything if you smile just right at him why he hasn't been at school. He said that someone called in for him, excusing him for the next couple of days. He said the old secretary kind of was in a trance when he was on the phone and just accepted it. It's just he's never gone that long without talking."

"He might have noticed how you've changed, and he wanted to break things off before you had the chance," Corbin said as he cleared his throat.

Clint approached the following subject as if he were walking up on a sleeping lion and was going to stick it in the nose with a pin. "Why do you want to get hold of him so bad?" He stammered, watching a couple of snails pass them by on the sidewalk.

Tamara made an indistinct sound and said nothing at all. Corbin shrugged at Clint, telling him she must not trust them or want help as she stared out the window, not looking at anyone in the car.

In the new uncomfortable silence, Corbin yelled, "You do know about how the gas pedal works in a car, don't you, Cody?" There was a short and tense discussion about Cody's knowledge of gas as a liquid or an aerosol.

Forty-Two

HALLOWEEN SHOULD BE A SCHOOL HOLIDAY

After another ten minutes, they dropped off Grant and Kayla. After both got out, Cody drove forward just out of sight, popped the trunk, and waited a moment. They waited until two soft taps told him they could go, as the trunk seemed to shut off its own accord. Clint and Corbin searched for any sign of their escort, who got out but saw nothing.

Both Corbin and Clint wondered how someone could disappear like that as they fantasized about the possibilities all the way to school. As they drove into the parking lot, they saw all the other students making their slow, miserable march toward the front doors. There was the same anxious feeling behind Clint's navel as he got out of the safety of the car. They had met nothing so far, and rather than being relieved, he felt a growing tension as if the worst was yet to come as time passed. He looked around at all the kids who were jeering and cheering now that Friday was here. Some younger kids joined the area as the rain started to sprinkle on them all. They talked excitedly about Halloween events that would happen later that day. It all seemed like it was coming from a previous life.

Some of Cody's usual group, who always waited for him, called him over in the light silver sheet of rain as he popped open the trunk just an inch. Cody glanced wildly at the car and then at Tamara, Clint, and Corbin, who stood by the car cautiously.

Cody focused on the space between them and the front door when he said lowly, "Just get inside and take care until school is out. Then we will get home and wait it out. It will all be over soon."

"Don't worry about us," Corbin said through clenched teeth so he wouldn't be too loud with so many people around them.

"Speak for yourself," Clint said to himself weakly.

Clint didn't dare look around, fearing that he might see something coming after them. He had a fleeting glimpse in his mind of five or so orcs tearing after them, breaking through cars and children alike, grimly tossing them around as if they were no more than leaves.

"Hey, Thamara," Zack called as they approached the front steps.

"Good luck," Corbin spluttered, not caring that anyone else overheard him. "You're getting attacked by all sorts of freaks lately. Oh, hey, Zack!" He still said loud enough for everyone to hear. Tamara didn't look back at Clint and Corbin as Zack started a feeble jog, waving at her. Clint didn't want to say anything but heaved his hand high as he slugged Corbin.

"Ouch! It has been a while since you have hit me. Like an entire five minutes… thanks for holding yourself back," Corbin said, rubbing his arm where Clint had hit him and lifting his bag higher on his arm.

Clint walked on, and as soon as he went through the inspection past the school doors, he breathed a sigh of relief as Corbin appeared by his side. He looked like he shared the same feeling as Clint now that they were inside and safe.

"Uh, is there anything else that uh, uh," Corbin muttered.

"Don't know," Clint whispered as he started to head off toward his first class. "I, I will see you at lunch, all right?" he said firmly, trying to sound normal. Neither could shake the look of misery on their faces as they went their separate ways.

Their classes testified to the amount of work they had all been about to do, how much they could commit their minds to their education, and the lessons they were having. Every time a teacher was going to ask a question, Clint's stomach did a horrible lurch as he shuddered to be called on. The one odd thing was some students remarked about seeing someone outside in the rain. They claimed only to see a head in the window. But when the teacher investigated, they found nothing besides the blazing hail of rain.

It was some relief when the lunch bell rang, and Principal Miller's drowning voice magnified over the intercom, talked about holiday events that had been interrupting classes. So far, it seemed someone had overflowed half the toilets while adding chemicals to make the water glow. Kids jumped out of vending machines and garbage cans to frighten other students. Restroom door signs were switched to classroom door numbers. Lockers were full of candy, live bats, spiders, cats, and mice on the loose, and one student was stuck in a locker surrounded by foam. Rumors spread that an air horn strapped to the old secretary's chair that went off as soon as he sat on it had killed him. Someone hotwired the PA system and announced aliens had delivered their usual lunch they would be having that day. Clint's favorite came right before the lunch bell as a student dressed as the headless horsemen rode a horse down the hallways throwing candy pumpkins.

Clint found that kids did all these tricks and almost forgot the trouble that was known only to his family and himself. He felt practically normal as he went to his locker first before lunch. He thought it would be better to finish getting what he needed before eating rather than wait the past two days he'd had to face anyone who found him at his locker. Then he nervously remembered the dance that night and feebly tried to think of what he would tell Melanie as a passing student handed him an obituary leaflet describing him. The school librarian had been dead for eighty years and yet still came to work.

This thought took him all the way to the lunchroom. As he went in, the pungent smell of the unidentifiable food hung in the air. Clint, having gone to his locker first, found the line to be very long and waited weighed down with the horrible consideration of what he was going to do when someone behind him started to talk to him.

"Hey Clint, what is going on with your thister?"

He didn't have to look around to know that it was Zack. It seemed that his waiting to avoid people had backfired on him as some of the school's most uninteresting people had edged behind him. Clint growled, not wanting to be caught in a place alone with Zack.

Clint's first thought was to pretend that he didn't hear him, but Zack's broad smile shone under his long, skinny nose as he checked out of the corner of his eye. Almost feeling like he was going to be sick, he turned to face Zack irritably.

"What are you talking about?" he said dully.

"Well, she has changed. Everyone in the offithe is talking about it. Well that and everything elthe going on. I even got some nothes from the teachers that she is now one of the best in the classth. Well, with Bill being gone, is she available? Do you know what she thinks of me? I could tell her that I have moved up two gradthes and percect gradesth. I am altho in charge of tonight. With a big thuprize. Would that impreth her? What do you think? If the secretary is dead. I bet I could get his job, because no one knowths the officeth better than me."

Zack said all this very fast as he tottered on his tip toes as his body vibrated. It was like having a talking backpack with an inferiority complex as Clint started to bounce one leg to calm his nerves. Clint didn't say anything back but grunted, sounding flustered. This didn't impact Zack's cascade of questions and comments. The line moved onwards, driving him into the lunch serving room. It was a surprise to Clint that there wasn't a light green haze in the air over the food as every lunch worker had dressed up in different costumes.

Clint got his food quickly and hurried toward his usual lunch spot. To his dismay and outrage, Zack had followed him all the way and sat down next to him as Clint sat next to Corbin. Those who regularly sat there were unhappy and bothered by Zack's presence. The reaction of the other kids did not sway Zack. On the contrary, he kept talking to Clint and Corbin as if they'd been his best friends all their lives. Clint started to feel angry as his ability to tune out what Zack was saying was beginning to wane as he asked what was wrong with Corbin.

"I forgot that I have detention after school today. I'm cleaning the gym before the dance and I have to help set up for it," Corbin said as if this was a nightmare come true as the rain was falling steadily on the windows unheard over the constant talking around the room.

"Oh, that is great!" Zack shouted. "It is going to be a tricky operation." As Zack went on, much to the exasperation of Clint and Corbin, he also took a long snort of nasal spray. Zack was just going on about what type of decorations were going to go up when suddenly he stopped. Clint looked up, wondering what miracle would bring this flood of useless information to a stop. Clint's mouth dropped as Tamara sat down on the other side of the table, making a young girl with blonde pigtails move over.

Tamara sat uncertainly and in a low mysterious voice, she asked if she could sit there.

"Please," Corbin said excitedly. Clint looked at Corbin and wondered where he had been hiding all this happiness that he was now showing when he was looking so fearfully miserable before.

Tamara bit her lip and smiled as her hands trembled to pick up her fork. All three of them were watching her in entirely different ways. Corbin was looking at her dreamy-eyed and used a soft tone when he spoke. Clint looked at her reprovingly, wondering why she wasn't with her friends. Zack's mouth had dropped as he peered over at her, and it looked like he couldn't get his mouth to close.

Corbin again came to Tamara's aid when he said, "Your old friends are having a hard time with you changing?"

Tamara looked up in relief as if she hoped to talk to someone about this as he checked the corner that she had been through during her previous lunch times so many days before. "I don't really get along with them very much anymore," she said heavily.

Zack found his voice once more and he said very airily and still not closing his mouth or even using his lips, "I know how you feel."

Clint grinned wickedly as he examined Zack as he barked, "I am sure you do." But no one seemed to be helping Tamara except Corbin when he said at once, "you are always welcome with us."

Tamara smiled again, which filled Clint with dread and seemed to melt Zack. How would it be to be seen all around school with his sister? This is when Tamara started to talk to him as she asked quietly, "I heard that you were going to go to the dance tonight with a few different girls Clint, but I didn't hear who you were going with Zack?"

At this question, Zack started to shake. He looked around as if he were scared out of his wits. He made a funny little noise that sounded like a pig snort and after hesitating for a moment he stood up so fast from the table he hit someone walking behind him and said, "I havth to go to the bathroom."

Clint saw Zack backing away making gagging noises as he started to look very ill on his way out of the room toward the hall. Everyone in the room watched him leave as he was acting very oddly. Tamara looked feverishly around for some reason for this strange action.

"Did I do something wrong?" she asked.

Clint was snickering at the stunned look at Tamara's face and couldn't talk past the uncontrollable urge to keep laughing but he did manage to squeak out, "he is just a little odd and he does some things like that."

"Nope, I think that Zack, the mastermind behind every A grade and brown nose to every teacher, couldn't take the thought of changing into Zack, the cool and suave man that we know he is. The change was too much for the poor fool," Corbin said looking on as Zack left the lunchroom at a sprint.

"Don't worry, Tamara," Clint told her laughing, "he is just allergic to good-looking girls."

As Clint chuckled, Tamara looked deeply impressed for a moment, which was also new. She usually would play it off that Zack's antics were a product of needing to eat more fiber. The new Tamara looked embarrassed as she said, "Thank you for the compliment, Clint."

Before they could say anything the first warning bell had rung throwing them all back into the reality of school. The whole room shifted as students swooped toward the doors and got ready for their next class.

"Any word from Bill yet?" Clint asked as a fresh surge of stress about his own problem resurfaced.

Tamara led Clint to her locker as she said, "no, but there was a note in my locker telling me that he was looking forward to tonight and that he should be feeling better. He has been ill for a while now."

Clint looked incredulously at her and couldn't help but see that she was worried. His mind was filled with the memories of when she came to talk to him and also what Nix had told him. As they reached her locker at the end of the hallway where there was hardly anyone else lurking around, Clint started talking before he could stop himself. "I know how you feel. There is someone I wanted to go to the dance with but now she probably thinks I'm toe lint because of what happened with Amber."

Tamara looked over at him as she opened her locker. She seemed interested and worried as if this was as new to her as it was to Clint. Her face's features softened. Clint felt like he had said too much and was about to apologize but Tamara said quickly, "I'm sorry, is there something I can do?"

Clint had a doom-laden expression as he didn't want to say what his mind was screaming to ask, "Why can't I talk to a girl that I like?" He was able to control that and instead asked calmly, "I don't know if anything can be done. Corbin admits that ship is sunk and is better left at the bottom of the ocean." He looked up and down the hall as his time was running out, feeling apprehensive standing with his new sister.

Tamara didn't say anything for a moment. It was as if she knew that there was something more that he wanted to say but he couldn't bring himself to do it. Her eyes were soft and compassionate as she shut her locker and waited for him to talk.

"Thanks for your offer to help, but I do need to get to class, and nothing so far has been normal with her or this week," Clint said finally as he started to walk away, but Tamara grabbed his shoulder before he could take two steps.

"Wait, what's the girl's name that you like?"

Clint turned around cautiously. Telling Tamara about his personal feelings was one thing but to tell her something that was one of his deepest secrets was something else.

Seeing how Clint hesitated she hit him on the shoulder as she pulled a single piece of paper and pencil out of her bag. "Come on, come on, we don't have much time here, lover boy."

Clint readjusted his bag, still unsure what she was going to do to him. "Just give it to me," she begged, her eyes twinkling.

Clint's head roved around checking who was close as if he were about to divulge some national security secret. His eyebrows rose, still looking and double-checking. Tamara was writing down something on the paper with the pencil flying fast. In a hushed, hurried voice Clint said, "Melanie, her name is Melanie." He felt his face turn furiously red as Tamara shrieked a soft giggle.

"Would you shut up?" Clint muttered.

"Now don't read this, just give it to her, all right!" Tamara said as she thrust the paper into Clint's hand and started to run down the hall.

"All right?" Tamara shouted as the last warning bell rang throughout the school. Clint stared at her beadily, as if he'd accidentally walked into the girl's bathroom and was being shouted at that he was out of bounds.

It took a moment for his blank mind to register that he had to get to class as Tamara was already on her way to hers.

He scrambled all the way to class, and for two days in a row, he was almost late and only made it on time by the skin of his teeth. His class went better that day, mainly because so many things were going on in his mind that he couldn't feel it all at once, nor could he really think of just one problem before another one came up. It was like putting ten puzzles together at once, and he didn't have a guide on what the picture should look like when he was finished. It wasn't until he was walking toward his last class when he saw Melanie walk in before him that he remembered the note Tamara had written to give to her. His legs kept walking as his mind raced to where he had put the letter. He had pulled his bag around to open it and walk simultaneously. It wasn't in there as he walked into the classroom.

He couldn't look at her as he was keen to get to his seat as soon as possible and find that note. What if he'd lost it? He didn't even know what was on it! He was suddenly full of memories of other students whose letters or notes had gone astray and might as well have their secrets printed in the school newsletter.

He was going through all his pockets when Corbin sat down, stripping off his bag. "What are you doing?" Corbin asked him as the bell rang, signaling the start of class.

Clint tried to sound normal as he replied, "nothing."

Mrs. Christenson was in rare form as if she were a guardian against any positive thought or child who desired to have fun that day. The atmosphere in class was almost a palpable feeling of excitement as school was almost over and Halloween night was about to start. Mrs. Christenson called on every student to answer complex questions and worked on them hard all through the class. They only had five minutes left when Clint had an opportunity to search for the note again as Mrs. Christenson was bent over, grilling a student for getting an answer wrong.

As he was feeling in his hip pocket a horrible voice called out. "Clint, what are you doing?" Mrs. Christenson called.

Closing his eyes, Clint felt his life fall away as the all too familiar steps of doom brought Mrs. Christenson closer.

"What are you hiding?" Mrs. Christenson blurted, bending over to place her face an inch from his.

Clint was frozen with fear. If she made him take out the note, she would read it to all the class. Clint started to breathe very fast as he almost felt like punching Mrs. Christenson in the face.

"Clint, you will stand up and turn out your pockets young man or I will, OUCH!"

Clint's eyes shot open as Mrs. Christenson jumped, bumping his desk as she spun around, turning on Corbin. Clint's sweaty face was horrified but he found Corbin was smiling. He was positively bursting with happiness as Mrs. Christenson wheeled on him like an angry bear.

"What did you just do, you little…" Mrs. Christenson stopped talking as she rubbed her hands over her backside. The angry lines in her face slowly softened. She slowly stood up and looked lost with a vacant expression. She moved, zombie-like to her desk, gathered her things, and left the room without so much of a word.

The bell rang and for the first time, every student in her class sat unmoving. Corbin was the first to stand and practically danced out of the room. Clint was the next to get up as he ran out of the room after his friend, leaving everyone else in their seats.

Clint turned into the hallway and bumped into Corbin who was still dancing.

"What did you do?" Clint blurted out, rubbing his stomach after colliding with Corbin's elbow.

"Demon dart," Corbin said sounding like Elvis. "I asked for one from Hobb when he was flustered on his way to the roof. He was in such a hurry he just gave me one and then pow! Been wanting to do that since we became her pets."

Clint was in a stupor of amazement as Corbin started dancing down the hall. "Hey, what were you looking for anyway?" Corbin asked, still doing his Elvis impression.

Horrified, Clint searched his pockets again. There! He must have absentmindedly put it in his back pocket when he was running to his class after lunch. Trying hard to figure out if he should give it to Melanie or not, he slowly walked past the waves of students all around him.

Suddenly out of the corner of his eye he saw the hair that he could never duplicate in his mind. His stomach tightened as he saw her walk down the hall. Biting his lip as he thought that things couldn't get much worse, he tore off after her.

It was as if he was a madman outside of himself as he called out, "Melanie, hey." She kept walking, apparently not keen to talk to him. When he caught up to her, he touched her shoulder. She turned sternly with a glower on her face. Clint felt like he was suddenly talking to his mother when she was in a bad mood. He opened his mouth to speak but nothing came out as he could hear Corbin now shouting down the hall amongst the loud chatter, calling for him.

"What is it?" Melanie snapped.

A minute later, Corbin got to him and grabbed his arm vigorously, shaking his head in disbelief. "We have to go. We don't have time for this."

Clint swallowed as Melanie now swung away angrily. Not having any control of himself he reached out and pushed the paper into her hand. Just then Corbin drove him down the hall, pulling on him hard to get out of the school as soon as possible. Clint could see Melanie standing there dispirited, with the paper in her hand, being drowned in other students before she was no longer in sight.

"You lovesick idiot! If you weren't so focused on her you would have seen Amber charging toward us. I was able to stop her and one of her cronies told me on behalf of her," Corbin screwed his voice to sound higher causing heads to turn toward them, " 'you tell him to be here at six if he wants to live. With two dozen roses, chocolates that she won't eat, three hundred in cash, a limo or helicopter, a lot of sanitizer, and no pictures.' I added the sanitizer."

"Great!" Clint said as he finished his locker combination, his fingers moving horribly slowly as he was trying now so hard to get out of school before this new threat of Amber and her posse could get to him now.

"Oh, that's not so bad if you think about it," Corbin said, consoling him. "You could have been like Zack this afternoon."

"What do you mean?" Clint asked as he finished with his locker and shut it.

"Well, Zack was just getting a little too friendly with your sister and I thought I should, well, that I would put a little salt on the worm. To help him out a bit."

"That's slugs," Clint said.

"You can call him that if you want."

"What did you do?" Clint asked slowly as if he was asking carefully.

"Well," Corbin suddenly sounded like he just won the lottery and was hoping to tell someone about it. "When he was sitting there, and you and I couldn't get rid of him, and he started going all walking dead on us when your sister came over. I just sort of, well, rubbed his leg with my foot as if Tamara was doing it every time she said something."

"You did what?!" Clint said so loudly that almost everyone walking by stopped to see what was going on.

"I got him to leave, didn't I?" Corbin said slamming his locker shut. "I thought it was a good idea."

"You are a genius!" Clint smirked. "But I would rather have you as my friend than my enemy with the things you come up with."

"That's why I am so special." Corbin was about to say more but Amber and her henchmen were cutting their familiar path down the hall towards them.

Clint and Corbin both ran out of school as fast as they could, not caring about attracting attention to themselves. Corbin ran as best as he could and with each exhale of breath he asked, "what, was on that, note, that, you, gave, Mel… a… nie?" Clint didn't respond to him as he ran through the halls, cutting a path through the milling crowd. They came out into the rain moving fast as they spotted the car and Cody waiting for them.

The rain had lightened and even rays of sunshine cut through the dissipating clouds. Clint took a moment to rest at the bottom of the steps to the parking lot, allowing Corbin to catch up.

As soon as he heard Corbin's feet clambering down the steps he started to jog toward the car. He was almost there when someone's shout split the sky. "Clint Holden!" Amber yelled angrily sounding like something out of a horror movie coming to kill him.

"Run for your life man!" Corbin yelled as they made a break for the car. Cody held open the door as they dove in.

"Let's go, go! Get out of here!" Clint demanded as he locked the doors with a click.

"Can't, Tamara isn't here yet. What is it? Are they here?" Cody asked searching them for anything that would help him pick up on what was going on.

"No, it's, it's, worse," Clint stammered.

"Clint Holden!" Amber cried again.

"It's her!" Clint finished in a trembling voice, lowering his head into his lap. He acted like he was bracing himself in a plane that was about to crash.

Cody turned to look out the window, "Dang, man she is mad. She is even getting wet in the rain and not allowing one of her servants to hold an umbrella over her."

Tamara tapped on the window on the other side of the car causing them all to scream in fear.

Corbin was yelling, "start the car!" over and over while Clint fumbled on the door lock to let Tamara in. Cody was panicking also as if Amber was another orc coming after him. It was odd but the orc and Amber, both did resemble each other as they both looked like they were out for blood. He seemed to have finally been pushed over the emotional edge and was screaming now too.

The door opened. "GET IN!" Clint yelled as the car's engine roared to life as Amber was only one parking space away. Tamara sprung into the front of the car and slammed her foot down on Cody's, causing the car to race out of the parking lot.

All of them were screaming, Cody in shock, Tamara with glee, and Corbin and Clint in terror as the car bounced over speed bumps and the dip between parking lot and road causing the car to lurch, Amber looking daggers at them all the way as they sped off down the road.

They picked up Kayla and Grant and after allowing an awkward moment of waiting for the trunk to open slightly and close they returned on their journey home. Everyone's spirits seemed to lift the closer they got to their home.

Forty-Three

I WAS ONLY TRYING TO HELP

"I can't believe we made it!" Cody said briskly as they pulled into their garage with the door closing behind them. "I mean all we have to do now is wait, we don't have to leave anymore."

"Speak for yourself," Corbin groaned as he urged Clint to open the door, so they could get out.

"Why, what is it?" Tamara pleaded.

"Owww," Clint and Corbin said as they both remembered that they hadn't told anyone that he had detention. Their happiness dropped as they told Cody when he opened the trunk, allowing a wet Transun and Ravin out. They both looked a little sick as they pulled themselves upright.

"What?" screamed Cody. "You have to go back to school, are you crazy? We just barely got out of there alive!"

"I wish you would say that every morning," Clint moaned.

They all walked into the house in a feeling of disarray. Transun walked in first calling the all-clear as Corbin's eyes were low as he slowly walked in. Cody was next into the house as Tamara followed him and Clint behind her.

"So?" Tamara asked eagerly. "How did it go?"

"What?" Clint said stupidly as he followed Corbin's eyes staring at the floor. He was about to slap Corbin to revive him when Tamara finished, "the note, how did she take it?"

"Oh, the note," Clint said slapping his head, thankful that he didn't have to comment on what he was thinking concerning Corbin and his detention. "Well, the note, I, uh, I sort of gave it to her," he said as he came into the house feeling stupid.

"And? Did she read it?" Tamara encouraged.

Clint was still fumbling with his words, "I don't know, I didn't see."

"But you are sure she got it?" Tamara asked, very pleased with herself. She had just shut the door and walked in.

"Yeah, she got it, but I don't know if she read it. Hey, what was is in that thing anyway?" Clint asked now, wondering what was going to happen next.

Just then Cody came into the kitchen and pointed toward Corbin who was by the stairs. "Ask him," he said facing someone who was out of his sight on the far side of the kitchen.

Through the silence Banks walked into view looking very much like Clint's mother coming to talk to one of her kids after a sleepless night. Everyone bustled out of the way to allow Banks to talk to Corbin together, alone in the office. They all were going their own way to their rooms as Clint waited for Banks to finish talking to Corbin while Tamara said she would talk about it later. Clint looked over at O'Neil who was crying, watching the television with used tissues all over the floor. The sounds of the movie Finding Nemo could be heard over his sobs.

When they were done talking Corbin came out of the room alone while Banks stood staring at his family's portrait. Clint's patience was finally rewarded when Corbin said, "he wants to see all of us to go over the plan for tonight."

Corbin didn't give Clint time to ask anything else as he walked away to get everyone with an uneasy look on his face. Clint leaned on the tree as Nuts, O'Neil's squirrel came rushing down it and jumped on Clint's shoulder then bounded his way into the office, with the familiar sounds of his little claws on the floor with soft skitters and then his squeaks.

Banks came rushing out of the room as he called out, "Clint, get out of sight. O'Neil, we have someone coming in one of their car things, it's a single male that we haven't seen before."

Right on cue, everyone took up defensive positions around the windows and door, weapons in hand. Clint sprinted out of the lobby and made his way into the kitchen when more footsteps and a voice from downstairs brought him to a stop.

Jamie was coming up the stairs calling, "no one get it, it's for me. I'll get the door."

Clint looked over to Banks who was looking slightly put out as he frantically waved everyone off. They all took cover hiding behind the couch, chair anywhere as Clint felt a nasty pain of guilt watching Jamie see those who were protecting them dive undercover. Jamie walked into the hall and looked at him uncharacteristically doggedly when she saw the tree.

Clint gave her a weak smile as he queasily followed her and turned toward the office when Jamie went to the front door. When she opened it, she squealed with pleasure. Clint saw outside in the sprinkling rain an old beat-up car pull up and came to a halt right by the front door. Clint panicked, as Banks, Chiowood and Ravin ran out of the office into the television room silently out past him as Jamie leaned on the open doorframe. Each moved stealthily behind her with frightened looks, going for the back door.

O'Neil and Hobb, who were also going to make a break for it was just outside of the television room when Jamie ran to the far side of the car and could see them. They both spun around looking for a place to hide as the car door opened. Jamie wrapped the man up in a huge hug when the driver stood up. O'Neil and Hobb would have been seen any moment as they ran uneasily up the stairs pushing each other.

"What was that?" the boy who was hugging Jamie asked as his head peered around hers.

"Oh, that is just my brother," she muttered holding him close, not bothering to look.

Clint could see that the boy was tall, as tall as Cody as his black hair emerged from around Jamie when she finally loosened her grip on him. He had nicely shaped features and all at once Clint thought he had a kind face. Clint saw Cody and Kayla come down from upstairs wondering what was going on. They must have been informed by O'Neil because they were both looking around frantically when they came down and saw Clint. Their eyes searched Clint for answers, wanting an explanation. Clint could only shrug his shoulders.

Jamie was coming into the house holding onto the man's arm who was stumbling forward. "Your parents are not here?" the man said, looking worried.

"No, not yet and I, well I haven't told them," she said uncomfortably.

"You didn't tell them I was coming?"

"Well, I haven't told them about some things," Jamie said, looking shy.

"What?"

"I neglected to tell them some minor details about you," she said.

"Like what?" he asked as she led him around the car holding onto his arm.

"Well, you. I didn't exactly tell them about parts of you. Well, all of you. OK, so I didn't tell them anything about you."

"What?" the boy said as he came into the house while Jamie shut the door behind him.

"Have you told anyone about us being engaged?" the boy said looking at her, extremely worried while his eyes glinted.

Jamie didn't say anything as she faced him sheepishly. "Well, I was waiting for a good time to let them know." Clint could see that she was trying to look slightly surprised as Cody and Kayla looked at the boy as if he was a mysterious ghost.

Clint was striving not to look too stupid as he noticed that his mouth was open. Jamie was looking down on the floor drawing an invisible line on it with her foot as she said, "I missed you."

Jamie's soon-to-be husband looked entirely out of place as he ran a hand through his hair. "Does anyone know that I was coming or about us?" he asked as Clint could tell that worry and uncertainty were coursing through his veins.

Jamie looked outraged as she saw Clint standing to the side and with a terrible grin, she turned, her eyes filled with malevolence. It made Clint's heart pound and go cold with dread. "Of course, I have told some of my family," she said with a fake laugh.

"Clint come here and meet my fiancé." The man turned away from Jamie and saw Clint and unfortunately the tree as well. He stepped back in surprise while Jamie held tightly to his hand.

Clint started to walk stupidly toward this man in his home, who was looking up and down at the tree. Jamie gave him a look that said he better move or when she got her chance, she would really let the boom fall on him. Utterly bewildered, Clint tried to force a smile onto his shocked face.

The boy continued to stare at the tree inside the house as he held out a hand to Clint.

"So, you're Clint. Jamie has told me a lot about you," he said, still preoccupied with the sight of something like a tree inside someone's home.

Jamie smiled only for a moment when she turned to her fiancé and that changed when she looked at Clint, once again threatening his life without speaking. She mouthed the words, "say something stupid."

"Oh yeah, Jamie has told me all about you, uh." Clint took his hand and shook it but was lost for words as Jamie tried to mouth the man's name silently. Clint read her lips and said keenly, "Bam?"

"Sam, I am Sam," Sam said now tearing his eyes away from the tree and looking at Clint as his smile genuinely grew.

Clint didn't need to look at Jamie's savage face to know he should keep going, "Oh yeah, yeah, Sam, nice to meet you at last."

Sam started shaking Clint's hand more vigorously as he looked up the stairs. Cody and Kayla had moved back to the landing with wide eyes and mouths open. Corbin appeared and looked on, watching everything from the top of the landing like a bird interested in a worm below him.

"You must be Cody and Kayla, is Tamara here?" Sam said looking thoroughly relieved to see more people.

"Yes, she is," Jamie said dully as Sam dropped Clint's hand. Clint could see O'Neil stick his head up from behind the couch as Tamara was coming out from the kitchen.

"Did someone call me?" Tamara asked.

This was the best part, Clint thought. It was Jamie's turn to be flabbergasted as she had stayed in her room like a groundhog and had not noticed the changes in Tamara.

Clint was euphoric as Jamie looked at Tamara as if she had never seen her before. Tamara smiled as she walked forward just a little, confused at Jamie's reaction on seeing her.

"Hello Sam, nice to meet you," Tamara said contagiously.

"Tamara," Sam said but very quietly, still unsure that this was her. "You're not really how Jamie described you."

"Well, Jamie's been a little behind on things in this house for the past couple of days," Tamara said smartly, shaking Sam's hand.

Jamie looked positively lost. Tamara seemed extremely pleased with herself, and Clint had to cover his laughter with a cough, unlike the three up the stairs, who did nothing to hide their laughter.

"Well you're taking this nice and smooth," Jamie said, regaining her composure and holding onto Sam's arm as if it were part of herself.

Clint kept coughing to cover up his laughter, while he overheard the definite hushed comments that came down from upstairs.

Jamie inclined her head upward, bearing one of her stares that would make animals cringe. The laughter and soft words stopped as if the people doing it had been eliminated silently. Just then Grant came up from downstairs. His face was buried in a book with his nose only an inch away as he read while he was walking. His eyes were moving over the words excitedly, not noticing anyone as he walked right by all of them.

"That must be Grant?" Sam said, thankful that there was something else to talk about.

"Yes," Jamie said refusing to drop her Jekyll and Hyde routine as she looked hotly at each one of her family and the next second gazed softly at Sam. Grant took no notice of them as he read on, moving toward the kitchen.

"I think that's everyone," Jamie said wheeling around away from Grant to face Sam as she looked at him flirtatiously. "Let's go down into my room so we can talk about tonight when my parents come home."

"What about this family that was supposed to come and stay with you? I wanted to meet them and find out where they are from. I was interested to find out if I have been to their country. Where are they from?" Sam said excitedly, looking around to see if he could find anyone that might be hiding.

"They are around here, somewhere, they keep to themselves mostly," Jamie said as her shoulders fell with frustration with Sam's interest in everything around the house except her.

Sam's eyes were still darting all around while Jamie was pulling on his arm when Cody asked, coming down to the lobby, "what do you do?"

"I am in the Navy," Sam said now looking at Jamie. "You didn't tell them?"

Jamie whipped around and this time she pulled so hard that Sam had no choice but to follow her as they both softly argued, Sam questioning what was going on as Jamie tried to quickly explain that her family was mentally challenged when it came to understanding anything new.

Everyone else's eyes were transfixed on Sam and Jamie as they made their way down to her room while Sam was trying to break free from her grip.

"What's next? Aliens? Earthquake? Government death ray? Giant mutant animals?" Clint shrieked.

"We already had the giant wolves," Grant said nonchalantly from behind his book.

O'Neil's head came around the corner to the hallway with his hair hanging low as he checked grimly if the coast was clear. As soon as Jamie's voice died out, he made his way as a burglar bent low toward the back door. As he passed Clint and Tamara he said, "I need tae inform Banks."

Clint pulled himself out of his panicked state, looking around to Cody for help on what to do next. Cody waved for all of them to go into the office. Without agreeing no one said anything until Corbin dashed from the landing upstairs and yelled out with all the dignity of a radio DJ announcing the newest top hit, "Whew, Jamie's getting married! Wahhhooo, all right!"

Everyone else downstairs shushed him fiercely at once. Corbin tottered on the spot, not understanding what was going on. With a considerable effort, he came down to join everyone else, saying,   "What's   the problem? So what if she is getting hitched? Why are all of you so unhappy?" Banks and O'Neil also came into the office right behind him.

O'Neil shut the door with a thud and faced everyone as they all sat down. O'Neil darted toward the nearest window and started to take up a lookout position. They all waited for Banks to talk as the rain pitter-pattered on the glass outside.

"This does complicate things, but I do not think that this new man makes much of a difference with what we need to do tonight. We will just have to avoid him until your parents return, open the safe and we return home." Banks looked like a general who had to call a retreat for a moment and Clint knew that what he was going to say next caused him great pain.

"If we can't, we will have failed in our mission."

"What?" Kayla and Cody said at the same time.

Banks raised his hand intently wanting quiet. "Please, let me finish," he said, slowly putting his hand down. Clint and Corbin exchanged worried looks, and both felt like the bottom of their stomachs had fallen away.

"We cannot dwell on that as we have more pressing matters," Banks said shaking his head. "Here is what we are going to do. Corbin must get to the school, but we have used the car enough that they may be anticipating that. So, we will have to get you there another way and get you back as well. Once that is done our plan is to open the safe and save our world if we can. It is our hope that the Fury will see and follow us, leaving everyone here alone. We will fight them all the way back to our portal and with luck, we will get home, and they will give up their efforts on trying to find anything here. Also, we can assume that they came to this world the same way that we did. So, they will also have to get to that farm for their return."

"Why did you want to go to the farm in the first place?" Cody asked before he could stop himself.

O'Neil spoke up not taking his eyes away from the window, "We could have made oot some information from any signs or tracks they left. When we got there, we couldnae mak' out anythin'. Either the tracks were destroyed in the rain or 'at Spell Binder took out aw their tracks by freezing' the ground."

"Either way, we have to do all this without bringing more attention to ourselves and make sure that we are seen by the Fury when we leave," Banks said nobly.

Clint looked down at his feet as he listened to his plan. He felt that there were so many things that could go wrong with it but he didn't want to point out problems. Clint barely had time to think about this when Banks started to talk once more, sounding like he wanted to get a move on, "all right, how can we get you to school without the car?"

They looked around searching each other's sober faces intently looking for an answer. Nothing came to any of them. Until Banks started to talk again, towering over all of them since he was the only one who was standing.

"Without using the aid of the druids, we will have to have you walk." He was looking at Corbin, "If you walk with someone else other than Clint that would be willing to go with you, we will have you followed to protect you and they will also keep an eye out for where the Fury is hiding." Banks took a deep breath as he started to tell them the bad news.

"It will be at great risk though. We would have to bank on that they will not attack because you are not with Clint, and you will not have anything with you that could be the Requiem. With any luck, you will get to school without a problem and back."

Everyone looked around at Corbin whose face had gone pasty white. Banks put it to him straight, "It's up to you Corbin, and at least one other."

For the longest time, Corbin couldn't say anything. The fear of going back outside only gave him the ability to give out a derisive sound. Clint remembered how Corbin had acted when the imp was after them and that he hadn't had any other encounters with death since unless he counted Amber.

"I will go with him," Tamara said bravely.

Corbin looked embarrassed and suddenly found his voice as he said very fast, "Yeah, I will go, yeah, why not, bring it on!"

Before anyone could interject Banks said over the sound of the rain spattering on the window, "It is settled, we will have O'Neil and two others follow you. Will you have the ability to use that phone thing that can contact others from afar?"

"I will call you when I get there," Corbin said quickly, now sounding like someone had taken a two-foot board and tied it to his spine, making him braver.

"Go to school as normally as you can, don't look around to find trouble, trust your escort to take care of you. When you get there, call, finish what you must and both of you meet up with O'Neil and the others at a predetermined spot and come right back here," Banks ordered quickly, "then when you are back, we will make ready to leave. The Light Bringers are almost ready just in case."

Corbin was squirming uncomfortably with the horrible fact that he would leave the house's safety while Banks and O'Neil talked about taking care of the house and making it ready to leave. The board that had seemed to be tied to Corbin's back to make him brave must have broken as Tamara looked at him. She appeared to be checking if he was a man or a mouse.

"Get your priorities straight, all right!" she groaned. "I am going to go get ready and do my homework till we go."

"Can you believe this?" Corbin asked with a defiant look of bewilderment on his face.

"What?" Cody said. "The fact that you might die on your way to detention or that fact that Tamara is doing her homework without being flogged?"

Clint was preoccupied with fear for his friend and proud of the changes his sister had made in her life. They all left the room, and the terrible time came in a matter of seconds for Corbin to go. He spent the time sitting on the stairs with Clint trying to do their homework. Clint said hesitantly, "you will need to get going if you are going to make it."

"Really?" Corbin said, trembling all overlooking unblinkingly at the door. Just then Tamara came down and hit Corbin on the head causing him to jump. O'Neil, Hobb, and Transun were standing ready in the kitchen talking lowly.

Clint watched Corbin get to his wobbly knees and decided to be brave for him and try not to think of what could happen out there. "Would you mind if I don't kiss you goodbye?" Clint said with a smile to Corbin as Tamara opened the front door.

Corbin didn't say anything back but just gave a weak laugh to Clint and walked out the door dragging his feet, stumbling on the door frame as O'Neil and the rest followed him out. Clint grabbed the closing door to watch them leave but as soon as his hand touched the door Banks' voice sounded from the far side of the kitchen, "They need to leave like there is nothing unusual."

Clint felt anger rise once more in him. How could Banks just let them go and say it's going to be just another day? It wasn't, it might be his best friend's last, he thought, noticing that he was gripping the doorknob so tight it could have broken off. Regrettably, he shut the door and stood there looking at it, wishing he could see through it.

The time went by mysteriously slowly as every clock in the house Clint checked went so slow that they must have all agreed to tease Clint by going backward. Jamie and Sam stayed downstairs, and Clint went down to check on them. Feeling restless he listened at the door and heard that Jamie was trying to explain why she didn't talk to her family about him. Everyone else stayed in their rooms working on their homework while Clint spent most of his time in the kitchen checking on the clocks and pulling out a variety of snacks. He nibbled on each one just a little, but none seemed to satisfy him or help. Nothing seemed to help.

Then the time came that they should be back. The first ten minutes after that time, then twenty, then thirty, then forty minutes past the time Corbin's detention should have been over. Clint started pacing until Banks came in with Nuts on his shoulder from the backyard in a hurry.

"Corbin is coming, and Tamara doesn't seem to be with him," Banks said hastily. Clint's heart turned over as he ran to the door looking through the window. Corbin was walking fast, clearly disturbed but was trying to move naturally. There was another sound of the back door opening and closing as Corbin was making his way up the driveway.

O'Neil was running in from the back. He was wet from the storm while Corbin was coming from the front not too wet but still moaning with emotion and out of breath.

Corbin almost fell in as Clint opened the door.

"Where is Tamara?" Clint shouted.

O'Neil went behind Clint quickly and shut the door for him. They all were waiting as the times compiled dark emotions and thoughts in their minds. O'Neil and Corbin were unable to speak as they were still breathing hard from their journey.

"She never came back to where we were waiting for her. We stayed there as long as we could and then I went back into the school to see if I could find her. She wasn't anywhere. Transun stayed behind at school in case she comes back but I couldn't find her. I just couldn't find her." Corbin was looking around in panic, his hands shaking.

O'Neil's voice turned up a notch as he said quickly to Banks, "she followed Corbin in and didn't come out. We couldn't follow 'er than, sir."

Banks took charge quickly clasping his hands together. "Corbin, go get everyone together except your grandmother, sister, and her boyfriend. Instruct Kayla to tell them that she will take care of them and explain that everyone else is going to the dance. I want Kayla to come as it will be safer to stay with us." He turned to O'Neil, "get everyone ready and Tremayne and Ohlwiler will stay on guard. I want those Light Bringers up, while the rest of us go and search for her. Also, place demolition charges on them if we are successful. No trace left, understood?"

O'Neil went straight down the hall after giving Banks a quick salute with Nuts scrambling to catch up to him. Banks then turned to Clint, "we need to blend into wherever we are going to. I need to have you get us ready, whatever it takes. When does this dance start?"

Clint looked at his watch, "It starts in about an hour. There will be tons of kids there in costume."

"What do we need to do?" Banks asked as Corbin tore off, looking blankly, following orders into the television room. Finding that he had run the wrong way, he took off up the stairs until he reached the fifth step. He slowed down considerably, leaning heavily on the handrail.

"Well we will be all right, the kids I mean but we can see what costumes will work for all of you," Clint said thinking hard. It wasn't easy to think of stuff with Banks standing over him like a parent wanting to know what they needed for a Europe trip. "What am I saying? You guys have the best costumes just the way you are."

Corbin turned up looking exhausted, with everyone behind him. He was telling everyone how Tamara was missing because she never came back when it was time.

"Clint, go and get those costumes you will need. I will explain the plan to everyone else," Banks said amused.

Clint leaped aside and ran determinedly into the garage. Frowning, he looked for a box that was marked 'Halloween'. He had to scan the pile of boxes on the first side where everything was stacked and stored, from old pictures to snow clothes. After looking for a moment he realized it was on the top.

Clint grabbed a ladder and found them. Taking one, he returned into the lobby and sat it down next to the tree. Cody assisted him as they brought the rest while Banks finished talking to everyone about their plan to take the car and do whatever they could to retrieve Tamara.

"What if they have her?" Kayla asked fearfully with her lip trembling.

"Don't worry, she will be all right," Cody said as they finished pulling the box to the center of the room and Cody gripped Kayla's arm reassuringly.

They opened the boxes as if it were Christmas. Clint hurried as he dug in, not wanting to let everyone else know what he was feeling. He could see in his mind the orc and imps dancing around Tamara tied up with the Spell Binder bearing down on her. It loomed over her, jet black except for those horrible white hands.

Clint scanned inside the box he opened but it was difficult to concentrate past his worry for his sister. He was saved from another idea when Banks's voice called his mind back.

"Clint," he waited for Clint's face to turn to his, "we are going in fifteen. Also, Tremayne will come with us and Ravin will stay. We will need both of their skills and we are having a problem on the roof."

"Uh, all right. What is a Light Bringer anyway?" Clint asked, slightly confused. Why would he tell Clint that? Before Banks could answer Kayla shot another question at him.

"What about your weapons? They won't let them in the school," Kayla said as it felt like a pillar was falling that was holding up their plan.

They were picking out costumes and throwing a great deal of them aside as they were each searching for something that would fit and also not be too embarrassing.

"We will have tae deal with that when we get there," O'Neil said sounding slightly anxious. They each grabbed costumes and changed quickly and came down to see Banks, O'Neil, Tremayne, Nix, Hobb, and Chiowood standing out getting their bows, arrows, armor, swords, and axes ready. The most unusual was the druids who have seemed to have made armor for themselves out of wood. Clint was looking at them in surprise, wondering how they did it when everyone else came out revealing what they were dressed as.

Kayla had found her Minnie Mouse outfit that Clint remembered she'd worn last year. Grant must have dug horribly in the bottom of a box for the cowardly lion outfit. It had a brown hairy mane that was around his head that was so heavy he had a difficult time holding his head up. Corbin had picked an old English nobleman's outfit not forgetting the wig, beauty spot, ankle tights, and white face powder. As Clint watched him in dismay, Corbin said taken aback, "It was the only thing that fit me."

"Indeed," Corbin continued, giving a stooped bow that almost tore his pants. He straightened up causing the buttons on the shirt to bulge threatening to snap off and shatter a window. Clint was lucky to find his Jack Sparrow costume that he'd also had last year.

Cody who avoided anything in the box because nothing in there would fit had run upstairs to Mom and Dad's room. He came down in an authentic Star Wars Storm Trooper costume.

"Where did you get that?" Kayla asked in amazement.

'It's Dads, he got it a long time ago and was saving it as a collector's item," Cody said holding the white helmet under one arm.

Forty-Four

YOU CAN'T FIGHT THE PARTY

They didn't have time to get the finer points of each costume on as they all rushed toward the car. Glumly, Cody got behind the wheel as everyone else piled in one on top of the other. Climbing in, Clint was squashed under the glove compartment while Banks' legs were pushing him into the heater. It was very difficult for everyone, especially with longbows and swords which were very sharp. Astonishingly they made it in with some measure of not breathing.

With the shocks bottomed out, they went down the driveway, the bumper scraping the road as they were off to the school. Cody drove oddly fast as Clint could see the strain in his eyes, his tension rising as they saw families walking around trick or treating. The last light of the sun died away behind the clouds that were only giving up a drop of two of rain, the added thunder, and lightning in the night sky, illuminating the evening eerily.

They got to the school without incident unless you count the moment Cody almost ran over two kids dressed as pumpkins, which definitely shook his fragile spirits. The school's parking lot was packed, and they drove around trying to find a parking place when Cody's worst fear started to come true. A police officer who was guiding cars was walking over to them.

"Everyone hide, get down, get down!" Cody yelled in alarm.

"Where exactly am I supposed to go?" Clint said blankly with his nose in the heating vent. Cody looked down at him grimly as the officer pressed forward, motioning for Cody to roll down his window.

"What am I going to say, what am I going to say?" Cody said instinctively frightened out of his wits.

"Tell him we are the band," Kayla said coolly, not wanting to draw attention to herself as her voice came from under Cody's seat.

Cody forced his face into a vague expression as he rolled down the window when the police officer descended on him and shined a flashlight in his face.

"I know what you are going to say, officer," Cody said with a groan.

"Oh, you do, do you son?" the officer said, scanning in the car suspiciously.

"This is the entertainment for tonight," Cody said hastily.

"Right," the officer huffed. "Is there any good reason why you only took one vehicle?"

"No apparent reason, sir," Cody said smoothly. "Can we go in now?"

"Not until I get something first," the officer said, leaning on the hood.

Cody looked like he was going to pass out as droplets of sweat started to roll down his forehead.

"Do you want to sing with the band as one of the Village People?" Cody wheezed. Clint shut his eyes in frustration. Cody didn't sound confident anymore. It could be because of his nerves or the fact that the steering wheel was jammed into his sternum because his seat had been forced all the way forward.

"That is not what I want from you," the police officer said thickly as he stood up to his full height and pulled something on his belt. There was the pull of a bow string somewhere in the back seat as Banks held up a hand to stop someone from shooting the officer. Cody started to shake with the thought that his life was going to end.

"Your name is Cody, right?" the officer asked as Clint could hear him scratch his pen on paper, writing something.

"Yes sir," Cody said glumly as he fought off the unbelievable urge to just die on the spot.

"Could I get your autograph?" the officer asked eagerly as he bent over, holding out a small notepad and pen for Cody.

"Uh, sure, sure thing officer," Cody said as Clint could see some of the color come back into Cody's face as he raised a shaking hand to sign the paper.

"That last game was fantastic! The last two touchdowns, unbelievable how you shot that ball in there. If I hadn't been there to see it, I wouldn't have believed it. Your team is going all the way this year. I love the grit iron," the officer said longingly.

Cody didn't interrupt the officer as he nodded and said, "Yeah, thank you," as he wrote very quickly on the pad of paper and handed it back to the officer.

The officer clearly looked happy as he gave them all a satisfactory smile, "you lot be careful tonight, a lot of strange things are going on."

"Sur, su, sur, si, shure thing officer," Cody said moronically. The officer waved as he pointed to the back of the school, "you can park over there with the other band. They have their own security and when you go home take more than one vehicle."

"Thank, thank, thank you off, officer," Cody stammered smiling as he drove off a little too quickly. Everyone took a long breath of relief which wasn't easy as they were all so crammed in together.

Just as the car slowed to a stop, the doors burst open. Bodies fell out on the pavement moaning in pain as they were so crammed, bent, and twisted. It was a tense moment as they all got ready for what they were about to do. Banks raised his hand and drew an invisible circle in the area. All of his group gathered around him as Clint could hear music playing from inside the school dance.

"Chiowood, you and Corbin go and get Transun and come back here," Banks said while still fastening his equipment around him. "If Tamara is there, send someone in to let us know. Everyone else, we will sweep inside for her."

The song from inside came to an end followed by an outbreak of applause, and shouts, from the students. Banks paused for a moment to listen before he wiped the sweat from his head before he continued, "once in, Nix you cover our exit. If there are any problems this is our fallback position."

Clint felt horribly alone standing in the dark as he scratched his scalp under his wig. It was making his head itch. Straitening it again to move the black dreadlocked hair and beads away from his eyes, Banks took an extra moment to match his gaze. The night seemed darker when Banks waved them toward the backdoors of the school.

"Cody, you take point! Grant and Corbin stay and watch over the car," Banks ordered in a low whisper. "Tremayne, you take care of the rear."

They were almost to the door as Banks waved his hand to the left and right of the door. O'Neil and Nix slammed into the wall facing the door on both sides. Cody went to open the door, but Banks stopped his hand for a moment as he waved everyone else to form a line behind him.

Someone with a high-pitched voice made an announcement for the band as Banks gripped a sword hilt without a blade in one hand, a dark short club in the other. Banks checked behind him and nodded to Cody to open the door to the cultural hall.

"That's right," sounded the magnified voice over the loud speakers as they moved in like a long centipede, "we are not done with them yet, they have another one." The voice said that Clint somehow knew. Clint walked in as O'Neil cut in front of him and held his shoulder. The heat of the room was like a slap in the face as soon as he stepped in.

"Hey, you can't come in," Wham! Clint just saw over O'Neil's shoulder that Banks had knocked out two security guards. The line had stopped as Banks moved the uncontested bodies aside. They had come behind what looked like a stage set up in the school's large auditorium and indoor sports courts. It was a massive room that was usually separated by large curtains that had been taken down for this evening's party. Cody helped Banks with the two guards as a third security guard came down the side stairs of the stage. Clint only felt a wisp of a breeze caused by O'Neil's arm throwing something by his head. Whatever he threw hit the large new guard in the head, also knocking him out. O'Neil maneuvered past Clint as he moved to grab the new guard who had just fallen down the rest of the stage stairs.

"Thank you, everyone. The nexth thong is, Move Your Body tho please do tho," the person said from the stage. "Just don't move too closthly."

"That's Zack's voice," Clint moaned as he helped stuff the guard under the stage.

Banks shushed him hastily as he parted the curtain that he was hiding behind to see the sea of students. Clint licked his dry lips as O'Neil started to dance next to him as the song began. Nix shut the door behind them as the lights above them and around the stage swiveled this way and that. Fog machines sprayed, coating the floor in a mist.

O'Neil pulled Clint to the back wall as he saw four other stagehands working behind the scenes. They were so busy that Banks and his compatriots remained unnoticed. Banks waved to Cody to join him and as he passed Clint, he gave him a wide excited smile. "That's Sia! That's really Sia singing. How did he get on stage with her?" he whispered, squawking like an excited young girl.

"How did they…" Clint started to say to himself as he leaned over to see the lead singer dance on stage as she moved to the enthusiasm of the crowd before her.

Clint was so focused on her and her singing that he hadn't noticed Banks had waved again to his left and right. O'Neil bent low, and left his side, running low to the right end of the stage still under it where he could be concealed from the students' view. Tremayne also followed him into the dark but flipped, spun, and rolled in impressive gymnastic moves in silence behind the band to the stage. The door next to Clint that they had come through opened as Clint panicked. He looked up and saw Cody tap Banks on the shoulder. Banks turned as quick as a snake and held ready a dagger, raising it high, ready to throw.

Chiowood's head poked through with Transun behind him. He shook his head negatively and came in gingerly with all his weight on his toes, moving fast, holding one arm out to balance himself.

Banks sheathed his daggers and looked down disappointed as he felt the eyes of Cody and Clint on him. Banks waved for Clint to join him and said, "Your sister didn't come back." Looking worried he looked at the floor before he turned his gaze back beyond the curtain to the music and stomping of dancing feet that echoed in the large room.

Banks waved Transun over and for Chiowood to go where Tramayne went, and then he looked very seriously at Cody and Clint.

"We will need to go out and see if she is in the crowd. You both will know her well enough to find her even if she is in disguise," Banks commanded. "I will go first around to the main entry door to the far end of the room. Then both of you follow on either side. If you see her, signal me and we will converge on her position for extraction. If you do not, make two rounds and return to this position. I will search outside of this room. I am trusting you two to go and get it done," Banks said as he gripped his sword hilt tighter. This time his longsword carried the appearance of a normal sword, and no flames or light surrounded it.

"Transun, join O'Neil," Banks said, turning to Transun. "Make a distraction for us. Both Clint and Cody should be in the main part of the dance when this happens, that's when you look for her, do not ask or call out for her. Get in and look for her and get out." Banks said all of this very quickly before adding, "Questions?"

"Uh," was all that Clint and Cody were able to get out of their mouths before Banks motioned for Transun to move. Clint watched Transun move cat-like across the floor and felt Banks go before he knew it. Clint and Cody saw Banks go around the corner of the stage into the farthest edge of the dance with the lights strobing, music gathering around him before he was out of sight.

Clint watched all the heads that were bobbing up and down as almost everyone from his school was dancing in a fury of different costumes. He could see some students sitting along one wall next to the refreshment tables on the other side of the room. It was odd to see so many of his peers doing something normal as he felt that he was a soldier in a war apart from them. Cody hit Clint's back causing him to jump. In watching the dance, he had forgotten Cody was next to him.

Cody gave an understanding smile to Clint that told him he understood his wishes that night to dance with his friends. Cody's eyes fell as the song ended with thunderous applause.

"Do you want another song!?!" Sia shouted, her voice blaring in the speakers.

More shouts and applause sounded from the crowd. "All right, all right, let's do another one. But I will need some help. How about Unstoppable?" she asked, turning to the band holding her arms up. The crowd yelled their approval.

"How did they get Sia here anyway?" Cody asked, shaking his head. Clint only managed a weak smile before Cody let Clint go and started to search on his side of the crowd. Clint saw Cody go and unlike the rest walked slow and upright as if he were one of the teachers looking over the crowd.

Clint froze for a moment as the music started. It felt difficult to breathe for a moment as his insides told him that he was about to go through an invisible barrier where both worlds would collide again. Not thinking, he straightened up and parted the curtain, and took two steps. Closing his eyes, he took a moment before he started to walk in front of the stage toward the far side of the room. He searched the crowd for Tamara, Sia singing behind him. As he investigated each face, he went to another for the one that was her. He just got to the corner of the room next to the stage when the song ended.

"Let's keep going you moving with a little Elastic Heart huh?" Sia called, starting into the next song, not waiting for the approval of the crowd which almost deafened Clint as every kid cried as loud as they could.

Clint saw Cody walking a little ahead of him by some students who had come without a date. No one was still as the music kept everyone moving. Clint was almost halfway through his search when he saw Banks at the far end of the room. He walked with such an air of authority that no one even gave him a second glance as he concealed his sword behind him.

Clint was almost to the end of the main body of dancers when a horrible feeling of terror came to him. What if he couldn't find her? He searched not out of duty but out of alarm. That one wasn't her, nor was that girl, nor that one. He was so frantic now that he even forgot that Tamara had changed and no longer dressed in black or wore such dark makeup. Cody was walking over to him quickly to his corner of the room and Clint noticed that he had put on his helmet. Cody waved his hands to Clint telling him to calm down as he started to slowly walk toward him.

"All right, Holbrook," Sia said at the end of the song. "We would like to do a special ladies choice dance, 'Never Give Up Girls'." The band started playing once more with applause sounding from the crowd while everyone started to dance once more.

"Did you see her?" Clint asked, unable to stop himself.

Cody shook his head negatively. "Why did you put that on?" Clint asked, returning his attention to the dancing crowd and the students lining the walls resting. "Some teacher is going to stop you, and have you take it off."

"Kids started to recognize me," Cody said but his voice had changed to sound like a Storm Trooper. "You go down my side and I will go down yours and meet where we started," Cody finished and started to search. Clint checked the last place he saw Banks and, not finding him, he watched

Cody dance while he walked, blending in a little. Clint watched him for a moment wondering how he could be so good on the football field but when it came to moving on the dance floor, he had no rhythm whatsoever.

Clint steadied his nerves by filling his lungs with air and wiping the sweat from his face before he started to search every girl that he passed. He wished that everyone wasn't in costumes, and they weren't moving so fast. He had a glimpse of what he thought was her but turned out to be another girl with the same color of hair.

"Every kid from the school must be here," Clint said to himself in frustration as he walked behind the students who were enjoying some food and drinks. Others were testing the vigilance of the teachers who were acting as chaperones by stealing a kiss.

A girl walking up to him with a smile on her face caused Clint alarm. He slid in between a tight group of dancers and tried to hide for a moment. As he straightened up, he saw the girl was the same one who'd tried to put a curse on him in the lunchroom. He put as many people between them as possible and circled her to resume his search when he saw her. There, about three couples from the center was Melanie, dancing in a beautiful Cinderella gown. She had taken down her hair and was wearing a small crown on top of it. Clint's stomach lurched as he forgot what he was doing, mesmerized. He didn't notice that the song changed to Cheap Thrills. She was the best-looking thing he had ever seen as time slowed down. He found his insides when he saw who she was dancing with. It was one of Cody's friends, the very same one who had let out that he was going to go to the dance with Amber, ruining his chances to go with Melanie. Clint let out a huff in protest as he was wearing his football uniform as a costume.

Red hot anger fueled him as he took a step toward them, but he remembered what he was there for when he saw out of the corner of his eye Banks leaving the room. He gave Melanie one last long look with a sigh and started to walk once more toward the side of the dance floor where could get away from everyone as quickly as possible. He didn't notice that he moved slower. He made it to the far corner of the room where another teacher was watching, swaying stupidly to the music. He didn't see Tamara as the band finished their song.

"I want to thank all of Holbrook and all of you for tonight and let you be the first to hear my next song!" Sia called out. Clint could barely hear her as the sound seemed to be coming from a different country.

It was difficult to swallow in the dry air as Clint watched the top of Melanie's head in the crowd. He saw Cody wave at him and work his way toward him once again, but Clint felt outside of himself. He didn't know why but he almost felt tears come, and pressure in his throat.

"Any luck?" Cody said when he stumbled next to Clint, still trying to dance as his voice was still being modified by his helmet.

"No," Clint said assuming that Cody hadn't had any luck either.

"What do we do now?" Clint asked stupidly. Melanie was out of his sight, but Clint watched with loathing at the bulbous head of her senseless date.

"We wait for the distraction from O'Neil, remember?" Cody said, watching Sia.

"Oh, right," Clint said feeling dumb. He was having a hard time keeping his mind where it was supposed to be.

"It's time Holbrook for you to hear," Sia said over the speakers. "' You're My Armor'." More applause and yells from the crowd in approval.

Clint and Cody both looked at each other. "An exclusive release of Sia's new song and O'Neil is going to carry out a distraction," Cody said. Even though his voice had been changed by his helmet Clint heard the whimper of distress in his tone. "This is typical for this week."

Sia started her song as Clint stated, "I can only guess. Maybe set off the sprinkler system? Other than that, what would he do to get everyone's attention?" He shrugged, unable to help looking over to see Melanie as the new song seemed to break the rock in his neck. All other thoughts left his mind as his mind cast all others out of the room. He was dancing alone with Melanie and as the song drew them closer, she closed the gap between them.

Just then the music slowed to a stop prematurely. Clint and Cody looked up at the stage to see what was going on as everyone stopped dancing. Sia looked awkward as she was talking away from the microphone, looking at someone just off stage. She waved her hands angrily as she walked off stage and out of sight. The spotlights over the band went off for a second as there were sounds of a struggle and some scuffling noises that were now coming through the microphone.

"What is going on?" Clint asked so only Cody could hear him over the grunts and moans of what sounded like a woman fighting.

His question was answered all too soon as the fog machines went off, covering the band and students with a low, thick fresh cloud of smoke. The sound of someone clearing their throat in the microphone and the stomping of heavy feet on the stage got the attention of every student, while the rest of the band's whispering sounded in the background, and someone grunted instructions. In the fog something was moving across to the front of the stage as there was a breathless pause only for a moment from the crowd of kids, followed by single spotlights which illuminated each member of the band until every one of them could be seen except the lead singer. With a loud crack, all the multi-colored lights came on over the stage showing the lead singers standing at the very center of the stage in a heroic pose.

"NO!" Clint and Cody said together in disbelief.

It was O'Neil and he had changed out of his weathered clothes and was now what looked like a heavy metal rock star with tight black leather leggings.

Clint's eyes went so wide they hurt as the drummer started playing. O'Neil made odd noises into the microphone that he held over his head. Then the guitar player joined them while Cody and Clint shook their heads in disbelief while the rest of the kids and teachers looked dumbfounded. Clint knew what was coming as his mouth fell to the floor when the band started to play, setting off O'Neil singing in a Scottish accent, 'The Greatest' by Sia.

"AAAaaahhhh!" Clint and Cody yelled together.

O'Neil's voice, magnified, stopped everyone from dancing, looking in disbelief at what was on the stage. "Uh-oh, running peched, bit I oh, ah, ah git stamina. Uh-oh, running noo, ah claise mah eyes. Well, och, ah git stamina and uh-oh, ah see anither ben tae climb but ah, ah, ah git stamina! Uh-oh, a'm needin' anither lover, be mine cause ah, ah, ah git stamina don't gie up, a wullnae gie up!

"He is mad!" Cody said stupidly.

Clint couldn't believe what he was seeing and hearing. Suddenly he remembered that he was supposed to be looking for his sister. Hitting Cody hard in the shoulder they searched the floor again. O'Neil was dancing now and singing all over the stage with everybody watching, not moving a muscle, eyes fixed on the dwarf. Cody and Clint were the ones moving as they merged into the large mass of kids who were statues now. Banks even peeked his head back into the room from the hallway to see what the horrible noise was.

Clint searched every face as fast as he could when O'Neil went off the stage. He seemed to have stopped for a moment but kept speaking into his microphone as a new voice came through it. It was the voice of Tremayne in his proper English tone,

"Are yoo runin' through waves of loove?" O'Neil asked over the microphone.

"What are yeh doing? We are supposed to distract 'em not try to kill 'em. What are yeh wearing yeh nesh?" Tremayne asked but only sounded faintly through the speakers.

O'Neil replied with a lot of breath in his voice, "I'm free tae be the greatest here tonight, the greatest."

"What?" Tremayne asked exasperated.

"Oh-oh, ah, git stamina."

"Give me that!" Tremayne shouted as the sounds of another small struggle offstage were taking place as the band looked on laughing but still playing on with even greater vigor.

Clint and Cody were in the center of the dance floor now where most of the kids were. Every face had a different expression, showing every feeling in the book as they all watched the stage.

"Stoop it! Ay git stamina," O'Neil shouted as he fell backward with a yell, falling back into view of the stage's spotlights. He was singing harder than before, moving every part of his body, pointing at the kids with vacant expressions on their faces who were closest to him. Clint and Cody were searching faster now as desperation was overcoming them. That wasn't her, that one wasn't her, maybe the next one. The next girl they checked, she had to be that one. No, nothing yet as they checked as many as they could see moving through the sea of young faces.

The band played louder as the climax of the ending. "Th' greatest, th' greatest alive…don't gie up, dinnae gie up, dinnae gie up; ah git STAMINAAAAAA!" O'Neil hit his last note as he did the splits, sliding on the stage, coming to a stop in the center, breathing heavily. If there was someone outside listing to the dance, they would have thought that everyone must have died in the room because of the absolute silence. No eye blinked and nobody said anything for what seemed like an eternity. O'Neil held his pose as the band looked on, letting their instruments hang low for a moment.

Suddenly one kid in the center of the dance jumped and screamed his approval and everyone else threw their hands into the air shouting harder than Clint thought was humanly possible. It was like a bomb going off, while O'Neil basked in his new glory. Clint and Cody were frantic to find Tamara now that they were running out of time and also girls to check.

Boom! A new heavy thumping sound came from the front of the room where the main door of the gymnasium was. Everyone turned, hearing another loud bang and saw the doors shake. Suddenly a man's body crashed through. He flew into the room, hitting a group of kids standing in the back, softening his impact. Even as the man yelled in pain Clint knew who it was. It was Banks.

The crowd wailed with screams of fear from the girls and loud gasps from the boys as everyone moved back in distress. There were loud thuds and bangs as the ground shook from the hallway beyond the door. Something appeared in the broken doorway where Banks had just been thrown through like a small rag doll. It was large, so large that Clint, who was only able to see over the tops of kids' heads, could just make out the bottom of a gigantic stomach heaving with breath on the other side.

Cody was moving fast, pushing people aside to get to where Banks was lying unconscious. Everyone was looking now at the doorway, giving off small whimpers of fear, some backing away, tripping over others.

Forty-Five

ENCORE!

Whatever it was in the hallway took a great breath of air and twisted its frame. Crash! It had hit the door frame causing what was left of it to shatter and crumble into large pieces. The closest kids ran, pushing everyone back while Cody was calling out Banks's name, trying to move against the wave of people moving away from the giant. The dust of the broken wall rose in the air as the giant moved into the room. Large legs the size of tree trunks came out of the dust and then huge round hands the size of one of the backboard basketball hoops that lined the walls of the room. It snarled and roared, lifting a gigantic club into the air.

"It's an ogre! Git out ay here kids!" O'Neil shouted over the microphone and threw it to the side causing squawks of feedback from the speakers.

Everyone ran toward the back door where Clint and his group had secretly entered the dance. Clint was being pushed back as the Ogre roared louder and charged the crowd of kids, holding its club high in the air. It was at least Eighteen feet tall, with deep green skin.

"STOP!" someone shouted over the mundane babble and screams for help.

It sounded so odd and out of place that whoever it was that had said it made the ogre stop and freeze where it was. All the kids also stopped screaming as a single person went to face the ogre alone. Clint pushed people out of the way to see who it was. Over a tall girl's shoulder, he could see that it was a tall, skinny kid dressed like a giant squirrel walking up to face the ogre.

"Zack, no!" Clint shouted.

"Ath appointed comity leader of thith danceth," Zack shouted at the ogre who was looking down on him in mild interest, "it is my duty to asthk you to leave this school premisthesth at onceth." Zack said, sounding strong.

Wham! The ogre hit Zack with his club causing his body to soar across the room and hit the wall with a bone-crushing thud and slide to the ground, dead.

Screams filled the room as the crowd sprinted, pushed, and pulled each other toward the back door. The ogre roared and charged toward the kids as Clint was calling out for everyone to run. Teachers and students alike were trampling each other to get out of the path of the ogre as two other large creatures came into the room through the smashed doorway made by the ogre. Clint recognized one of them at once. It was the orc that had crashed into their house and destroyed Tamara's room and almost half the city as it made its escape. The other looked just like his partner but was female.

Clint was still fighting to get to Banks when Cody finally pushed his way by the last few kids running into him from the opposite direction. He'd just got to the spot where Banks's body lay on the ground when the ogre turned toward him. O'Neil was running on all the refreshment tables, which was the only place he could run unimpaired by terrified kids blocking his way. He rushed, knocking over both food and drinks with his long ax, its blades of blue fire ignited in one hand and a club with metal edging in the other. The ogre started to charge, its powerful feet pushing its large body with the force of a freight train. Suddenly Clint could see over the head of a boy and girl who ran into him that Banks was on his feet running at the ogre, matching its roar with his own. The ogre swung its club again down at Banks with a great whoosh.

It missed as Banks dove toward the ogre, hitting it in the stomach. He thrust a dagger into its chest. Cody had taken off his helmet and was pushing kids out of the room and helping others that had fallen get to their feet. An arrow of light from Tremayne came from the corner of the stage and hit the male orc in the shoulder causing it to howl when the female orc had locked its short sword with O'Neil's mace.

"'Ere!" O'Neil shouted as he threw Banks his ax, narrowly ducking out of the way of the short sword's thrust from the female orc that almost took off his head. As soon as the axe left his hand the blades dissipated, and it was just a stick with an elaborate handle. O'Neil countered the strike with his mace, swinging it at the female's knees. She dodged it but also gave way by flipping somersaults back. Clint was almost through the mob of kids as he saw Cody help a very attractive girl to her feet when another light arrow flew. The male orc dodged it by diving into the chairs that students had sat in moments earlier. The chairs cascaded across the open floor. Banks ducked and rolled to where O'Neil's axe had slid across the floor next to him as the ogre's massive foot landed, almost crushing him. O'Neil was trading blocks and swings with the female orc, both dancing with their weapons swinging trying to score a hit on the other. O'Neil was only half her size but matched her in strength and skill with each move.

Clint was through all the kids now and ran to Cody. Tremayne soared out of nowhere with two short medal swords in each hand. His weapons met the orc, getting up from the chairs before it could defend itself fully. It was an incredible sight as all six were locked in combat with weapons swinging at each other, each trying to get past the defense of the other.

Clint once again didn't know what to do as Cody was next to him only for a moment. Banks was ducking and moving cat-like around the giant ogre, swinging the axe at whatever part he could hit, while the ogre's club could not be stopped, only avoided. Cody yelled in rage and started to run right at the ogre.

"Cody, no!" Clint yelled as he held out a hand to grab him but was too late.

Slam! Cody had hit the ogre in the leg with all his might just like he'd done so many times on the football field. The ogre was so preoccupied with Banks that it didn't prepare itself for the hit and toppled over on the smooth floor, kicking Cody hard causing him to fly back off his feet two meters away. He hit the gym floor hard, moaning in pain.

Something snapped in Clint as he also charged forward just like Cody. He picked up the dagger that Banks had exchanged for his long axe from O'Neil. To his right the male orc was fighting with a long sword in one hand, blocking the many swings from Tremayne, and held up a school chair in the other, returning blow for blow. To Clint's left O'Neil was swinging his club with all the force of a baseball player at the female orc as both danced oddly on the floor. Clint ran as fast as he could while the ogre was still on its back, swinging its tree-like club at Banks who was just out of reach but closed and hit the ogre with his ax. Clint jumped on the great ogre and drove the dagger as far in as he could into its chest right where its heart should be. The tip of the blade only penetrated the skin of the ogre less than an inch and was also next to the wound made by Banks. Clint only had time to marvel at how tough the ogre's skin was for a second when the ogre's club-free hand hit him with the force of a car, causing him to fall five feet away.

Pain erupted in his leg where he hit the floor as the ogre was on its feet again fighting Banks. Tremayne, O'Neil, and Banks were fighting more furiously now, each in a different style in close combat with their terrible opponent. Tremayne dodged a blow to his head and as he dropped his head, swung his short sword up and cut the male orc's arm but also was hit over the head with the chair with the orc's good arm when someone from behind them called out, "we found her!"

It was Transun back by the stage door. She was waving at them frantically repeating the words, "we found her! We found her!"

Cody was getting to his feet, holding his back, limping toward Clint. Just then O'Neil had somehow beaten his opponent when Clint looked up. The female orc lay on the floor not moving as O'Neil was racing to the aid of Tremayne, who was losing ground.

Cody helped Clint to his feet as a screaming pain started in his left foot and worked its way up his leg. He felt sick as if his leg was broken when he tried to put weight on it.

"Come on!" Cody called to him, putting one of Clint's arms around his shoulder to take the weight as he also gritted his teeth in pain. Transun ran past them to help Banks who had just been knocked back by a hit from the ogre. Clint and Cody limped and dragged each other to the door with their backs to the battle. Their path was clear of students. They could only hear the swish of the club, swords, and ax. The roar of the male orc and ogre clashed with those of dwarf, man, and elf as they fought on, and the laughter and taunting of O'Neil.

When they got to the door Cody opened it, and as he turned his body to go through, Clint could see the battle. Tremayne and Transun were fighting the male orc now. Banks and O'Neil were doing all they could against the gigantic ogre.

"Let's go!" Cody yelled as he moved to go through the door, but Clint held him back.

"Wait," Clint pleaded to Cody.

O'Neil was hit and with a bellow that sounded like a chuckle from Santa Claus, he hit one of the refreshment tables causing what food and drink that remained to spring off like a catapult. The food and drink splattered the ogre and made the floor at its feet slippery.

"I am mad now!" O'Neil yelled, shaking his head to clear it from the stars that he was seeing. Banks dodged yet another swing from the ogre's club, sliding on the floor with his knees.

As Clint watched on, helpless, holding on to the door frame with his free hand, O'Neil grabbed one of the few chairs from that side of the room and slid it across the floor toward the ogre. He ran after it as fast as his short legs would allow. Right before the chair hit the ogre, O'Neil jumped on it and propelled himself into the air, aiming right for the ogre's head. He held his club high over his head and started to bring it down aiming for the creature's forehead. The ogre was ready for him as it swung its tree-sized club at O'Neil. It hit him square in the chest. The blow forced O'Neil's short body to wrap around the club and hit the ogre with its own club with greater force right on its melon-like head. Banks had just swung his ax, hitting the ogre in the back of the legs. With their combined strength and the recoil force of the blow to O'Neil's chest combined, the energy of the club hitting the ogre's head increased tenfold. The ogre was stunned and started to fall back while O'Neil was launched like a baseball toward the stage on the other side of the room, laughing all the way. He hit the drum set, smashing it to pieces.

Someone yelled in protest as soon as O'Neil disappeared behind the stage. Clint was surprised when he found out it was his voice. Cody started to let Clint off his shoulders, "hold the door," he shouted as he went for O'Neil. Clint almost collapsed without the help supporting him. Banks had now started to help Tremayne and Transun fight against the male orc. Now with three fighting him, the male orc retreated into the hallway as the ogre started to stir and began to get to its feet. Clint turned to the other side of the door frame to support himself as Banks and Transun helped a wobbling Tremayne flee. O'Neil surprisingly was carrying Cody on his back down the stage stairs. O'Neil was so short that Cody's feet were scraping along the floor. All of them were making their way back to the doorway that Clint braced open.

"They should have played 'Evacuate the dance floor'!" Clint gasped as Cody went through the door.

The Ogre let out a thunderous roar that shattered all the windows in the room. Banks was the last one through the door, grabbing Clint and supporting him to the car. Everyone else was already in the car. Clint practically collapsed into the driver-side door. He saw Tamara lying down in the backseat on everyone's laps with Nix holding her head in his hands. Once again there was little room with everyone in the car before and now to squeeze one more in was even more difficult. This time Chiowood was in the open trunk, readying weapons like a rear gunner.

"I can't drive with my back like this," Cody yelped. Another roar from inside the school shocked them all. Cody was hunched over and every breath he took seemed to cause him pain.

"Just get in! O'Neil, you drive?" Banks ordered as Cody and Clint both fell into the front passenger seat. Tremayne got into the trunk with Chiowood and Banks as well, as O'Neil got in behind the steering wheel. Everyone else sat in the backseat trying not to move Tamara. Cody was shouting at O'Neil how to drive. O'Neil was yelling back, "It's a'right! I have played all yoor games at home. I knoow wha' tae doo."

Clint gripped his leg at the knee rubbing it hard, trying to ease the pain. He turned to get a closer look back at Tamara. He could barely see her face over the seat headrest. Their door was still open, so the interior lights illuminated her pale face.

"What's wrong with her?" Clint pleaded, wincing with the pain in his leg.

Bam! Another explosion came with the crash of the school rear wall exploding. The ogre lunged out at them, hitting the pavement, cracking it under its huge feet. Someone from behind Clint was shouting for O'Neil to go, go, go and drive! Over all the cries and shouting Clint heard Nix saying softly, "she has been bitten by a vampire," to Banks.

"GO! GO! GO!" Cody yelled as he reached over and turned the key, causing the car to scream to life, and with a pull of the gear shift into drive by Cody, O'Neil hit the gas, causing the car to peel out. Unfortunately, they roared onto the soccer field that was behind the school.

The ogre howled, once more giving chase. The car bounced and swerved as O'Neil turned this way and that trying to get a feel for the car on the rough ground. Cody was screaming out instructions as Clint could hear the massive feet of the ogre thundering behind them over O'Neil's laughter. Clint saw in the side mirror the blurry huge green body charging at them. It held its club high and mouth wide and was gaining ground. Nix was cradling Tamara's head, trying to keep her steady whispering, "hold on. Take long steady breaths."

O'Neil swerved hard right, pointing towards the far fence. Cody squealed as if someone had ripped out a toenail, grabbing the wheel and turning it sharply to the left causing the car to spin out of control. They missed the fence as the wheels dug up chunks of dirt and wet grass that flew up over the car. Suddenly the car was hit and leaned terribly to one side. The ogre's club connected with its left side. The windows shattered, and the doors buckled.

Cody and O'Neil fought over control of the wheel and were able to straighten the car. They circled the ogre and raced back the way they came toward the parking lot. Clint let go of his leg and clung to his door as he held on tightly. The parking lot was almost empty but in the distance of the bouncing headlights, he saw people running away. He saw movement in the mirror again while those giant green legs had taken the ogre too far off balance as it swung and missed the car. It slid in the grass, crashing into the metal fence line, crushing it as if it were made from twigs. The ogre gripped the grass on all fours and sprung after them again, roaring in frustration. It sprung out of the ripped fence as if it were a fly escaping a spider's web.

A hard bounce brought Clint around. "What can we do for her?" he yelled at Nix as Tamara turned her head, showing her neck. The hard bounce was the car hitting the pavement, causing them to rise out of their seats. Clint felt a slight tug behind his navel. He could see in the glimmering light from the parking lot that there were two small wounds in Tamara's neck.

"We need to get her out of here," Nix called back, trying to hold her steady as the car went zooming around the remaining parked cars as some kids were running away.

"Hit the brake!" Cody yelled as the car practically flew onto the road, the front bumper connecting with asphalt, causing sparks to fly under and around the car. The car turned up the road, and as it did, Clint could see the ogre still chasing them, hitting vehicles with its tree club, bashing them out of his way like toys.

With the headlights leading the way, the engine roared up the road. There were shouts from the trunk as those riding back were shooting light arrows at the great beast chasing them. O'Neil was swerving the car in and out of the two lanes as other cars were coming and going in front of them. With Cody's help, they managed to swerve around them, only nicking one and the ogre trampling over another, still running at least thirty miles an hour to get to them. As they reached the hill crest, the headlights suddenly showed trick-or-treaters crossing the street in front of them. O'Neil pulled the wheel hard left while Cody grabbed it, trying to pull it hard right. The result was the car sped straight at the kids, with everyone in the car screaming. Trick-or-treaters dove out of the way as they ran a red light.

O'Neil let go of the wheel shouting, "Fine with it, yoo drive." He folded his arms leaving Cody still driving over his shoulder, pulling the car to the right, making it mount the sidewalk on two wheels and run over people's front yards. They hit bushes, fences, and lawn ornaments alike until Cody struggled to turn the wheel. He pulled them back on the road nearly missing a kid dressed up like a monkey who managed to dive out of the way, throwing his candy bag into the air, hitting the windshield. O'Neil looked disappointed that they'd missed the monkey as he had not once yet taken his foot off the gas.

Everyone except Tamara was locked in a never-ending scream as O'Neil asked smugly, "do yoo want me tae drive again?"

"Take the wheel," Cody howled. "Take it, take it, take it. PLLLEEAASE!" O'Neil rubbed his beard while Cody swung the car around two more. Finally, O'Neil took control again as if he were doing so against his better judgment. Cody kept yelling instructions and moaning about how the car was getting beat up, calling it his baby, as Tamara took sharp intakes of breath from pain, and Nix tried to help her. Clint kept hearing the small snaps of bow strings from the back of the car as everyone in the trunk kept firing arrows at the ogre. O'Neil, howling with laughter, joked, "I'm actually aiming fer the dumpy-looking kids."

They turned left, right, and another left, taking out several mailboxes, gaining speed, finally on a straight road as the ogre was slowing down. Clint watched as it grew smaller in his mirror until it was gone out of his sight.

"I think we lost it for now," Clint said loudly over everyone else's screams and yells as O'Neil almost flipped the car when taking a turn too sharp.

They kept going fast for another couple of blocks until they were almost home. The car slowed down and so did their heartrates as they were driving up the park road to their house. O'Neil didn't stop laughing until they pulled up the driveway and into the garage, safely away from anything that was after them.

Forty-Six

I WOULD BLAME THE NORMAL KIDS

They were a bruised group of oddities that got out of the car, especially those who were in the trunk. O'Neil opened his door only to find that it had fallen off the car. O'Neil acted like this was perfectly normal as he jumped down onto the door that was lying on the garage floor. He was still chuckling softly, while Cody was crying, not in pain, but when he said lowly in a hush, "dad is going to kill me."

They all hurried to get Tamara into the house. Clint hobbled behind them, refusing help from anyone to support him while he was struggling not to throw up now that the ground was stable under his feet. They moved into the television room and laid Tamara down on the couch.

"How did you find her?" Cody asked with a note of urgency in his voice. Tamara was paler now than she'd looked when she was in the car.

"It was Grant," Corbin said proudly. When we were left alone, he wanted to look around. I told him not to, but he started off and I didn't want to go and help."

Grant took another deep breath from his inhaler and started to talk when Kayla hurried in to join them. Grant sounded more confident than Clint had ever heard him before. "I just wanted to help, so I started walking around the parking lot. I saw Bill running away when the police officer wasn't looking. I went to where he ran from when the officer saw him and started after him, saying something. I found Tamara in the front of a car that he was running away from."

Clint started shaking as Tamara began to talk so softly and weakly that everyone had to stop talking to listen. "I am sorry," she said meekly.

"I went with Corbin and when we got there, I waited for him but when the sun was out of sight, I saw Bill. I went to tell him everything, everything," she coughed making her skin even whiter. "Before I knew it he hugged me and then I felt pain in my neck. Then I was in the car alone. Grant, Grant…" Grant poked his mousy head over to see her.

"Thank you for finding me," she said smiling feebly.

"What can you do for her, Nix?" Banks said quickly. Everyone turned to Nix at once all with hopeful expressions.

"She has been bitten too long ago to do anything directly. We will have to revive her when the time comes and keep her safe till daybreak," Nix said rubbing his chin.

"What do you mean?" Cody demanded.

"Have you ever heard of a vampire in this world?" Banks interjected.

"Yeah, but there is nothing like that here, they are just make believe," Kayla said, staring sharply at Nix and Banks.

"Before we do anything else those of you who are all right take up lookout positions. Everyone else stay put while Nix takes a moment and helps those injured. They will probably be coming for us."

"What about Tamara?" Clint asked furiously.

Banks looked over at Clint with calmness, but he took several breaths as if he didn't think there was time for this right now. "When a vampire bites someone they don't always give them venom. They sometimes just feed and let the person go. If they didn't feed too much, the person will live. When the venom is given, Nix can save them if he can get to them as soon as it happens. In the case of Tamara who has been bitten some time ago, we have to wait to see what happens."

"What do you mean?" Clint said unpleasantly.

"She will die." Banks said plainly, and without allowing for anyone to say anything else he said quickly, "If she dies during the night there is nothing, we can do to save her, she will become a vampire. If she dies during the day, we can revive her, and she will be all right."

"But you are leaving tonight!" Kayla said desperately.

"I know," Banks said indifferently. "Everything will be fine. We will not leave you without help but we must do what we can to save all of you and our own world. You will understand sooner than you think." Banks sighed. When he said this O'Neil suddenly looked worried like Banks had said something that he shouldn't have.

"Bring everyone up," Banks ordered Transun.

As Transun left, Nix started to work on Cody's back as he was helping him take off his costume. Clint watched Nix and turned back toward Tamara.

"I have done all I can for her," Nix said on tenterhooks. "She will be all right for now as long as she isn't moved, or gets too excited. We need to keep her heart rate down and keep her spirit high. The fight is up to her."

Nix was working on Cody's lower back when everyone came in to see Banks, who was leaning heavily on the front door. Banks motioned for all of them, even Nix, to go into the office leaving Clint with his family and Corbin. Clint felt alone as he limped over to Tamara who was asleep now but breathing unsteadily.

Cody was the one who spoke, helping everyone to know what to do. "Let's change and get out of this stuff. Please, those who can, help those who are hurt."

It was a painful process for Clint as Kayla went upstairs by herself while Corbin was taking off Clint's pirate boots. Corbin kept apologizing but unfortunately, that didn't help the pain when he was changing his pants. It couldn't have been done soon enough for Clint until they finally put on a clean shirt over his head.

Corbin went over to help Grant with Cody's shirt, as his back was still very painful, preventing him from bending. They had just helped him get his jeans on when Kayla came downstairs with her red book in hand. She sat in her father's study chair, once again writing fast. Clint stretched his leg painfully and saw that she still had her costume on. Clint tried to force himself to relax but it was all in vain as he watched Tamara take each one of her breaths, wondering if it was going to be her last.

It took at least twenty minutes for Banks and his group to come out of the office. Clint searched their faces for a trace of their conversation to give him a sign of what was going to happen next. They all walked to the kitchen to go out the back door except for O'Neil and Banks as Nix rushed over to check on Tamara. Apparently satisfied that she was going to be all right for now, he went over to help Cody.

Banks came out of the darkened office and was about to talk to Clint when the sound of a car came from up front. Banks jumped to the door as O'Neil went over and slumped to see out of the bottom part of a window.

"It must be yer parents!" O'Neil said and for the first time, Clint thought that he sounded fearful.

"What ur we gonnae do?" O'Neil asked sounding like a child having a party with his parents returning home too soon.

Everyone looked around, unable to speak in fear of what a fresh pair of eyes would see. Tamara lying half-dead on the couch. Cody and Clint were wounded, with Kayla still in a Minnie mouse costume writing as fast as she could. Banks and O'Neil are still in full combat gear standing next to a tree growing in the house. Every eye found its way to Banks as Clint expected him to run and hide, but oddly he stood his ground. Clint opened his mouth to say something when the front door opened and there were his mother and stepfather. They both were laughing warmly, holding some luggage under their arms as they came in. Their smiles and laughter left them as quickly as if they were just force-fed milk that had been left out for about eighty years. They dropped their luggage as Clint could see their eyes popping as they traveled from the tree that was in front of them, to Banks who was battered and bruised and armed. They looked at Clint who was leaning heavily on the stair railing. Then to Cody whose shirt was held up to his shoulders with Nix still working on his back, taking no notice that someone had just come in.

"What is going on?" Clint's mother demanded as she folded her arms.

Clint was petrified with fear as if the orc was back. He couldn't move anything but his eyes.

"You must be Mr. Holden," Banks said, stepping up to face him.

"Yes, and who are you?" Clint's stepfather said, swallowing.

O'Neil, who was behind the door, shut it slowly, and when it clicked shut, Clint's parents jumped and screamed, spinning around, almost falling over their luggage that they had dropped. O'Neil also screamed and jumped in surprise at their reaction.

"I have to speak to you now!" Banks said urgently. "It is a matter of life or death."

"I want to see my children first, and who are you?" Clint's stepfather shuddered as he took a step forward. Banks held up a hand to stop him.

"I must insist; we have no time," Banks said as he slowly lifted a hand to rest on Clint's stepfather's shoulder and with his other hand, he took out the piece of old paper that he had pulled out before, that he said contained names on it and that he alone could see. Banks looked at it once more, turning it so he could read it, and then lowered it as if it could turn to dust in his hand.

"It has to do with your work," Banks said honestly. "It has to do with your project, Red Thorn."

John stiffened instantly. "Where are the rest of my kids?" Clint's mother shouted so loud that everyone looked at her; even Kayla poked her head around the corner of the television room to see them.

"No, wait!" John said sharply. "How do you know about that, no one except seven people in the world knows about that?" Clint's stepfather's eyes were working hard, examining Banks all over.

"There is no time," Banks said once more. "I must talk to you two alone, now!"

"What is project Red Thorn?" Clint asked.

"It is my work," Clint's stepfather said as if his stomach had dropped about a foot. "We had a break in but no leak. How could you know about Red Thorn? Is it out? Is it contained? If it gets out it will change the world. The consequences are incalculable." John spoke very fast.

"There have been rumors about it on the news, but it has to do with my work and what I discovered with my partner Kevin Ferney. It's top secret and to have this man know…"

"This way please, I must talk to you now," Banks said, almost shouting as he started gently moving Clint's parents to the office.

"I want to know what is going on and that my family—"

"They are as well as expected," Banks interrupted him.

"O'Neil, secure this room," Banks ordered as Clint stood there with his mouth open. "No one comes in."

Clint watched as Banks gently maneuvered his parents into the office and shut the door. O'Neil swelled importantly as he folded his arms, standing in front of the door barring anyone's way.

"Na, don't try me on these, boy," O'Neil said rather harshly. "Yoo will understand later. I was told soon afta we got here, and Banks just told everyone else."

Clint looked at him and then checked everyone else behind him, looking for support to try and find out what was going on. Kayla must be writing again as Clint couldn't see her and Nix was asking Cody to move around now. Grant and Corbin were pacing around the television room. Cody started to walk around arching his back, which seemed to not hurt him, but he was definitely stiff. Then he looked back at O'Neil who hadn't moved an inch.

"What did he just tell you and how did you survive that hit from that ogre anyway?" Clint asked in frustration.

"Ah, we dwarves ur soft on the inside but as tuff as granite on the ootside. On what Banks has said, yoo will fin' out when yoo need tae," O'Neil said, hitting his chest with his fist.

Clint itched his head as he readjusted his hurt leg on the stairs. The silence was horrible as he worked hard to hear anything from the office. Not finding any help or relief he had to break the silence.

"And what exactly are an ogre and an orc?" he asked O'Neil.

O'Neil smiled painfully at this and rubbed his beard before he stated, "They were men like yoo and me once, ur their parent's ay grandparents were at least. That is what happens tae those who do wrong, that is how the Reclamation works. Don't yoo remember me tellin' yoo these before? Those who do anythin' that they know is wrong, change a wee bit at a time ay sometimes all at once." O'Neil's eyes started to go out of focus as he stared at nothing.

"It's nae like on yer games or yer shows here boy. It's nae like yoo go oot and get some bad guys tae make yer day all better." O'Neil's voice sounded inward and emotional as he went on.

"These ur your brothers, people like yoo and I who choose tae do things that they know ur wrong and keep doin' it and dinnae come back tae what is right. Don't yoo see that could be yoo out there, ur yer brother Grant, or yer sister Jamie. They can come back, and we need tae give them that chance. They can aw come back." O'Neil looked almost pleading for Clint to understand. "Yoo need tae know that noo, I guess tae praepair yoo."

"What?" Clint's asked, his mind racing. Clint was going to ask what O'Neil had just said but before he could, Nix came and tapped his good foot.

"Let's take care of that leg," Nix said smiling. Clint thought for a moment that Nix gave O'Neil a worried look. Nix had a very friendly face and as he helped Clint down the stairs, he looked like a doctor who was about to give him a shot. Nix had him stand in the hallway as he worked on his leg and this time he wasn't talking. As he rubbed his leg Clint couldn't talk either, as he concentrated not to scream because of the pain.

Nix was rubbing it hard causing Clint to close his eyes when he suddenly said after a few minutes, "put a little weight on it and walk on it."

Clint hesitated, but did so; amazingly there was no pain, but his leg felt like it was in a splint. Nix gave him a reassuring smile and said, "I have to go out back to check on everyone else." Before he left, he looked over Tamara once more and then went on his way out to the kitchen.

Clint tenderly walked up and down the hallway. It seemed that his leg had been covered in a stiff clear gel. It felt like super glue around his knee. He paced on it for another ten minutes before he heard a few keys of the piano play from the office. Everything in the house went silent for a moment as everyone listened. No one moved. Then the doors of the office opened, sounding louder than normal as everyone's ears pricked up. Until the door hit O'Neil in the back of the head with a soft thud. Clint's parents came out as O'Neil stood aside as Clint hobbled around the corner. He saw that his mother had raccoon eyes and a red nose from crying. All the kids and Corbin too stood up and came into the lobby, with Kayla being the last one in.

Without saying a word, Clint's mother swooped down and hugged Clint, crushing him as John started to speak. "I need you to listen and not to ask anything." Clint's stepfather's face went from a new tan to a pasty white. He appeared to be forcing himself to say something that he really didn't want to. Banks hovered oddly behind him, standing in silence.

"Kids, first I want you all to know that your mother and I love you more than anything else in this world," John said keenly. "We will have to go to dinner, and we do want to know what has been going on with all of you these past few days and we want to let you know everything that we have been doing." He suddenly looked older and tired as he lowered his heavy head. Much more tired than Clint had ever seen him before.

"I need you to do whatever this man says, is that understood? Whatever this man says!" John was vigorously pointing at Banks who stood upright at attention. Clint's mother released him from her hug and went to Cody, Grant, Kyla, and even Corbin before she leaned softly on the couch that Tamara was on. She was careful not to disturb her as she gently fixed her hair lovingly as more tears fell from her face.

Clint looked back and forth from Banks to his stepfather glumly wounding what in the world they talked about in that room. Tears were coming up rapidly into John's eyes as his bottom lip quivered. Clint could see behind Banks that the family portrait was open showing a safe door behind it.

"Robyn, we have to go!" John said bravely.

"No, I can't do it," she whimpered.

"Robyn please, everything will be all right. We will see them again, you know that."

It was a strange moment as Clint felt like his mother was looking at him as if it was going to be for the last time. Every one of the kids felt the same way as Clint's stepfather had started to help his mother to the door. He opened it for her and was almost out the door when Kayla ran up.

"Here!" she said clutching onto the red leather book and forcing it into John's hand. "I have written everything that has happened in there as best I could."

Without a warning Clint's stepfather fell on Kayla, hugging her tight as tears fell fast from his eyes. Clint could hear his mother wailing from the other side of the door as Banks cleared his throat.

John turned quickly to Banks for a moment and without another word he shut the door behind them and was gone. Silence fell over the hollow feeling house. Everyone shared the weight of what had just happened.

"What happens now?" Cody asked softly. "And what is this Red Thorn thing? Why can't you tell us?" Cody was sounding more deranged than concerned. Banks pursed his lips not saying anything as he watched them in silence. O'Neil went to the window once more to keep an eye out as

Clint's parents drove away. It was a silent standoff between those who had questions and those who had answers.

Corbin seemed to have made up his mind as he sat down on the floor and asked, "do you think they will do another school dance this year?" Everyone looked at him as if he'd just performed a very bad magical trick.

Something turned on in Clint's mind. "This is about my father's work and my family. You're not going to tell us what's going on," he said now with a hint of anger in his voice. "What about Corbin? What has this to do with him, can't he go?"

"He cannot go," Banks said just as low as Clint did. "You have to think how the Fury knew about you in the first place? Where was your first encounter with the Fury? How did they find us here?" He gave time for Clint to think.

Clint watched him but didn't think for some time as his emotions seemed to be overwhelming his brain. Finally, he was able to conclude an answer, "they had to be informed about us from someone from our world," Clint said coldly. Banks gave him a warm smile like a teacher who'd just got an answer to a question posed to the class.

Clint was thinking hard but Banks came to his aid. "The disappearances, Tamara's boyfriend missing, being led into a trap. We have to assume that the Fury knew everything about us." Banks' face contorted in worry. "Our best hope is that Tamara hasn't told them that we do not have the Requiem and that we intended to lead them away with a fake one."

"But you have it," Clint shouted. "The safe is open!"

"That is not it and you are missing a point that you don't understand."

"What, Tamara?" Cody asked loudly sounding like he was hurt for being left out of the conversation.

"She may not have been able to help herself, vampires can be very persuasive and there could be worse things that the Fury have brought here," Banks said, now looking toward the wall lost in thought.

"What are we going to do then?" Clint said, now feeling like he was going to lose his mind.

Banks smiled once more warmly as he bent low to look at Clint face to face. "You will have to trust me and know that what we are all doing is right. You don't understand the change and how it can betray someone to themselves, but if you did you would know that I am doing what is right to save us all."

Clint looked into his warm eyes and didn't understand what he was saying, but for one of the first times as his throat tightened, he believed Banks as a leader.

"We have kids comin', not Fury," O'Neil said cautiously.

Clint found that he was smiling as he was still looking into Banks's eyes. Blinking he said, "they are probably just some trick-or-treaters, we will just give them some candy and send them on their way."

"Well, that just happened!" Corbin said drily. "I'm going to do something I should have done when all this started."

"What is that?" Kyla asked.

"Watch TV and eat candy. It's Halloween y'all."

"But Tamara…" Kyla said brashly.

"I'll keep the volume down," and with a click, he turned it on.

"I hope you all have clean underwear handy because we made the news again," Corbin said weakly as if trouble was expected.

Clint staggered and went to watch the news as Corbin turned up the sound just enough. It was the same woman that they had seen before from the news.

"The oddities that are being reported from our area continue. You have just heard from our on-site correspondent at Kingston hospital reporting on the unpleasant event that took place there the other day that led to the savage death of one of those who helped the injured. Now we take you to what seems to be another Halloween prank as many sports stores in our area were broken into last night. Oddly the only reported items that were stolen were their entire stock of bows and arrows."

Clint was shocked at this and wondered if there was a connection to everything that was going on and was eager to hear more but his focus was taken off the news as the doorbell sounded threatening.

Kayla was the one who jumped up and ran to the kitchen to get some candy and then opened the door with O'Neil covering her. What Clint heard next was one of the most terrible sounds that he had ever heard in his life.

"Clint Holden? Where are you?" Amber yelled in through the open door. Clint closed his eyes as his blood turned cold. Corbin started to laugh out loud as Clint looked desperately around for a place to hide. Corbin's mickey mouse laugh seemed too extended beyond its range and lifted everyone else's feelings of dread.

Then a new sound appeared that made Clint change his feelings faster than Cody could change the television channel from a soap opera to find a football game. "Is Clint here?" came Melanie's soft, warm voice.

Clint hit the floor, hiding low out of view when Corbin helped his best friend by shouting, "yeah he's in here," as he was laughing harder, causing him to drop the remote and roll on the floor. Clint was groping around on the floor to feel where Corbin was and kicked him. This only made Corbin laugh harder.

"What are you doing?" Cody called as he leaned on a shelf. "You can't invite them in here!"

Quick footsteps sounded in the lobby towards the television room. Clint closed his eyes, realizing that there were more than just two sets of footsteps coming for him as he rolled into a ball on the floor.

"Turn it off and get them out of here!" Cody barked, sounding disappointed.

With a soft click the light and sounds of the television stopped as Corbin set the remote down and sheepishly said, "sorry, I didn't think of that." He was no longer laughing.

"Where is he?" Amber demanded. No one had time to answer her as they moved fast across the lobby and suddenly there was a shout of, "Ah-ha!"

Clint jumped up to his feet, smiling, agitated but anxiously trying to look calm. "Hi," he said joyfully.

It was probably for the best that so many kids started to talk at once. Clint couldn't understand a word from anyone. It sounded like they all wanted to know what was going on. Amber stood towering before him, much like Mrs. Christenson did when she was out for blood. Thankfully, Melanie was right behind her with six other students with them that Clint didn't know. All the kids looked dirty and disheveled in their Halloween costumes as if they had just come out of a bomb shelter that almost failed. Amber shifted what little weight she had to spare, putting her hands on her hips. When she did, Clint could see and recognize that the boy behind her was the football player who had taken Melanie to the dance. Clint noticed out of the corner of his eye that Banks had waved to O'Neil to retreat into the office.

"Hold it, hold it!" Cody yelled, shutting up all the kids except Amber. It was not a good thing for Clint now that she was the only one who could be heard.

"How dare you! If you are not into me at least you can treat me with respect! You little attention-grabbing self-made moron! What, that little moment we had might have been crazy and cute for you, but this is like, really wrong just to make someone grieve. It's like we are not even on the same planet!"

Clint swallowed as the sensation that he had never been in worse trouble before poured over him like cold tar. Corbin suddenly hit the floor again, overcome with silent giggles.

"Like, you are perfect for a really strict boarding school. You are just too immature for me Mr. amateur hour. You should know that you should keep me happy and when you don't, AHHHHHHH!" Amber kept telling him off until her eyes fell on Tamara. Amber started to dance in place as she screamed, trembling. Grant, who was closest to her ran and on his toes held her mouth, muffling her scream.

The scream caused Banks to tear out of the office with O'Neil rushing right behind him. "What is it?" Banks called out as he drew out his large longsword, bringing it to life. Every new child who just came in started to scream loudly, turning around and seeing two men charging at them, weapons drawn. Kayla jumped up between them and yelled as loud as she could, "everyone, stop!"

Clint was shocked that everyone obeyed her at once, even Amber. Banks and O'Neil slid to a halt while a profound silence misted over them.

"Shut it up down there!" their grandmother called. "You're making me miss Mel Gibson. I was almost married to him, no thanks to you!"

Kayla waited a moment as everyone's eyes first rolled up, looking up the stairs and back to her told her they were processing what they'd just heard. "Now, every one of you listen," Kayla shouted. "No more screaming.". It didn't help that Melanie's date chose that awkward moment in the quiet to try to ease the tension by saying stupidly, "Nice tree."

Another awkward moment followed as everyone looked at him in disbelief. "Clint," Melanie said with quiet fear behind her voice, "what is going on?"

Clint could only shake his head, examining the carpet. Corbin, probably still feeling guilty, spoke up to save him, saying, "What if you go first and tell us what happened to all of you?"

She was looking at him desperately for answers but nodded smartly, "We, we ran out to the dance. No one answered when we called nine-one-one. We went to the police station, but when David went in," she indicated her date, "he said that all the police were dead. So, we ran to my house, but my parents weren't there. We went to Amber's, and when we went to Corbin's, no one was there either." She started to shake as a single tear came down from her right eye.

Melanie sniffed and continued, "All our parents were supposed to be home tonight. We can't find them, and no one is answering their phones. The doors to our houses were unlocked and it was like they had just vanished. Some of the houses don't even have power… even, even at the police station."

Clint didn't know what to say as Banks suddenly looked more worried when he said, "They know."

"They know what?" Kayla asked in horror.

Banks took control as he ordered O'Neil, "Get the others," and then he addressed all the kids who came in. "You all have to stay here with us; your parents, family, and law enforcement are more than likely dead."

The silence that came after Banks said this was so electric that Clint thought that he couldn't take anything else that night.

"What are you talking about? How would you know, and, like, who are you anyway?" Amber said snobbishly. Just then all of Banks' group came in, wearing their armor and weapons. They marched single file into the lobby next to the tree and stood to attention. This caused all the kids to retreat further into the TV room, especially the new ones who were not really used to seeing someone with blue skin, even on Halloween.

Clint suddenly found himself between worlds again. To his left, there were his classmates, friends, and family and to his right, his protectors and new friends now brought a different world with them. Each group put pressure and fear on him as he struggled to figure out what to do. He was thinking of anything that would save them all. Any answer that would give a solution to mend both worlds that were pulling on him. He couldn't come up with anything, as he looked over at Tamara.

"What's going to happen?" Cody asked with a heavy throat.

Banks looked at him past all those who stood between them and then at his group. He looked at each of them with a stony face, brow down in thought. When he had finished, he looked each of them in the eye before he turned to Clint.

"I said that I would protect you at all costs," he declared taking a deep breath. "And that is what I am going to do. If I lied to you that would be a fate worse than death." He looked into Clint's heart through his eyes for only a moment then turned to his men still standing at attention.

"But what say you?" he asked them all. Everyone from O'Neil, who was at one end, to Chiowood who stood tall on the other, looked taken aback at being asked this. It seemed to Clint that being asked what they thought was best was not something that happened to a soldier every day. They looked at one another with mixed feelings showing on their faces until each one took a step forward proudly.

"We didnae come all this way for nothen," O'Neil said, looking down the line.

"Would someone speak English, like, now?" Amber said as sharp as a whip crack.

Banks turned to her and said blandly, "Ma'am, if you will allow, trust our judgment. We will do all we can to keep you safe and get what we came here for."

"I have had enough things going on on my weirdometer today, thank you very much," Amber said as if she were addressing a scoring on her cheer squad that she didn't agree with. "I have, like, been, almost killed, parents gone, broke a nail, like, got really dirty, had some, like, green people on steroids break up my dance." Amber seemed to be getting angrier with every word. "And like that weird fog followed us here, and for the first time in my life I have been stood up!"

She had started to turn red as if being stood up was about as bad as losing one's limb. Clint felt like Amber was about to explode when Banks lunged forward, shocking Amber into compliance.

"What?" Banks asked taking everyone by surprise except Amber who looked like she was glad to get an ally who understood how much she hurt.

"I know, like, who would ever think to stand me up, me, MEEE," Amber said giving Clint a ferocious look like a lion stalking its prey.

"No, what fog?" Banks demanded, facing her down.

"Oh, like, that was just creepy, to be walking and, like—"

"I need an explanation I can understand now," Banks interrupted. This only seemed to make Amber angrier, seething with sharp breaths.

"We came up here as fast as we could," Melanie said quickly. "Mostly 'cause we were just scared I guess, but there was this cold fog that seemed to follow us," she said sounding very brave, Clint thought as he watched her mouth move without blinking.

"O'Neil, check it," Banks said, sounding worried.

O'Neil who was already close to the door took two steps and was at the window by the door moving the shade ever so slightly. Clint moved close to O'Neil to look out as well. Clint put his face right next to O'Neil's hairy one and peered through the small opening which O'Neil was holding with his fingers. Clint also heard some footsteps from the TV room as he could see an eerie, milky fog slowly devouring the entire park outside his front door.

Forty-Seven

RUSH OF EVIL

A crack, whoosh, and a pointed scream of pain made Clint jump right onto O'Neil's legs and fall back. There were screams from all the girls. Clint got to his feet and looked over the couch where Tamara lay asleep still. He saw someone lying on the floor. The head of whoever fell was just visible around the couch corner. Clint couldn't determine who it was at first because his eyes were drawn to the arrow sticking through the person's neck. Blood started to pool on the floor underneath him into the carpet. A trembling hand rose as the person reached up around the arrow and held it like he wasn't exactly sure what had hit him. Clint moved over just enough to see the person's face already turning pale from the loss of blood and found that it was Melanie's date, David, convulsing on the ground.

"Everybody down, now!" Banks yelled.

Crash, crash, crash! Everyone fell to the floor as low as possible. Nix crawled right over Cody who was now on one side of the floor next to the couch watching as the pool of blood got bigger.

"Stay away from the windows, stay down, stay down!" Banks yelled again over the sharp cracks of glass and wood from the deathly wall of arrows destroying everything around them.

"David!" one of the girls cried out as she too was bawling along with all the girls except for Melanie who was watching Clint. Her eyes seemed to desperately pull on his heart for answers.

"Hold on little man, hold on," Nix pleaded when he got to David and started to work on his neck, lying in the boy's blood.

"Transun, Hobb, we are past the point of safe return. Get the two from downstairs! Dall and Ravin, get the grandmother! They will be on us any moment. Ohlwiler, Tremayne, go dark. O'Neil, get going with that diversion," Banks ordered quickly over the crying and screaming as an arrow connected with the chandelier over the tree in the lobby, causing it to come plummeting down. It smashed against the tree and crashed into the ground, barely missing O'Neil and Clint. Both covered themselves as crystal showered around them.

Clint lay flat on the wood floor with his hands over his head. His house was being shot to pieces as if thousands of tiny meteors were falling at the speed of light on his home. Everyone in the lobby was moving at once, staying on their bellies except for Tremayne and Ohlwiler, who were hitting all the light switches as best as they could without standing. They threw whatever rubble they could at to break the lightbulb to extinguish the lights that were too dangerous to try and reach.

There were shouts of protest as Sam and Jamie sounded like they were being forced up from downstairs unwillingly. Nix was working fast on David while Clint's grandmother was being brought down the stairs. She was outraged and seemed not to notice the impending death showering around her as she hit every living thing that she could while muttering, "I knew you were going to take me to a home eventually! This is my house. Where's my dog and pudding? Mel? Mel, where are you? Take your hands off me, you delinquent! Not one of you is in the Will anymore!"

"Nix and Ravin, you stay here. Keep them down and together," Banks called out as he crawled, keeping his head low to the door. "O'Neil, you're on me. We go down the center! Tremayne and Ohlwiler, you get those Light Bringers going."

"They are not ready, sir," Hobb shouted over the sound of arrows cascading around them.

"Go!" Banks bellowed. "Hobb, left sweep, left flank, Chiowood, take the right flank. Transun, you are in reserve and cover this door until O'Neil can get that fake Requiem out of here. For us all."

"What are you doing?" Cody yelled as he ducked, a fragment of the ceiling falling, hitting his shoulder.

Banks wasn't listening but made his way toward the door now in the completely dark house. The visible light which was shining was the electrical panels of their DVD player, stereo, arcade machines, and the weak light from outside lampposts. The light poured in through the shattered windows and the growing number of countless holes from the endless arrows that kept coming.

Jamie and Sam were yelling something down the hall that Clint couldn't understand. Cody responded with, "What are they doing? There are no police, Sam. We can't stay here."

"We don't know what's out there," Nix replied as he pulled something out of a pocket that glowed like a glow stick as he worked feverishly on David's neck. "We need to engage the enemy as far away from the house as possible. Now, stay down and keep quiet." Nix roared over his shoulder just when he broke the arrow in two and was gently pulling it out of David's neck.

"What?" Cody shot back at him in unbelief.

"They are not ready to hit us yet. If they were, they would have been on top of this house quicker than O'Neil could finish a flask." He stopped for a moment as an arrow nearly missed his left ear. Ravin pushed them to keep low close to Sam, Jamie, and grandma, who was hitting her as they all lay in the hallway.

Nix was pleading with David to keep his eyes open as O'Neil wormed his way across to the office and came out holding the strange octagonal instrument that Clint first saw his stepfather with earlier that week. Everyone else who was going to join the attack outside made ready their assault by the front door. They were almost lying on top of one and other under the sharp thuds of arrows that didn't seem to end. Some had the power to penetrate the outer walls of the house while some came in part way. Clint could see hundreds of arrow heads protruding partly through the walls all over as if his house were turning into a porcupine. Some arrows made it through the walls and windows and shattered everything in their path. Pictures were crushed, the furniture sliced and punctured, keepsakes on shelves shattered, and movies and electronic devices blasted apart all over their heads and came falling on them without mercy.

Banks reached up cautiously to the doorknob as he lay as close to the ground as he could. Sam and Jamie kept low, giving shouts of protest and never-ending questions as the girls in the television room whimpered. Nix continued pleading for David to stay alive as he worked on him with one hand and with his other, he started to pull Tamara down off the couch that was now being shot up. Cody and Corbin gave aid and laid her unconscious body down on the carpet just as the pads on the couch bust free of their fabric restraints by several arrows that hit just where her body had been. Everyone pressed themselves further down onto the floor, crying in fear.

Clint wiggled like a worm as an arrow carved through the wall and cut the sole of his left shoe in half, thankfully missing his skin by centimeters as he moved to the side window by the door. Banks nodded and with a whoosh, he opened the door and rolled aside out of it. No sooner was the door opened when arrows started to fly through the door above them, hitting the staircase wall, tree, and pictures that were once hanging there. Banks' team followed likewise one by one, down low to the ground, rolling like potato bugs on the ground as arrows without number flew over their bodies.

Over the shouts and screams from all around him, Clint heard something new as an arrow shattered glass frames through the open door, showering the stairs with glass. It sounded like someone was trying to start what was an old lawnmower on the roof. The lawnmower sound whizzed, sputtered, and died. O'Neil was the last one through the door, holding the strange object close to him.

"Shut the door behin' me laddie. Coody, open the garage door while stayin' low," he ordered before he whisked out of sight.

Clint couldn't move as arrows impacted all around him. He was frozen with fear. Time and time again, he reached up until finally, with a shaking hand, he slammed the door shut. The door protested as the thuds of more arrows were stopped by it. It sounded like the world's worst hailstorm outside, turning his house into a shooting range. Clint pushed himself back against the wall and window as he saw Cody moving across the floor with one arm and the other holding his stiff back when an arrow whizzed right in front of him, missing his nose by an inch. Cody moved just out of sight of the hallway, and with the sound of the garage opening, light spilled in from the open door when an arrow struck just where Cody's shadow was.

Clint could see light peeking through the door as arrows shot in the hallway just where Cody's shadow was. New screams came from down the hallway, and the door slammed shut as Cody crawled back, holding his left hand. Cody clutched his arm close to his heart as he fell back into the hallway. Clint saw that he looked shaken but not critically hurt, and when he saw Clint, he gave him a weak smile past the pain.

New shouts and screams of battle came from outside while another grinding fail of what sounded like a lawnmower clanked from the roof. Clint, unable to stop himself, had to see what was going on. He moved his head back to the window and parted the blind when he heard something that made him snap his back the other way.

"I am losing him," Nix cried, "Corbin, hold his neck here, Grant, you hold the other side."

Clint wouldn't believe his eyes while they showed him what couldn't be real. Nix was wiping David's mouth as he was coughing blood and convulsing. Nix moved to the other side of David, blocking Clint's view. A new sound ripped through fear and reason from outside. It sounded like a thousand taps on metal. Horrified, Clint watched Banks rushing toward one of the stone pillars on the edge of their driveway, shooting his short bow, with Hobb rushing after him. Arrows were hitting the ground all around them and cutting tree branches and leaves. Another figure moved into the night, melting into it, and went left, hurtling over the stone fence and taking up position by Mrs. Hutchings's house. They were shooting longbows and seemed to be taking small pieces of wood no more than a foot long out of one of their many bags and making them longer in their hands by at least four to five feet, throwing them like javelins into the fog.

To the right was another figure moving fast, staying low with their longbow, firing without stopping or breaking their stride as they made their way across the yard toward their neighbor's home.

Clint peered with only one eye through the broken window to the war zone park. The fog rippled with soft poofs of fog billowing up here and there with each volley. It was like watching rain disturb a pond as every few meters something stuck its head up exposing itself long enough to order shots fired toward the house or Banks's party. Clint tried to count the arms and heads concealed in the fog but there were too many. The

Fury were shooting all around and must have had hundreds of shooters out there while Banks only had six.

Crash! An arrow hit what was left of the glass on the other side of the door, shattering it while the arrow embedded itself in the wall on the far side. Everyone jumped again as Clint ducked down with more debris falling around him. His fear forced him to stay down as there were more shouts and screams from outside. The twinge of a bow, the whoosh of an arrow cutting air, and the thud of it hitting flesh, tree, or ground came from outside. Inside, shouts and continued screams under the hail of fire were all around them.

There was a new sound as Clint looked into the park again. He could see Banks and everyone else shoot their arrows and then dive or roll to another position that would give them cover before they attack again. Arrows, daggers, and spears were hitting all around them. The sound didn't come from the outside but from the side of the house, toward the garage. It sounded like one of his stepfather's Harley-Davidsons starting up.

Over the shouts and cries from behind Clint of some fighting to save David and others wanting to know what was going on or why they couldn't escape out of the back, Clint heard Cody yell, "No! Not Dad's bike too!"

The roar of the motorcycle engine sounded as a single light pushed the dark aside. Clint watched O'Neil riding his stepfather's motorcycle down the driveway with the octagonal ball under one arm. When the headlight turned on, the enemy targeted him. Arrows flew all around him as if he were leaving a path of them behind him. O'Neil hit the road hard with a bounce and parted the fog like a low-flying plane, splitting it like a knife.

The fog swallowed him, and under its thick blanket, it moved fast toward the motorcycle. The sound of O'Neil forcing his motor harder and faster hung as a steady cry over the bellows of war. The distorted headlight turned sharply around something large, causing the fog to move all around it. As O'Neil went on, Banks yelled, "Push the line!"

Clint lifted his head again to see Banks rush from his cover into the fog, slinging his short bow and drawing his sword. Clint watched the motorcycle headlight go further away, going, going, going until it was swallowed in the fog that was as thick as mashed potatoes. The swells and waves behind him testified to the things pursuing him relentlessly.

Clang! Another arrow hit a window, but this one was the one above Clint's head. The arrow shot down the hall, missing Sam's ear as glass fell around Clint and in his hair. There was a sharp cry from somewhere out in the park, "Fall back!".

Clint stayed low at the growing sounds of thuds on the door and around the house as shouts and footsteps grew closer and louder. Suddenly the door burst open, hitting Clint hard in the leg as Transun dove inside, scrabbling to get undercover. It seemed like arrows were being dropped right behind her, hitting the wood floor causing it to splinter as they followed her inside. Then everyone else piled in one by one breaking the arrows stuck in the floor as they also took cover in the office or behind Clint. Banks was the last in and shut the door hard behind him, bracing it closed with his weight as more arrows hit it.

"Everyone, check?" Banks called as he covered a nasty cut over his right eye that was bleeding.

Nix was the first to speak, "I can't save him." There was a moment of silence from everyone except for David's gargled breath and groans of pain as the life he was fighting to hold on to left him as the thuds of arrows hitting the house and wall and the shattering of objects above them continued. Without looking back, Nix dove into the lobby to help everyone else. All the girls except Amber and his grandmother whimpered in despair. Corbin and Grant crawled away from the dead body in shock.

A new low moan turned into a scream to Clint's right. Chiowood was moaning as he turned over Hobb who had three arrows sticking out of his stomach.

Hobb never made a sound but smiled until the light left his eyes while Chiowood held Hobbs's face shouting, "No! Stay... stay," as his eyes filled with tears. Chiowood split the night with a monstrous cry. Everyone else looked on helplessly, keeping their heads down.

Banks was the first to notice that the thuds of the arrows hitting around them had slowed and then stopped. Banks grabbed Chiowood's shoulder hard and nodded to him. Chiowood wouldn't let go of Hobb until Nix appeared, pulled Hobb away from him, and started trying to resuscitate him.

There was a hissing sound from outside now that made Clint's skin crawl. Banks urged everyone to be quiet. "SSSHHHHH." The hissing sound came again, but Clint couldn't understand it. Unable to stop himself, Clint whispered, "What is that, and what is going to happen to O'Neil, and—"

"SHUSH," Banks repeated irritably.

The noise came again but this time Clint could understand it. Clint started to shake all over now that he heard that low rasping voice.

"Give it to us," it called from outside.

All the blood left Clint's face as Banks moved to the broken window on the other side of the door and looked out of it. Clint could see his eyes widen as he said softly, "It's him."

Clint whipped around to look out as well. It was a horrible sight as the fog was being pushed aside out of the park to the road, like a boat making a wake in water. It was coming toward the house, slowly parting the fog as it went with an army of figures behind it walking in the clearing it was leaving. It washed its way right up to the sidewalk on the other side of the street. The Spell Binder stood in the center surrounded by a dozen different creatures of different shapes and sizes. Clint squinted in the dark to see as the fog dissipated, rolling back itself to see. The Spell Binder's group was accompanied by many normal-sized people in the park. Clint lifted his head instinctively to see their dark outline in the night. The number of enemies in the park increased from hundreds to thousands of murky silhouettes.

"Give it to us," the Spell Binder called once more.

"What is that, what is that?" Jamie cried, panicking.

"Shut up!" Banks yelled as he rolled over and got his bow ready.

"Everyone get to a window and get ready to shoot, they are coming. I need those Light Bringers, or we are dead. Kids, fall back as far as you can but don't go out until I give the word. Ravin, stay with them; keep them down. Move, move, move!"

Everyone panicked and moved hurriedly, except Clint who sat watching on with paralyzing fear as the Spell Binder called again, "Give… give it."

"Why didn't they follow O'Neil?" Clint whimpered in fear.

"They probably did," Banks huffed as he worked fast to get his gear ready around him. "It doesn't matter since they are coming."

Another thought stabbed Clint's mind shaking away the fear. "Wait a minute," Clint said, sounding normal. "You ordered O'Neil out with what you called the fake Requiem. Is that not the…"

"Not now!" Banks shouted as he pulled out every dagger he had and set them around him. "I need those Light Bringers or we are all dead. Nix, pass the word and get back here on the double." All the kids were moving clumsily, most still in their costumes as Nix went over and picked up Tamara from the couch and followed everyone else into the kitchen, before he went upstairs like a shot. Everyone who was left in Banks's group went to a window and set daggers and arrows around them getting them ready for easy retrieval. No one seemed to notice Clint sitting unmovable, shaking, and gripping the floor as if his life depended on it as they moved around him when the voice came through once more.

"Banks!" the Spell Binder called.

"Banks, we don't have Light Bringers yet; they are trying," Nix wheezed as he came down the stairs and went to the kitchen.

"Banks," the Spell Binder said lovingly. "Banks, we have your scent from when you escaped us on the mountain. We can follow you anywhere you go." Banks peered out again as little as he could, keeping his head down so as not to present it as a target.

"Give it to us and we will let you all go, we will let the boy live," it shrieked.

Banks turned his brown eyes away from the night and towards Clint and then his men. He looked back to Clint as if he were weighing his options. The look was as if a father were searching his son before saying goodbye for the last time. The clocks stopped while the sounds of everyone else breaking glass or getting their weapons ready stopped for a moment. Clint locked eyes with Banks as they just looked at each other.

"What if it was your call, Clint?" Banks asked. "You think that they would give up or do you want to live for something more in your life?"

Clint licked his dry lips and felt a tear fall down his face, suppressing the feeling of cold death over him. Looking at Banks, he started to feel a strength in his chest. He began to feel anger as he looked over at Hobbs's body and the blood that he could see from David in the other room. He stopped shaking, and with an anger that he had never known, he turned toward the broken window and shouted as loud as he could, "Drop dead, you frozen freak!"

Wham! Arrows hit all around him at once as Banks called out, "Fire!" Everyone started to shoot back out of the house as Clint hit the floor as an arrow just hit the collar of his shirt.

"Clint, get back here!" Melanie and Kayla yelled from the kitchen.

Clint started to crawl but the stained-glass window above the door was hit, showering glass everywhere once more as arrow after arrow flew in through the broken windows and thudded against the side of the house and door. Banks was shouting out orders, "Watch the left, concentrate, fire," and, "They are using the dead as shields; aim for the feet."

"Watch the right, watch the right, three coming up!" Another voice called as Clint ducked.

"I got em!"

"They must have a vampire with them controlling the dead, some coming up the middle, watch it!" They all were crying to one another as arrows were flying out of the house to stop the oncoming wave of intruders.

The door was now getting shot with so many arrows some heads were starting to break through. Clint shuffled on the ground as chips of wood and glass still cascaded on top of him. The house was getting torn to pieces. Everything was getting shot up as if a hundred machine guns were firing on his house at once. Unable to feel safe or get to the kitchen Clint fell back and looked out the open window with one eye and watched wave after wave of what looked like corpses were making their way toward the house.

"What in the world are those?" Clint yelled as an arrow hit right beside him making him jump and duck down again.

"The dead, now get back! Stay under cover." Banks shouted as he shot out of the window again. "Vampires can control the dead," He shot again as Clint heard the arrow he just fired, hitting something with a thud. "They gain enough strength; they can call any dead from an unblessed grave."

Clint looked out the broken window, sticking his head up, and saw dead bodies everywhere. Some on the ground had stopped and fallen when an arrow or spear had hit them. Others were walking, shuffling their way up to the house as some stayed back behind the Spell Binder, shooting arrows at the house. Clint also could make out from the light arrows being fired back, right behind the Spell Binder the shadowy forms of the ogre, orcs, and some others that were not dead.

The corpses were coming closer. The few arrows coming from the house were unable to stop the continued wave after wave of undead marching oddly up to them. Some of the lifeless held broken off limbs wielding them like clubs, others had tree branches or rocks in their bony hands. They didn't look slimy, or gooey but bones and dead skin were coming at him without care for pain or self-preservation.

"Fire flasks!" Banks yelled, bringing Clint out of his stupor as some of the corpses were getting so close to the house that they were throwing limbs that they had broken off or things that they'd picked up. Clint watched as a very larger uncoordinated skeleton threw their mailbox at the door when Banks picked up something that looked like a vial of soft light out of one of his bags and threw it out of the window.

There was a soft sound of glass breaking outside and a whoosh of fire like a bomb had gone off when the flask hit the ground. Light erupted in front of the house as flames shot up wherever Banks's party threw out the fire flasks. They reached ten feet high, blowing some back and burning anything they touched. This only held off the undead momentarily as they kept coming, even trying to go through the flames and falling, burning as if they had no feeling. Clint felt the heat on his face as the sound from the roof came again. This time, the sound sizzled and popped before it roared to an even hum.

"WHOOOHOO! Banks yelled. "Pour it to them!"

Suddenly the air was bright above them from the outside of the roof. The humming and popping steadied and two sturdy streams of light arrows shot out from the roof down to the walking dead's front lines. They burned, cut, and stopped everything in their path as they swept their yard, the street, and the front of the park. The enemy's lines were crumbling. There were shouts and cries of joy from the house and groaning from the dead in the park.

For an instant, Clint felt a spasm of safety until something dark appeared in the air above the park with a loud grunt. Clint watched the dark outline fly in the air toward them until it disappeared above the house. Clint thought about the image against the night sky and figured that it was the outline of one of their dead.

"D.P.G.!" Banks yelled as he leaped to cover Clint with his own body.

Clint was crushed under Banks's weight when there was an almighty boom. Everything went fuzzy after that. Banks rolled off Clint and all he could hear was a high-pitched whistle in his ears. It felt like he was underwater as he tried to look around. He saw a blur of a person grab him and twist him on his side as hands felt him all over. This whistling dimmed, and he heard someone talking as if they were far away.

"Clint, are you hit?" Nix shouted. Clint didn't understand him as he felt his ears to see what was covering them. He didn't feel anything when Nix started to shake him. It was as if someone turned a light on inside him with an adrenaline rush. He screamed while Nix held him still. "You're all right, you're all right," Nix called reassuringly.

"Sir, sir?" Clint heard with his ears still ringing. "Hold on, sir, hold on." Clint saw through a cloud Nix hopping over Banks who was in a ball next to Clint.

"What's wrong with him?" Clint asked, still shaking to clear his head. He couldn't believe his eyes when he saw above him a tremendous hole in the roof. The night sky opened above him as pieces of the roof and ash fell over him.

"He is not hit," Nix shouted while he shined a light in Banks' eyes. "He is having another attack."

"What?" Clint asked still not hearing clearly.

"This is his second attack here that I know of," Nix stated as he helped, rubbing Banks' arms and legs to relax.

"Sir, we need you," Nix yelled as Banks started to come around. "Sir we have one K.I.A. Both Light Bringers are down. Tremayne and Ohlwiler are all right and are coming down now. Orders, sir? Sir, come on, sir?"

"Ravin," Banks whimpered. "Ravin, Ravin!" Banks called, now sounding normal.

Ravin rushed down the hall slipping on shards of glass, broken wood, and arrows stuck in the wall and floor. Banks rolled to his knees as everyone started firing from the house again.

"Get them out," Banks said as if they were anywhere other than a war zone.

This was the first clear thing Clint heard. Ravin whipped her head around causing her long, pretty hair to whip into the air as she grabbed Clint by the shirt and pulled him close.

"You have to run. You all have to run, NOW!" she yelled as she pushed him toward the kitchen with remarkable strength.

Sharp twinges of arrows cutting the sky came in again. The enemy had opened fire on them once more and this time dark plasma arrows burned holes and showered sparks where they hit.

"Nix," Banks yelled, returning fire as he just barely ducked out of the way of an oncoming arrow. "Nix, get them out of here! We will hold them back. Ravin, you have to get ready Final Judgment and bring the heat. Go now!"

Clint didn't have time to hear more as an arrow hit the wall a foot to his right. Ravin pushed him while he was down on all fours crawling through the hall toward the kitchen where Nix was already leading everyone else out, holding Tamara on his shoulder. Everyone was already in the backyard with Nix shouting out instructions where they should go. The sounds of pain and war were coming from the front of the house. Clint was just going out the back door when he heard Banks command, "Fall back!"

Clint sprinted into the backyard and before he was out of earshot, he could hear shouts of, "There's too many of them," "I'm hit! Get me out of here!"

"Here they coooooooooooome!"

Ravin was right on Clint's heels as he ran as fast as he could with his stiff leg acting more like it was made of wood than flesh and bone. He had made it to the other side of the yard where Nix apparently had broken down the fence leading up into the woods away from the neighborhood and toward the steep hills devoid of homes. Clint looked back as two dark figures were coming out of the house, one being supported by another under their arms.

Clint jumped through the broken fence trying to see the sparsely wooded area in the dark where not even moonlight could aid him with the clouds overhead that refused to rain.

"They have a goblin, get down!" Clint heard Tremayne yell from somewhere around the house when a massive explosion erupted. Clint looked on and saw wood, flame, and his roof shot up into the night sky as if someone had just let off a bomb blowing his house open.

"Move!" Ravin yelled, pushing him hard in the back. There were more shouts and sounds of bow strings firing as parts of his house that were shot up into the sky from the tremendous force of the explosion started to plummet down to the ground. Clint ran on toward the screams of his family and friends who were running for their lives through the woods in the dark up the hill. Behind them, what once was their house fell around them. He couldn't make out very well in the dark the shadow he was running after. Clint was coming up to them fast, closing the gap between them as a bed landed to his right, tearing apart the tree that it landed on.

"Nix needs you," Cody's voice shouted from up ahead in the night. Ravin zoomed forward as if propelled by a rubber band. Clint limped in pain to keep up but felt his way being poked and prodded by the low tree branches and weeds. He ran and ran, losing track of time. There were more shouts and yells from behind them followed by another large explosion. Clint couldn't see it because of the trees now blocking his way but he could hear the footsteps and shouts were getting closer.

"Come on!" Cody yelled. Clint saw his dark image at the top of the hill before it disappeared. He followed them as they went up a hill behind their house and then down it on the other side, which had fewer trees but more undergrowth. Through the tree branches down the hill, Clint could see the irrigation stream in front of him at the base of the hill. They had come out on the far side of the golf course. Between the golf course and the hill lay a large field or open high weeds and marsh.

More shouts and then a sharp scream of pain from behind. Clint pushed his sore leg to go beyond its capability as he ran. A flash of light from behind him made him look over his shoulder. The pain in his leg from being twisted was suddenly too great. Clint stopped running and watched everyone else sprint on before him and in that second, he turned around and watched the top of the hill. He only had to wait a moment as he rubbed his throbbing leg to find Chiowood scrambling over the hilltop running with his bow in his hand followed closely by Tremayne and Ohlwiler. As soon as Chiowood flew over the top of the hill he turned his red head back the way he came as he stopped and fixed an arrow. Before Clint could see what, he was shooting at, he fired hitting a corpse that just appeared, then another and another.

Tremayne grabbed Clint, shouting something at him as he lifted him. Ohlwiler right next to him was limping badly but also forced Clint onward. Clint couldn't see behind. He could only feel Tremayne's powerful body driving him like a plow as they were running down the hill. Clint's leg couldn't take the pressure and gave way. He stumbled and fell. Before he hit the ground Tremayne grabbed him and flung him over his shoulder.

"Where is Transun?" Chiowood yelled past the sounds of his bow.

"She didn't make it!" Banks bellowed from above them.

Clint's heart fell as he was bouncing up and down on Tremayne's shoulder. He pushed himself up to see what was going on as something very solid hit him on his right shoulder and leaves brushed his body scraping his back, arms, and face.

"Stay down!" Tremayne shouted as Ohlwiler shot more arrows up the hill. Arrows were now flying over Clint's head as it sounded like Tremayne was running over anything he could to get down the hill as quickly as possible. There was a sharp whiz of an arrow and a thud. Before Clint knew it, Tremayne fell to the ground dropping him. He hit the ground legs first, his head spinning as he saw trees, sky, and ground all twirling as he rolled down the mountain. A tree trunk stopped him as he slammed into it with his right arm with a bang. His arm was sore, but it still worked. He looked around with the world still spinning. Tremayne was clutching his right leg and even in the dark with everything still spiraling Clint could see an arrow was sticking through it. Ohlwiler stopped next to him and in between shots he broke the arrowhead from the shaft and pulled the arrow out. He picked up some dirt off the ground and rubbed it in the holes when Chiowood came rushing down the hill by them. He was holding his shoulder where his shirt was soaked with blood.

"Come on, get going Clint," Chiowood shouted as he grabbed Clint, bolstering him to his feet. Just then there was a loud scream of a woman further up the hill. Ohlwiler fell backward and slid down the hill with an arrow in her chest. Tremayne held his leg as he slid down to her with arrows hitting around them. Chiowood was pushing Clint to run but Clint still saw Tremayne check to see if Ohlwiler was still alive when Banks came rushing down, showering them all with earth and dust.

"Reform the line at the waters and field's edge," he shouted as he also turned to shoot.

"Get out of here!" Chiowood yelled at Clint, pushing his injured shoulder hard. Clint turned his head once more up the hill. Stumbling down he saw the same outlines of those following the Spell Binder in the park. The ogre and orc alike emerged at the top of the crest with the moon shining behind them. His ankles began to wobble and give way but the hail of arrows and rocks flying all around him kept him moving. Before he made it to the bottom there was a loud grunt from the top of the hill and the sound of something whizzing through the air.

"Look out!" Chiowood yelled. He seemed to come out of nowhere as he dove forward, grabbing Clint's shoulder causing him to fall once more against rock and dirt.

With an unbelievable smash, a huge boulder hit the ground right in front of Clint. It crushed everything in front and pounded everything down the hill it rolled over.

Clint temporarily lost his senses but was pulled to his feet and pulled forward like he was a stubborn animal. "What was that?" Clint coughed while he was wrenched around the scar in the ground that the boulder had left. He watched it roll down the hill, clearing a path for him breaking tree and bush alike.

"It's that ogre, keep moving!" Chiowood cried, pushing Clint hard in the back ahead of him. Clint heard over the mayhem Chiowood returning fire up the hill behind him.

Pain erupted on the left side of Clint's head. Screaming, he instinctively lifted his hand from his throbbing leg to his ear which was split. Another grunt sounded from up and behind him as Chiowood pushed Clint to get down.

With his hand over his ear, he didn't hear the soft grunt of the ogre launching another boulder into the air over them. Nor the cry of Chiowood before impact. He did feel the ground shudder and his already wobbly legs threaten to give under the new strain. Clint did hear Chiowood's sharp bellow as the side of his leg was crushed.

"Chiowood!" Clint heard Tremayne from behind him. Clint didn't turn back, and he was unable to dwell on Chiowood for even a second. His mind seemed to stop working as his body kept moving.

The atrocious clouds seem to have parted allowing the moon to shine brighter. With Clint's tongue baked with dust, his lungs filled with dirt, he saw the boulder that made a path for him at the bottom embanked against the canal. Clint could see the shimmer of rainwater moving in the canal and the dark figures of almost all his family and friends by it. A spasm of hope grew at the sight of them but was snatched away when an arrow hit one of the kids in the leg right above the knee. Clint couldn't make out who it was as he rushed to the water's edge. In the field beyond Clint could see the trails of the rest of his family rushing on through the field's rows of weeds and cattails.

Clint collapsed onto the water's edge caring not for the cold. Chiowood dove in right in the water. Clint rolled into the water and from its touch, it felt like his ear had been sliced all over again. His sore stubborn leg refused to work, causing Clint's head to submerge more than once.

"Incoming," Clint heard someone roar muffled under the water. He was halfway to the concrete edge when the boulder hit the water, forcing a wave to push him forward. It also washed over his head as if someone had thrown a wet blanket over him. Gasping for air when his head broke through, arrows were falling thicker now around him.

It felt like he was grabbing sandpaper when his hands hit the rough concrete side of the canal. He tried to pull himself up but slumped back down. He tried again but his body refused to rise out of the water. Chiowood was suddenly there by his side and pulling him out. Before Clint was on his feet, he saw the shock in Chiowood's eyes when he was struck with an arrow in the same shoulder that was already bloody.

He shouted in surprise and fell back, tumbling over the side of the embankment of the canal. Clint crawled to him, helping him to his feet, and watched Chiowood return fire up the hill even with the arrow in him.

"Go, Clint," Chiowood shouted. Clint ran, not thinking, only feeling. The tall weeds made his arms and face itch, the pushed back weeds showing him the way others went for him to follow.

"Coming over!" Clint heard Tremayne call as he rolled over the crest of the canal all wet.

The arrows would not stop falling as Clint held his leg, still throbbing in pain and cold. Banks was next coming out of the water, his head covered in blood from a terrible gash on the top of his bald skull. He turned to shoot his bow up the hill with Chiowood and Tremayne Clint looked back to see the flashes of light trailing up the hill at the army of dead descending it. Fear overwhelmed Clint as he watched the war on the hill over his shoulder behind him. In the light of the arrows, it was as if the hill was swarming with ants.

Running on in the cover of the long grass and weeds he could only hear the whisps and dull thuds of arrows falling all around him. Suddenly, he fell once more as he tripped over something. It caused his leg to hurt even more as he got up and started limping away and only noticed at the last minute that it was a dead body he'd tripped over.

There was another yell from Banks who called out, "Fall back, back!" Clint turned and froze for only a second before an arrow struck a foot behind him. The shouts and yells seemed to be all around him, closing from everywhere.

The arrows were now not falling around him but coming horizontally at him. He looked back once to see someone's outline turning to shoot their arrow back the way they were running from.

He reached the edge of the field and was coming up the side of the dirt bank when something grabbed his hurt leg from behind. Clint kicked at it with his good leg as he fell and met a horned head. When he kicked it squealed like a pig and fell over. It was back on its little feet and lunged at Clint, drawing a long knife. Clint saw it all in slow motion as the knife was driven into his right shoulder, the pain causing him to scream louder than he ever had. He hit the imp right across the jaw with his left hand causing the imp to squeal once more and roll off him. Then there were footsteps in the dirt from behind him and over his head. Something heavy hit the imp hard enough to make it fly twenty feet, squealing like a pig all the way through the air until it was lost in the field. Clint looked up and saw Ravin hurrying toward him with a golf club in her hand.

She reached down and pulled Clint onto his good leg. Clint struggled to breathe from all the pain. He reached up in disbelief and felt the knife sticking out of his shoulder. There was another thud as an arrow hit something close by him. All at once Ravin pulled the knife out and thrust it into Clint's hand.

"Get going, go straight, you're there, we made it," Ravin shouted breathlessly.

Clint didn't wait as he went up and over the mound of earth onto the golf course. A hundred feet away in front of him was everyone else huddled around a large wooden shack. Cody and Sam were struggling to open the large, locked doors. Clint hobbled his way toward them feeling warm blood now trickle down to his belly.

Cody broke the lock and hurried people inside the shack. Nix had his grandmother when Cody noticed that Ravin was not with him. The Fury was close enough now that arrows were hitting the old wooden shack and crossing just above them. Clint turned to see that Ravin was kneeling on the mound of earth edge he had just come from. She was waving her hands from side to side and slowly pulling them in close to her body. The arrows were too close, she was going to get hit.

"Ravin," he called weakly. When he shouted, it made his chest hurt sharply.

She paid him no attention as she kept moving, almost dancing. A single body came over the mound right by Ravin. It was Chiowood.

"Come on Banks, come on," he shouted.

Clint started moving to the shack as the curtain of arrows slowly lowered. They were now arching over the earth mound separating them and were whizzing around everywhere. There were so many coming that Clint didn't think he was going to make it. By some miracle, he made it to the open wooden door and shielded himself behind it as watched in terror through a crack in the door. Those who were shooting them would be on top of them any minute. Ravin was still sitting exposed with Chiowood screaming for Banks when an arrow hit the wooden door close to Clint causing splinters to sting his hand.

Someone was coming over the mound when Nix grabbed Clint around the middle and shouted, "Get down!"

"But they are here!" Clint shouted, hitting the ground another time.

"Ravin's going to set it all on fire," he shouted to Clint and called back to every person in the shack, "Get down!"

Nix covered Clint like Banks had in the house. As soon as he hit the ground, he was thankful it was the soft grass of a fairway when he saw a body come over the mound and roll right next to Chiowood.

The arrows were everywhere. The Fury was almost on them. Clint could smell them as he had his nose in the dirt when Ravin stood up, a strange glow in front of her illuminating her outline.

Boom! Clint and Nix were both thrown back even though they were on the ground as a blinding light came from where Ravin was standing. A tremendous shockwave deafened Clint's ears and muffled screams of pain. He covered his eyes and head from the blast wave and blinding light until there was darkness on the other side of his eyelids.

When he opened his eyes, Nix squirmed back on top of him, shielding him once more. He could see two figures stirring on their side of the wall of dirt and earth. On the other side of the wall of dirt, a wall of flames burned. A massive cloud of smoke flew up to the heavens from what looked like the entire field. Nix got off Clint and started running over to where Ravin was now kneeling. The fire was rolling over everything like a tidal wave of destruction, devouring everything in its path. It had started where Ravin was and had spread to the hillside in only seconds. Even with Clint's ears still muffled from the blast wave, he could hear the cries of pain coming from the corn field. Ravin was now hunched over, lying on her side, her body illuminated with the light of the fire. Clint hobbled after Nix, watching the two men that had made it over in the nick of time get to their feet.

Clint instinctively followed Nix, limping on his hurt leg. When he was close enough, he saw that they were Chiowood and Banks. Both were leaning heavily on one another but were moving over the crest of the mound to see what lay on the other side.

It was difficult work for Clint to get back up the soft earth, but when his head reached a height to see the open marsh, his mouth dropped. There wasn't anything left. Tiny embers of the fire smoldered in pockets, reflecting a soft glow on the ash floating in the air. Everything that was in that field had been completely cremated. Clint limped over to Chiowood and Banks, who were still leaning on one another. Nix had turned Ravin over to check her and found an arrow stuck in her chest.

"H, h, how?" Clint asked.

Banks looked over at Clint with his good eye that wasn't covered in blood. "Ravin was a mage, Clint. Final protocol almost takes the life of the one doing it. The time it took her, killed her, and saved us all."

Clint did not understand, nor was his mind working. He looked out over the blackened field and let out a sigh of relief that nothing was hunting them at that moment. His eyes fell on the canal. "Tremayne?" Clint asked weakly, already knowing the answer.

"He never left the water's edge," Chiowood choked.

Now Clint knew what that thud had been when she was helping him up. He started to shake with the thought of everyone who had just died. He wasn't given much time to think about it when a new light came up from behind him. He turned and saw a soft white illuminating ball. It was the color of a flame tip emerging, rotating around on the ground next to the arrow-riddled shack. His family and friends were coming out of the hut to see it. Clint stopped shaking as their faces reflected in the sparkling, growing light.

"What is that?" Clint asked, sounding worried.

"It is our way home," Chiowood said, wincing in pain.

Nix had picked up Ravin's body and started to descend the mound of earth while everyone was still coming out of the shack. Clint counted each one as they came into view. There was Kayla, she was the short one. Next to her was Grant, and Sam and Jamie holding each other. Then Corbin and Cody both were helping their grandmother to stand. The one closest was Melanie, and Amber was taking a selfie. By her were the rest of her friends he didn't know. Without words Banks, Nix, Chiowood, and he were all slowly walking over holding their wounds. Melanie was the first to notice them. She rushed over and hugged him so hard that his chest felt like it was going to burst, both from the wound in his shoulder and his heart that was beating so fast with her arms around him.

The light from the portal was larger now and much brighter. It was almost impossible to look at it straight, but it was simply beautiful. Melanie helped Clint over to stand and look at it when Nix looked at Banks.

"What about Tamara?" Nix asked as he indicated the shack where she lay down on a golf cart seat.

Everyone looked over at Banks who was wiping the blood to see out of both eyes, adding a smirk. "This is going to be difficult," he said while they all were breathing deeply hugging one and another.

"We will take care of her and all of you. Nix, take quick care of me and Clint then check everyone else for extraction," he moaned, not meeting anyone's eye.

Nix made quick work of Banks and Clint at least to stop the bleeding. "I will have to bring her closer into the light," Nix added hastily. Even with the pain, Clint thought that was strange as there was just as much light where she was. Nix went toward the shack now as Clint was still very sore, but his movement was manageable.

They had done it, Clint thought, giving a deep sigh of relief. Melanie was holding him. All his family was going to be all right and alive. Nix was bringing Tamara over and Clint could see her in his arms, and she was still breathing. He laid her down next to Banks and straightened her hair, almost like a parent with a child who was taking a nap. She was still very pale but had a smile on her face. Clint looked up and saw smiles on everyone's faces—all except Amber, who was frowning at her messed-up hair. Banks was testing his dexterity after being quickly treated and held up his hands to gain everyone's attention.

CHAPTER

Forty-Eight

AND I THOUGHT COCKROACHES WERE TOUGH

Whoosh! Something flew past Clint so fast that he thought it was a bird and was larger than an arrow. Everyone looked around at each other to see what it was. Grant suddenly fell to his knees with something that looked like a piece of glass in his hands over his heart.

"NO!" Banks yelled as Clint discovered that it was an icicle sticking out of his chest. Grant opened his mouth in a silent scream. His hands were shaking as he pulled on the slippery ice shard while everyone looked around helplessly. Grant fell on his side, his large glasses falling off as his head hit the ground.

"NO!" Clint cried. He spun his tender body around and could see a prominent, black-cloaked figure with whisps of steam rising from its frame standing on the mound of earth that separated the golf course and the scorched marsh.

"Everyone into the light, NOW!" Banks ordered.

"We can't go there," Cody bellowed back as the dark figure tentatively limped down toward them.

"You stay and you die!" Banks yelled as he grabbed Melanie by the neck and threw her in the light. She screamed and in a flash of light, she was gone.

"Melanie!" Clint shrieked. He tried to reach her but fell because of his stiff leg. He hit the ground watching Nix run into the light holding Tamara in his large arms. There was another whoosh as a thrown icicle barely missed one of the kids that Clint didn't know as they also dove into the

424

light, pulling on the others that they were next to. Everyone made a mad rush into the light save for Clint. One after the other images swirled and were gone in the blink of an eye.

Clint watched the last members of his family and friends vanish. Banks turned to the Spell Binder who was shuffling quickly toward them.

Bank's hands faltered as he pulled out his longsword because of the pain from the arrow that was just removed from his back. The Spell Binder was closing, fifty feet, thirty, twenty feet. Banks held his weapon defensively, bringing a blue flame around the blade. He stood his ground between the Spell Binder and the portal of light.

"Give it to me!" the Spell Binder demanded, making the night air almost freeze.

"It is almost gone," Banks said bravely as he moved his feet apart to lengthen his stance. "You've lost. If you don't hurry you will be stuck here, and I haven't seen a place here that would serve you a meal. You might find employment in food storage though." He started to laugh painfully.

Banks' laugh was interrupted as the Spell Binder's white hand rose and slowly lifted its black hood. Clint was transfixed to the ground in fear as the hood was lifted, revealing a marble-white face. Its breath was fast and angry, its fragile skin stuck to its skull so tight it was almost transparent. The hood fell back, showing no hair on the Spell Binder's head, and then the entire cloak fell to the grass. Now Clint saw why the Spell Binder always leaned to its right. Its horribly lopsided skeleton frame bore black, tattered, and torn rags hanging around it. Its left arm was feeble, average length. Its right arm was at least two feet longer than its other. It was as thick and muscular as a grown man's leg. The fingers of its right hand were lengthened as well, and they almost touched the ground. Its fingertips weren't rounded on the ends. They appeared sharp, like five slender blades glimmering in the reflection from the portal light.

Banks stood his ground, sword at the ready, while Clint tried with all his might to inch away from the Spell Binder, who laughed horribly. Then, in its long, terribly oversized hand, the air seemed to be turning and gathering as a heavy, thick ice handle was growing from its palm. A giant heavy sword of ice slowly emerged, and in the smaller hand, an elegant longsword started to grow out of thin air. Once formed the Spell Binder swung them around with ease around him.

"Finally," it hissed, laughing. Before Clint could react, the Spell Binder hurled toward Banks, propelled strongly with its muscular leg. Its ice blades moved so fast that they were a blur in Clint's eyes. Clint expected that it would shatter as soon as the blade joined with Banks's in a crash, but it chipped slightly and became instantly sharp once again as if the blade could heal itself.

They fought with a ferocity that Clint had never seen before. Each one swung their weapons as if it were a part of themselves, twirling around each other, each trying to gain a hit on the other but blocking or dodging with each swing. The shouts with each force sounded like a karate demonstration.

The Spell Binder was swinging hard and strong with its heavy arm and with its smaller, it would lunge and parry. Banks was quicker and his style lighter. He gave ground but was able to withstand each and every swing. The Spell Binder swung right, left, up, right, straight; it was so fast, and its body moved smoothly but favored the one side, depending on the weapon it used. Clint twisted and could barely breathe as Banks moved away from the light and into the golf shed.

Banks blocked a sharp thrust by spinning out of the way and defecting the sword to the right, kicking the Spell Binder's white face with his right leg-spinning in a roundhouse. The Spell Binder fell back as Banks pushed the attack as his foe's footing was off. He charged the Spell Binder from the right and at the last minute fell low as the Spell Binder swung his slender ice sword just where Banks' head should have been. With a swoosh, it flew over Banks as he rolled onto his side and drove his sword into the Spell Binder's mid-section. The Spell Binder screamed in pain and hatred as it swung its large sword down where Banks lay on the ground. The icy edge cut into Banks's shirt but missed his flesh as he crawled out of the way.

With its normal-sized arm, the Spell Binder felt the cut as it lifted its rags, showing its paper-thin skin clinging to its ribs. It looked like the skin was not cut but broken like ice on a lake's edge. Banks rose to his feet holding his injured shoulder and leaning to one side. The Spell Binder laughed more terribly and started to conjure new, bigger swords letting the old ones fall and melt away. As soon as the air stopped turning it pressed the attack on Banks faster this time. With its left hand, it fenced with a sword that was no thicker than a pencil and drew heavy blows with its right as if it were a club. Banks was blocking, dodging, and even attacking here and there but he was starting to show signs of fatigue as the shorter blade sliced his arm, cutting a long gash in it.

Clint, overwhelmed with pain, felt helpless when something else moved into the portal's light. It shuffled its way toward the wooden shack's doorway. It was one of the Fury. It was battered and bruised, and at least part of it was severely burned. It was limping heavily to one side and had one hand holding its stomach. It looked around, and in the light, Clint could see it had a long overlarge nose and many different earrings reflected in the light. It stopped and watched the battle in the shed as Banks moved in close, elbowed the Spell Binder, and then hit him in the face. The Spell Binder only seemed to grow stronger as Banks grew weaker.

The newcomer moved closer to the shed and leaned against one door. Then it pulled a long dagger from its opposite side with difficulty in its burned hand and then held it out in front of it as if it were taking aim down the barrel of a gun, just waiting for the right moment to fire with one good eye while the other eye had a large leather patch over. Banks either didn't notice or was so busy with his current fight that he didn't show any signs of reacting to this new threat.

Clint summoned all his strength and with every muscle slowly pulled himself away from the light on his belly. He pushed and pulled himself by Grant's lifeless face and couldn't bear to look at it as he moved toward the green figure holding the dagger. He had no thought of what he could or would do as he moved along the grass toward the shed. His shoulder screaming in pain and his leg refusing to move with strength slowed him down as the battle dance kept going fiercely in the shed as the Spell Binder was swinging and destroying everything within its reach.

Just as the Spell Binder cut off the top of a golf cart while Banks dove through it, Clint felt something cold and hard in the grass. With the only light behind him and his shadow in front of him, he couldn't see it until he raised it up. It was the dagger from his shoulder stained with his blood. He had dropped it when Grant was struck. Gripping it tightly he used it to help him move, driving the blade into the soft earth and pulling on the hilt, looking like a mountain climber crawling on the ground as if gravity had shifted for him. He came up behind the green man with the dagger so close now that he could smell him and see the terrible burns and wounds covering his skin.

The Spell Binder and Banks were fighting in the center of the shed and one swing from the Spell Binder caused Banks to dodge under it, exposing a clear shot for the dagger to be thrown right into his back.

The assassin with the dagger saw his chance and lifted the dagger behind its green head. It started to bring its arm forward just as Clint brought his dagger down into the green foot of the cutthroat.

The dagger thrower howled in pain and started to fall over. Clint's dagger had been driven all the way into the foot up to the hilt. The assassin had thrown its dagger, but the shot went astray to the right when its heavy body hit the ground with a thud. Banks swung around to see Clint rolling away and struck out hard against the Spell Binder, giving recoil to add time to take his attention away from his current opponent. Clint was scurrying to get away as the fallen figure was howling in agony, grabbing his leg.

Banks only had a moment to spare as the Spell Binder was on top of him again pressing the attack. The green figure's foot was stuck to the ground with the dagger still in it when its eye fell on Clint.

"Get out of here, Clint!" Banks yelled as he blocked two hits from the Spell Binder.

Clint didn't need to be told twice but he couldn't stand or even crawl very well as he tried in vain to get away. All he could do well was roll but as soon as he started, he could hear the troll scrambling to get to him. It was only a foot away and would have him in a second. Its hands scratched Clint's arm as it dove for him but couldn't get him as it was still stuck to the ground. Clint stared on in fear into the troll's eye as it bellowed in hatred trying to grab him as a mad dog held back by a chain.

The troll bent over and grabbed the dagger and with another cry of pain pulled it out. Just then Banks was in trouble as the Spell Binder had cut his leg, causing him to fall to the ground on one knee. Clint stopped rolling and watched as Banks fought as best as he could, but after five or six blows was disarmed. His sword flew out of his hands and hit the wall of the shed.

The Spell Binder pointed the tip of its short sword right at his throat, laughing madly. The troll was free now and was on its feet. It fell to its knees discovering his foot was too painful to bear his weight and like a mad dog, mouth wide, it charged at Clint. It was almost on him and raised the dagger and held Clint pinned to the ground with one of its green knees.

Clint saw the tip of the dagger start down right to his eye when suddenly from inside of the shed there came the voice of the Spell Binder.

"Spare him, Voscass!" it called.

The dagger's force was too great and, when redirected at the last possible moment, hit the ground, cutting his already wounded ear slightly. Clint barely felt the cut due to the tremendous pain from his chest and shoulder with the troll on top of him.

"Bring him here!" the Spell Binder called eagerly.

The troll picked Clint up with such strength that he felt like a puppet being pushed around by a master. The troll grabbed him by his injured shoulder, and with pain, it pulled him forward into the shed. Clint stumbled twice, his poor leg refusing to hold him, and each time, the troll dug his strong fingers into his wounded shoulder, lifting him and pushing him on until he dropped beside Banks, who was sitting on his good leg. Banks weakly held his injured leg with his hands to stop the bleeding while the Spell Binder's blade held steady on his Adam's apple. Clint noticed Banks's neck changing red and blue from its cold edge.

When all four exhaled, the water vapor in their breath condensed into thick clouds. The Spell Binder's white skin refused to move as it smiled over them. The troll forced Clint to bow in respect. Clint looked up into the strange black and white eyes and felt fear like he never had before. The cold air seemed to be pulsating from those black robes that washed over him just as if someone had poured a bucket of ice water on him.

"Where is it?" the Spell Binder asked, still sounding amused. It turned those eyes between them. Clint and Banks said nothing.

"I will kill the boy," the Spell Binder said as it brought the larger blade over Clint's head. Clint's panic grew in his chest and settled somewhere in his neck. All the Spell Binder had to do was to drop the ice sword a foot and he would be dead. Clint's lungs were colder as his breath quickened. His hands were oddly sweaty, the stabbing pain in his leg and chest only grew.

"Where is the Requiem?" the Spell Binder yelled, shaking in frustration. Frost erupted on the grass and painted the weathered wood of the shed.

Clint caught Banks's eye without moving his head. Banks was looking at the Spell Binder through his one good eye. Banks, sensing Clint's gaze, turned, showing his other covered in dried blood. Banks pursed his lips and spit before he gave Clint a wry smile.

"Sorry, kid," he said as he winced in pain. "Best laid plans."

"So be it!" The Spell Binder twisted its lopsided body to lay a killer blow. It locked its cold, lifeless eyes with Clint's. Suddenly, it looked up as a roar and new light filled the shed and Clint's ears. The Spell Binder's arm stopped high in the air as Banks hit Clint, falling over sideways. Clint felt the hand of the troll fall away as it spun around. The Spell Binder stood ready to strike at the new sound as its eyes were filled with the light of O'Neil's motorcycle. A crazy scream of laughter drowned out everything else over the motorcycle's roar as it zoomed by Clint and Banks and hit the Spell Binder. It was over in a flash as O'Neil drove into the shed wall with an almighty crash. Everything fell off the shelves above and on top of them, covering the wrecked motorcycle.

Before Clint could catch his breath, Banks set upon the troll, struggling and kicking to get control of the dagger that they both had in their hands. Each held and pulled on each other's hands and arms to force the blade into the other. Clint moved away from the fray as best as he could when something started moving underneath the pile of parts and twisted metal.

Banks and the troll stopped struggling as each eye looked on and ear perked up to hear which one had survived the crash. A short head and a cackle of laughter came from under a plastic tire as O'Neil pushed it off. He was dirty and messy but was laughing as he'd just had the best day anyone could have asked for. He pulled himself out of the rubble and held out the octagonal ball.

Banks took the troll's distraction for his opportunity. He hit the troll across its green face with his elbow. The stunned troll let go of the dagger and found his error in Banks's hand, which was pointed at his chest. Breathing hard, Banks got to his feet, holding the dagger firmly pointed at the troll's heart.

"O'Neil, get something to restrain him," Banks called over without looking at O'Neil, who was coming now, walking toward them almost drunk with laughter, swaying left and right in a daze.

"Whaaaaaaaaaaaaaaaaaaaaaaaaaaaaaaaaaaaaaaaaw! Whit just happened?" O'Neil asked, going cross-eyed. Their heavy breath, misted in the cold, ebbed away the warmth slowly returning.

"You saved us!" Clint said in shock. He saw a roll of twine that had fallen from its perch among the wreckage around him. He slowly and painfully retrieved it and tossed it to Banks.

Banks was quickly tying up the troll when O'Neil's path finally straightened, approaching an uneasy halt before Banks.

"Ah did?" O'Neil said, tipping dangerously forward. Clint grabbed his strange frame to straighten him.

"Gees O'Neil," Clint huffed under O'Neil's weight. "You are moving like Jack Sparrow."

"Don't you remember?" Banks asked while finishing several layers of twine around the hands and feet of the troll and tying it all off. The troll's arms were completely restrained from movement like a prisoner in chains.

"I was just trying tae find out how yoo slow 'at thing down. I never git tae figure that oot when I was playing that game ay yers," O'Neil sputtered while tipping backward. Clint was out of position to help this time as O'Neil fell back with a thud. Banks and Clint looked at one another worriedly.

Banks unexpectedly started to laugh and Clint, despite being sick with pain, couldn't help but laugh as well. It felt wonderful. It rushed through him as if he had been in a desert for days and finally was able to drink cool refreshing water. Clint and Banks were still laughing freely as O'Neil tried to get up but kept falling. It was on O'Neil's third try to get up that Clint felt it. Something was wrong.

Forty-Nine
WHO PLANNED THIS ANYWAY?

Their laughter left the air as Clint saw the joy in Banks's face diminish. They both looked over to see yet another large, motionless cloaked figure standing in the shed doorway, the light of the portal shining brilliantly behind him. It was as if he had magically appeared giving no indication of his approach. The only sound between them was O'Neil's drunken moans of laughter.

"Is, is that another Spell Binder?" Clint asked, his voice shaky.

"It's larger," Banks said breathlessly.

Banks turned on the troll and used him as a human shield, facing the hooded figure.

"Get behind me, Clint!" Banks shouted as the cloaked figure just stood, making no movement to compensate for theirs. Clint got behind Banks as fast as he could while O'Neil stopped laughing and also picked up the light octagonal ball.

"Banks," the figure growled, "give me what I want, and I won't taste your flesh." It snarled again. It didn't sound like the Spell Binder, and it didn't make the night cold when it spoke. Its voice was more profound, and Clint could barely understand it, as if it had difficulty forming the words in its mouth. Clint held fast to the back of Banks's shirt, squinting to see the portal light behind it.

"Just try it!" Banks shouted, jerking the troll hard with the knife at his throat. "There are three of us and we have one of your men. Why don't you get back to your portal before it's too late?"

"Uh, Banks," O'Neil said, suddenly walking up to stand next to Banks "Excuse us a wee moment," O'Neil said to the dark figure with a wave. Clint was shocked and thought that O'Neil must have hit his head because he was acting like he was talking to old friends and nothing to be worried about.

"Maybe yoo huvnae checked the score ur yoo got hit in the head one tae many times but we ur fresh out of motorcycles, an' whatever is under 'at hood is a loot bigger than yoo."

Banks's expression didn't change' he was acting like he didn't hear. Clint was looking around Banks's shoulder when the hooded figure took a step forward. In the soft light, Clint saw that it had a massive leg, that was covered in dark fur. The cold feeling that had died away with the Spell Binder was replaced once more giving an unnatural cold about them. It seemed to Clint that it was moving from behind them towards something next to the portal. Was it his fear? The cold dissipated once again just as quickly as it came.

"Don't you want to know how you escaped from us? How did you survive that night on the side of the mountain?" the dark hood asked as it took two decisive steps. Its movements were strong, like a lion crouched low, moving in for the kill.

"How do you know about that?" Banks asked and for one of the first times, Clint could hear fear behind his voice.

"No, dinnae ask him questions?" O'Neil groaned, waving his hands in the air, falling back behind Clint again.

The hooded figure straightened for a moment. Its shoulders outlined in its large cloak were rising and falling with each breath. They all were looking at it when the hood moved up sharply and then in an ear-splitting howl it cried out like a wolf bellowing at the moon. The cloak fell off it as it rose to its full and considerable height.

"Werewolf," O'Neil and Banks said together. The difference was O'Neil was laughing mockingly after he spoke while Banks was not.

The werewolf was massive, filling the entire doorway. It looked like a man and wolf had joined, taking from each the most powerful traits. It had long pointed ears, dark eyes, a long snout with inch-long teeth, and a massive body concealed under a coat of thick fur. Its muscular form ended in sharp claws on its hands and feet. It reared, arching his back, standing taller, watching them as a smile rippled around its large teeth.

"I could kill you all," it said, licking its lips like a dog smelling a bone. Banks and O'Neil never moved. They didn't even breathe as they all just looked at each other, holding one another in a standoff.

"You do not disagree," the werewolf growled. "I will let you all live if you give me the Requiem and that troll."

"Why should we trust you?" Banks shouted back, gripping the troll harder.

The werewolf took another long step forward with its pigeon-toed hairy foot. "You know when I lie, and it was I who saved you from the Fury!" The werewolf barked as drool started running out of the side of its open mouth. Clint watched in horror as that jaw across from him began to pant excitedly.

"I was sent to make sure you got back and that you would come here," it continued as if it hated everything that it was saying. "It was I who have been watching you until now when I knew you would have the Requiem. It was I who kept the others to spare you till now. I have been sent by the gods to finally free the Fury and take back what you stole from us."

"Enough!" Banks shouted.

"Oh, now yoo say it," O'Neil coughed. "If yoo didnae listen it wouldn't have talked sae much. If it didnae say sae much it wouldnae have worked up sae much of an appetite."

"O'Neil," Banks said simply. O'Neil fell silent, lowering his chin in shame.

The werewolf laughed and howled as it drew out its long claws that looked sharp enough to cut a cow in half. Clint leaning heavily on one side in pain trying to reposition his weight.

"What is it talking about?" Clint asked Banks, struggling to figure out how a werewolf fit into all this as well. Clint's eyes were rolling watching each one of them, wondering what they were going to do.

"They sent two groups!" Banks said as he started to comprehend. "You set this all up from the beginning. Whenever the Fury would have us, you stopped them. It was you who cleared a way for me to get away from the hunting party from the start."

"It was yoo who took me number away that night," O'Neil said as if he just now comprehended something. "I couldn't look another pint drinker fer a week since that."

"O'Neil," Banks said dryly again. O'Neil fell back in his shamed stance.

"Yes," the werewolf said happily, "I so wanted so much to taste your flesh, but the gods commanded me to let you live. To let you bring us the Requiem."

Banks started to move back away from the werewolf, dragging the troll to follow. Clint shuffled to keep out of his way and to move back as well. O'Neil was looking all around the shed for anything that would save them.

"There is no escape," the werewolf growled as he held out a long hairy arm. "Give it to me."

"What do you think, O'Neil?" Banks said.

O'Neil moved slowly to the far side of the shed to give them space. "I dinnae know, I was hoping that yoo could handle it. He likes yoo and yoo have been doin' sae well sae far."

With a heavy heart Banks loosened his grip on the troll and lowered the knife from his throat and pointed it in his back. The light behind the werewolf started to flicker and fade slightly more.

"Looks like you have to hurry if you are going to make it home in one piece," Banks said as he nodded to the portal with a smirk. "Time is not working for you and me, you need to make it to your portal before you are stuck here."

The werewolf snarled and dropped to all fours. It bared its large fangs and dug its claws into the ground, preparing to strike. Clint jumped as he saw the werewolf's eye fall on him. Banks and O'Neil responded quickly by centering their bodyweight under their feet.

"Wait!" Banks cried as he pushed the troll to move up closer to the werewolf. "We will give it to you, and the troll." Clint moved behind Banks and hid his face in his back.

"First, back up!" Banks ordered. "Or O'Neil will smash it and I will kill the troll, either way, you will lose something you want. Even you are not fast enough to get both. So back up."

The werewolf snarled once more, making the old shack rattle. It moved back one foot and then the other, still eyeing them and looking like it would pounce at any moment. The werewolf gave way and as it did Banks moved forward, coming out of the shed. The light of the portal was growing dimmer and dimmer with each passing moment. Clint's mouth was dry as the standoff went on while they emerged out of the shed into the night. The werewolf stopped moving just past the portal but not so far to let Banks have any chance to make a break for it and get to the portal. Banks pulled the troll to a stop while it was limping on its one good foot, left snorting in pain and hatred.

"Here is how it is going to happen," Banks said and at that moment he faltered in his step. The werewolf jumped an inch but stopped itself.

"Here is what we are going to do," Banks went on, sounding more in pain than when he was before. "We give the ball to the troll here and he takes a step toward you. We take a step to the portal. If he moves too fast, we will stop him, and he won't move again. Agreed?"

The werewolf lowered itself flat on the ground and nodded, reminding Clint of a cat ready to spring into the air at its prey. Clint couldn't help but look under Banks's arm at the werewolf's claws, dig into the ground with ease and imagine his own skin being cut that easily.

Banks held out one free hand behind him toward O'Neil. O'Neil looked the situation over and moved in close to Banks before he gave him the globe. As he did so, Banks looked over his shoulder to where Clint was hiding behind him. He whispered so low that Clint could barely make out it all when he said, "It will be all right, kid. We have what we came for. He can feel it when you lie, and I am telling you it is all right," Banks was almost pleading, "So don't be afraid."

"Afraid?" Clint huffed "I'm petrified and hurting beyond belief. I'm just proud that my pants are dry. Wait, what about the Requiem? They can't have it."

"Just think about yer dry pants, boy," O'Neil whispered back.

The troll looked over his shoulder in disgust at O'Neil.

"Oh, what is it?" O'Neil spat back. "Like yoor pants be dry now trolly. Best be off with the ball before I toss him it and pull that long nose over behind yoor heid."

Banks quickly took the globe from O'Neil like taking a toy from a troublesome toddler. Clint only had a moment to think on this before the troll took one weak step away from the fading light and Banks reached around and grabbed his throbbing arm, pulling Clint to follow.

What if the werewolf struck? It must have been forty feet away. Could they jump that far? They each took another step. With each step, the feeling was terrible as the werewolf subtly got itself into the best position it could to leap toward them. Clint held on to Banks's back for dear life with each move. The light was getting dimmer and softer by the second. Was it going to close before they got there? What was he going to do? Was he going to be forced through? Was he going to stay here? Would his family have time to come back? Another step then another. Each one they took caused him great pain, countered equally with a feeling of freedom.

Suddenly, just when the troll was almost halfway the werewolf sprung into the air. "Get down!" Banks yelled as he pulled the dagger up to defend them. The werewolf soared through the air snarling, flying ten feet, twenty, thirty! It was sure to land on them as Clint hit the ground. O'Neil fell on him to shield him when the werewolf landed on the ground right between them. The troll fell forward letting the werewolf sail over him. Clint astonishingly was fixed on the feeling of hatred in its terrible red eye, watching to see who the werewolf would kill first.

What happened next was so fast Clint could only play it back in his mind slowly to understand it. With one fast swipe, Banks was thrown back as the werewolf's claws slashed him across the chest. Its claws starting at his belly cutting up to his chest. The strength of its blow caused Banks's feet to leave the ground. Before Banks hit the earth, the werewolf cut the twine ropes binding the troll with his other clawed hand and lifted the troll onto its shoulder. With blinding speed, it picked up Grant's body with his other arm.

Before any of the three could get off the ground and act it was gone in the night, taking gigantic jumps that drove it through the air like a rabbit jumping in a field, the troll bouncing over one powerful shoulder and Grant's lifeless one flopping under his other. Even in the soft light of the portal, Clint could see the globe, the Requiem, still clutched tightly in the Troll's green hands. There was Grant's motionless body as well, being swallowed by the night until they were gone.

Fifty

WHY DIDN'T YOU SAY THAT IN THE FIRST PLACE?

"Yoo all right?" O'Neil pleaded as he helped Banks to sit up. "Did it bite yoo?"

"No," Banks replied but as Clint saw, Banks was barely conscious. O'Neil examined him up and down, then tore on of his long sleeves off his shirt. He quickly wrapped it around Banks's chest.

"Yoo'll be alrigh' me buck'oh," O'Neil said. Clint heard didn't hear that familiar tone of joy in O'Neil's voice.

"Git heem through the portal!" O'Neil ordered Clint as he stood up.

Clint panicked as he saw Banks drop the dagger and looked like he had barely enough strength to hold his head up.

"What about my family?" Clint shouted back. "How do they get back?"

O'Neil grabbed Clint's shoulder raising him to his feet. He tightened his grip as he looked into Clint's eyes. O'Neil's seriousness didn't seem to fit him. This was not the man he had been with these past few horrible days. O'Neil sounded like Banks when he said, "They arenae coming back, these was the plan aw along."

"What?" Clint shouted in disbelief. "Why did he take Grant? What plan?"

"The Requiem isnae here boy. There is nothing that can be done fur Grant now," O'Neil said loosening his grip on Clint. He sighed as the portal went dimmer still. "Yoo ur the guide tae the Requiem. We came here tae get yoo. Banks told me when we firs' arrived. He only told the rest right befor' yer parents arrived. We all came here tae bring yoo tae our world and fur yer family tae help us find it. It was yer names on the piece ay parchment, it was written that yoo lot would lead us tae the Requiem."

"No, I can't help you," Clint shouted back as tears fell down his face, "You bring my family back!" His hands were balled up into fists. He started to pound O'Neil's firm chest with each word. "You bring them back! You give me my life back. No more I can't take it anymore."

"They can't come back," Banks said weakly from below him. Clint looked down at him, anger filling him with the thought of all his family gone. It hurt him that only days ago he wanted nothing but to get away from his family and now all he wanted was to have them back.

"They cannot come back, not now. I explained this to your parents when they left and told them what was written. You must follow your family if you want to save both our worlds."

"What are you talking about? You bring my family back home!" Clint yelled as he pounded on O'Neil's solid chest. O'Neil didn't move but took each hit with a show of regret behind his eyes.

"You lied to me! You lied!" Clint yelled. Banks tried to sit up but faltered. O'Neil grabbed and supported him. The light of the portal flickered on and off now beside them.

"I did not lie. Your family's lives depend on you and the lives of everyone in this world and ours."

Banks lifted his tired eyes that were full of pain up to look into Clint's and with his face covered in blood he smirked, "You haven't got it yet?" he coughed softly, "This world and ours are the same."

"What?" Clint said, not wanting to hear this.

"We don't have time fur this. Clint, help me get Banks through that portal before it closes. If it does, we fail. If we cannae get Banks help he'll die. Ur before that werewolf comes back," O'Neil spat, trying to help Banks to his feet. O'Neil had the strength easily, but Banks had to be moved with the care of more than just one.

"We have to go now, or everyone will die and our future, your future is lost," Banks pleaded as he tried to pull himself up.

"Help me, please, Clint," Banks moaned as he fell over on top of him while the portal's light started to flicker on and off again. "Help us save you. Save us all."

"He will die if we don't git 'im through," O'Neil pleaded from the shed.

Clint was feeling so much his mind started to go numb as he tried to decide what to do. There were so many thoughts and feelings that he was overwhelmed and stood shaking and trapped. Then he looked down into Banks's eyes and compassion won him over, as he also remembered his stepfather's last plea to do what Banks said. With the last bit of strength, he had, he grabbed Banks's hand and pulled him over, so his weight would be on his good leg. Banks stood up and leaned heavily over on Clint who was buckling under the weight.

He started with one step only, using his strong leg while the last light of the portal was fading. Clint was under Banks's left arm and O'Neil under his right.

"Oh, peanut pints!" O'Neil spat. "Hold him a tick, boy." O'Neil quickly maneuvered Banks over so Clint could hold him. Both grunted in pain as O'Neil ran back out of sight toward the motorcycle. Clint couldn't twist to see what was going on as he gave every ounce of strength to hold Banks. The sounds of rummaging through the shed and crashing came over O'Neil muttering something to himself.

"We must get through before it closes," Banks pleaded, gasping in deep pain as he tried to move under his own feeble strength.

O'Neil arrived once more under Banks's other arm holding him up with a bag, a suitcase in his hands, and a stereo under his arm, with a disheveled, angry Nuts on his shoulder.

"What was so darn important?" Clint gasped.

"Yer music yoo got 'ere, Pepsi, toilet pepper, one of them autographs from Sia, some of at heid lotion yoo saw at yoo like and I had tae save me Nuts!" O'Neil heaved as they moved into the remaining light.

Three of them and the squirrel moved arm in arm, each supporting the other. Limp by limp, pulling, pushing one another as the light was growing fainter and fainter. Clint saw it going as he struggled to move; each step was excruciating, his shoulder beyond pain as every move made it hurt more than he ever thought possible. The light was going, they weren't going to make it, and then O'Neil shoved all three of them into it right as the light gave way and was gone into the night.

"For us all," were the last words one of them said softly.

Epilogue

"Good evening, this is Nicole Wilsonland for your Channel Ten News. Halloween was anything but dull for teens and students who attended what is left of Holbrook school. The Halloween dance that they held was said to be terrorized by a horrible prank that not only cost a young man his life but also caused everyone to run in fear and many haven't been found yet. If this wasn't enough, law enforcement was slaughtered by what authorities are calling a massive, coordinated terrorist attack. Yet no one group has claimed credit for the attack on police officers and those who worked in the local station who were all found murdered. Many speculate that this was carried out by the protesters against the President and the upcoming Olympics, now enjoying the preparations for the starting ceremonies which will be coming in a few months.

Before we go to our live feed to the construction of the Olympic Los Angeles Memorial Coliseum, we have a foreign family that has come to our nation with hopes and dreams of starting a new life but found the home they were going to stay in blown up in ruins and most of the family missing. The parents of the family were not able to comment but had the utmost confidence that their children were safe and sound wherever they were. Next to their home was also the scene of some extensive prank, but further investigations into this matter have been met with difficulty due to obstructions to tampering with evidence. There are strong rumors that it was the parents who were responsible for the missing children, but having the president as a close friend has cleared them of any investigations into the matter. If anyone has any information on the missing children or knowledge of what happened that night, you are strongly encouraged to contact the authorities. As this has largely not been explained, many are considering a curfew. Some heads of state have been discussing declaring marshal law to rectify the situation quickly and ensure safety for all families here. While most oppose this action, it does not sway the fact that something must be done to maintain freedom and protection for us all, for us all."

About the Author

RJ PARKER was born in Bountiful, Utah. As his father was a safety manager, he had to move around until his senior year of high school when he came to Cache Valley, Utah, to stay. He married the most wonderful woman in the world, and they are the parents of four fantastic kids with two crazy dogs thrown in.

RJ played various sports and was an outdoorsman until an accident brought him to writing. A writer since high school, encouragement brought his stories to life.